I0685152

Praise for TOXIC WATERS
By David G. Ferguson

"Take an Ontario conservation officer and put him on a sailboat on Lake Huron. Mix in the crooked owner of a waste management company who is secretly dumping barrels of toxic material in the lake. Add a beautiful environmental activist and her father, the judge.

Now you have the makings for a fast-paced tale of suspense and adventure. In his first novel, Ferguson, a retired conservation officer, delivers the goods."

Shawn Perich – Northern Wilds Magazine (Minnesota, USA)

"Congratulations. I just finished reading Toxic Waters. What a great read. Good story, complicated plot, interesting characters. At one point I thought it was turning in to an Errol Flynn film. Well done. I will recommend it."

Murray Finn, Elliot Lake, ON

"Dave: I just wanted to drop you a line to say how much I enjoyed your book, Toxic Waters … I look forward to your next novel. And thanks for presenting our Ministry as the "good guys"!"

Bill Thornton, Deputy Minister (Ret'd.) Ontario MNRF

Praise for BEAR RUNNERS
By David G. Ferguson

"Looking for an **absolute thriller** that combines your love of the outdoors with great story telling? Then pick up a copy of David Ferguson's *Bear Runners*. When you start to read this book, you will find it impossible to put it down."

Gord Pyzer – Outdoor Canada Magazine

"A young conservation officer takes a posting in Ontario's far north where he meets a young and beautiful bush pilot and encounters an elusive polar bear poacher.
…. A great bedtime read, although the story moves so quickly you might not want to put it down…."

Shawn Perich – Northern Wilds Magazine (Minnesota, USA)

"I picked it up in the morning and never put it down until I finished reading at midnight. **That's what makes a great story**."

Gary Jolicour, Stratton, ON

"Just got back from a remote cabin in the Yukon where I finished Bear Runners. Loved it! A bit freaky reading about the murder in the remote cabin when I was sitting alone in a remote cabin in the middle of a cold winter…."

Greg Derbyshire, Brantford, Ontario

Praise for UP HALFWAY CREEK
By David G. Ferguson

"**A darned good read.** The details woven into this novel brought many memories of places and events from my five years as a Conservation Officer at Moosonee. Believe me the settings, people and happenings are authentic. At the same time the topics dealt with are right out of today's news. You won't be disappointed."

Pat Brown, Retired Ontario Conservation Officer

"**Another entertaining and action-packed wilderness crime adventure** with the duo Rob McNabb and Samantha Williams; but it's also a standalone story if you haven't yet read Bear Runners.
I enjoyed the survival-in-the-wilderness aspects of the book and the thorough descriptions of the Ontario landscape and various equipment (airplanes, boats, ATVs) instrumental to the excitement in the story. The story flows very well and the various storylines are woven together nicely."

J.E. Schwartz, P.Eng. San Diego, California

"**Good read! Kept me up half the night to finish it!** Well written. Characters and plot rich in interesting detail and well developed. Nice for us northerners to be in familiar territory. Sensitive treatment of difficult issues involving abuse of children."

Roland H. Aube, Elliot Lake, Ontario

Double Back Fur Run

David G. Ferguson

Published by
North Channel Novels
705-849-8238

To Ralph Grant, my good friend and former partner officer.

Acknowledgements

My thanks go to Ralph Grant for inviting me to co-drive with him on January fur pickup runs over the past twenty years. The weather challenges we faced, the mechanical breakdowns we endured, and the camaraderie of many thousands of kilometres together were essential elements for the nucleus of the idea that became this story.

And the managers at Fur Harvesters Auctions in North Bay, Ontario also deserve my thanks for those experiences. Despite the challenges we faced on the road, the fur always arrived at the auction house, safe and sound.

And special thanks go to Carol Piper Curtis and Norm Brown for providing their very helpful comments following a pre-read of my manuscript — a cruel responsibility to impose on friends. And to Marnie Ferguson, Principal at Note Editorial and Publishing Services, http://noteeditorialandpublishing.ca/ for her evaluation, editing and helpful encouragement, as she steered me, once again, from raw manuscript to finished story. This book is our fourth such collaborative project.

Novels by David G. Ferguson

Toxic Waters

Rob McNabb and Samantha Williams Wildlife Crime Series:

Bear Runners
Up Halfway Creek
Double Back Fur Run
(And coming in 2024: Moose Down)

Part I

Chapter 1

Christmas morning – New York City

"Well, open it, sweetheart," the man urged his wife.

The woman untied the ribbons and tore open the colourful wrapping paper. The sharp intake of her breath emphasized the exclamation that followed.

"Oh Arnie! ... It's *absolutely* gorgeous. Where on *earth* did you get it?"

Inside a one cubic foot glass display case was mounted a hand carved, ivory reproduction of Mont St. Michel, the historic French island near St. Malo. The entire island above the high tide line, not just the monastery, was reproduced in careful detail.

"It was carved by a Chinese craftsman at an art colony in Canada. They specialize in custom ivory pieces." The pure pleasure of seeing his wife's reaction was worth more than anything to the successful bank mogul. He didn't tell her how many thousands of dollars he'd spent on it — made no mention of the high premium he paid for the illegally imported work of art, unlawfully crafted from the tusk of a majestic mammal. A majestic mammal, murdered to satisfy human vanity.

"I thought it would bring back fond memories of our honeymoon. And your brother did a really professional job on the display case." He unlatched the glass cube from its oak base and smiled as his wife picked up the carving with great care. Turning it over, she read the words inscribed on the bottom: *To Linda my Love. Let's do it again. Arnie.* And beneath that, the artisan's neat printing: *Hand Crafted at Jimmy Lee Specialty Arts – 44°38.9'N 78°40.3'W.*

"Just one thing, sweetheart. We can't tell a soul ... can't show it to anyone here in America. Not even our closest friends. Chuck has seen it, of course, when he built the case. But I've sworn him to secrecy. If word ever got out, agents from the Fish and Wildlife Service would come down hard on us, just for possession alone.

"Once we've moved into our place in the islands it will be safe to put it on display. Kiribati isn't bound by the international endangered species convention.

"In the meantime, when anyone asks what I gave you for Christmas, just tell them, 'A trip to France.'"

"I'll pack it away right now, Arnie. It will be safe with the taboo Navajo art we're taking with us."

—

Monday, January 27, 0945 – Highway 1 near Broadview, Saskatchewan.

Eighteen wheels locked up. Eighteen tires chattered on the bare pavement, smoking, despite the bitter cold prairie wind. The white Kenworth tractor came screeching to a stop barely a foot from the massive roadblock. The driver and his two passengers stared wide-eyed at the six law enforcement carbines aimed directly at them.

Forty-five minutes earlier, the driver had failed to stop at the westbound weigh scales near Moosomin, Saskatchewan. And just five minutes after that, he ignored a Highway Patrol officer's order to pull over. Completely disregarded the government pickup truck's glaring red and blue emergency lights.

Twenty minutes later, the Kenworth driver blew through the first roadblock, smashing two police cruisers out of the way, just like they do in the movies. Two constables were now being rushed to the nearest trauma unit with serious injuries.

The Mounties were in no mood for a re-run when they chose the location for this final roadblock. They'd picked a highway construction site just west of Broadview. Work had stopped for the winter, so there was little chance of what the military calls "collateral damage."

Two police SUVs had moved to block the westbound lanes just minutes before the transport came into view. As soon as it became obvious that the driver of the big rig planned a repeat performance, RCMP Corporal Jacques Dupuis signalled to the driver of a Euclid earthmover that sat idling in the snow-covered median. The diesel monster, awakened from its winter shutdown, belched a dense cloud of black exhaust as it rolled across the road, completely blocking the westbound lanes. It provided a nearly impenetrable barrier between the rampaging transport and the police vehicles.

Within seconds of getting his rig stopped, the Kenworth driver threw the automatic transmission into reverse hoping to do a backing, jackknife U-turn. Not willing to give up yet, he figured he'd go back to a secondary highway they'd just passed. It was a desperation move.

But the police weren't about to let that happen. A Caterpillar D-8 bulldozer from the construction site, clattered onto the road behind the transport. The operator pivoted the dozer, closing the gap, and boxed the rig in.

The six officers stood protected by the front and rear

ends of the earthmover, and they held their pose while the corporal used a megaphone to address the road warriors.

"Driver … turn off your engine and exit the cab. *Do it now!*" The man behind the wheel looked at his companions, and then reluctantly complied.

The next order: "Face down on the ground. *Do it now!*"

Before advancing on the man, Corporal Dupuis followed the same routine with the two passengers. When all three were lying prone on the freezing cold pavement, they were arrested, handcuffed and thoroughly searched. The search produced a loaded 9 mm handgun, several knives and a can of bear spray. A search of the sleeper cab produced no more perpetrators but yielded a Ruger Mini-14 semi-automatic rifle, complete with a fully loaded twenty-round magazine. Classed as a prohibited weapon in Canada, it and the pistol had been smuggled into the country from the United States.

The takedown team consisted of the Mountie corporal and three constables as well as two Saskatchewan Highway Patrol truck inspectors and a conservation officer. The latter three had recently been given full police powers.

The four Mounties loaded the prisoners into the police SUVs while the three provincial officers moved to the back of the transport trailer. They were curious to see what cargo was worth avoiding an inspection at the weigh scale. The manifest taken from the cab read "mixed freight – 15,000 pounds." Not a heavy load. If that was all that was in there, they'd have most likely been waved over the scale without having to stop or undergo any further inspection.

After the bulldozer backed clear of the doors, one of the highway patrol officers took bolt cutters to the padlock and the boxcar seal securing the load. His partner and the conservation officer covered him with their pistols drawn. They all stood back as the doors swung open to reveal a load of large white, woven plastic bags. The bags were stacked three high and three across and covered all but the back ten feet of the fifty-three-foot trailer. The conservation officer was the first to speak.

"Huh … smells like beaver."

The highway patrol officers chuckled.

"C'mon guys, the four-legged, fur bearing … oh, forget it." He grinned and said, "What I mean is, it smells like a shipment of raw fur pelts."

"Yeah, yeah." More amused chuckles. Two highway patrol officers to one lonely game warden was an open invitation to some friendly ribbing.

The CO shook his head and climbed into the back of the trailer. He opened a half dozen bags. If all the heavy-duty fur bags in the trailer contained the same product, then it was a cargo of beaver pelts, just as his nose had detected.

"If that's all that's in here, it's a mystery as to why they would have avoided the weigh scale. The only thing missing is export permits for the fur."

"It's an Ontario truck," the highway patrol officer with the bolt cutters said.

"Yeah, their COs will be more than a little pissed if these guys are moving this much fur without any paperwork. They could be missing out on a shitload of royalties. Can one of you check the cab again? I'll go and have a chat with the driver and his buddies."

Chapter 2

The office headquarters of Overnight Shipping Logistics sat in a shabby industrial park, wedged between a complex of modern big box stores on one side and a pair of tired looking 1960s era apartment towers on the other. It did not make for an inspiring work environment. But the tense atmosphere inside the office had nothing to do with its dreary surroundings.

Overnight Shipping Logistics did not have a fleet of trucks on the road — just the one that was now tied up in legal knots in Saskatchewan. Most of OSL's business — the above-board part of the business — was facilitating freight transportation for others. "Big load or small, we handle them all," was the automated telephone greeting clients heard before a live operator came on the line. If a shipper had five thousand or fifty thousand pounds of goods to go from a Toronto warehouse to a Walmart store in another city, OSL would find a truck and arrange for it to pick up the shipment and get it to its destination, usually before the next business day.

The front office was a drab room about twenty feet square. The room was divided roughly in half by a worn, chest high customer service counter. Behind the counter were three mismatched desks. The desks on the right and left faced the one in the centre. The centre one was pushed up against the counter.

Bea, the matronly middle-aged dispatcher, sat at the right-hand desk. She was on the phone; her fingers flying across her desktop keyboard as she arranged transportation for another client's freight. She was very good at multi-tasking. She had fine-tuned those skills in a previous dispatch position years earlier. In addition to being a whiz at her own job, she had the uncanny ability to simultaneously keep her ears open to other goings on in the office.

"Overnight Shipping, how can I help you?" Bea took the next call.

Sylvia, the boss's gorgeous personal secretary, was an anomaly in the otherwise shabby surroundings. She sat at the middle desk. At the moment, she was busy filing her nails. To a frequent visitor, that might have appeared to be the extent of her duties — she always seemed to be filing her nails. But monitoring the progress of the company's own transport truck and answering general phone enquiries did come first.

Twenty minutes ago, she'd alerted the boss to a possible problem. The GPS tracking information on her desktop screen showed the company's truck stopped for over three hours somewhere in the middle of the prairies. Way too long for a lunch break. More likely a breakdown or a road closure. She'd listened in on her extension when the boss tried to call the delivery crew — and heard him gasp when the phone was answered by an RCMP corporal.

Now her phone rang — inside line — the boss.

"Get Raymond in here *right now!*" Derek Cheney was livid. Cheney was the company's owner, and when things got this badly screwed up, he was entitled to be livid.

Raymond Conn was the occupant of the third desk. He didn't need Sylvia to relay the message. He'd heard it all too clearly. He stepped into Derek's office, nervous, but supremely ticked off as well. Raymond was entitled to be nervous. Not because Cheney was the muscle-bound, tattooed tyrant that he was — Raymond was built like a bulldog himself and could hold his own if push came to shove — but he was nervous, because when something got screwed up, it was usually his fault. At least it was, as far as Cheney was concerned. But the boss's attitude was feeding a slow burn that had been festering in Raymond for months, stoked a little more with each negative encounter between the two of them.

"Those three idiots you sent west with the load have got themselves into a deep pile of shit. Missed a weigh scale and ran a roadblock somewhere out on the prairies. They damned near killed a couple of Mounties and now the truck's been impounded.

"What the *fuck* were those shit-for-brains boneheads thinking? All they had to do was drive over a weigh scale like all the other truckers and move on. Light load like that wouldn't have sparked anyone's interest if they'd just acted normal. *Shit!*" He ran a hand over his greying crewcut, then looked at the sweat on his hand before wiping it dry on the leg of his jeans.

"We need that truck back *A*-sap, Raymond. And I need it to arrive on schedule. I don't want to miss out on this shipment. That Chinaman doesn't sell his products on credit. The ship arrives out there in less than ten days. You do whatever it takes to meet that boat on time." For security purposes, "out there" was all he could tell his people until they got close to the west coast, and even then, only on the day of the transaction would they learn the exact destination.

The ship's captain never told his clients the exact rendezvous location until the last possible moment. Not one soul in North America knew exactly where he would land until he was confident that the coast was clear — literally.

As much as the boss always heaped the blame for any

screw-ups on his second in command, Raymond was still the only person who could manage the demanding logistics of this side of his business. And Raymond always got things done. Or he had, at least, until the COVID virus had sidelined his regular delivery crew. And now the B team had just got an F.

Out in the front office, on the other side of Derek's closed door, both women could hear the conversation clearly. Sylvia wondered if it would even qualify as a conversation when only one person was doing all the talking — more like yelling.

Chapter 3

Conservation Officer Rob McNabb grabbed his parka and started to leave the office for lunch. But the desk phone warbled before he made it to the door. Any thought of letting the call go to voicemail lasted no more than a millisecond. That wasn't his style. His dedication to the job wouldn't allow him to walk away from an incoming call — no matter how hungry he was.

"Enforcement, McNabb speaking." He sat back down and laid his coat on the desk.

"*Someone has been dumping garbage on my trapline.*" The voice, a woman's — Cree accent — and familiar to him. "What are you going to do about that?"

"May I ask who's calling please?"

"*You know damn well who I am, Robert McNabb. It's Martha Trumpeter. Just look at that call display in front of you.*"

"Okay, Martha, you win," he smiled to himself. She was a regular visitor at the office; a tough as nails old bird, well into her sixties, but easy to like and usually a reliable source of local information. Just the same, he liked to jerk her chain at least a little. She would be disappointed if he didn't. It was a ritual they shared.

"Now, how do you know someone's been dumping garbage there?"

"Because there's a pile of bagged garbage in the middle of my trail and I didn't put it there ... rookie!"

Time to get serious. "Human tracks there, Martha?"

"Yes, but I don't know whose, if that's what you're asking. And Skidoo tracks ... pulling a wide plastic toboggan, not a sleigh on runners. The tracks lead right back to town where they got buried by the road traffic."

"Well then, I'll go over and see if I can find some identifying information," he told her. Although he had a near perfect track record for solving littering cases of this nature, he hated digging through garbage bags for evidence of ownership. At least the worst smelling, gross items were usually frozen solid at this time of year. But sorting through it was never a pleasant process.

"You are a good man, Robert McNabb. Someday you'll make a fine amisk hookimaw."

"I sure do appreciate your confidence, Martha. Thanks for calling. Bye now."

Amisk hookimaw was a title that the Cree people had conferred on conservation officers in Ontario for generations. The English translation was beaver boss. After solving his first major case, within months of arriving in the district, McNabb had been embraced as Moosonee's own amisk hookimaw for most of his three years there. In everyone's mind but Martha's.

He made a quick call home. "Sam, sweetie, I won't be home for lunch. Just got a complaint that could be time sensitive if it snows again this afternoon. Garbage bags to search and a possible tracking job."

"Okay, Robbie. Stop by and pick up your sandwiches on the way. They're already made. And I'll fill your Thermos before you get here." Samantha Williams wasn't flying today, so she'd already left for lunch ahead of him. Sam was a provincial air service pilot. She was stationed in Moosonee to fly the MNR's Turbo Beaver.

In a vast district with no year-round road systems to connect the coastal communities either to each other, or to the outside world, the bush plane was the primary mode of transportation for anything other than local work. As a result, this particular aircraft was specifically earmarked for Moosonee District. And because more than eighty percent of flying in the district was enforcement related, McNabb and his partner officer came to think of the Beaver as their own patrol vehicle.

At twenty-nine years, Williams was three days older than McNabb. Despite being only five-feet four-inches tall and possessing a modest figure, Sam was a woman who could carry a load and fly a bush plane as well as anyone. The green-eyed, curly haired redhead rarely wore makeup. A light sprinkling of freckles on her cheeks and nose, gave her an almost girlish look. Sam could be feisty if someone pissed her off, but she strove to please everyone she worked with, and was a favourite among her colleagues.

Sam and Rob had first worked together tracking a dangerous polar bear poacher when McNabb was still a rookie. A series of life-threatening events they faced during that case had drawn them together, and now they were a married couple with two daughters — an eighteen-month-old of their own and an adopted teen.

—

Sam was leaning over the dining room table, helping Mae Ling, their fifteen-year-old adopted daughter with a math problem. Schooling at home during the COVID plague.

"You can work it out in either metric or imperial measure, Mae Ling. But since the four dimensions are given in imperial, my preference would be to stay with imperial and then convert your final answer to metric. But you can do it either way."

They paused when McNabb's government Skidoo rumbled into the backyard. They could hear him come up the back porch steps, two at a time. The instant he opened the back door, he was almost bowled over by the family's big orange tabby. The cat was in a hurry to escape the clutches of little Lottie.

Once safely inside, Rob reached down and scooped up his little girl for a hug, then hoisted her up to touch the ceiling. The six-foot dad had discovered that the toddler went into laughing hysterics every time they played that game. It was always a treat, hearing those happy sounds fill the house.

Cradling Lottie on his hip, he pulled the snowmobile helmet off. His sandy brown hair was long overdue for a cut. He used his fingers to comb it out of his blue eyes, then kicked off his snow boots and walked to the counter where he attempted to stuff his lunch into his day pack — but that would have required at least one more free hand. Sam came to his rescue and snatched the baby from her dad, then returned to watch Mae Ling's progress. The Turbo Beaver pilot could do complex math calculations in her head, and Mae Ling appreciated having her own in-house tutor.

Rob pulled his boots back on, blew kisses to his women, and when he opened the door, almost tripped over the cat who was now in a hurry to escape the frigid temperature out in the yard. McNabb rushed down the steps and headed the Skidoo toward the railway station at the top end of First Street.

Martha Trumpeter's trapline started at the edge of town, and after crossing the railroad tracks, McNabb slowly followed her snowshoe trail as it wound through the black spruce forest along the banks of Store Creek. Someone else had run a snowmobile along her trail and the tracks were fresh, over top of last night's dusting of snow. They'd been pulling a plastic toboggan, just as she'd said. Martha's snowshoe tracks on top of the snowmobile tracks were the only other sign of activity.

Martha didn't own a snowmobile. "I don't want one of those screamin' machines," she said. "Can't afford one anyhow." She got around in the bush on snowshoes as she had her entire life. An old wooden toboggan was all she needed to haul her gear.

McNabb continued following the trail for almost a kilometre to where it turned away from the creek. Right around the next bend in the trail sat half a dozen black plastic garbage bags. They were heaped beside the trail in a random pile. Two ravens flew off a short distance, scolding him for interrupting their take-out lunch. He mimicked their squawks and they answered with more, a conversation he continued with the intelligent birds while he hurried through a sandwich before starting his search.

A few folks claimed there was a raven in town that could mimic human speech. McNabb didn't entirely doubt their claims and occasionally put the birds to the test. But he hadn't met the right bird yet. So as he opened the first bag of trash, he began to recite his favourite Robert Service poem, but the ravens continued in their own conversational cluck-and-squawk.

"*There are strange things done in the midnight sun,*" he called out to the birds, "*By the men who moil for gold* … aw shit, got dirty diapers instead." He was sure that the ravens were laughing at him now. Sounded that way, anyhow.

Digging through other people's garbage was not a pleasant part of the job. But there were usually rewards for his persistence. And sure enough, beneath the second layer of undesirables, he found a soggy telephone bill and an empty prescription drug bottle.

The same person's name appeared on both items and was someone he'd previously charged for littering — at a different location. The name showed up on several documents in a couple of the other bags too, so after taking pictures of the scene, he loaded whole mess into the sleigh behind his machine.

There would be no out-of-court settlement available to the guy this time. As a repeat offender, the jerk would be getting a court summons, and the local Justice of the Peace, an outdoor enthusiast herself, played rough with repeat offenders.

Chapter 4

After returning from the littering complaint scene, McNabb spent the rest of the afternoon preparing court documents and a case summary for the Crown prosecutor. And he made a point of calling Martha back to thank her for the lead. He was busy typing a violation report, two-fingered, into the provincial information system when his supervisor entered the room. James Bird didn't speak until the CO looked up from his work.

"Checked your email yet this afternoon, Robbie?"

"That's my next 'to do' James. Why?" McNabb turned back to his desktop PC and switched screens. And then he groaned. More than a dozen new messages sat waiting in the inbox. He'd already cleared out all the new messages just before lunch.

"There's one from head office you might want to check out. Let me know if you are interested. I don't think there are many other COs in the province qualified to drive transport trucks," Bird said as he turned and left the room.

His parting comment piqued McNabb's interest, as intended. With the district enforcement budget just about drained for the year, James figured that one officer working out of district on the provincial tab for a few days would get them a few days closer to the new fiscal year — and a fresh budget.

McNabb found the email from head office. It read:

URGENT — PROVINCEWIDE
To ALL Conservation Officers:
Immediately require one CO with A-Z driver's licence.
TASK: Retrieve seized transport and load of illegal fur from Saskatchewan and deliver said seizures to secure storage in North Bay.
CO Rick Webb already in Regina working on the investigation. Webb will accompany load on return trip. Please reply to the director before end of business today, if possible.
Dorothy Fitch, Chief, Enforcement Branch

—

Rob stuck his head in the boss's office minutes after reading the message. "I'd love to do it, James, but I've got to check with Sam first. She's scheduled to fly moose surveys beginning on Monday. She'll really be pissed if I screw that up."

"Okay, Robbie, go check with her. The last thing we want is to have an upset pilot."

"Be right back." McNabb raced up the stairs to Sam's office. He worried about confronting her with a scheduling challenge of this magnitude on such short notice, but she was surprisingly unperturbed by his request.

"I don't see a problem, Robbie. Katie's already isolating with us while her furnace is broken down." Katie Burke, an elementary school teacher, was their closest friend and their next-door-neighbour. "And with the schools closed again because of the current COVID wave, she is pretty much running the household for us already. I expect she'd love to take care of the girls while we're out of district. But I'll give her a call just to make sure."

While the birth of Charlotte Jean, eighteen months ago, had been expected, the adoption of a teenager just four months later, had not. Rob and Sam had been involved in the rescue of Mae Ling during a life-threatening encounter with her abductor at the conclusion of what had started out as a poaching investigation.

At thirteen, an orphan and victim of human trafficking, she had been sold by an uncle and smuggled into the country for the purpose of prostitution. When the dust had settled on the case, it was determined that Mae Ling was eligible for refugee status. If deported back to her home country, she would most likely have been resold into the sex trade. Rob and Sam learned that as a refugee, she would face the remainder of her teen years as a ward of the province, in foster care. They couldn't bear the thought of that and had jumped through a myriad of bureaucratic hoops before being allowed to adopt the girl. Now she was a full-fledged member of their family.

"Thanks Katie, you're a life saver. We'll be home shortly. There you go, Flyboy. Now you can dig out your cowboy boots and fancy belt buckle and go truckin."

"Thanks Sam, but I think they expect me to show up in uniform. You can buy me the boots and buckle for my birthday, though." It was almost quitting time when he hurried back downstairs to Bird's office with the news.

"Okay Robbie, I called the director as soon as you said you were interested … I know Sam well enough by now that I guessed she would agree." He gave Rob a flash of his spontaneous Cree grin. "Anyhow, the director said you were the only volunteer so far. I'll call her back and let her know that you'll be heading out tomorrow. You go and make your flight reservations. It'll probably be a long day, what with layovers in Timmins and Toronto before the flight to Regina."

—

At the same time – on the Pacific Ocean 2400 nautical miles west of British Columbia

The Chinese flagged vessel, *Ocean Princess* came nowhere close to living up to her regal name. At ten thousand tons, the cargo ship was much too small to be a major player in the modern world of intermodal container shipping. Fashioned on the design of World War II Liberty ships, she was now little more than a bucket of rust on her last legs. Badly underpaid, her Indonesian crew lacked the incentive to carry out even the most basic maintenance and her officers lacked the initiative to inspire them.

At her best speed, *Ocean Princess* could no longer make the sixteen knots she did when she was launched forty-five years earlier. On a good day she could average almost fifteen, but in heavy seas, Captain Chang never pushed her over ten knots.

Ocean Princess carried a small cargo of containers bound for the port of Vancouver, British Columbia, or thereabouts. Only the captain knew the exact place she would dock. Security was important. The containers she carried were not shipped by big name Asian manufacturing facilities. Major corporations expected timely deliveries and insisted on dependable modern vessels. *Ocean Princess* struggled even to play in the minor leagues.

In fact, the cargo on this crossing was a mixture of legal, but third-rate, manufactured goods, some counterfeit designer goods and a container carrying an illegal mixed load of heroin and African ivory. She also carried a container accommodating twenty-four illegal migrants expecting a fresh start in a promised land but destined for a degrading life of enslaved servitude.

At the moment, *Ocean Princess* was plodding eastbound, across glass calm waters, making her best "almost fifteen knots."

Chapter 5

When Rob McNabb emerged from the arrivals gate in the Regina airport, he was approached by a uniformed Ontario conservation officer he hadn't previously met.

"McNabb? I'm Rick Webb."

"Hi Rick. Good to meet you. Boss told me you'd be here to greet me. How are you doing?"

"Not bad for an old guy." At forty-one, Webb was far from being over the hill, but sometimes he felt his age when meeting the next generation of enthusiastic young officers. "It's good to meet you too, and thanks for coming on short notice."

"Glad to be able to come. I'm here as a cost-saving measure at the suggestion of the boss. But I *am* here voluntarily. My partner and I have just about burned through our budget for the year, so while I'm on this project, I'm not costing my own district anything."

McNabb had flown with just a carry-on bag, so they bypassed the baggage carousels on the way out.

"James Bird says you are on the Great Lakes team, Rick. So, what are you doing investigating wild fur out here in the middle of the bald-ass prairies?"

"Same thing as you. The money pot's run dry, and with the lake mostly frozen over, boating's no fun and the snowmobiles don't float for long." Several inches shorter than McNabb's six feet, Webb led the way toward the exit as they talked. He had been a CO since graduating from college eighteen years earlier.

Like McNabb, he kept himself in good shape, not through any workout plan, but by leading an active outdoor life. His brown hair was tinged with early shades of grey. Unlike McNabb, his hair was short, courtesy of a buzz cut recently administered by his wife.

"So how is James, anyhow? He was our acting staff sergeant for six months just before he transferred up north."

"Man, I couldn't ask for a better boss. He's the kind of guy you work with ... not for."

"Yeah, I can believe that. He did a great job in the short time he was with us in Parry Sound. Couldn't have been easy stepping into a short-term acting position. A bit like being a school supply teacher."

"I remember those," McNabb chuckled. "Us kids *always* gave them a rough time. Cruel little brats."

"Sounds familiar," Webb agreed, smiling. "And James arrived just in time to clean up a mess left by the guy before him. Low morale ... everyone going off in their own direction ... without any direction. To make things worse, we had a couple of real rednecks on the team who figured James was given the job because he was Indigenous. They called him our Token Indian. And that was when they were being polite about it.

"But he didn't rise to the bait. When he arrived, he just sat down with each of us for a quiet one-on-one chat to learn our strengths and interests, and then a week later, he called a group meeting with the whole team. The session was geared to going forward. Not a word said about past issues. Within days, everyone was on board, working as a real team and enjoying their jobs again, including the rednecks, who completely changed their tune."

Webb and McNabb zipped up their parkas as they stepped out into the cold night air and headed for the parking lot.

"So, what's the story on this mission, Rick? About all I got from the director's email was, 'A seized transport and its load of fur needs a driver. Come quick.' Couldn't they just hire a bonded driver to bring the rig back?"

"It's a strange story, Rob, and I get the feeling we don't know the half of it yet. But a trio of tough-looking characters from Toronto blew past a government weigh scale with a load of fur that has no export permits or any other documentation. When they finally got snagged at a heavy-duty roadblock, they told a Saskatchewan CO that the load was going to a big furrier's shop in China. Then they lawyered up.

"We checked it out, and the Chinese officials have been helpful. But it turns out that there's no such shop ... no such address, even. All we do know is that the shipment originated in Ontario. But we don't yet know who bought the fur from whom."

"How big's the load?"

"Saskatchewan guys counted a hundred and sixty bags, more than three-quarters of which are beaver. At fifty pelts per bag, those are heavy. Wolves, bobcat, marten, otter and black bear make up most of the rest of the load and there are four polar bear hides aboard too. Of course, other than beaver, most of the rest require CITES permits, which again, they didn't have."

Shipping any product of a species listed under the Convention on International Trade in Endangered Species without permits meant big trouble. There was a federal agency responsible for that, but the provinces were on the front lines as usual.

"The only document in the cab was a generic manifest declaring fifteen thousand pounds of general freight," Webb continued. "But dividing that by a hundred and sixty bags would average a little over ninety pounds per bag. The few beaver bags I've opened and checked are at least that heavy."

"That's still a light load for a big rig, Rick. But I understand, you aren't an A-Z driver?"

"Nope. You're it. I'm riding shotgun. And as it turns out, our departure has been delayed by a day. The Mounties didn't finish their forensic work on the rig until early this afternoon. Only then did they release it to the Saskatchewan Highway Patrol guys to do a safety inspection.

"Their mechanic is coming in tomorrow. The plan is to check it over before it goes on the road again. He says he needs a hand to remove the crash bars from the front. They got bent when the bad guys rammed the police cars at the first roadblock. He can't tip them forward and therefore can't raise the hood to check for mechanical damage inside. So I volunteered you.

"He's reasonably confident that other than some broken fibreglass bodywork, it will be okay. It was driven from Broadview to here under its own power, but he won't sign off on it until he's done a proper inspection.

"Also, I've got a few more things to nail down on the case here with their COs, so we're looking at a late start, tomorrow afternoon, at the earliest."

"If it's okay with you, Rick, I'd prefer to start first thing the next morning. I looked it up, and it's about twenty-four hundred kilometres from here to North Bay. I'm allowed thirteen driving hours per day. *If* we could average one hundred kilometres per hour, had perfect road and weather conditions and no mechanical problems, I'd need every minute of two days to get there legally. But that'll never happen. Murphy's law." He was referring to the commonly quoted saying that goes: If anything can possibly go wrong, it probably will.

"So, we're looking at a good portion of three days on the road."

"No problem, Rob. You're the driver. You choose the route and set the schedule."

They got into Webb's rental car but stayed bundled in their parkas. At -38° C, it was as cold inside as out until the car began to warm up after a few kilometres.

After they stopped at a drive-through to pick up supper for McNabb, Webb drove them to the hotel where he'd been staying. All restaurants were closed for dining in again due to the COVID pandemic. They shared a double room and talked about families and work experiences while Rob ate his burgers.

"So, James tells me that you met your wife on the job too, Rick."

"Well, job related. I was just beginning a sailing vacation, and on my second day out on Georgian Bay I ran into a hazardous waste fiasco that I couldn't ignore. It could have turned out to be the vacation from hell. The bad guys were determined to eliminate any witnesses — of which I was one — and they roughed up my boat pretty badly, but I met Erin during the ordeal, and we haven't looked back since. And by some odd coincidence," he smiled as he spoke, "our little Jimmy came along almost exactly nine months later. Go figure.

"Now Erin is expecting a little sister for our boy. Due in three months. I think Jimmy is as excited as Mommy and Daddy are. So aside from the pandemic panic, life is good, Rob."

They turned in after watching the late news. There would be a few long days ahead before either of them got back home.

—

Friday, January 31, 0830 – government garage, Regina, Saskatchewan

Rick Webb dropped McNabb at the Saskatchewan Highway Patrol complex on his way to finish his business with the local conservation officers. Rob met the government mechanic in the front office. The man introduced himself simply as Arnold. A slender, silver haired man in his fifties, Arnold spoke with a slight German accent.

"Here are the keys," he said as he led McNabb into the garage area. "It is out in the yard. Unhitch from the trailer and bring the tractor into this bay. The block heater has been plugged in all night, so it should start alright.

"I have to get some equipment ready before you drive it in. I was originally planning to remove the bent crash bars, but I think we can straighten them in place." The man was referring to the heavy-duty protective rack attached to the front bumper. Members of the trucking fraternity often called them moose bars, roo bars or bull bars, depending on where in the world one was driving. They were designed to protect the tractor's hood and forward bodywork in the event the rig hit a moose, a kangaroo or domestic livestock. As solid as a highway tractor might appear, the forward bodywork on most transports is fibreglass and on modern trucks, the radiator is just one of several vulnerable heat exchange devices housed right behind the grillwork.

Ten minutes later, following Arnold's precise hand signals, McNabb inched a big white Kenworth tractor into place and shut it down. He was opening the door to dismount from the cab, but Arnold told him to get back in and wait for instructions. Rob ran down the power windows, partly so he could hear the man, but primarily to let some warm air from the garage into the freezing cold cab.

Arnold hooked one end of a length of heavy chain to one corner of the bent push bars and the other end to a steel eyebolt anchored in the concrete floor. Then he had McNabb start up and ease the truck backward several times. Each time the tractor jerked the chain tight, it straightened the push bar frame a little closer to its original alignment. At one point, the mechanic relocated the chain to a new position and had McNabb repeat the process several more times before he was satisfied with the result.

"Good. That's enough. Now get down and give me a hand. If you don't want to get your uniform dirty there are coveralls hanging over there." The lower five feet of the cab's bodywork was covered with road salt and grime from the winter drive west. McNabb pulled on a set of blue coveralls and joined Arnold at the front of the truck.

"Now, we pull forward on the bars." With more force than would normally be required, the heavy-duty grill protector tilted forward. The two men had to stand on the bars to force them the last six inches down to the floor. Arnold sprayed some lubricant on the hinge points before they moved on to unlatch the hood and tilt it forward. Even before it came to rest, Arnold spotted trouble.

"There's a breakdown waiting to happen." He pointed to the tail end of a screw that was beginning to chafe a hole into the outer layers of a radiator hose. The screw, which fastened some of the fibreglass bodywork together, got shifted back almost half an inch. That was all that was needed for it to contact the hose after the truck had hit the police cars. It would have worn a hole right into the hose long before the truck got to North Bay.

Not about to repair the bodywork, Arnold simply removed the screw and turned it end for end. Now the rounded head was next to the hose — but not touching it.

"Arnold, when I started it up outside, the ABS light came on, and it stays on. I had brakes okay, but I don't know how serious an antilock brake issue might be. Didn't have it on the old rigs I trained on."

"It is possibly just the circuit breaker, or a relay. It sometimes happens on these big trucks. The fellow who drove it here said the same thing, so we'll check it out."

While he continued his inspection of the engine compartment, Arnold handed McNabb a tire pressure gauge. All the tires were within several pounds of the same pressure, but when he was finished, Rob reported that the two outer tires on the rear axle appeared to have inner tubes in them. All the rest were tubeless. He could tell the difference by the shape of the valve stems.

Arnold had Rob start the truck again and roll slowly forward while he examined the tires that had the tubes in them. "The tires are okay. They may have had slow leaks around the rim. This was their fix. It is not uncommon to do that."

While Arnold continued his detailed inspection and reset the anti-lock brake system, McNabb found some strong cleaners and rags. He gave the filthy seats, steering wheel and control surfaces a wipe down and swept half an inch of sand and gravel off the floor mats. When he had finished, it was by no means a sterile environment, but was much improved over the condition it was in when he first climbed into the cab. These OSL guys lived like pigs. No, scratch that, he thought. It would be unfair to brand four-legged swine with the same label.

Following a road test, first with the tractor alone, then with the trailer attached, the rig passed its inspection. They plugged it in for another cold night outdoors and Arnold gave McNabb a ride back to the hotel. He was in the shower, ridding himself of the OSL crew's grunge by 2:20 pm.

Chapter 6

Toronto, Ontario

Douglas Bowman, the provincial police commissioner, sat at his desk shaking his head. He and Staff Superintendent Stan Farrell were suffering through a phone call from the deputy minister overseeing the federal agency that was funding the Overnight Shipping Logistics investigation. Farrell was in charge of the Major Case Section. They didn't dare piss the federal guy off, because he controlled the purse strings for this project. But they sure didn't like dealing with the desk-bound senior civil servant. The only reason that they were involved with the federal government was because it had originally been an RCMP case before they passed the lead to the province — the primary suspects being from Ontario. So, the commissioner and the superintendent listened to the man drone on.

"We'll continue to fund your project for now, but I'm not happy that you've taken these game wardens into the mix. Those people are nothing more than glorified dog catchers," the deputy minister grumbled. *"I've read their files. One of them set some guy's tugboat on fire in order to arrest him and the other emptied his pistol into a poacher when the poor fellow wouldn't stop. They're a pair of damned loose cannons if you ask me."*

"The poacher wouldn't stop shooting at the officer's pilot, sir," Stan Farrell responded, "I believe that if you read the reports to the end, you would find both of these conservation officers were responding bravely to extremely difficult situations. And the actions of each officer were cleared by our provincial police watchdog agency."

"Swept under the carpet, no doubt, Superintendent. People like that are likely to leak information on a highly sensitive investigation such as this. In any event, I don't want them briefed on the finer details of this project. If you can promise me that, we'll approve the funding to continue. We just don't know if they can be trusted, and you know the old wartime saying: 'Loose lips sink ships.'"

The commissioner replied this time. "We'll do our best, Deputy Minister. But at some point, we'll likely have to take them into our confidence."

"Damned well better not." And the call suddenly ended.

"That guy's a real asshole, Commissioner. I don't understand his paranoia. Those two COs have got outstanding records, and McNabb has already worked on several task force operations with our people."

"Look Stan, just carry on as we planned. Hold back what you can from the two COs without endangering them. The man is probably scared to death that having already gone overbudget, he's going to be on the hot seat if this case falls apart. So now, he's busy picking bodies to throw under the bus to save his own skin should it happen."

Farrell didn't look happy. "The team is not going to like this, but we'll try to make it as painless as we can. I'm concerned that if part of the team is working blind, it poses a risk not only to the outcome of the project, but also to the safety of everyone involved."

—

Raymond Conn was at his desk, printing out masterfully forged substitute vehicle registrations and insurance slips for the Kenworth and the trailer while he waited for a phone call from Willie and the road crew. He had already gone home and packed his travel bag for a week on the road.

Chapter 7

The prisoners sat in front of a camera in a small room in the city jail, waiting for technicians to establish a video link with the courthouse. The judge, the prosecutor, the defence lawyer and the court clerk were in the courtroom across town, waiting for the same thing to happen. It would take a couple more minutes.

The judge looked at the clerk. "Is this to do with those idiots who ran the police roadblock the other day?"

"Yes, Your Honour."

"Stunned assholes." Nothing was being recorded yet.

"Alleged stunned assholes, Your Honour," came from the counsel for the defence. He sat at the defence table smiling as he leafed through some documents in front of him.

"Maimed a couple of our badly overworked Mounties and wrecked two expensive government vehicles, Mr. Clark. You know full well what I'd do to them if we weren't constrained by the law."

"Allegedly maimed, Your Honour. And yes, I *could* envision you standing over them while you made them dig their own graves."

"Alleged ... damnably overused adjective in this business Mr. Clark." The judge looked at the Crown attorney. "Madam prosecutor, what condition are the 'alleged' victims in?"

"The police vehicles are totalled but the constables are recovering, Your Honour," Jennifer Burdsall replied. She too was smiling. Away from the ears of the public, the judge and James Clark carried on like this on a regular basis — probably did it all the time they were out on the golf course too. They were next door neighbours and good friends.

Clark parried: "I do hope you don't take your personal feelings out on my poor clients, Your Honour."

"Mr. Clark, you've been before this court enough times by now to know that the sleazy characters you defend will get a perfectly fair and unbiased hearing once court is open. Madam clerk, please open the court."

The clerk pushed a button. The video feeds went live. "All rise." Burdsall and Clark, stood behind their tables. They were the only people in the courtroom besides the judge and clerk. "This bail court hearing for the Province of Saskatchewan is now in session. His Honour, Judge Neil McKechnie presiding. Please be seated."

The judge took it from there. "In the matter of William Eardley, Zachary Graham and Jason Mead, I see they've been jointly charged with criminal negligence causing bodily harm and possession of one restricted and one prohibited firearm." McKechnie looked up at his monitor. "Are those the defendants on the screen, Madam prosecutor?"

"Yes, they are, Your Honour."

"Hmph. Can you gentlemen hear us alright, there?" Three heads nodded and mumbled affirmative replies.

"Speak up please. Can you hear us? The clerk can not record bobbing heads."

"Yes, sir ... ah, Your Honour," One spoke for the three of them.

"You are aware that these are indictable offenses? Your

lawyer has gone over this with you, has he?" He glanced at his monitor again to catch their replies. "Then I see a bunch of summary offenses listed here too, boys. Not as bad as the criminal charges, but very serious matters when taken as a whole. What does the defence have to say, Mr. Clark?"

"I've spoken with the defendants and with their employer, a Mr. Derek Cheney, Your Honour. He assures me that these three men are not likely to offend again and are not a flight risk. They are gainfully employed, and Eardley and Mead have been with his company for almost five years. Graham is a nephew and has been working for him just over two years. He also assures me that he will be paying for their return trip to court as soon as the pandemic shutdown is loosened, and a trial date scheduled. I see no reason to refuse bail, particularly under the COVID Temporary Release program."

"Cheney ... Cheney ... there's something familiar about the name. A careless hunting case if memory serves ... a few years back maybe," he looked at the young prosecutor. Ms. Burdsall shrugged. "No? ... Oh, well, probably some other shady character I'm thinking about.

"So, Mr. Clark, you're recommending a release on this COVID Program they're pushing at us?"

"Yes, Your Honour."

"Goes totally against my better judgement ... but ... on their own recognizance...."

"Your Honour," Burdsall jumped to her feet. "Perhaps the court would allow some input from the prosecution?" And without waiting for the judge's permission, she dove right in. "Even more grave than the firearms offenses, Your Honour, these defendants recklessly endangered...."

"Allegedly," Clark interjected.

".... Endangered the lives of two police officers,

35

injuring them badly in the process. If the court intends to turn them loose at all, then that fact alone merits them posting a substantial bail. The Crown asks for at least twenty thousand dollars each."

"Mr. Clark?" the judge looked at his golfing buddy.

"Your Honour, that's a lot of money to expect mere truck drivers to come up with. Our position remains, as you began to say, that they be released on their own recognizance."

"Shall we split it down the middle, then?" Judge McKechnie asked. Neither Burdsall nor Clark looked happy with the compromise but they each consented.

Turning toward the camera, Judge McKechnie addressed the defendants. "The prosecutor and your attorney have agreed to allow for your release on ten thousand dollars bail. That's ten thousand for each one of you. If this COVID business hadn't brought the court system to a standstill and if it were entirely up to me, I'd 'a kept you locked up here until your trial. But bail will be set at ten thousand dollars. Understood?

"Yes, Your Honour," the defendant, Eardley spoke for the three of them. They knew that the boss was going to post their bail.

"So ordered." The judge's final two words came out as a weary sigh.

—

1455 – Regina City Jail

As soon as he got his cell phone back, Willie Eardley went to a corner of the booking room and placed a call to Raymond Conn. While the desk sergeant was processing Jason Mead's release, she overheard bits of Eardley's urgent conversation.

"…. Don't *worry*, we'll *get* the fuckin' truck back…." was the comment that most caught her attention.

—

1710 – The COs' hotel room in Regina

"What kind of shape is this truck in?" Webb asked when he got back to the hotel.

"Dirty … inside and out. Human neglect inside. Road salt on everything we touched outside, and a bit of body damage to the front end. The front bumper has a crooked smile if you look at it from head on. And it'll take two of us to open the hood. But other than that, it's good to go. Runs nice and it's only five years old, half a million kilometres on it. For a big rig, that's just barely broken in. So, other than needing fuel and DEF in the morning, it's ready to roll." Diesel Exhaust Fluid was the product added to the exhaust system on all modern diesel engines so that they no longer blew black smoke or smelled like, well, like a diesel.

"Okay, that sounds encouraging. What time do you want to get started? It's supposed to snow tomorrow."

"Yeah, I know, but they aren't predicting much. So, I checked online, and sunrise here comes at about ten minutes to eight. If we can plan to be at the truck by then, I can do my circle check when it's light enough to see the beast. We should be wheels rolling within fifteen minutes. The night security guard will let us in and open the main gate when we're ready to roll."

"Circle check? Right after getting it certified mechanically fit?"

"Hey, we went over both the tractor and the trailer with a fine-tooth comb today, but regulations call for a daily circle check … the logbook's got entries to be made. Sure, I could cheat, but as a law enforcement officer, I'd have to live with a guilty conscience till the day I die." McNabb made a mock serious face as he picked up one of the takeout dinners Webb had just carried in. "Oh, great! Chinese. Thanks."

Chapter 8

Willie Eardley crouched between two rows of commercial dumpsters in a waste management company's storage yard. The short, thickset truck driver watched his boss's transport truck sitting parked on the other side of a high chain link fence. Despite the dirty white road salt covering the lower portions of the cab, the big white Kenworth looked impressive under the orangey pink glow of the rising sun. The promised snow hadn't started yet.

He shivered in the early dawn. At -22°C, the temperature had risen dramatically overnight, but despite being bundled up in the best available winter parka, the raw east wind seemed to cut right through him. Maybe shaving his head last week had been a bad choice. While his bushy, black beard helped protect his face from the wind, the cold nylon liner inside the parka hood seemed to draw any warmth from his scalp. But he was tough, and it was all for the cause. And an important step toward getting off Cheney's shit list.

He had already called his buddies when he discovered that the two men taking possession of the rig were armed game wardens. The simple hijack that he and the guys had planned had just gotten a lot less simple.

The rig had been driven to the secure government

compound the same day that he and the guys were arrested. Yesterday afternoon, after their release from jail, he had called Raymond at the office. Even though it was asshole Zak who'd been driving, Raymond had given Willie a royal chewing out for screwing up the delivery and losing the truck. Unless he and his buddies got the truck back and met the ship on time, their lives wouldn't be worth shit. The only saving grace was that, according to the ship's revised schedule, they still had five or six days to grab the truck and get out to the west coast.

They were under no illusions of being able to retake the rig from the secured government yard, so while he watched the truck, the other guys were taking care of some last-minute logistics. And if the truck moved out before they got rolling, that wasn't going to be a problem. A call to the office would get them it's exact location at any given time. Sexy Sylvia was being paid overtime to track the Kenworth's GPS locator until they got the rig back.

Raymond had assured him that his Regina contact said only one of the drivers was licenced to drive a transport. So, if these guys stuck to the rules, one guy driving the whole shift would get pretty tired as the day wore on. And in winter conditions, that fatigue would set in long before his shift was up. That would be the time to retake the rig — late in the afternoon, somewhere on a cold, desolate stretch of the Trans-Canada Highway in northwestern Ontario. Now he just needed his buddies — and the nice warm pickup — to come and pick him up.

He watched the game wardens begin their circle check with an inspection in the engine compartment. When the hood and moose bars were latched back in place, one of the officers climbed into the cab. Half a minute went by before the starter motor turned the big Cummins diesel over. The beast came to life. Lights went on, and the officer climbed down again to check lights, tires, air brake fittings and the fifth wheel connection. It seemed to take those guys forever to do what he usually did in a few minutes. But both men finally climbed into the cab, and from where he watched, Eardley could see the driver making entries in his logbook.

"Fuckin' logbooks. Pain in the ass."

—

At the same time — In the Regina basement of a freelance firearms entrepreneur

The man's gun shop was not listed online or in the yellow pages, nor did he have a storefront operation, nor was he known to the police — as far as he knew. Jason Mead had tracked him down through the friend of a friend.

"You got a couple of AR-15s?" twenty-six-year-old Mead asked. The wiry, six and a half foot tall, dirty blond, was the group expert on firearms.

"Yeah, I've picked up a few of them since the ban was announced." He paused to spit excess tobacco juice into a spittoon he carried everywhere around the room with him. The container was a grubby old metal coffee can. It was corroded to the point where it looked as if it could spring a leak at any time. And it was more than half full.

"My business got a real boost after the government outlawed 'em. Mind you, there's pissed off guys all across the country say they'll refuse to give 'em up … plan on burying 'em in their back yards, hiding 'em in their walls or whatever.

"But some are in a hurry to sell, too. Some of *those* guys would've held off till the government buy back started, but there's lots of folks out of work these days, and with the virus scare on and the gas and oil industry gone for shit, they can't afford to wait. God only knows when Ottawa will start the program. So the guys come to me. You say you only want two?"

"Yeah, and I want a shotgun," Zak piped up. "A real short one." Graham was short and skinny, in his early twenties with an acne-ravaged face. He was a bit of a loose cannon. He was the one who drove the transport past the weigh scale and through the roadblock, causing everyone so much grief. The only reason he had the job in the first place was because Derek Cheney was his uncle. It was an inside connection that constantly chafed at Raymond Conn.

"Don't have any like that … that would be illegal," the dealer said with a conspiratorial grin. "But I've got an old double that a handy fellow could make short on short notice."

A few minutes later, the two rifles and a beat-up double barrel 12-gauge shotgun lay on the fellow's worktable along with a generous supply of ammunition. Jason counted out the payment from a wad of cash Conn sent them on the road with, and everyone was happy. They left the man's house with their purchases in a large gym bag and climbed into the pickup truck Jason had rented on the company card.

Chapter 9

Having tentatively passed its circle check, the Kenworth rolled out of the compound and out of the city, eastbound on Hwy 1. Webb sat in the passenger seat, searching through the operator's manual, trying to determine the meaning of an amber warning light — not flashing — on the dash display. It indicated an exhaust emissions issue, but the truck was running well, and all the traditional dash gauges were approaching normal readings. He found the reference he was looking for just as McNabb slowed and signalled to pull into a truck stop for fuel a few kilometres east of the city.

"It's okay, Rob. It's doing some kind of exhaust system regeneration. Book says the light will go out when it's finished."

"Okay, that's good to know. Next issue: Did you notice the ripe odour in here?"

"I wasn't going to say anything for fear of offending your standards of personal hygiene. But yeah, it smells like someone pissed himself in here … last summer."

"Smelled it yesterday too, but I thought it would smell better after my quick spit and polish job. After that, we were busy dealing with all the safety related stuff, so it slipped my mind until now. If you'd be so kind as to find a dumpster and drag the mattress off the bunk while I fuel up, I think it will smell much better in here afterwards." The Kenworth's cab was a sleeper unit with a bunk behind the front seats. "The personal hygiene habits of some long-haul truckers leave a lot to be desired. I think the OSL guys fit into that category."

Twenty minutes later, they were eastbound with a handful of Pine Tree air fresheners spread around the cab. The outside temperature had risen a couple more degrees and the cab began to warm up inside. McNabb was down to his vest, but Webb kept his parka on. Rob reached forward and plugged his MP3 player into the tractor's sound system. Willie Nelson started into *On the Road Again*. McNabb laughed. Webb frowned.

"Honest Rick, it's set on random. I had no idea that would be the first of my eight hundred songs to come up."

"Eight *hundred? All* country?" Webb didn't sound enthused.

"Naw, mostly 60s and 70s pop rock. Not even ten percent hurtin' truck driver songs."

"Well, okay, but as senior officer and navigator, I've got the right to veto."

"Okay, boss."

Conversation between them was an easy back and forth on any number of topics. At one point, the conversation returned to family life. Rob asked Rick about his somewhat late start at a family. The silence that came from the passenger seat caused McNabb to look over at Webb. He immediately regretted having asked.

"Sorry Rick … I guess that was out of bounds."

"No, not your fault Rob. It's something I don't normally talk about, but it's no secret, either. I was married before I met Erin. My first wife, Melanie, was killed in a car wreck when she was on her way home to tell me that we were pregnant. I wasn't with her when she died, and it took me about eight years — and meeting my second wonderful partner — to get past it."

"Oh, shit," McNabb felt awful. He'd sure put his foot in his mouth with that question. "That must have been really tough," he said. With a sympathetic lump in his throat, he added, "Having almost lost Sam in a plane wreck when we first knew each other, I can almost understand, but to lose your newly pregnant wife ... man ... I can't begin to imagine how that would feel." The conversation died away for a while as Rob reflected on several life-threatening events that he and Sam had experienced on the job in their three years together.

During the pause in the conversation, Webb's cell phone rang. While he carried on a serious sounding discussion with whoever had called, McNabb let an empty car carrier tear by them before he pulled out to pass a Manitoulin Transport unit. They were back in the driving lane when Webb disconnected the call. He said nothing at first, and he looked concerned.

"What's up Rick?"

"That was Jacqui Morin, one of our detective COs at the Major Case Unit in head office. The word is, someone's taking an unhealthy interest in our load." The ministry's special investigations team — they were often called secret squirrels by field COs — maintained close ties with the intelligence units of other enforcement agencies, and information on special operations was often shared to avoid accidental interference with each other's covert activities.

"For starters, we might have a tail. Seen anything suspicious back there?"

"Not that I've noticed. Any hints?"

"The three guys they arrested when this rig was seized, were released on bail yesterday. Yeah, imagine that. They crashed through a roadblock, almost killed two Mounties, and now they've been released on bail and told to come back to court when the plague has ended. Something to do with a COVID early release program."

McNabb shook his head. Like most folks in law enforcement, he was frustrated by a justice system that seemed to be guided by a bunch of bleeding heart politicians.

"Anyhow," Webb continued, "one of them rented a pickup, a silver Ford F-150, and they've disappeared."

"Haven't seen one of those yet." McNabb began a more conscious scan of the mirrors. More conscious than the frequent casual glances needed to keep track of overtaking traffic. There were no distant followers back there at the moment. "Maybe they are just headed back to Ontario ... it would be a logical requirement of their bail."

"If that was the only bit of information, it could be construed that way. But the officer handling their release yesterday, overheard parts of a phone conversation to the effect that they are looking to retake the rig. And it gets worse. The squirrels advise that a source who can't be compromised, messaged that the owners of the truck, down in Toronto, have expressed the same intention. Problem is, if the police do anything overt to help us, some undercover operative's cover will get blown. There's something big happening there, but they say it's not related to us. That's what they say ... but it *is* tied to the same outfit. Kind of hard to believe that we aren't somehow involved."

"Oh boy." McNabb blew out a breath before continuing. "So, it appears we picked up a hot potato when we volunteered for this run," he mused. "I doubt that these guys will just ask for the keys ... or be satisfied with our promise not to tell anyone when they take it back, will they?"

"Highly doubtful."

"Now that Sam and I have kids, we promised each other that we'd avoid excessive heroism after our last near-death experience. She calls it our Post Apocalyptic Vow."

"Yeah, it sure puts us in a bind, Rob." They both sat silent. Several kilometres of snow-covered prairies rolled by before Webb spoke again. "I understand you are the go-to guy for resourceful solutions."

"Sure. Your Skidoo's broken down out in the bush? I can deal with that. No problem. This shemozzle? That's a whole different ball game. But James told me *you* were the king of resourceful solutions. He told me how you handled that toxic waste gang a few years back."

"Yeah, we did alright that time. I had a great crew aboard. But like you said, this is different … I'm out of my element here. Seems I come up with my best inspirations when I'm on a boat."

McNabb smiled as he scratched his head thinking for a moment. "How be we just pull into the next major centre, Brandon I guess, and leave the rig at a truck stop? Just walk away."

"They might guess we've been tipped off. The undercover person could get burned."

McNabb wasn't about to suggest that it was better to burn the undercover operative than themselves. Those people must live in hell for extended periods while trying to bring down the devil himself. Instead, he asked, "You got your passport with you? I could get Sam to fly mine to Winnipeg and by tomorrow morning we could deke down through the States. It's actually a bit shorter to go that way, too." He was sure the secret squirrels could authorize the flight he was suggesting.

"I like the idea, but my passport's at home … and expired." The conversation lapsed again as the Kenworth pulled them eastward.

"There are secondary highways that parallel this one," McNabb was thinking out loud, "but after Winnipeg we'd still be forced back onto Hwy 1, the one and only eastbound route into Ontario. And then we'd lose a bunch of time dicking around on the lesser roads."

"Yes, I think we'd be wise to keep making good time here on the freeway until there are better opportunities to zigzag. Our first chance to properly mix up the route won't come until after Nipigon, though." Webb paused before asking, "Can you drive this thing any faster?"

McNabb smiled. He already had the truck running at its full governed hundred and four kilometres per hour. "It's going flat out. It's got a governor. And I think we'd need a laptop with the right app to reprogram the thing." Speed limiters were required by law in Ontario, and the owner of this particular rig had forbidden his drivers from deactivating the device at any time, even when they left the province. There was nothing McNabb could do to speed up their schedule. A glance in his side mirror brought their problem to the forefront.

"Hang on a sec. Got a silver Ford pickup coming up behind us now. Could be anyone, but this one is acting erratic."

Webb watched through the mirror on his side of the cab. Caught occasional glimpses of the pickup as it weaved back and forth across the lane behind them. It was right on the tail of the OSL trailer — only a few yards back. Both officers were beginning to feel the tension. McNabb drew his pistol from his shoulder holster and set it on the console within easy reach. Webb gripped his weapon, but left it holstered. He wouldn't have a clear line of fire until and unless the pickup passed and pulled in front of the rig.

"Here they come," McNabb said. As the silver truck pulled out to pass, he ran his window down. If the bad guys started shooting, he didn't want to be showered with broken glass. And if he had a chance to shoot back at them, he didn't want the window in the way.

"Hold the wheel, Rick." McNabb picked up his pistol but didn't hold it up to the open window — yet. The silver F-150 pulled up even with the Kenworth's cab. He got a good look at the occupants. "Well shit." He shook his head, holstered his pistol and took back control of the wheel. "Distracted driving, To Wit: unlawfully receive blow job while in control of motor vehicle," he said, chuckling.

"Not our boys."

"Nope. And seeing as how this is presently our workplace, it would probably be improper for me to comment on the woman's really nice butt."

"Highly improper. I'd probably have to report you." They watched the silver pickup weave its way ahead of them, gradually opening the distance between them. Webb caught a glimpse of the action as they went by. "Eyes front, McNabb. Definitely a distraction.

"So anyhow," McNabb returned to their original topic, "If the OSL gang are thinking like truckers, they'll expect me to keep running until I time out … somewhere this side of Thunder Bay … probably around Ignace. Not many places to hide this thing overnight in a small town like that. The only motels I know of are right along the highway there. So maybe we should think of pulling off earlier, either in Kenora or Dryden? That is, if they aren't already on our ass when we get there."

"Might throw them off our scent for tonight, Rob. But there's something else I just thought of. It's possible they might be able to track this rig electronically, in which case, any evasive manoeuvres we try won't help."

"Call Jacqui back. Ask her if there's any way to find out

if we are sending out a signal. Or is there maybe some universal tracking system that comes standard on these trucks … something that we could disable? When I trained for my licence, the instructor didn't cover that. You should have seen the old Mack beater I trained on. I don't think GPS had been invented when they built that old road tractor."

Webb had the phone to his ear before McNabb finished. When he cut the call, he looked over at McNabb. "Jacqui says we need to disable the GPS. Most of the modern big rigs are tracked by their navigation systems, but in the meantime, she's making some inquiries. She'll get back to us with any other possible bugs we might carry."

"Can I suggest we don't disable it until we get to Winnipeg? Shut it down while we are skirting the city … or even start down a highway leading to the US border and shut it off after we look to be well committed. Then do a U-turn and get back on the Trans-Canada."

"Good ideas, both. But with your second option, if they discover we've backtracked, that could tip them off that we know. I think we'll go with your simpler suggestion … just shut it down as we go."

Chapter 10

Same time – In the silver F-150

"There they are!" Willie gave a triumphant yell, emphasized by a fist pump. It woke his napping passengers. He had been pissed off at the guys for taking so long to pick him up in Regina. How in hell could they have gotten lost in a small city that was laid out almost entirely in a rectangular grid? Then again, with Zak navigating, maybe it was inevitable. But now that the rig was in sight, all was forgiven. More or less.

"Which one?" Zak asked. "I can see the back end of three white trailers up ahead. And all their plates and back doors are covered in snow."

"The one with the top centre clearance light that keeps winking. How long have we been at Ray to get the wiring looked at?"

"Good thing he didn't get round to it." Jason Mead entered the conversation, yawning from the back seat. "But how the fuck are we going to take them down surrounded by all this traffic? Shit, looks like a holiday weekend in the summertime … 'cept it's mostly commercial."

"We wait until traffic thins out. Late afternoon, probably. Like I said earlier, we'll probably be into northwestern Ontario before we get the chance."

Although their pickup was legitimately rented on a

company credit card, Mead and Graham had stolen the licence plate from a silver F-150 they'd found parked behind an autobody shop in Regina. Now they were driving with a Saskatchewan plate instead of the Tennessee plates it came with. It looked a lot less conspicuous in this part of the world.

After leaving Regina, Zak had done an efficient job of shortening the shotgun. Efficient, but not pretty. Sawing the barrel and buttstock by hand with a hacksaw, but no workbench vice to clamp it to, made for a rough looking job. But it was still a shotgun. And it was very short. The company credit card would have to eat the cost of the damage done to the back seat fabric.

—

In the Kenworth

McNabb and Webb discussed various ways of dealing with potential challenges to their possession of the truck as the morning wore on, and then suddenly they were in Manitoba. And just as suddenly they were met by a wall of driving snow.

Within minutes, Rob was driving the rig through whiteout conditions. The forward visibility was down to less than forty metres, traffic slowed to less than sixty kilometres per hour. Even drivers who would normally ignore the hazardous conditions, were down to a crawl and most were staying in the one visible lane. Heavy snow pellets smacked against the windshield, almost drowning out the music coming from the speakers.

Jacqui called from secret squirrel headquarters. *"Their tail is on your ass, Rick. A couple vehicles behind you. Stay sharp."*

"No way they'll try anything right now, Jacqui," Webb

replied. "We're driving through whiteout conditions and surrounded by other slow-moving traffic. But thanks for the heads up."

A transport hauling a load of scrap steel ripped by them on the snow-covered passing lane, going close to the speed limit.

"Shit! Look at that asshole go, Rick. Had to be moving at three times the speed of everyone else." As suddenly as the truck was there, it disappeared in the swirling vortex of snow ahead. The idiot had to be driving blind. McNabb slowed further, waiting for the impenetrable curtain of riled up snow to settle.

Ten minutes later, the traffic ahead slowed to a stop and go crawl. When they got to the cause of the slowdown, they saw that everyone was having to squeeze between a transport on the left side, and a farm truck and trailer loaded with round hay bales on the right side. The transport trailer was half in the median ditch and leaning heavily to the left, and the tractor was jackknifed at right angles to the road, the front-end blocking half of the passing lane. It was the crazy idiot in the scrap steel hauler. The hay truck was jammed into the snowbank but still half in the driving lane. Only one line of traffic could squeeze through the gap.

Two large men, one armed with a hammer and the other with an axe were beating on the scrap truck's cab and had already made a mess of it. Headlights smashed, mirrors beaten useless and the guy with the axe was going at the radiator, despite standing only inches from the passing traffic.

Desperate to get away, the scrap driver began rocking the truck between forward and reverse, trying in vain to get the rig back on the road.

"The aggrieved farmer and his son in discussions with the transgressor, I'm guessing," McNabb suggested.

"Yeah, looks like dispute resolution in its purest form,

Rob. Can't say I blame them either the way that rig flew by us. Let's keep rolling."

McNabb picked up the pace to stay with the rest of the traffic. He was just barely past the scrap truck when it gained enough traction for the tractor to shudder its way onto the snow-covered pavement and then grind to a stop. A broken drive shaft immobilized the rig and effectively closed the road to all the traffic behind him. Everything came to a standstill, including the OSL road crew in the silver F-150.

"Looks like the boys are going to be tied up for a while, Rob."

"Yeah, I see that. Sure hope it buys us enough time to stay ahead of them 'til we pull off for the night."

"Could be there for hours ... or not."

The Kenworth continued through the heavy snow, until five kilometres later, as quickly as the squall had started, it backed off. Now just a dusting of light flakes fell. Visibility rose to over half a kilometre, and rather than accumulating on the road, most of it blew clear. High above the road in the driver's seat, the ground level blowing snow was not an issue for McNabb.

Chapter 11

In the F-150

Zak Graham was ragging on Willie Eardley for letting them get jammed up in the traffic with the OSL rig getting farther away with every passing minute.

"It's that fuckin' scrap driver's fault, you idiot!" Willie came back at him. "Our rig was the last one to get through. If we'd been right on their ass, that jerk up there would have mashed us between his front bumper and the hay trailer."

"I've a mind to stick this sawed-off up Scrappy's ass and touch off both barrels."

Jason Mead shook his head. "Zak, as well as being a shitty navigator, you're an idiot. The farm boys up there are taking care of business. Meanwhile, we should go and see what we can do to help get them back on the road once they've finished … or murdered the guy. I don't see much chance of getting tow trucks out here to clear this mess for hours."

He left the pickup and trudged through the snow past the car and the SUV they were stopped behind. A quick look at the situation told him it was more complex than just pulling the farm truck out of the snowbank. The base of the fifth-wheel hitch on the pickup was broken — not irreparably — but it wouldn't be safe to move it until it was repaired. Willie joined him, while keeping an eye on the irate farmers.

"Need a welder, Willie. We're on the edge of oil country. We've passed half a dozen mobile welders on the road in the last hour. I'll walk back along the line and see what I can find."

"Yeah, right. In the middle of a blizzard? Good luck. I'm going back to sit in the warm and dry."

Fifteen minutes later, Mead arrived back as passenger in a heavy-duty Ram 3500 pickup with a big electric welding unit mounted on the bed. The driver got out and took a quick look at the broken hitch.

"Close to an hour's work. Have to use the trailer front jacks to lift and hold it in place. And I'll need cover overhead, but yeah, I can patch that up."

Meanwhile, Willie was on the phone, explaining their delay to Raymond.

—

Just before noon

The Kenworth was rolling along at its best governed speed again, but no more than a couple hundred metres past the Virden exit, a loud bang — more like an explosion — startled both officers.

"…. the hell was that?" from Webb.

The front of the cab dropped six inches on McNabb's side, and the tortured sound of a blown tire slapping the pavement, told the story. "That was your first lesson in truckin' Rick. Just when you think things are running smoothly, think again." He pulled the rig over onto the highway shoulder and came to a stop.

Almost immediately, a pickup truck with tire company logos on the doors pulled up and stopped right in front of the

Kenworth. A short skinny fellow got out. Rob climbed down from the cab to meet him. If the guy was curious about the CO's uniform, he said nothing. Webb got out too, and waded through the snowplowed bank on the passenger side to join them in front of the rig.

"Lookin' for a tire shop, I bet."

"It wasn't on my to-do list for today," McNabb replied. "But I like to keep my options open."

"I'm just headed home for a bite," the man said as he put his phone to his ear. "Hey Slim ... got a big rig down on the highway, right in front of the cement plant. Easy job ... front tire on a Kenny." He listened a moment, then tucked the phone back in his pocket and said, "He'll be right over. Our shop's just back in town."

When the service truck arrived ten minutes later, the driver parked in front of the rig in the same spot the first guy had just left. Slim was anything but. He was also very tall. In his winter parka, the giant would have dwarfed both Paul Bunyan and Big Joe Mufferaw — both of them put together. Less than ten minutes saw the cab jacked up and the front wheel off. Slim tossed the rim and what was left of the tire up on the service truck's deck with the ease of a smaller man handling a bicycle tire.

More shredded remains of the tire lay strewn along the edge of the highway for several hundred metres back in the direction they'd come from. But Slim paid no attention to them. None were big enough to cause a wreck, and the highways crews would eventually pick them up if a snowplow didn't fling them into the ditch first.

"I'm not mounting a new tire here on the roadside ... not this close to the shop. One of you wanna come up with me? We can stop for a takeout lunch at Tim's or McDonalds on the way back if you want."

"A couple of Big Macs and a pint of milk would hit the spot for me, Rick. You've got the bigger company credit card. I'll wait here with the load. Give me your spare ammo. If those assholes catch up and want to challenge me for possession, five magazines will be more convincing than three."

"Tell ya what, Flyboy, I'll give you one spare mag. I might have to surround them if I get back in time." Somewhere around Broadview, Webb had heard the story of the nickname Samantha had given him during the bumpy start to McNabb's love life.

Chapter 12

The truck was back on the road again. The tire replacement and roadside lunch had set Webb and McNabb back just under an hour.

The Brandon exits rolled by a short while later. About two hours and fifteen minutes left to get to Winnipeg. They expected to run into the back of a cold front east of the city. But so far, the outside temperature had gradually warmed all day. It was just below freezing now and still snowing — but still not accumulating. The road surface was wet and dirty. Windshield washer fluid would need a top-up long before their next refuelling. Should have bought some at the truck stop.

Webb took another call from Jacqui, then said. "Word is, the OSL road crew is currently hung up in a snowstorm behind a bit of road wreckage. But despite the excitement at the OSL office, it's good to know that the mole is still able to communicate."

"I guess the scrap hauler did us a favour, Rick. I shouldn't have been so hasty in my criticism of his driving. Have to send him a thankyou card."

—

On the Trans-Canada Highway, near the scene of the wreck

Willie Eardley and his buddies were moving again in the rented Ford pickup. The road wreckage had delayed them by almost two hours, but between Mead, the welder and a handful of guys with pickups, heavy jacks and tow chains, they got the farmers' truck repaired and back on the road. The highway shoulder and a partial lane were open just enough for light vehicles to pass. The scrap truck would have to wait for commercial assistance and transport traffic would have to wait for him to get moved.

Sexy Sylvia kept them up to date by phone on the whereabouts of the Kenworth, and despite their delay, they were gaining on the rig again. Its unexplained one hour stop at Virden had helped and possibly had something to do with the scattered remains of a blown-out tire they'd passed on the roadside there.

The snow had quit, and Willie pushed hard to make up time. They were only about thirty-five minutes behind the OSL rig, and Jason calculated that they'd overtake it before they got to the Ontario – Manitoba border. Traffic was light the farther east they drove, so a hijacking should be no problem — especially armed the way they were. The two officers' pistols would be no contest against the two rifles and the shotgun they'd bought.

—

1610 – In the Kenworth, passing Winnipeg

On their way around the city on the Perimeter Highway, Rick Webb figured out how to disable the truck's GPS. He worried that if he just turned off the display, there was the possibility that the unit would still send out a signal. The GPS on his Lake Huron patrol boat was like that. But inside the Kenworth's electrical panel, he found the fuse for the navigation system. A trial disconnection didn't appear to affect any of the truck's other functions, so he planned to leave their tracking signal unplugged. Neither officer needed the GPS to find their way to North Bay.

"If we want to appear to be having trouble with the GPS, Rick, maybe you should restart it and shut it down several times before we disappear completely."

"Good thinking Rob. They may twig to our ruse anyhow, but if it appears to be an intermittent fault, they are less likely to think we've suddenly unplugged them."

—

1615 – Hwy 1 near Cartier, Manitoba

Willie Eardley's phone went off. Call display showed Sexy Syl. "Hey Sylvia, we just passed the exit for an invisible town called Cartier. How's our rig doing?"

"We've lost them Willie. They were going around the Winnipeg bypass and the signal quit. It shut down a couple times, came back on again for a minute each time, but then it disappeared completely."

"Shit. The GPS did that to me once when I was going through Detroit. Don't ever get lost in Detroit, Syl ... so they were still headed east, right?"

"Uh-huh. They were and they hadn't got as far as the Trans-Canada East exit when it quit. That was just ten minutes ago."

"Okay then. That's the only way to North Bay from this part of the world, so we'll keep on keeping on. Jason figures we're less than half an hour behind them now. I'll step a little harder on the pedal and we should catch up with them before they get into Ontario.

—

1714 – Hwy 1 near Hadashville, Manitoba

McNabb kept the Kenworth motoring along at the truck's maximum governed speed. The cruise control took care of that detail. All he had to do was steer and stay out of trouble. It was getting dark in the last of the evening twilight. They were still eastbound on the Trans-Canada Highway, which was Hwy 1 in Manitoba but would become Hwy 17 in Ontario. Webb had agreed that they should pull into Kenora for the night. If the bad guys didn't catch up by then, hopefully they would overshoot and miss them entirely. Little did they know just how close their tail was to catching up.

They were approaching the Pine Grove rest stop when they passed a beat-up looking tractor trailer carrying a poorly secured overload of logs. In fact, Webb was sure he saw several logs shift as McNabb hurried to get past. 'Hurried' as in, he didn't dare slow down.

They both watched in the mirrors as the log truck fell behind, but nothing catastrophic happened while it remained in view. Just after rounding one of the few curves on that stretch of highway, the Kenworth rolled over a frost heave in the road — one so big that McNabb's air ride seat bottomed out and then stretched his seatbelt to the limit on the rebound.

"Ouch!"

"Ha … shit! You've got the soft seat Rob. I'm the one sitting on the bench. That hurt. Didn't you see the 'Bump' sign?"

"Sorry, Rick, but we've been seeing bump signs all along. You sort of get used to ignoring them, because the road's usually no worse where it's posted than it is at all the unmarked imperfections."

—

1717 — in the F-150 approaching Hadashville

Willie Eardley had the F-150 running well over the speed limit, eastbound on Hwy 1. They ripped past the Pine Grove rest stop doing close to 130 km/h, certain that they were closing on the Kenworth.

Just around the next curve they picked up four-way flashers ahead. Willie cancelled the cruise control, and the pickup began to slow as they coasted toward the blinking lights. Even as their speed fell off, the three were almost airborne inside the pickup when it lurched over a major frost heave in the pavement. "Fuck!" was the common curse from all three.

Ahead, they saw that a load of logs had broken free from a log truck and spilled across the highway. The road was blocked from snowbank to snowbank. Another pickup was already sitting there, four-way flashers on, the driver just stepping out onto the road. The log truck driver stood on the running board of his cab yelling into his cell phone. Over the past hour the temperature had dropped to -28°C. They were well into the back side of the predicted cold front. Nobody was pleased with the prospect of a long delay.

Chapter 13

McNabb left the Kenora Bypass and took the old highway into town. After they stopped to grab a takeout dinner, he wheeled the transport into the Super 8 Motel parking lot. Webb had phoned ahead to reserve a room and had been assured that there were working electrical outlets for plugging in the truck overnight. McNabb parked the rig on the far side of a FedEx train pulling two trailers. He was satisfied that the seized transport was obscured from view to anyone passing by.

While Webb checked in, McNabb did up his logbook, shut down the engine, and after verifying that the electrical power was truly live at the outlet, he plugged in the block heater. Modern diesels were much better at unassisted cold starts than earlier engines, but even a new diesel would balk at a -40°C start up if it wasn't plugged in overnight. And the radio promised a very cold night.

McNabb kicked the snow off his boots as he entered their motel room accompanied by a cloud of rapidly condensed humidity. Laying his overnight bag on the nearest of the two beds, he took off his parka and hung it up. He sat on the foot of the bed to take off his boots and looked over at Webb. Rick noticed the puzzled look on his face and waited for the inevitable question.

"So, I've been trying to figure why these guys are so eager to get this load back, Rick." He tossed the first boot onto the door mat and started unlacing the other one. "Doing the math, I come up with a ballpark value in the range of two hundred thousand bucks for the fur ... maybe as high as two-fifty ... but the fur market is kind of shaky this year, so it could be quite a bit less, too. And the rig might fetch another hundred grand at the most, in this market. Now that's a lot of money for a family guy like me. But assuming ... based on the fact there's supposed to be an undercover operative involved ... assuming these guys are part of some criminal organization, is there something in that trailer that's maybe worth a whole lot more?" The second boot made it halfway onto the mat. Close enough.

"Been bothering me too, Rob. And from the outset, the Mounties and the Saskatchewan guys wondered what was in there worth running a roadblock for, so they had a drug sniffing dog go through the load. It came up empty. Then they opened every bag on board ... again, nothing. They inspected the trailer floor and the whole tractor-trailer combo for hidden compartments ... nada. So, it's a puzzle for sure."

There seemed to be no reasonable answer to the problem, so after a few more minutes of speculation, they let the subject drop and ate yet another takeout meal while they watched some TV. But everything on the tube was reruns. So they both dug out the books they'd been reading — a James Patterson novel for Rob, and Rick was halfway through a copy of *Toxic Waters*, a novel by a retired game warden.

"Hey, I read that one a couple of years ago, Rick. Great story."

"Sure is, and it takes place in a setting familiar to me."

They caught the ten o'clock news — just more COVID-19 coverage, so McNabb took a hot shower.

While Rob was in the shower, Webb phoned home. Erin sounded tired when she answered.

"*Jimmy's been bouncing off the walls ever since supper tonight. I made the mistake of feeding him a hotdog. Don't know what they put in that stuff ... well, scientifically, I guess I do. But I have no idea why.*" She had a degree in biology and had participated in a study on the effects of various food additives on humans and livestock.

"*So, if you are still thinking we should get a dog, I think I'll train the dog and you can tend to Wonder Boy.*"

"Feed him beef, broccoli and potatoes, Erin. The boy, not the dog. The beef will keep him growing, but he'll sit there staring at his veggies until bedtime ... give you some peace and quiet. It worked for my mother when I was that age. If he starts liking the broccoli, substitute turnip. Guaranteed to work."

Erin wasn't impressed to learn that the owners of the transport wanted to take it back, but she knew her man wasn't about to back away from a challenge. All she could do was tell him to be careful — and hope that he would.

"Oh, by the way, the new diesel has been shipped. It should arrive in a day or two." Webb was in the process of repowering his antique sailboat. Expired old gasoline engine to new diesel. "I'll get them to drop it close to the garage."

When Rob was finished in the shower, he called home too. Everyone there was fine, but Sam wasn't happy either, to hear that their mystery load was coveted by others — especially since the others included the guys who rammed a police roadblock.

"*You be careful Robbie. Some truckers can be really rough, and if there's criminal activity involved, they can be just plain dangerous.*"

"We'll be okay, sweetie. We're both uniformed and armed, and Rick qualified top shooter in his group, just like I did. Honest, we'll be okay. I'll call again tomorrow night. I think we should be able to get to Hearst if everything goes well."

"*You just be careful Robbie. And remember our Post Apocalyptic Vow.*"

"I will sweetie. Love you. Give hugs and kisses to the girls for me and tell Katie I said 'hi.' Good night." He looked over at Webb, who'd dozed off with the TV remote in his hand — but awoke the instant Rob tried to sneak it back. "Guess we'd better get some sleep, old man," he said. Webb grinned and turned off the TV, then the bedside light.

—

2015 — Near Hadashville, Manitoba

It took almost three hours to get the highway cleared of spilled logs and the disabled truck. When the Mounties had finally showed up, they called a contractor with a self-loading tandem axle log truck. It took him more than long enough to get there too, but when he did, the operator immediately began to unscramble what looked like a giant's game of pickup sticks. He loaded as much as he could carry onto his own truck and set the other half of the load off to the side of the road for later. The old transport that had lost the load was declared unfit for the road and a heavy-duty tow truck had to be brought in from the city to take it away before the highway could be reopened.

Meanwhile, Willie Eardley spent some time on the phone with Raymond Conn. Raymond was not happy, but he didn't spend any energy chewing out the delivery driver. He said the spilled load of logs came under the heading "shit happens." Instead, he went into delegation mode.

"*Unless you've got horseshoes up your ass, you'll never find them tonight. They'll probably be off the road for the night soon anyhow, so when the road opens up again, you guys push on through to Nipigon. Find a busy spot there with a view of the highway. A truck stop would be best. Wait there 'til they go by tomorrow and call my cell as soon as they do.*

"Then you follow them but stay far enough back not to spook them. I'll be heading north with Kyle. Whichever route they take after the highway splits past Nipigon, we'll find a spot to take back the rig. Got it?"

"Sure Ray."

"Now, when you're going through all those one-horse towns along the highway up there, keep an eye at the truck stops and motels. If you find them bunked down for the night somewhere, it'd be real easy to just slip in and drive off. You've got your spare keys for the rig, right?"

"Yup, got 'em boss."

"Okay. Call me with any updates."

Chapter 14

Sunrise was still almost two hours off when Rob McNabb fired up the Kenworth. It was bitterly cold. The snow squeaked beneath his boots with every step while he unplugged the truck and coiled the stiff extension cord. The local radio station reported the temperature at -43°C. Coldest it had been there in a few years and a record for that date.

While the engine ran at high idle, he and Rick Webb performed the circle check. Back in the cab, the check engine light came on and another warning light too — an amber triangle, but neither was flashing, so he backed away from the motel wall, wheeled out of the lot and started toward the centre of town. The warning lights would probably go out when temperatures came up closer to operating range. The guys needed a takeout breakfast, and they wanted large coffees to get them started. So Rob headed for the Tim Horton's, a little past the Canadian Tire gas bar. They would grab their go-juice there.

The truck was not feeling its usual power as they crossed through town, but McNabb wasn't planning to push it until the engine and transmission temperature gauges began to rise off their pegs. It was just as cold inside the cab as out. They wore mittens and snow pants in addition to their parkas.

When they got to Tim Horton's, there was no suitable

space for big truck parking. What might have been large enough in the summer, was piled high with mountains of snow. So, like a regular trucker, Rob just stopped at the edge of the roadway and put on his four-way flashers while Rick hurried in to buy breakfast. As soon as Webb returned to the cab, Rob released the brakes and started forward.

The first uphill grade leading out of town began several hundred metres past Tim Horton's. It wasn't a particularly steep grade, but McNabb knew right away that something was wrong with the Kenworth. It didn't have anywhere near its usual power. On the next hill, longer and steeper than the first, the automatic transmission stayed in second gear just to crawl to the top.

"Shit, I think the fuel's freezing up on us, Rick. Can you google local truck repair places? Now that we've made it up the hill, I'll keep rolling, but if I find a good place to turn around, I'll hold there until you've got something."

Webb had his phone out, fingers flying on the touch screen. "If they're open on a weekend, we may be in luck, Rob. Keep rolling. Godbout Auto Repair ... just a couple of klicks ahead. Think we can make it? If not, it says here they've got twenty-four-hour towing and they're equipped to tow big rigs."

"It's not getting any worse, but at thirty-five kilometres per hour, we'd be over a week getting to North Bay. More likely, we'd just end up frozen solid, somewhere in the middle of nowhere between here and Vermillion Bay."

Several tense minutes went by. Up ahead on the left, someone had mounted an old Volkswagen Beetle on long pipe legs and painted it bright yellow to look like some kind insect — a beetle, maybe. And right there was the Godbout sign. "Good omen Rick ... the gate's open."

McNabb wheeled the transport up the driveway and

stopped in front of the facility. It had the look of a Department of Highways depot built back in the 1950s or '60s.

It wasn't yet seven a.m., but there were lights on inside, so Webb and McNabb left the cab and tried the front door — which was locked. Rob knocked. Nothing happened. Rick knocked harder.

A man wearing a heavy parka overtop of blue coveralls emerged from an interior doorway into the office area and held up one hand while he picked up a telephone — spoke briefly into the phone, then came to let the two uniformed COs in.

"Got a search warrant?" The name patch on the outside of his parka said *Gilles*.

"We're searching for a mechanic, Gilles. Do we need one for that?" Webb asked, smiling.

"Naw, I think you're good. Just let me take this call. Coffee's on back there," he indicated with a nod to a hallway. But they already had their Tim Horton's coffee waiting in the truck, so they stood at the counter while the man finished on the phone.

"Let me guess. Fuel freeze-up," he said as he cradled the handset.

"Yes, sir. At least that's what I think it is," Rob said.

"Heard you coming in. It's a sound I've heard many times before and I could smell it through the bay doors. Exhaust gives an odour strangely unique to diesel freeze-up. Drop your trailer out back, and then I'll get you to drive it in the back door, farthest bay on the right. Don't shut it down until you are inside. My diesel guys are both at home, self-isolating from the virus, and I've got a couple of other jobs going today but we'll get you thawed out and going again. Job like yours usually has to be done in stages. Thaw a line, pull it off and blow it out, thaw out the next section and so on. Make yourselves at home, it'll probably

71

be well into the afternoon before you roll out of here."

"Okay, we're at your mercy," McNabb said. "We've both done 'hurry up and wait' before. And thanks for fitting us in ... sure appreciate it." They went back outside and moved the rig to drop the trailer in a large yard behind the complex. By the time Rob pulled the Kenworth up to the large overhead door, Rick was back inside, pushing the button to raise it. McNabb eased the unit in, shut it down and exited the cab as the mechanic came over, carrying a couple of portable electric heaters with him.

"First thing is to get some heat on the subject." The three men wrestled the bent moose bars to the floor. McNabb released the latches and opened the hood and Gilles set up the heaters in strategic locations. Other than the somewhat warm engine block, almost everything under the hood was covered in thick white frost. "If I try to undo some of those fittings before they warm up, something is bound to break."

The two officers took their cold breakfasts to the lunchroom and nuked everything back to life in the microwave.

—

0915 – Godbout Auto Service

"Hello," Webb answered his cell phone while he and McNabb sat in the lunchroom drinking coffee and reading old copies of *Car and Driver*. "Yeah, we're just coming into Superior, Wisconsin," he said, and as he talked, he scribbled a message on the back of his magazine, passed it to Rob and pointed at the wall phone.

Call Jacqui in head office. Use the landline. This

might be her, but she sounds a lot different. Got to make sure.

McNabb checked his own phone to get the number, then punched the number into the wall phone and waited while it rang.

Webb heard: *"Hang on a sec, Rick, I've got a call coming in on the other line...."*

McNabb heard: *".... M.C.U., Jacqui speaking."*

"Rob McNabb here, Jacqui. Are you on the phone with someone else?"

"Yeah, with Webb. What, you guys don't trust me?"

"His idea. And maybe we should stay here on the landline … in case cell phones can be monitored." Webb disconnected his call and Rob closed the lunchroom door, then switched the wall phone to speaker mode.

"Are you guys really in Wisconsin?"

"Sorry about that, Jacqui, but you didn't sound like yourself," Webb explained. "And no, we're not going that way. We're still in Kenora … frozen fuel lines."

"Ten-four. Came down with a bitch of a cold overnight, so you're forgiven for wondering about the strange voice. Kudos for the quick thinking.

"Anyhow, shutting down the GPS worked. The bad guys don't know where you are right now. Our source says they drove through the night to get to Nipigon. They're holding there for now, waiting for you guys to pass by.

"Unfortunately, that's not all. A couple more guys are headed up from the south to help the original crew with whatever they've planned to get back their rig. They'll be driving a black Chevy Silverado. I'll get the plate numbers to you as soon as I have the info."

"Nipigon's the obvious place for them to watch for us," Rick commented. "It's the only highway between eastern and western Canada at that point ... and it's only two lanes wide there. So, do they know that we know? Can we get some police help now?"

"*No, they don't know. And no, the police don't want to provide any backup yet. The informant's cover is tenuous. So the other agencies are telling us to hang tough and act as if we have no idea ... while you do your best to finish the run.*"

"That's just great. There'll be five of them and just two of us. All we have is our pistols ... we're not ideally equipped for blockade running."

"*Rick, I agree, but I've got two major police agencies telling me to back off. In the meantime, I'll see if I can arrange some unmarked green and white support starting in the morning ... not to look like an official escort, but eyes on the road ahead of you. Can you manage with that?*"

"Well, it's no longer the simple mission we were sold on ... or that Rob and I sold our wives on ... but if that's the best you can do, then I guess that's it ... for now." Webb looked at McNabb, who was leaning toward the phone to add something.

"Jacqui, if this trip turns to shit and those guys show up loaded for bear, Rick and I are stepping off into the bush ... the bad guys can have their truck back. Got it?"

"*Roger that, Rob. It'll become a full-blown police matter if that happens, anyhow. Looking forward to your updates. Stay safe.*" The call ended there, and McNabb helped himself to another cup of Godbout company coffee before sitting back down.

"Okay, Rick, revisiting our conversation from last night, did the Saskatchewan guys empty each bag? Or just open them and riffle through the contents?"

"They had their looksee before I arrived Rob, so I can't say how thoroughly they looked. How be I call my contact there and find out?"

"Okay. If it was anything other than a pelt-by-pelt

inspection, I'd like to suggest we go and freeze our butts for a few hours. There has to be something really valuable somewhere in those hundred and sixty bags of fur."

Three minutes later, Webb disconnected the call and gave Rob the highlights. "He says the Mounties were in a hurry. It was cold that morning and I guess it sort of went down like you suggested … they opened the bags, peered inside each one, tied it up and moved on. Not much of a search. Guess we've got some time to kill, so let's go and do it right."

Out in the trailer, Webb and McNabb got down to the business of opening every bag of fur and checking every pelt. It was bitterly cold work, and it couldn't be done while wearing heavy winter mittens. Thin driving gloves worked for Rob most of the time, and he used his heavy mitts to kneel on — he had to work on the floor. Rick preferred to work bare-handed, pocketing his hands for warmth any time he got ahead of McNabb.

They had the back ten feet of the trailer floor free to work on and after opening the tie on each bag, Rick slid the pelts out and Rob checked the contents. The flattened, oval beaver pelts were packed skin to skin and fur to fur. Turning each hide over, like pages in a large book, the cardboard-stiff pelts stacked up in one pile as the other pile diminished. The case skinned pelts — furs skinned like removing a body suit, not slit open and lying flat — Rob checked inside every single one for hidden objects. It wasn't a complicated procedure. He just slid a hand in to the far end of each one and quickly moved on. That took longer than the beaver pelts, but he went through the piles almost as fast as Rick could untie, dump and repack the bags. They were more than half of their way through the load when they locked the trailer and went back inside the shop to warm up at noon.

The mechanic was eating a bowl of chili when they

arrived in the lunchroom. "Lots more of this in the slow cooker over there, guys. Help yourselves. Wife made some bread you can throw in the toaster if you want, too, and there's a pop machine in the hall … or the coffee."

"Thanks. That sounds like a perfect meal on a day like this." McNabb began ladling out a bowlful for Webb and another for himself while Webb tended the toaster. "Making any headway on our rig, Gilles?"

"I'm about a third of the way there, but the rest won't take any longer than the first bit now that the heat is beginning to loosen things up. Fuel's gone slushy all the way through the system. Ice crystals from a build-up of condensation on the walls of a near empty tank, I'd bet. Then you probably fuelled up from underground storage … the relatively warm fuel melts the ice and carries it into the system. Cold night like last night, everything thickens up and turns to slush. Lucky you had the power to get it here."

"I kind of thought it would be something like that," Rob said.

"You can go a long way on those big tanks, but to avoid freezing up again in these cold conditions, I'd fuel up each day if you are shutting down at night." There was a lull in the conversation as they each tied into their chili, then the mechanic spoke again.

"You guys rearranging your load?"

"Looking for something, but we don't know what," Rick answered.

"Ah, a mystery then, is it?"

"It's an ongoing investigation. First part was obvious, but it goes deeper than it first appeared."

"Don't worry, I won't pry. Some of the tow calls we go on are also crime scenes. If we see something out of place, we point it out to the cops and then don't touch anything until they tell us we're clear. Makes for a lot of hurry up and wait, too."

After lunch, Rick and Rob returned to finish their search in the trailer and Gilles returned to the frozen truck. He was interrupted briefly when a trucker came in to ask him to diagnose his rough running diesel. Needed it fixed yesterday, of course.

While Gilles was putting the guy off until tomorrow, the guy asked about the OSL rig. "What's that in for?"

"Fuel freeze-up, but I'll have them rolling in a couple of hours. Got a couple of other jobs to finish this afternoon before I go home. Tomorrow morning's the best I can do for you. Got a ride home? If you run it into this next bay, it'll be nice and warm for me to start on it first thing." The guy agreed, and Gilles got back to work on the Kenworth.

Chapter 15

"Yeah, unless they've had a problem, they should have been through there by now." Raymond Conn was on the phone with Willie Eardley. Eardley and his buddies were parked at the Petro-Pass truck stop in Nipigon where they'd been sitting since they'd arrived, early in the morning.

"But it's winter, Willie. They could have been delayed somewhere ... breakdowns, road closures, you know how it is."

"We've been listening to the radio and talkin' with some of the other drivers and haven't heard of any road closures, Ray."

"Well, keep your eyes and ears open then. Meanwhile, I've put out the word to some of our trucking buddies. They're watching for them too. They'll let me know if they meet them on the road somewhere. You just hold pat until you spot them."

He disconnected and was about to say something to his passenger, but Kyle Roach had reclined his seat and was already snoring. Raymond was always impressed by the way the guy could do that. But then, the guy always said it was easy falling to sleep with an uncluttered mind. Kyle was a doer — he left the thinking to others.

Raymond took the Highway 144 exit to head north to Timmins. All the issues he faced as the man in charge of logistics at OSL swirled non-stop in his mind. He constantly weighed the pros and cons of every aspect of an operation as it unfolded. He was always looking for the tripwires that could lead to problems, large or small. And for each problem, he would consider every option. When he made a decision, he never second-guessed himself. He was good at what he did. That's why Derek had hired him in the first place — before they began to get on each other's nerves.

In the last two years, OSL had made six runs to meet the Chinese ship on the west coast. But while each trip had been completed without a hitch, Conn knew that their luck was bound to run out one day. In reality, after the roadblock screw-up in Saskatchewan, they should have backed off. The odds were no longer in their favour — at least, not without a long pause.

In discussing the situation with Derek, Raymond had argued that with the company's lawyer working on it, they would have gotten the truck back through legal channels sooner or later. They could lease a replacement in the meantime. But no, Derek was determined to get them out there in time to buy the shipment that was already on the way.

The idiot's getting careless, Raymond mused, shaking his head. Except for Zak Graham, the guys on the B team weren't bad. But Graham was a loose cannon. He was the bonehead who'd skipped the weigh scale and run the roadblock. Well, if retaking the rig worked out, Raymond was going to cut that pain in the ass character from the roster and Roach would join them for the run west. Cheney might not be happy about it but fuck him. Besides, if things didn't work out, they'd all probably be bunking together behind bars, with little chance of bail next time. Cheney's anger would be the least of their problems then.

—

1830 – Hwy 17, Dryden, Ontario

Gilles, the mechanic, hadn't declared the Kenworth fit to travel until he'd taken it out for a road test. It had passed to his satisfaction.

Webb and McNabb had finished their detailed search in the trailer almost an hour earlier, but aside from the load of pelts, they'd found nothing of value. They were back in the lunchroom, still puzzling over the problem when Gilles came in with the bill. Rick's government VISA card did the trick at the counter while Rob went outside and hitched the tractor to the trailer. The two of them made an abbreviated circle check before they were finally on the road again.

It was dark when the lights of Dryden came into view. The pulp mill produced the brightest display. Caught in the facility's glare, steam rising from the mill gave the appearance of the venting hot springs at Yellowstone Park on a frosty Wyoming morning.

Rick was on the phone to head office. "Hey, Jacqui, we're entering Dryden. It's been a long day. We're thinking of doing the next leg during daylight hours."

"Good idea Rick. Talk to you in the morning. Might be Norm or Sara sitting in for me if this cold gets any worse."

"Not COVID is it?"

"Don't worry, you can't catch it over the phone. And no … it's just a good old-fashioned head cold. Been going through the family for the last week and a half. In any event, the others will see my notes in the log if I don't make it in. Good night."

Webb had already called ahead for reservations, and McNabb pulled the eighteen-wheeler into the parking lot at the back of the Town and Country Motel, out of sight of the highway. If their intelligence was to be believed, the bad guys were still over four hundred kilometres ahead of them, but bad guys have been known to be sneaky on occasion. The COs weren't taking any unnecessary chances.

The temperature had moderated to -30°C and was supposed to hold in that range for the night, but the condensed vapour of their exhaled breath still hung in the air around their heads when they stepped down from the truck. And the snow still squeaked underfoot, and the truck still got plugged in. After they checked into their room, they walked across the road for takeout dinners — pizza tonight — and they watched the COVID news on TV while they ate. Webb took a hot bath to drive out the cold that had settled in his core during the long hours of searching through fur bags in the trailer. McNabb followed with a shower. He came out of the bathroom in his long johns as Rick's phone began to ring.

"Hey, Jimmy, how's my big boy?"

"Guess what, dad?"

"What?" Rick put the phone on speaker. He knew from experience that his four-year-old was about to launch into a story of some sort. "Here, Rob, something for you to look forward to in a couple of years."

"A transport truck came to our house, Dad. And guess what?"

"What, Jimmy?"

"The men put a diesel enjun on the elevator platford at the back and put it down on the driveway."

"That's the new engine for the bo...." but he got no chance to finish.

"And guess what, Dad?"

"What, Jimmy?"

"Grandpa got Buddy to bring the forklift from the marina to carry the diesel into the grodge. And guess what, Dad?"

By now, McNabb was chuckling, and Webb wore a grin

81

that only a proud dad could wear.

"I'm guessing it's time for your bath, Jimmy."

"Nooo! The cat pooped on the basement floor! Bye Dad."

Rob was still chuckling as he took his shaving kit into the bathroom. Rick killed the speaker and started an adult conversation with Erin. Jimmy had neglected to mention that he'd parked his big Tonka dump truck in the cat's litter box.

Rick told Erin the events of the day and she wanted to know more about the bad guys looking to take back the truck. He assured her that Rob was proving to be a top-notch partner and the two of them had agreed to abandon the rig in the event of real trouble. They would stay on their toes, he assured her. She didn't share his optimism, but let it go. No point causing him extra worry.

By the time McNabb finished shaving and brushing his teeth, Webb had turned off the TV and the bedside light on his side. McNabb followed suit. They were looking at another dark and early start in the morning.

—

Monday February 3, 0130 – Nipigon

Willie Eardley was having a tough time staying awake. In half an hour it would be Jason's turn to watch for two hours. He had the feeling that the government guys wouldn't run the rig at night, but they couldn't risk letting it get past them unnoticed. He was almost nodding off when his phone sounded. The *Rocky* theme song. It woke up the other two guys as well.

"What's up, Ray?"

"A guy I know, he found the rig."

"Hey, that's great. Where is it?"

"*It spent all day at a truck service centre in Kenora. Fuel line freeze up. Their driver will have used up most of his duty hours sitting around waiting, so they won't have gone far. Probably spending the night either there, or in Dryden.*

"*In a couple hours, you guys head back that way. Hold up around Ignace if you don't come on them beforehand. I don't want you overshooting them. Then when you find them, don't fuckin' loose them. Keep me posted.*"

"Sure thing, Ray."

Chapter 16

Webb and McNabb were eastbound on Hwy 17 out of Dryden. The truck was running well but both men were on edge. There was not as much friendly banter as there had been during their first day on the road. Despite knowing that two fellow COs were running ten minutes ahead of them in an unmarked pickup, they knew that at some point after they passed Nipigon late in the morning, the gang from Overnight Shipping was likely to make a move on them. Or maybe something could even happen before then.

McNabb left his ministry walkie-talkie sitting on the console, tuned to the enforcement channel. Same channel as the guys out front. It was a scrambled frequency. He turned up the volume in case the officers ahead saw any sign of trouble. They promised to provide eyes out front as far as Upsala. At that point, Thunder Bay officers were supposed to take up the lead.

On the never-ending stretch of highway between Ignace and Upsala, Rick was watching the seemingly endless forest roll by while Electric Light Orchestra sang *Evil Woman*. At the same time, Rob's mind wandered to an ongoing family discussion back home. Their adopted daughter, Mae Ling, seemed to feel that taking an Anglo-based name would help her fit in better with the other kids at school. It wasn't that she didn't have any friends, but she kept asking if she could make the change — wanted to be more accepted by the popular girls. Mary-Ann was the name she wanted to take.

Rob was of the opinion that....

"Moose, *moose*, **moose!**" Webb's sudden exclamation snapped McNabb's attention back to the road and the massive bull crossing their lane just ahead of them. He hit the brakes hard. Eighteen wheels locked up and eighteen tires screamed and chattered at the abuse as the big truck slowed. The antilock brake system had tripped its relay switch again.

The noise caused the moose to pause in the centre of their lane. The opposite lane had oncoming traffic in it, leaving Rob no option but to keep on the brakes — and cross his fingers. The moose just stood there, broadside to the truck, glaring at it, daring it to come any closer. And it did. When the transport shuddered to a stop, the grill was just inches from the big fellow.

"Shit! ... Thanks Rick. I almost missed that."

"You almost didn't."

"Well ... there's that, too." He exhaled a huge sigh of relief. They sat in the truck with the Cummins diesel idling and the moose showing no interest in moving from its claimed spot on the pavement. The oncoming vehicles — a pickup and a car — stopped in their own lane to watch the standoff. Rob tooted the airhorn, but the moose just changed his stance to face the truck, head-on. With his antlers shed for the winter, he didn't represent a great threat — not to a big highway tractor — but still, he refused to move out of the way.

"I always wondered what the moose bars were for," McNabb said, easing off the brakes. The truck crept slowly forward, daring to nudge the animal's chest. That caused it to turn end for end with lightening speed. It gave the Kenworth's front bumper a swift, one-legged kick, destroying one of the fog lamps before moving across the road to challenge the pickup truck. The driver of that vehicle hit the gas, steered around the beast and sped away, and the moose took off at a trot to follow, leaving two women in a tiny Toyota taking videos of the departing wildlife with their phones.

"Well, my heart rate's edging back below the danger zone now," Webb sighed. "I think we might as well move on." He waved at the awestruck women as Rob accelerated the transport away from the scene.

—

0810 – Moosonee airport

Samantha Williams finished her pre-flight inspection of the bright yellow Turbo Beaver and then climbed into the cockpit to begin the prestart checklist. C-FOEY was a stretched, eight-seat modification of its original six-seat de Havilland configuration. The Ontario Provincial Air Service bush plane was fitted with large, convex side windows for improved aerial observation, and it was mounted on wheel-skis for winter operations. The aircraft could be flown either from runways or snow-covered lakes.

This morning, Sam was headed to Hearst to pick up a team of observers before beginning aerial moose surveys between there and Geraldton. But as much as she loved flying moose surveys, this morning she was a little distracted — worried, in fact.

The last conversation she'd had with Rob had left her feeling uneasy. Driving the seized transport truck across northern Ontario, knowing that the owners intended to take it back — no doubt by force — was an invitation to trouble. She'd picked up on her husband's concern despite his attempts to downplay the whole thing. He had assured her that they would walk away from the rig if they were challenged for possession by the bad guys.

She could just picture his response to an actual confrontation. "Yeah, Robbie, I just *bet* you'll do that … *NOT.*" Walking away from a job he'd volunteered for — a job he hadn't yet finished — that just wasn't his style. "You've forgotten our Post Apocalyptic Vow, Flyboy," she muttered.

Even worse, the police weren't to intervene. In fact, they had even been told to avoid being near the rig unless the bad guys made an obvious move to take it. Somewhere in the mix was an undercover operative whose cover could be blown if the criminals suspected that their plans to grab the truck had been discovered.

So how, if the police were supposed to stay clear of the truck, were they going to respond to a call for help in a timely fashion — even know where to respond to — if they were supposed to keep away? Especially on remote northern Ontario highways, miles from the nearest police detachments. There were too few cops in the region as it was.

But as soon as Sam began the engine start up sequence, she shut out the distracting thoughts and became one with the Beaver. She had a history of being able to put personal baggage completely aside as soon as she took charge of an aircraft. Five minutes later, she called Moosonee airport for clearance to takeoff, and moments after that, the six hundred and eighty horsepower Pratt and Whitney turboprop was pulling her southwest, toward her first stop.

—

0815 – Hwy 17, west of Upsala

Not long after the moose confrontation, McNabb and Webb were talking shop. Oncoming traffic was still light. Many of the big rig drivers would be stopped for breakfast now. Rob probably wouldn't have noticed it if the driver of the oncoming pickup hadn't touched his brakes just after going by. But the brief flash of brake lights in the side mirror was hard to ignore.

"Oh-oh. Trouble coming, Rick. A silver Ford pickup just went by. Touched his brakes. Maybe, *the* F-150 ... wait a minute." The truck appeared to continue away from them still westbound. "Or, maybe not. False alarm, I guess." But he continued monitoring his rear-view mirror.

When the silver pickup was almost out of sight behind them, the brake lights came on again. Now Webb could see it in the mirror on his side of the cab too. The pickup's tail lights became daytime running lights as the driver pulled a U-turn. The pickup was now beginning to follow them.

Webb got on the walkie-talkie. "Green leader, we've picked up a follower. Can you drop back and run behind us?"

"*Ten-four, Rick. But unless it's really urgent, maybe we'll go the last ten klicks to Upsala and hand you off to Bernie and Chuck. We're almost there now. But it's your call.*"

"Roger, Green, they're staying almost a kilometre back, so if Bernie can drop in behind us after we go by the gas station, that'll work. He just has to look like any other traffic. We don't want these followers to think they've been spotted."

"*Rest assured, Rick, Bernie will blend in with the local traffic better than anyone can.*"

Chapter 17

The OSL transport rolled through the scattered community at the seventy km/h limit. They passed the XTR gas station and restaurant. The parking lot was full of big rigs, their drivers enjoying a good homestyle breakfast. Two pickups were stopped by the far entrance, the drivers engaged in a quick conflab.

"There's Bernie," Webb said, pointing at one of them. "They were right. That truck of his won't give any hints as to who they are."

Bernie Sanders was a big man in his thirties. Out of uniform, with his bushy beard, he could pass for the scruffiest bum in the woods. In uniform, he commanded a whole lot of authority. He and CO Chuck Ransom were dressed in plain clothes for the occasion. A tough looking pair of locals, for sure.

Webb called them on the walkie-talkie. "Is that an official unmarked government pickup, Bernie?"

"*Brought my own battle wagon this morning, Rick. Everything at the office looked way too official. And after we were briefed last night, we did a bit of staging. I think we'll pass for local traffic okay. We're loaded for bear, and we've got your ass covered. So we'll fall in behind you once we get eyes on the competition ... and ... there they are now.*"

Webb and McNabb watched in the Kenworth's mirrors as Bernie's flat black, diesel-powered GMC 3500 pulled out of the restaurant parking lot. It was a big pickup riding on oversized tires. Dual wheels on the back. It was built for heavy work and built before the era of DEF emission systems. Webb laughed as the air behind the big beast turned black, the diesel exhaust momentarily blotting out the image of the OSL guys in the silver F-150.

—

"What the fuck is *that?*" Zak Graham asked from the back seat of the F-150. The black exhaust cloud thinned out when the big pickup ahead of them reached highway speed. It had pulled away from the restaurant lot and was now halfway between them and the OSL transport. In the bed of the black dually sat a beat-up old Skidoo Tundra from the 1980s. To help build on the backwoods image, a couple of filthy diesel fuel jugs were half-covered in snow and a plastic milk crate stacked with animal traps was strapped to the snowmobile's cargo rack.

"Fuckin' country bumpkins," Willie said, laughing.

"Not so funny," said Jason from the driver's seat. "Traffic's light, and this would be a good stretch of road to try for a takedown. But not with the Beverley Hillbillies as witnesses."

"Bet they'll turn off at a sideroad before long and go trapping," Willie offered. "When they do, we'll pass the rig and be ready to take it back if the right situation comes up."

"Just blow by the bumpkins now, and I'll take out the driver as we pass," Zak suggested.

Out of the corner of his eye, Willie saw Zak drop a couple shells into the breeches of the shotgun. "Unload that fuckin' thing, for shit's sake, Zak. *Jesus!* You've got it pointed right at me. *Asshole.* And that's not how we are going to do this. We wait until there are no witnesses other than the game wardens and if we do it right, no one fires a shot … unless they shoot first."

Jason kept driving. Stayed a couple hundred metres behind the black pickup. But the driver kept speeding up and slowing down. Despite the bitter cold, he had his window down, and every few minutes, he would slow down, reach out and point at something in the swamp on the north side of the highway before resuming highway speed. All three of the OSL guys were getting pretty tired of this, so Willie finally made a decision. "Just pass the fucker, Jay. He's so busy looking for places to set his traps, he won't give a shit."

There was nothing coming the other way. Jason put his foot down and their rental truck leapt forward, accelerating to one hundred thirty km/h.

—

In the cab of the flat black GMC dually, Bernie Sanders and Chuck Ransom kept an eye on the silver F-150 behind them. Sanders was doing his best to drive like a hick, and they could imagine it was beginning to piss off the guys following them. But he kept up the act, doing his best to gradually fall farther behind the transport. It was a good four hundred metres ahead of them now, and gradually gaining ground.

In his side mirror, Ransom could see the Ford begin to close the distance. "Uh, they're going to make a run for it, Bern," he said. "Coming on fast." He left Sanders to handle the driving and picked up the government issue carbine rifle resting against the seat beside him. A quick check assured him that the magazine was locked in. He hadn't chambered a round yet. Wouldn't until it was needed, but he could see through the clear plastic side of the magazine that it was loaded. He was ready.

"Hang on, Chucky. Here we go!" Sanders kept checking his mirror, timing his move to the second.

—

In the F-150

When Jason Mead was about to pass the big dually, it belched out an opaque cloud of black diesel exhaust. By the time he could see the road ahead again, the other truck was three hundred metres ahead of them and moving like a rocket sled.

"Look at that fucker go!" came from Zak. "That old Duramax isn't smoking because it's worn out. That guy has done some serious fuckin' tweaking."

Past Raith, the highway got hilly and curvy, and the traffic increased. Breakfast was over and the big rigs were back on the road in force. Willie's crew had lost any opportunity to initiate a takedown for the time being. They were resigned to following the flat black dually. They figured the trapper must have left his trapping area, because now the guy set a steady pace more than a dozen car lengths behind the OSL transport.

Willie called Raymond to report the situation and was relieved he didn't get yelled at.

"*Comes under 'shit happens,' Willie. At least you found them again. Just stay with them for now. Grab it if they both leave the rig, but if they don't, there will be other opportunities later today. Derek's got a plan. I'm not so sure about it, but it might work.*"

—

1010 – East of Thunder Bay at the Pass Lake truck stop

"Time to top up the fuel, Rick," McNabb said as he pulled the Kenworth off the highway and headed toward the diesel pumps. "Still got plenty onboard, but I don't feel like spending another day getting it thawed out. And a coffee sure would go down well. You might as well order our lunch too. We'll be out in the middle of nowhere when it's noon."

Other than the confrontation with the moose, they'd made good time from Dryden. Their CO escort pulled in at the diesel pump next to the rig. With the guys in the silver F-150 watching them from across the parking lot, the four COs carried on a conversation that looked as innocent as strangers making small talk during a break in their travels. Webb bought coffee for himself and McNabb, and Chuck Ransom bought for himself and Sanders while McNabb and Sanders finished filling their tanks. Rob topped up the windshield washer fluid, too.

"The Nipigon truck that was supposed to take over from us here suffered a breakdown somewhere out in the boonies," said Sanders. "Frozen gas line. Go figure. Anyhow, we can stay with you as far as Nipigon, but after that, you're on your own … unless the Nipigon unit gets going again."

That was an unwanted hiccup in the day's plans. They were headed right into the lion's den now. The north highway was the last part of the route that was remote enough to try for a hijacking. It was the stretch where they really could have used extra eyes — and bodies. Webb returned to the restaurant to pick up their lunches, and twenty-five minutes after they arrived, they were on the road again.

There was enough heavy-truck traffic to provide safety in numbers for the time being. And while it would slow their progress by a kilometre or two, Rob dropped in between a

McKevitt rig and a Day and Ross double trailer train.

Sanders and Ransom had left five minutes ahead of them and dawdled until McNabb saw the intermittent belching of black exhaust about a kilometre ahead. Webb passed the word and Sanders sped up to position his black battle wagon half a kilometre out front of the Day and Ross rig and set his cruise control to match their speed. In the unlikely event of trouble, he could be back to help in less than a minute. Willie and the boys followed behind the convoy, still unaware of any connection between their rig and the scruffy trappers in the flat black GMC dually.

Chapter 18

1132 – Nipigon, Ontario

Willie Eardley pushed the rental truck's Bluetooth phone button. "Call Raymond," he said. The call went through, and Raymond came on the line. The OSL transport was about a half kilometre ahead. Willie didn't try to catch up. He had to remain well back — still needed to remain inconspicuous. Didn't realize they'd been recognized several hundred kilometres ago — back in Upsala.

"*Well, what's happening?*"

"We'll be at the Highway 11/17 junction in a few minutes. I'm betting he goes north on 11. It's supposed to snow later, and most of the long-haul drivers avoid the Lake Superior route in bad weather if they can."

"*We were betting on that too, Willie, so we came up Highway 11 as far as Hearst. But we can drop back down to 17 in a couple hours if he goes that way.*"

A minute passed as they waited to see which way their rig was going.

"He's just crossed the suspension bridge … and … he's signalling left. We've got them boxed in, Ray. They're headed your way."

"*Yeah, well it's a mighty big box right now, but we'll head out toward Longlac. There's a spot I have in mind where we can cause the road closure before you get there. And when we've done that, we'll get you to do the same thing behind them, just like Derek planned. No traffic, no witnesses. See you in a few hours."*

—

1300 – In the Kenworth between Jellicoe and Geraldton

The snow-covered boreal forest and frozen lakes rolled past as the kilometres wore on. Vince Gill's voice filled the cab with the haunting strains of *When I Call Your Name*.

Rick Webb spoke as he watched the scenery going by. "You know, there's something about country music...."

"Okay, I can change it." McNabb conceded.

"No, no, leave it on ... let me finish. I never thought I'd be saying this, but there's something about country music that goes well with the drone of the diesel in a big rig. I'm beginning to like it. *Some* of the songs are a bit ... uh ... *too* country for my liking, but this guy gives it class. He sort of tugs at the heart strings, doesn't he?"

"Yeah, he does," Rob agreed. "Tightens the chest muscles ... like waiting for the OSL guys to make a move. Man, not knowing what's going on is the shits."

"Can you see them behind us, Rob?" They had been uncomfortably aware of the silver F-150's presence, trailing discreetly behind ever since their escort had left them in Nipigon.

"Occasional glimpses of a vehicle about a kilometre back of us. Pretty sure it's them, but they're riding farther back than before. But still, no way to be sure it's the silver pickup ... unless ... I try this...."

The OSL rig had just crested the top of a long hill and

was starting down the other side. The view of the distant vehicle behind them was temporarily obscured. McNabb stepped down on the brakes, bringing the transport's speed down under seventy km/h. By the time the following vehicle cleared the hill, it would be a whole lot closer. Webb approved of the move but said nothing.

By the time the Kenworth rolled out on level ground at the bottom, their follower popped over the hilltop — and it was much closer.

"Silver pickup, for sure, Rob," Webb watched it in the mirror on his side. "Sure looks like a Ford. Not a hundred percent sure, but if I was a betting man, I'd roll the dice on it being our tail."

"Comforting to know." McNabb hit the cruise control resume button and the big rig worked back up to speed. "It would be nice to hear from the undercover contact. I mean, there's not much traffic up here and if they are going to pull something off, they'll have to do it sometime this afternoon. The sooner the better, for them. Between here and Hearst is the last truly remote stretch of highway. After that, while it's still sparsely settled, a lot of small communities pop up between the bigger towns. Lots of local traffic, too."

"You're right, Rob. And thinking about those guys *is* tightening up part of my anatomy ... you suggested a tight chest, but I was thinking farther south."

"Huh, yeah. Don't feel bad. Now that I've got a family of my own, I've sort of lost my sense of youthful immortality too. Why do you think I pulled on my snow pants after our last pee break? Sam might think I would stubbornly hang tough and protect the load, but if this has the look of any kind of trouble we can't settle peacefully, from inside the cab, I'd seriously suggest we abandon ship. Might have to ram a pickup or two to clear the way, but if those guys are armed and deadly serious, I say we chuck it and run for the bush. Get all your cold weather gear on, or at least, close at hand. We can turn the heater down to compensate."

"Good idea," Webb said as he reached back into the bunk to grab his snow pants. "I'm guessing they'll probably try to block us in between the two pickups and wave some firepower in our faces. If that's the case, then yeah, you shove the pickup in front into the snowbank. Then we'll bail out. If they fire so much as a single shot, we lay down a curtain of lead ... both of us firing ... first mag, all seventeen rounds, rapid fire. You shoot forward and I'll hose down whoever's behind us as we scamper into the trees. If we take the initiative, the element of surprise should play in our favour. We can reload and use our extra mags for more strategic fire if it's needed after we hit the bush line."

"I think they'll just want to grab the truck and leave after that," Rob suggested. "No point in them hanging around to hunt us down when they could be making tracks for the coast again."

"You may be right. We'll just have to see how it plays out, but they might want to eliminate witnesses. Anyhow, once we're into the trees, the advantage goes to us. They'll be the ones out in the open." Each man lapsed into silence. Each mentally refining his exit strategy. For Webb, who had a paper roadmap open in his lap, another option opened up. The more he considered it, the more he liked it.

"Rob, as you had so wisely put it earlier, the stretch between Longlac and Hearst ... it's almost two hundred kilometres without a settlement ... it's their last best chance to hit us. But just past Longlac there's a secondary highway that winds its way down to 17 through Caramat and Manitouwadge. I was thinking, if we get that far and nothing's happened yet ...."

McNabb picked up on Webb's idea. Nodded his approval. "Yeah, if we cut down there, we'll only have the silver pickup to deal with. Whoever is waiting ahead in the Silverado is either going to be out of the picture, or at the worst, going to have to fall in behind with the other guys."

"My thoughts exactly. And they'd be behind us on a narrow twisting highway that probably doesn't have many places for them to pass. I'm betting that if they tried, you could easily force them off the road."

"Okay, but by taking an obscure secondary route, isn't that still going to give them the hint that we are onto them?"

"You know, Rob, I'm getting past the point of caring. We've allowed the armchair quarterbacks to get us into this, way over our heads. Someone's screwing with us and they've given us dick all for background information. If the cops have got someone working undercover, this is big time dangerous shit we're involved in. It can't just be about a small load of dead beavers. Gotta be more to it than that. A whole shitload more."

"We've got a cell signal here, Rick. Why don't we phone home and ask Jacqui if we can divert?" McNabb wasn't happy either, about the position they'd been put in, but at the same time, he worried about endangering somebody's imbedded mole. At his last enforcement course, an undercover police operative had given a half-day presentation on the topic. A lot of the time those folks tread a fine line between life and death. The slightest miscue can blow their cover.

Webb agreed to touching base with the squirrels' nest and McNabb told the Kenworth to call Jacqui.

"*What's up, Rob?*" she asked. And he and Webb told her their concerns and Webb's suggested workaround. "*Hmm, I don't know, guys. Hang on a sec while I talk to the boss,*" she said. Two minutes passed. "*Call you back in a few. We're working on something here.*" She disconnected the call.

Ten minutes later, she called back. "*Okay guys, the cops aren't happy about it, but they've just announced the closure of Highway 11 from Hearst to west of the Hornepayne junction due to a bad accident. They've assured us that the news will get to the appropriate ears. Your shortest route now is to take the secondary highways down through Caramat and Manitouwadge. Not much cell service through there, so check in with us whenever you can. You'll still have one on your tail.*"

"Thanks Jacqui, and pass our appreciation along to the pissed off cops for us, will you?"

Chapter 19

Zak Graham was driving the silver Ford pickup. They'd rotated drivers during a bladder break near Jellicoe. Willie had put him behind the wheel to keep his itchy trigger finger off the shotgun. Willie was in the passenger seat beside him, engaged in a phone conversation with Raymond. Jason Mead was sprawled in the back seat, mostly on the passenger side, dozing.

"We're going by Geraldton right now, Ray. The rig is almost a kilometre ahead of us."

"Okay, you know what to do. We've been to Longlac and got what we need. Now we are headed back east of town. I've got a spot picked out. It's out of cell tower range, so no one can call for help when shit starts to happen. We'll block off our end a few minutes after the time you should be passing the town. With no phone service, we've got to do it based on timing, so make sure you don't it screw up." The call disconnected.

"Asshole's got no faith in us," Zak said. Willie remained silent. In twenty minutes, they would be passing Longlac. As soon as they were clear of the town, he would have to block the highway. He was certain that the transport following four hundred metres behind them would stop. Facing three guys standing in the road with guns pointed at him — or her — the driver would have to stop. Then they would block the road with the rig and disable it. Derek had come up with the idea and the guys had gone over it while they travelled. After they left the roadblock rig disabled across the highway, they would switch the stolen Saskatchewan plate on the F-150 for a set of Ontario plates they'd picked up while they were waiting at the Nipigon truck stop overnight. Then they'd be free and clear.

Zak, who would be driving the pickup home with its new identity, would be one guy, not three, caught waiting for the highway to reopen. Just another hapless motorist stuck behind the blockage.

In the seat behind him, Jason stretched, sat up and looked around. Ahead of them a snowplow pulled into a snowplow turnaround, and as they approached, the driver got out and walked around the back of his truck — in a hurry — working eagerly to unzip his fly.

"Quick, Zak, pull over and let me off beside the driver's door on that thing. There's our roadblock!"

Zak glanced at Willie who shrugged and said, "Sure." Zak stomped down on the brake pedal and pulled up beside the parked snowplow. Jason hopped out of the pickup, took three steps, opened the door on the big dump truck and hoisted himself into the driver's seat. The engine was still running. Without pausing, he put the truck in gear, released the air brakes and started forward. Zak had already pulled out onto the highway and was accelerating away.

In the passenger side mirror Jason could see the driver hurriedly zipping up his pants and running after his stolen unit — too slow, too late. And the guy's phone was on the dash, plugged in to recharge. He wouldn't be able to call for help, at least, not until the next vehicle with a cell phone came along, and even then, not until they got into cell tower range. Lots of dead zones in the region. The transport that had been following the F-150 had already gone by. But they wouldn't be needing it now.

When he got up to highway speed, Jason began to realize why snowplow operators drive so much slower than the rest of the traffic. With the massive steel plow and all the supporting hardware mounted out front of the cab, the steering was heavy and sluggish. At every heave in the pavement, and there were lots of those, the front end of the truck bucked like an amusement park ride. It was a proper pig to drive.

Something else he soon noticed was that the fuel gauge was bobbing on empty. If it ran dry before he passed through Longlac, he wouldn't be able to manoeuvre it to block the road. But now, he was driving on a long straight stretch, about halfway between the two communities. There was no traffic ahead or behind, other than his team in the silver F-150. This would be as good a place as any, he decided.

Coming to a stop in his own lane, he cranked the steering hard to the left and backed the truck into the opposite lane — the first leg of a three-point turn. When the back of the dump box was overhanging the snowbank on the far side of the road, the raised plow at the front was almost touching the snowbank on the eastbound lane. He straightened the wheel and moved forward several feet to even it up, then dropped both the front and wing plow blades to the road surface and shut off the engine. He got out, threw the keys as far as he could into the snow-filled ditch and walked toward Zak, who was coming back to pick him up.

Zak had been almost half a kilometre ahead of the plow when it stopped. Instead of doing a U-turn and driving back to pick up Jason, he threw the pickup into reverse and floored it.

While he was doing that, Willie phoned Raymond to tell him that their roadblock was in place already. But Ray wasn't answering. His line was busy, and he never used call waiting. Willie left a quick a message, explaining the revised roadblock and disconnected the call.

Driving in reverse at fifty kilometres per hour, Zak didn't anticipate that the steering would become twitchy. He didn't anticipate either, that when the passenger side tires left the pavement briefly, they'd pull the truck to the right and cause it to dive backwards into the plowed snowbank. But it did just that, and when it came to rest, it was totally hung up, unable to drive itself out — not even in four-wheel drive.

—

On the short drive east from Longlac, Raymond was on the phone with Derek Cheney. It was a call he wanted to make before he lost the cell signal.

"We're just about set up to grab the truck back. But I still don't like your idea of this double-ended roadblock. It's going down where no one can use their cell phones to call for help. Problem with that is, I've got no contact with Willie and the boys for the same reason. Bad shit could happen if this doesn't go like you planned."

Raymond had no problem with what they had planned for the game wardens. He never shrank from violence. A bit of bloodshed was entirely likely. But what if the cavalry came along at just the wrong moment — the police or a truckload of hardened lumberjacks or even a busload of grannies returning from a casino — unknowingly caught between the two roadblocks and coming up on the highjack scene? What then? That shouldn't happen if Willie and the boys did their part, but in Conn's experience, Murphy's Law was always lurking close at hand.

"I don't need you criticizing my decisions, Raymond. I pay you to make things happen, so just make it fuckin' happen."

Raymond shook his head as he pictured his asshole boss sitting in his comfy office chair more than eight hundred kilometres away. Nope, he's not risking *his* skin on this job. If this takedown goes all to hell, it'll be me and the guys who will be wearing the handcuffs. Derek will have time to grab his secret cash stash, fold his tent and disappear into the night.

"Just tell me when you've got it done. And I want that rig turned around and headed west again as soon as it's done. No witnesses."

"Don't worry. We'll get it done," he replied with a minimum of enthusiasm. He cut the connection just before the phone signal dropped completely.

When he arrived at the turnoff to Caramat, he pulled off the road behind the log truck they'd appropriated from the mill yard in Longlac less than an hour earlier. Seeing that there was no traffic in view in either direction, Raymond flashed his headlights, and the log truck pulled onto the highway.

Transport tires are good at handling sudden changes in direction on bare pavement. But tall loads of heavy logs prefer to continue travelling in a straight even when the truck beneath them changes direction in a hurry. It's called inertia. So, when Roach steered the log truck first, halfway back onto the shoulder of the road, then executed a tight U-turn across the highway at thirty kilometres per hour, the tractor made it most of the way around the turn, but the trailer, with its high load of logs, tipped up onto the wheels on one side and teetered, balanced there briefly, then tipped the rest of the way, falling over onto the highway.

The trailer's weight pulled the tractor over onto its side at the same time. Logs broke loose from the load and scattered everywhere. Roach had released the tiedown chains while he waited for Raymond to show up. Now the highway was blocked. Snowbank to snowbank.

Roach had left his side window open. Now he calmly undid his seat belt and climbed up through the window opening, crawled forward on the side of the cab and slid down over the hood, onto the road. He'd performed the same stunt several times at truck rodeos with old beater trucks on their last legs. He knew just how to time the manoeuvre. He was the best driver on the OSL A team.

Raymond pulled up close with his black Silverado, and as soon as Kyle got in, he turned the pickup around and headed west for more than a kilometre to the place he had chosen for the highjack. He pulled onto the shoulder to wait. Derek's Kenworth rig should be along in less than ten minutes. If there were any other vehicles running just ahead of the company rig, they would go past him and bunch up at the overturned log truck — not here, where he set up for the highjack.

After they took back their rig, they would change the company logo on the cab doors and switch licence plates, then turn the truck at the snowplow turnaround just behind them and head west. Just as Zak would have to wait at the eastbound blockage, the renamed OSL rig would wait patiently at the westbound blockade. Just another hapless transport waiting for the road to reopen. It wouldn't take forever — this was the Trans-Canada Highway, after all.

Chapter 20

Samantha Williams and the two observers in her Turbo Beaver had finished the last transect line of the moose survey in the wildlife area south of Highway 11. The next survey on the list lay north, across the highway and a few kilometres east.

They hadn't covered as much territory today as they'd originally planned. One of the observers — his first ever moose survey — became violently airsick shortly after starting the first transects in the morning. Something to do with circling in tight wingtip turns while they tried to determine the sex of a moose they'd spotted. They had to return to Hearst to drop the poor fellow off, and one of the local conservation officers joined the flight as a substitute.

Sam flew the Beaver northeast toward their next starting point. As they approached Highway 11, Ralph Shortling, the CO sitting in the co-pilot's seat beside Sam, pointed down to the right. "Something going on down there, Sam." He was looking at a string of westbound traffic stopped behind a load of something spilled over the highway. Sam banked the Beaver to the right so she could see, then nodded in agreement.

"We'd better take a closer look," she said. "There's next to no cell signal up here ... probably none down at ground level. They might need someone to call for first responders." She pulled back on the power, circling as she descended toward the blockage. It appeared that a log truck had overturned, spilling its load. The highway was completely blocked, but there didn't appear to be any sign of panic at the crash site. People were standing around. No sign of excitement whatsoever. Then, as she circled, something else caught her eye, not far to the west.

"Train your binoculars on that black pickup, Ralph." She banked the plane into a left turn, and he looked in the direction she indicated. The truck she was looking at was parked facing west on the highway shoulder, over a kilometre west of the blockage. Just sitting there. She was down under five hundred feet now.

"Looks like a Chevy or a GMC with at least a couple of guys sitting in it. They don't appear to be signalling those couple of eastbound trucks headed for the wreckage. They're just sitting ... waiting for something."

"Oh, *shit*. A black Chevy ... just waiting." Sam gave him a troubled look. She had already told him about what Rob and Rick were up against. "We have to see if we can find the guys before they get to that truck." During his fuel stop at Pass Lake, Rob had told her on the phone that they hoped to be going through the Geraldton – Longlac area around this time if all went well. She advanced the controls back to full cruising power and headed the Beaver west. She kept to the same altitude above the highway.

"Keep your eyes open for a white tractor-trailer, Ralph. There's no company logo on the trailer. Plain white. Just the company name ... OSL ... on the cab doors, Robbie says. We've got to stop them." While she flew, she got on the VHF radio to the Geraldton MNR office and asked the clerk to notify the police of the overturned log truck.

They passed over Longlac without seeing any sign of the

rig. Hardly any other traffic on the road, either. Then, about a dozen kilometres west of town, they spotted a lone white tractor, towing a white trailer, road salt spray up the sides. Neither Ralph nor Sam could read the company logo through the grime.

Sam pulled the cell phone from her breast pocket. "Call Robbie," she told the device. She overflew the transport while waiting for the call to connect. The connection was slow. She had to verify that it was him — would feel badly if she panicked an uninvolved, unsuspecting driver with a low altitude flypast. There was no sign of the silver pickup that was supposed to be following them, but it made sense that the bad guys would hang back, well out of sight. She kept following the highway west while she waited. As the phone finally began its ringtone, she saw another disturbance in the distance on the road ahead and pointed it out to Ralph, who had already seen it.

"*Hi Sam,*" Rob came on the line. "*Any moose around? That's us you just flew over down here.*"

"Stand by a minute Robbie. You've got trouble brewing ahead of you at the Caramat junction, and something's going on behind you too. Going to check that one out. And while I do, there's a little lake just a kilometre or so ahead of you on the left side, comes right up to the road. Stop there. I've got something here you might need … really soon."

"*Sure Sam. Just don't get stuck in the slush when you land. We'll try to check it out near the shore before you get down.*" Deep snow on a frozen lake can weigh the ice down to the point where water seeps up into the snow to form a layer of slush. Dry snow lying on top of the slush acts as an insulating layer, so even in bitterly cold weather, the slush doesn't freeze. Sometimes the slush can be over a foot deep — deep enough to get even a powerful Turbo Beaver thoroughly stuck once it loses speed. And sometimes the ice beneath the slush isn't very thick — not thick enough to support an aircraft.

Ralph had his binoculars trained on the activity down on the highway ahead of the Beaver. "Snowplow sitting crosswise, blocking the highway, Sam, and ... a silver pickup ... looks like it's stuck in the snowbank this side of the blockage. Backed in," he chuckled. "Oh yeah, I mean *really* stuck."

Sam, on the phone to Rob: "Looks like they've blocked the highway behind you, too Robbie. These guys mean serious shit! Stop at that little lake and we'll pick you up. They can have their damned truck. I want my man back. Remember our Post Apocalyptic Vow? No more hero shit!"

"We're stopped at the lake now Sam. I'll take the item you were going to give us, if it's what I think it is, but we're not giving up the rig yet. If things get rough, then they can have it. We do have an exit strategy. But we'd prefer not to give it up till we've figured out why they want it so badly. And there's another player depending on us to keep going.

"Meanwhile, I'm pretty sure there's a forest access road running south from Longlac to somewhere around Terrace Bay. We'll ask in town if it goes all the way through. If so, then we'll change our route and go back down to Highway 17."

McNabb parked the rig on the highway shoulder. The two COs got out and crossed the road on foot, slid down the short steep road embankment and made their way out onto the ice surface. The snow was knee deep near the shore with a layer of ankle-deep slush under it, but both the snow depth and slush became less as they walked the first hundred feet out onto the lake. The wind offshore had a better sweep there, blowing loose snow toward the edges of the lake.

Another fifty feet farther and the snow became ankle deep with no slush at all. Rob speed dialled his phone and told Sam that conditions were good. No chance of getting stuck.

Two minutes later, she was taxiing up to the two officers standing on the ice.

Sam and Ralph piled out of the Beaver's front doors. They made for an interesting sight, Ralph being a whole foot taller than Sam's five-foot-four. Rob gave his woman a tight hug, then dug keys out of his pants pocket and reached in the back door of the aircraft. He said "hi" to a woman who was sitting there, eating her lunch. She was the rear seat observer, covering the pilot's side of the plane during the moose transects.

He made quick work of opening the lock that secured the .30-06 hunting rifle that Sam had been permitted to carry in the aircraft when she transferred to Moosonee. Working in the remote Hudson and James Bay Lowland, often alone, it was prudent to have one aboard for survival purposes.

A quick round of introductions was taking place behind him while he opened a locked ammunition box and took out two loaded magazines and an unopened box of ammunition for the rifle. He dropped them into his parka pocket as he turned to join the conversation.

"Hey Ralph, it's good to finally meet you. We've got adjacent patrol areas but still work three hundred kilometres apart. I knew we'd eventually cross paths." They bumped elbows — COVID prevention convention.

"Good to meet you too, Rob. I was up your way for a fall goose hunt two years ago, but they said you were up checking non-resident hunters near Peawanuck that week."

"Yeah, with only two of us to protect a district bigger than the state of Minnesota, we can't always be at home. I don't want to sound rushed, but do you know anything about the road that runs south from Longlac?"

At that moment, Webb dropped out of the circle to take a call. It was Jacqui at the MCU.

"The Catlonite Road," Ralph said. "It's a gravel forest access road, wide and well graded. Open year-round. The log haulers and wood chip trucks roll along at a pretty good pace. They can usually average seventy klicks or so. It goes right to the mill in Terrace Bay.

"To get to it from here, you take the first right off the highway when you get to Longlac." He noticed McNabb nervously watching the highway, expecting company to pull up at any moment. "Don't worry, Rob. If the silver Ford is the rearguard for your bad guys, they really buried that pickup. They were running back to the snowplow to grab shovels when we flew over them. And with the highway blocked, no one on the other side will be able to get around it to pull them out."

"So, Robbie," Sam reopened the discussion she'd brought up each time they'd talked on the phone over the last two days — the question both he and Rick were racking their brains to answer. "What *is* it about this truck that makes it worth those guys closing down the Trans-Canada Highway to get it back?

"There's *got* to be something you haven't found … something different or unusual about it. Maybe diamonds in the air filter, or a solid gold engine oil pan … something inventive like that. C'mon, use your practical, problem-solving mind."

"I just don't know, Sam. The Mounties went over it inside and out, and we've been back over it too … we can't find anything. Didn't check for gold or diamonds, though." He thought about it, not knowing if the police had tried angles like that. He and Rick could look next time they did their circle check, but he doubted that it would be anything like that.

Rick rejoined the group, and without excusing himself, changed the subject.

"Jacqui made the call, but it was the chief who spoke to

me. The undercover operative just passed the word along that the OSL gang is just about to get their truck back … which fits with our own moose survey intel.

"So, change of plans. Our detour through Caramat and Manitouwadge is out of the question now. Until the bad guys actually contact us, the police are still staying out of the way … other than dealing with the highway obstructions. So, Sam and Ralph, as of now you two have been pulled off moose surveys. You have become our designated air escort. As senior officer, I have been instructed to tell you to go fly your kite … and clear our path down the Catlonite Road. We'll see you at suppertime, somewhere in Terrace Bay. There's no cell service most of the way, so we'll keep our walkie-talkie on."

"What about our back seat observer?" Sam asked.

"She's got family here in Longlac," Ralph said. "Hang on a sec." He stepped over and put his head in the Beaver's back door to speak with the woman, then turned back to the group.

"Rob, if you guys can drop her off at the Home Hardware store on your way through Longlac, her father works there. You'll drive right past it. I'll call the office and have someone from Hearst drive her back when the highway reopens." They broke from their brief conference, and Sam was starting her takeoff run by the time McNabb, Webb and the woman observer began struggling up the highway embankment.

Chapter 21

"Should have been here before now," Raymond looked at his watch. Then he checked his phone. Remembered that he had been talking to Derek about the time Willie would have called. There was no signal — just as he'd planned it. The kind of detail that could come back to bite you on the ass.

Kyle Roach sat unconcerned in the passenger seat. Kyle had done this sort of thing before. His department was doing, not planning.

"So, remember, no bullet holes in the truck," Conn filled the void with a rerun of the instructions he'd given several times in the last few minutes. "We do it without firing a shot … if we can. There's five of us and only two of them. So, like we agreed, we grab them as they climb down from the cab, knock them out, break their necks … whatever … I don't give a shit. When we've got 'em, we throw them in the trailer without their coats. They'll be solid blocks of ice by the time we get out west. We'll roll them off a cliff into the Fraser River out there at night and no one'll ever find them." He looked at his watch again.

"Shit, they're running late … C'mon guys."

"Maybe the guys in the rig pulled off in town to get something to eat," Kyle suggested. It was a possibility, but again, with no cell service, there was no way of calling Willie to find out.

—

1440 – On the Catlonite Road, several kilometres south of Longlac

Rob had just eased the truck across a narrow Bailey bridge that marked the end of the town of Longlac and the beginning of the Ginoogaming First Nation. Children were having a blast sliding down a hill on inner tubes. The hill ended at the edge of the road. He slowed quickly when a pair of laughing kids looked as if they might slide out onto the road in front of him. Instead, they fell off before they reached the road, but their carefree ride triggered a sudden thought.

"Damn, Rick, we missed it … I saw it and it never clicked … the one place in this rig I bet no one thought to check."

"Okay, you've got my attention. What did we miss?"

"The inner tubes. Arnold, the mechanic, said that inner tubes might be used in tubeless tires if there was a slow leak that they couldn't fix … usually a leak between the tire and the rim. But all the tires on this rig look pretty new, and the rims … certainly the two with inner tubes … both look in good shape too. And what are the odds that both outer tires on the same axle, but none of the others, would be afflicted by the same problem?

"Maybe they've got something stashed in those tires and are using the tubes to keep whatever it is, firmly in place. With a tire pressure of a hundred and twenty pounds per square inch, anything hidden in there would be wedged tight in place."

A knowing smile broke out on Webb's face. "I like that. Yeah, sounds like a good avenue to check out."

McNabb picked up the walkie-talkie and made a call.

"OEY, this is Flyboy, do you copy?"

"*What's up, Robbie?*" Sam came back.

"Inner tubes, Sam, regarding the unfinished conversation we keep having. We might have the answer, but we need the skills of a trustworthy mechanic when we arrive at tonight's destination. Can you pick Ralph's brain and hopefully make arrangements to meet one?

"*Roger, Robbie. Caught your drift ... will do. Out.*" At the instant she signed off, Rob was startled by the image in his rear-view mirror.

"Oh shit, that guy came up fast," He pulled over to allow a following wood chip truck to cannonball past him, then he picked up his own pace to take advantage of the guy's familiarity with the road. Rob had been rolling along doing around sixty km/h, getting used to running the big rig on a winding, snow-covered gravel road. But the travelled surface was wide, and the steeper hills and tighter curves had been thoroughly sanded, so he began to feel more confident averaging seventy while he followed the load of tree chips.

—

1455 – In the air over the Catlonite Road

"Shouldn't be a problem Sam." Ralph was an abundant source of local knowledge; and for him, local encompassed much of northeastern Ontario. "Carol Swain is the CO in Terrace Bay, and her husband, Bill, is a mechanic at the mill. They work on big trucks there all the time ... and log trucks are hard on tires. I'll call her while we've still got a signal."

—

Same time – Hwy 11, Twelve kilometres west of Longlac

Jason Mead was taking a break from digging packed snow from underneath the silver Ford pickup. They had only found two shovels on the snowplow, so they took it in shifts. While Willie and Zak were hard at it, Jason saw a black Chevy Silverado approaching from the direction of Longlac. He figured it had to be Raymond, and he strained to see if it was being followed by the Kenworth but couldn't see it — yet. And then, he saw not one, but two heads in the Silverado.

"Oh, fuck. The shit's about to fly now, guys." The other two straightened where they stood, thigh deep in the snow filled ditch, and they all watched Raymond pull to their side of the highway and run down his window.

"Where's the rig boys? And what the *fuck* are you doing parked ten feet off the goddamned road? Can't you dumb shitheads get anything right?"

"Didn't it come to you?" Willie asked.

"No, it didn't fuckin' come to us. You assholes were supposed to be on their tail as soon as you blocked the road. Not fuckin' around making snow angels! Jesus Christ, what a fuckup. And how come you set up your roadblock here? You were supposed to wait until you passed Longlac."

Willie looked at Jason, who provided a suggestion that didn't really answer the question.

"They must have stopped in the town … pulled in to eat, or something," Jason suggested.

"Well, I see the cops are just arriving at your roadblock," he nodded toward the snowplow three hundred metres down the road, "So you'd better hook my tow chain onto your ride,

117

and I'll see if we can pull you out of there before they come walking up here with five pairs of handcuffs. *Fuck me*, what a *screw-up!*"

It took four solid jerks on the tow chain for the Chev to pull the Ford off the snowbank, but ten minutes later, the two pickups were cruising the streets of Longlac, looking for the company's eighteen-wheeler. After touring every street in town — it didn't take long — they met out at the mill yard. Not there either. The two trucks pulled up, side by side, window to window, for a conference.

"There's no road out of here other than the highway." Raymond was looking at the GPS in his truck. It showed a gravel road leaving town to the south, but his GPS showed it ending at an Indian Reserve. The rented F-150 didn't have a GPS, but Jason had picked up a cheap Ontario road map at the truck stop during their long layover in Nipigon. The map showed no roads leaving town other than the main east-west highway.

Someone from mill security drove out to see what the two pickups were doing there. They were a little jumpy after having had a fully loaded log truck stolen from under their noses earlier in the afternoon. Raymond took the lead in dealing with the guy.

"Highway's blocked both ways, so we were hoping to find a detour. Got a meeting to get to in Thunder Bay in the morning."

"When you leave the yard, turn left. The Catlonite road will take you down to Terrace Bay. 'Bout a three-hour drive."

"K, thanks, buddy." They headed south, almost fifty minutes behind Webb, McNabb and the company's Kenworth.

—

1535 – Overnight Shipping Office, Scarborough, Ontario

"You're going to give yourself a stroke," Sylvia spoke just above a whisper. The comment, directed toward Derek's open office door, was not really meant to be heard. Cheney was in the middle of a telephone yelling match with — no — *at* Raymond Conn but had paused long enough to listen to Ray's reply.

"*We think they stopped in town for a bite, and the word got out about the overturned load. Some of the truckers up here have satellite phones because of the crappy cell service. Either they already knew about this logging road, or someone told them.*"

"Look, Raymond, the double ended roadblock was a foolproof plan. It didn't work because *your* guys fucked it up. Plain and simple."

"*That's bullshit, Derek. There were too many moving parts. Too much chance of something going wrong. We're going back to my original suggestion. KISS ... you remember that saying, right? Keep It Simple Stupid?*

"*Willie has his spare key, and we coulda grabbed the rig back the first night if the fuckin' GPS hadn't quit trackin'. But now we'll follow them close enough to keep an eye on them. Then we just take the truck when they stop for the night.*

"*If one of them stays with the truck, we can still do it. With one or two of our guys as lookouts, one game warden won't have a chance against three or four of us. We can bundle him into one of the pickups and dump him in the bush somewhere. If anyone happens to see it going down we tell them the guy had a stroke or a seizure and we're rushing him to the hospital.*"

"Idiot! How are you going to do that? You don't even know where they are now."

"*Well, they're obviously somewhere between here and North Bay. A whole lot closer to us here ... and close to the end of their duty hours by*

119

now. So, when we get to Terrace Bay, we'll split up and start checking every hotel, motel, restaurant and gas bar along the way. We won't stop for the night until we've gone at least as far east as White River. That's a good place to sit and watch. And if you want us to try that roadblock shit again, you can just forget about it. It's not going to happen. It was a dumb fuckin' plan. There's not many cops up here, but all it would take is one to land us all in jail."

Raymond cut the call before Derek could reply, so he banged down his telephone handset and threw his stapler against the wall.

Sylvia returned to talking on her cell phone and reading an online article about the lack of available food and restroom facilities for truckers during the pandemic.

Bea was on the line with a client. "Just a second, another truck just became available. It's much nearer than the first one. Hang on while I stick a hold pin in it, then I'll get your details."

She paused to send a text, her thumbs flying over her phone screen while the screen on her computer refreshed. Then she returned to the client.

"Okay, they're available any time after four-thirty. What time do you want it picked up?"

Chapter 22

1805 – Terrace Bay, Ontario

Webb and McNabb could tell they were getting close to the pulp mill by the glare in the evening sky. As they came around a bend in the road, they pulled up to a stop sign at the T intersection with Mill Road. A tall, stocky, middle-aged woman stood beside a conservation officer enforcement truck. She flagged them down and walked up to the driver's side window.

"Hi, I'm Carol," she called out over noise of the idling diesel. "We're going to get you to park your rig in Bill's shop. Don't worry, it's secure. And then we'll all come back after supper to perform what he calls a 'tubal' on those tires," she chuckled. "Follow me."

McNabb fell in behind the CO's pickup and snaked past several large mill buildings, all pumping out industrious volumes of steam and noise. As they approached an enormous warehouse structure, an overhead door began to rise. Carol drove in ahead of them. McNabb paused until the door was fully open. He could see a similar door at the far end of the cavernous drive-through service bay. Once inside, he stopped the Kenworth behind her pickup.

Carol and Bill approached the truck as Rick and Rob climbed down to the floor with their COVID masks on and introduced themselves.

"You guys are staying with us tonight. Sam and Ralph are already at the house. Bill put one of his famous monster moose stews in the slow cooker this morning, so we won't starve." They all climbed into the pickup and she drove out the other roll-up door, pausing behind the building until the door was fully closed.

—

1935 – In the pulp mill garage

The four COs, plus the pilot and Bill Swain, gathered beside the Kenworth tractor where it sat in the enormous repair shop. Tire repairs were common jobs on log trucks. Swain could do this stuff with his eyes closed. After McNabb cranked down the trailer landing gear to take the weight off the Kenworth's fifth-wheel, Bill ran a jack under the back of the tractor and had the first wheel off in minutes. Rob removed the tire valve to let the air out while the mechanic ran a second jack under the other side.

When the first tire lost its air pressure, they rolled it under a pneumatic press to break the seal. Bill slid a long-handled tire iron inside the tire and began to work the first edge of the tire off the rim. Peeking through the gap, Rob gasped at what he saw.

"Oh, yeah! *This* is why they're so eager to get their rig back. Take a look." The others gathered round to look. Inside the tire were banded packets of United States one-hundred-dollar bills. Each packet was tightly wrapped in a sandwich bag and stuck with double-sided tape to the inside of the tire. Packets of bills were stuck side by side all the way around it. The tube, when inflated, kept all the packets pressed firmly in place.

The double-sided tape was simply to position everything until the tube was inflated.

Webb reached in with a latex-gloved hand and pulled one of the Ziploc bags free of the tape. "Someone count the remaining straps ... that's what each packet is called in the banking business. Normally there are a hundred banknotes in a strap. I'll count one as a sample."

Rob and Ralph each counted the remaining straps of money inside the tire.

"I count forty-four," McNabb said. "And the top note in each strap is a one-hundred-dollar bill."

"Agreed," said Ralph.

"One hundred bills here," said Webb. "They're not new, and they've got randomly different serial numbers. It's not likely counterfeit."

Sam didn't even have to think to do the math. "Four hundred and fifty thousand. Sort of leaves you feeling a little breathless."

"And behind door number two," Bill said as he pried open the second tire, "another fortune here."

They sampled one strap from the second tire and came up with the same total. Rick took pictures of the stash before placing a call to the secret squirrels at head office. The office had already been alerted that there might be a break in the case. After describing their find, Jacqui told them she'd have to talk to the police agencies working on the bigger case — whatever it was.

Ten minutes later, Webb's phone went off again. It was Jacqui, and once again, the chief was present to take over the call. "*Do you have access to a landline there?*" Bill gave her the number for the lunchroom phone. His office was too small to sit six, regardless of social distancing. The phone rang almost before they were all seated. Bill put it on speaker and Carol immediately addressed the chief.

"Everyone's here ma'am, but did you want just the primary officers involved?"

———

Major Case Unit, MNR Head Office

"No, I need to speak to everyone who was involved in discovering the money, Carol ... including your husband ... he's the mechanic who opened the tires?"

"*Yes, ma'am.*"

"Okay, call me Dot and let me get right down to business.

"We appreciate everything you people have put into this project so far," she said. "The Canadian equivalent of more than a million dollars is an impressive find, folks. That's really good work. But no one is to talk to anyone outside this group about the cash. *Not ... to ... anyone!* It's strictly a need-to-know situation, and nobody but us and the police agencies we're working with, needs to know. Got it?"

The group in the office of the pulp mill's garage all agreed to keep it so.

"Okay, now don't kill the messenger, but we've been asked to tell you to put everything back together exactly as you found it, and tomorrow, while continuing to appear to be delivering the truck as directed, you will allow the OSL people to take it back, if and when they find it."

The response from the group in the lunchroom was predictable. "*Awe, c'mon, you've got to be kidding.*"

"Just a minute, I'm not done yet. We now know the money is intended to finance a major illicit goods transaction. Some drugs ... that's this guy's usual line, but he's also expecting a shipment of raw ivory. I know, bulk shipments of wildlife parts are usually being exported … polar bear hides, black bear galls, etcetera. But he's apparently come up with a domestic market for something that doesn't grow in this part of the world.

"The police have been working on the drugs angle with this crew for several years, and not only do they want to take down the Ontario end of the operation, but also whoever it is brings the drugs to the west coast. So, the truck and its money stash are needed out there to close the deal at a location as yet unknown. Unknown not only to the police, but even the buyer remains in the dark until the last possible moment.

"Environment Canada is in the loop now because of the ivory, and officers from their Wildlife Enforcement Directorate will join in for the takedown out on the coast."

"Of course, there is still your load of undocumented fur that needs to be dealt with. So, Rick and Rob, if you are willing to continue, your revised mission, after the truck is taken over by the OSL people, is to team up with the police and follow it to the undisclosed location out west. And after the police and federal wildlife officers have completed their takedown, you two seize the fur once again and proceed with appropriate legal action.

"Are you willing to continue, or do you wish to pull out?" She overheard the two officers talking between themselves and the occasional input of a woman's voice — presumably Sam's.

"*Rick here, Dot. Okay, Rob and I agree that we signed up for the original delivery, so we're committed to carry on at least until the truck is back in the hands of the bad guys. And if you can assure us that there will be a significant police involvement, then we'll see it right through to the end.*"

"Okay, thanks guys. The police will have several detectives in unmarked rental vehicles joining you tomorrow. Given enough opportunity, we hope the bad guys will take it back when it's unattended, and immediately turn it around and head for the west coast.

"So, concerning immediate logistics: Tomorrow happens to be the day the province is allowing restaurants to open up once again … with limited seating … social distancing and masks remain in effect. To give these guys an opportunity to take back their rig, you take your time during stops for all your meals, fuel stops and breaks. Remember, we still don't want them to know that we know, so don't offer them the keys if you see them looking longingly at their truck. But don't make it difficult for them, either.

"Once the OSL guys have taken it back, you'll each team up with a detective to provide a minimum two-car tail. The police will arrange frequent fresh rentals along the way. Our provincial police will liaise with police agencies along your route, and they promise keep this office in the loop.

"Samantha, we'd like you and Ralph to provide air cover as far as Wawa tomorrow, then you can return to Hearst and resume your moose surveys."

"*Sure, we can do that.*"

"Thanks Sam. And thanks, Carol and Bill, for putting the team up for the night and for your participation in the excitement. While it screwed up the simple return of the load of furs from the west, your help finding that cash sure put things in a new perspective."

"*No problem Dot. We're glad to have the visitors. These guys are the first company we've had here in over a year.*"

"Rick and Rob, because of severe staff shortages, the police agencies involved are relieved to have you two along. I've been assured that you will be treated as equal partners, not excess baggage.

"That about wraps it up for me. Any questions?"

"*What time is our police escort arriving in the morning, Dot?*" Rob asked.

"They're not … at least, not there. They're leaving from the Soo in the wee hours and will wait for you to go by at White River. That's why I've got Sam and Ralph riding shotgun to Wawa, giving you a hundred kilometres of overlapping protection. You're not likely to be stopping for any breaks before that, I assume."

"*Coffee and an early lunch in Wawa would be the first planned stop,*" Rob said.

"Good. Then I'll leave it to you folks to get organized. Call the secret squirrels any time you need anything. Good night."

———

Rick and Rob helped Bill Swain reinstall the tires and Sam commandeered a ladder and a can of orange boundary marking paint she saw sitting on a shelf. She climbed up on top of the trailer and sprayed a bright orange circle several feet in diameter on its roof. "There, Robbie, you guys should stand out from the crowd from a couple thousand feet. We won't have to fly just above the treetops looking for company logos."

Once finished, they returned to the Swain house for the night. While the group sat around the basement woodstove over a nightcap, Sam reminded Rob that he would have to get the rifle back into the Beaver before she left in the morning. And Rob realized something else.

"If they retake the truck at a stop along the way, we don't want them driving off with our personal belongings. We'll have to send our bags with you, too, Sam."

But Rick could see a potential hitch in the plan. "Those

guys aren't supposed to suspect we know about their plans. Somehow, the cab still needs to look lived in."

"A bit of subterfuge is in order here, boys," Carol piped up. "And I know just how we can do that. Bill, get that old sports bag I keep threatening to throw out. I'm going to run over to the office for a few things. I'll be right back."

Ten minutes later, the sports bag sat empty in the middle of the basement floor. When Carol returned with a ratty old government backpack, she proceeded to dump its contents on the carpet.

"There. The CO that I replaced, retired from here and left his whole uniform … and his emergency dry clothes in case he went through the ice on patrol. It's been taking up space in a closet at the office ever since. We'll just put a few uniform pieces and a pair of emergency long johns and socks in each bag, and your bad guys won't likely twig to it."

McNabb was sorting through the clothes on the floor. "Hey, my pant size exactly … the shirts too, and some of these look like they've hardly been worn. I think I'll contribute several of my old worn items to the cause and commandeer the newer ones to wear tomorrow."

Webb chuckled. "Yeah, I always put half worn-out stuff in my emergency clothes bag. This guy's socks and long underwear look brand new. Rob's got the right idea. Besides, two guys who've been away from home for almost a week aren't going to have a bag full of clean clothes, so we'll give them our dirty laundry."

"I've got a couple of dull disposable razors upstairs," Bill said, and he left the room for a minute. Along with the razors, he returned with a crumpled, empty toothpaste tube salvaged from the bathroom garbage and another, a different brand, down to its last few squeezes. And he handed them each a used

Ziploc bag. "Sorry, but these are all I can think of to use for shaving kits," he said.

"I've got a couple of worn toothbrushes in my gun cleaning kit," Carol said. She disappeared into the utility room for a moment and returned with the brushes.

Sam burst out laughing. "You guys have pretty much replicated Robbie's regular travel luggage." Rob's glare quickly dissolved. He knew she wasn't far wrong.

Chapter 23

There was a raw wind blowing from the east. The temperature had risen five degrees in the hour and forty minutes since they'd left Terrace Bay. But at -15°C it still was not the sort of day you'd want to be stranded by the roadside.

Despite making an early start, Webb and McNabb were running close to half an hour behind Rob's estimated time to the Marathon turnoff. The Trans-Canada Highway between the two communities takes a winding route over not the highest, but some of the most rugged granite hills of the Canadian shield. There are some spectacular vistas to take in when travelling the route in daylight, but sunrise was still almost half an hour away.

For almost half the distance, they'd followed a string of transports caught behind a slow-moving snowplow. It was laying down road salt on the worst hills and curves before the day's anticipated snowfall. The few passing lanes on the route were located on steep uphill grades and most were too short to allow more than one or two trailing rigs to get past the plow. The average speed of the convoy was barely sixty kilometres per hour, and Rob was becoming impatient with the slow pace.

"This is frustrating Rick. At this rate I'm going to be as old as you are when we stop for lunch in Wawa."

"Don't worry, Rob, it's all pensionable time."

"Wasn't planning to retire this soon."

"Fret not, my friend, brake lights up ahead. He's turning off." And in his side mirror, Webb could see an assortment of twenty or more vehicles, large and small, bunched up behind them. "Now we'll be the slowpoke rig that everyone else is anxious to pass."

At 0845, they made it through the reduced speed zone at White River and were back up to speed, bound for Wawa when Sam's Turbo Beaver passed several thousand feet above them. Rick noticed it out of his side window. Rob's phone rang. It was Sam.

"*I hope you guys weren't waiting for me. I've been circling just behind you for over forty minutes and you're holding up the traffic down there.*"

"Caught in the morning rush hour for a while, Sam. But I never could figure out why they call it that. Anyhow, now that we're clear of it, this is as fast as she goes."

"*Reason I called … just after you guys went by the hotel on the right-hand side, two pickups pulled out onto the highway. They're eastbound. Can't tell their make from two thousand feet, but one is silver and the other one black. Do you see them?*"

"They're a good piece back, Sam, but I think so," Rob said as he studied the driver's side mirror for a quick moment.

"*And I don't know if it's your other escort, but one car just came out of the A&W, headed in your direction, and another pulled out from the motel on the other side of the road to follow it. One dark blue and one white. They seem to be holding back, behind the pickups.*"

"Well, I hope they don't mind us stopping for lunch and a pee break in Wawa. Carol's coffee is starting to look for a way out. How's the weather looking?"

"*Supposed to start snowing around Wawa and get heavier as you go south along the lake.*"

"Crap. No way I want to tackle this highway along the

131

Superior coast in a snowstorm. I think we'll head across to Timmins on 101 instead."

The rugged eastern shore of Lake Superior could be a transport driver's worst nightmare. When it snowed there, it snowed hard. The two-hundred-and-twenty-kilometre section between Wawa and Sault Ste. Marie was often closed due to winter whiteout conditions — or road wrecks caused by whiteouts. Rob had heard stories of trucks stranded on the big hill at Montreal River for many hours — occasionally for days. That was the worst spot, but there were other bad hills too.

—

Raymond's black Silverado ran about half a kilometre behind the Kenworth, and Willie and his two companions followed a few hundred metres behind him in the silver F-150. They paid no attention to the cars pulling onto the highway behind them. Didn't even notice them. This was the Trans-Canada Highway. It would be unusual if there wasn't any other traffic.

—

0950 – Wawa, Ontario
McNabb was pulling off the highway and heading into town when Sam called again. "*You're not going to like this, Robbie. Highway 101 is closed. There's a train derailed at the Hawk Junction crossing. I'm over it right now and there are rail cars lying on their side, right across the highway.*"

"You're a real ray of sunshine, sweetie. Thanks a lot. We're headed into town now anyhow, so we'll stop for lunch as planned. With any luck, we'll be westbound again after we eat, and the bad guys can break trail for a few days. Are you landing here, or moving on?"

"We're stopping just long enough to transfer your real bags to one of the police escort cars. Jacqui just called to say she'd arranged it. Then we're headed back to Hearst. You guys take care."

"Okay, love you Sam. I'll call when I can … and I'll see you when we finish this job. Fly safely."

McNabb ended the call as he drove slowly up Broadway Street past the North of 17 Restaurant. The whole main street in that part of town was angle parking only, so he took the rig around the block in three left turns and parked on the side street nearest to the diner. The truck blocked a residential driveway, but the house looked as if no one had been there all winter. He'd risk a parking ticket. Didn't really matter anyhow. If it did get ticketed, Overnight Shipping could add another count to its growing list of court transactions. Maybe — hopefully — this would be the place the OSL thugs would take back the truck, then no one would have to drive south through a snowstorm.

As they walked around the corner toward the restaurant, Rick gave Rob a slight nudge with his elbow. "Silver F-150 up ahead just turned the first corner we took to go around the block."

"Sorry, I was busy admiring the black Silverado, parking across from the diner. Got the right licence plate, too. This might be the place, Rick. With the forecast calling for a major dump of snow, and the closure of Highway 101, I'm really beginning to root for the bad guys."

"Yeah. No point in them dragging it out any longer. The farther we go east, the farther they'll have to backtrack. I bet their boss is a little miffed that they missed us yesterday."

"Would have been interesting to be a fly on the wall when he found out."

—

Willie Eardley took the third left turn around the block as soon as Raymond phoned to tell him that the game wardens had entered the restaurant. He pulled over and parked alongside a four-foot-high snowbank, one driveway behind the Overnight Shipping rig.

"Hand me the bag," he said to Zak, who was sitting in the back seat. The sports bag landed with a thump on the console between Willie and Jason. Willie unzipped the bag to check its contents.

"Shit," Jason stiffened in his seat. "Fuckin' cops."

Willie looked up, and all three outlaws watched as a police car turned off Broadway onto their street and parked opposite the Kenworth. The constable was engaged in a lively conversation on his cell phone. There was no way Willie could just walk up to the rig, get in and drive off with it, not until he modified its identity, and certainly not with a uniformed witness sitting less than twenty feet from it. Not even with the uniform being distracted by his phone conversation. Way too risky.

Surely a phone call wouldn't take that long. They could wait. And Raymond was watching the front of the restaurant. If the call ended soon and the game wardens were still inside eating, the magnetic signs and replacement licence plates wouldn't take long to slap in place. They'd done this before. He could be in the cab and on his way just minutes after the cop drove off. But that wasn't to be, either.

A second black and white pulled up alongside the first. The driver got out with two takeout coffees in hand. The first cop ended his call and ran down his window. The newcomer handed him a coffee and leaned against the side of his cruiser. The OSL guys couldn't know what they were talking about, but it looked like they were in no hurry to leave.

"They forgot the fuckin' donuts," Jason said.

"Fuck," Willie said. He started the engine, put the truck in drive and squeezed between the second cruiser and the Kenworth, then pulled out onto Broadway and parked beside Raymond's pickup.

—

1030 – North of 17 Restaurant, Wawa

Webb and McNabb had just finished eating and were contemplating a final coffee refill when a man entered from the street, looked around the room, then proceeded to the counter where he ordered a coffee to go. He was an ordinary looking guy, maybe about five foot eight, with a couple of days of red whisker stubble on his face, but he walked with the gait of a cop.

The fellow paid for his coffee and walked toward the exit. He brushed up against their table as he passed to make way for a waitress headed in the opposite direction. In doing so, he placed a business card, face down, beside Rob's empty breakfast plate. McNabb picked it up and read it before handing it to Rick.

The card identified the man as Detective Constable Ian Selkirk. On the back of the card, he'd printed a brief message:

"No point hanging around. Bad guys spooked by a black and white. Might as well continue south. Sorry. Call me when you are rolling. Ian"

Webb read the card and slipped it into a pocket. "The day's a-wasting, Flyboy. You get the heater fired up and I'll settle the lunch tab."

Chapter 24

The black Silverado was gone when McNabb left the restaurant and the Overnight Shipping transport still sat where he'd parked it. He began hoping that with a major dump of snow coming, the police might have closed Hwy 17. If that happened, he could park in front of a motel, pretending to check in, and give the OSL gang a chance at a re-do.

Maybe on any other snowy day that might have happened, but it was wishful thinking on his part. When Webb climbed back in, they headed out of town. They arrived at the Highway 17 junction and the Trans-Canada was still open, still accepting southbound traffic. He activated the left turn signal and headed the rig south.

Rob McNabb loved driving, and the Kenworth was a real pleasure to handle. But the fresh snowfall was bound to prove challenging on some of the big hills along the Lake Superior coast. He wasn't looking forward to that. At least he had the antilock brake system back online. Bill Swain had reset it last night in the service bay and it was working fine this morning.

The rig wasn't up to speed yet when he saw a couple of transports up ahead waiting to pull out from the Esso truck stop south of town. So, he slowed and flashed his headlights to let them in. By staying behind, he would have tail lights and tire tracks to follow as a visual reference if conditions worsened.

While McNabb drove, Webb was on his phone with

Detective Selkirk. When he finished the call, he updated Rob on the situation.

"So, the detective is ahead of us in a blue Mazda. After the bad guys took off, he managed to stick a short-range tracker on us. It's mostly for when the OSL guys get the truck back. His sergeant says the two pickups are behind us. For now, Selkirk is going to keep his distance ahead of us and give us a warning of any problems with road conditions or highwaymen."

"Selkirk says there's no need to push beyond your comfort level. You set the pace. Our other escort car is a white Camry. The sergeant is driving it and staying back. She'll tail the two OSL pickups. Selkirk suggests that when we get to the Soo, we should head to the Husky restaurant for our next break. There's plenty of big rig parking at the back, out of sight of the restaurant. The sergeant will call ahead and make sure there are no cop cars to spook them this time."

After the first twenty minutes, McNabb was beginning to feel comfortable with the pace set by the Bison transport he was following. With police riding shotgun ahead and behind, his only responsibility now was to drive.

The informal convoy soon caught up with a snowplow and they followed it at sixty km/h for over half an hour before it pulled off to turn around at the Lake Superior Park headquarters. But none of the vehicles that had stacked up behind it made any attempt to pass after they left the plow behind. Visibility was the pits, and the other side of the highway hadn't been plowed yet.

Even after the snowplow left the parade, the pace didn't pick up by more than five km/h. Conditions were that bad.

From Wawa it took an hour and a half to reach the Montreal River hill — thirty minutes longer than it would have if the road conditions had been good. The Bison rig slowed way down before beginning the long steep descent. Rob was pleased he'd chosen to follow a more experienced driver and he kept more than a truck length behind. But if he rode any farther back, the trailer ahead of him was lost in a blinding swirl of snow.

Rick's phone went off just as they started down the long steep grade. It was Selkirk with an urgent traffic report. Webb put his phone on speaker, turned up the volume and held it close to McNabb so he could hear.

"*There are two upbound transports stuck on the top third of the hill. The one in the lead is half on the shoulder and half on the road. The one behind him is halfway into the passing lane and there's another idiot right behind them, still crawling and about to pass them both. Your lane might be a tight fit by the time you get down to them.*"

"Did you get that Rob?"

"Oh, yeah, I got it alright." He was already downshifting and working the brakes when the brake lights on the Bison trailer switched to four-way flashers. "Ohhhh *shit!*"

The Bison was slowing more quickly than Rob. He applied more brake, but the rig began to lose traction. The ABS warning light came on. The antilock brake system failed now when he needed it most.

"Shit. ABS failure, Rick. Hang on." He continued feathering the brakes and had the rig down to less than twenty kilometres per hour. His closing speed with the Bison unit was less than a slow walk, but McNabb knew he was about to rear-end his leader's trailer. "Shit, shit, shit, shit."

"Don't worry, Rob. No one's going to get hurt at this rate of closing." Rick tried to ease McNabb's obvious anxiety.

"I can't see ahead … I might shove him into something he's trying to avoid."

It looked as if the moose bars on the Kenworth were going to get another workout. They couldn't be more than a foot from impact now.

With just inches to go, the gap suddenly stopped shrinking — it actually grew slowly wider as the Bison rig stopped braking. But now, air horns were blaring up ahead, so Rob stayed on his brakes until he finally came to a stop. Behind him, a silver pickup truck — an F-150 — lost control and bounced off the snowbank a hundred yards back, then spun a complete 360° circle before coming to rest in the snowbank in the opposite lane, just inches from the front bumper of the transport that was half off the road.

Ahead of Rob, the eight-and-a-half-foot wide Bison trailer squeezed through an eight-foot gap between an oncoming transport and the snowbank. The driver's side mirror from the upbound rig was lying on the pavement. The Bison truck stopped fifty yards downhill past the bottleneck, on a slightly less steep grade. The four-way flashers were on again. The driver exited the cab and headed back up the hill on the run. A large, solidly built woman, she looked about ready to tear the face off the jerk who'd just ruined her twenty-five-year safe driving record.

"Oh, shit," Rob said. With his four-way lights flashing, he locked the air brakes and opened his door ready to leave the cab.

"No, you're blocking the road there," the woman yelled at him. "Go on down and park behind me. I've got a beef to settle with this shit-for-brains idiot first," she pointed at the driver whose truck was occupying fully half of the single downbound lane. Traffic behind them was already stopped, but Rob obeyed the woman, released the brakes and began to inch forward, through the tiny gap that Lady Bison had just opened up.

Webb phoned Selkirk and told him of the delay. "Park down at the bottom of the mountain, Detective, and we'll let you know when we are rolling again. We weren't actually involved in anything, and Rob kept us close enough to the rig ahead that we couldn't witness whatever did happen, but he feels he has to smooth some ruffled feathers before we leave. We shouldn't be long."

McNabb threw in: "That is, if the lady wrestler leaves enough of me to get behind the wheel again." He squeezed past the offending transport with no more than two inches to spare and didn't get stuck in the snowbank on the other side. After rolling past the upbound rig, he parked a comfortable six feet behind the Bison transport and walked back up the hill to apologize to the dragon lady.

When he got there, the driver of the offending truck was cowering inside his cab and the woman was pounding on the side of his handsome Peterbilt tractor with his own broken mirror set. While Samantha could provide some salty language from time to time, Rob had never heard a woman spit out such a continuous string of crude vitriolic curse words. He was beginning to wonder at the wisdom of coming back to apologize to her.

The abusive tirade suddenly stopped, and the woman showed the driver a middle finger as she turned her attention on McNabb. He had always thought that if he died on the job, it would be of exposure after falling through the ice in a remote location, or in a bush plane crash, or even a gunfight, but he'd never contemplated being beaten to a pulp on the Trans-Canada Highway by a lady trucker. Sam had been right. Some truckers can be tough.

"So, young fellow ... ah, Officer young fellow ... you know you got a little close back there, don't you?"

"I'm really sorry Ma'am. I was trying to make as much space as I could, without losing sight of you before starting down the hill. But you were on the brakes before I was, and my ABS system blew a relay." He didn't dare mention having received a traffic update by phone just before the beginning of it all.

"Well don't worry about it. No harm no foul. That asshole was still creeping ahead and would have closed our lane completely if I hadn't let off the brakes when I did. The idiot couldn't have gone anywhere with us in the lane anyhow, but he still wanted to keep coming. Now he can explain a thousand dollars worth of bodywork and a day's delay to his dispatcher as a reward for his aggression.

"You drive regular for that outfit?"

"No, Ma'am." And as he explained about delivering the seized rig to North Bay, they started walking down the hill, chatting all the way — she gave him a COVID elbow bump when they came alongside the OSL cab and told him to stay on her tail. Said she'd keep him centred on the road the rest of the way to Sault Ste. Marie. "They'll be shutting down the highway now between Wawa and the Soo with the hill in a mess like this. So in about an hour we won't have any oncoming traffic to mark the opposing lane. Gives us more room, but when the whiteout's really bad, it can be disorienting without tire tracks on the oncoming side for visual reference."

"You're not staying here?" he asked.

"Naw, it was his fault … just a scratch on the corner of my trailer and there's less than two grand damage to his rig, even with the dozen new dents in his door. Mirror's fucked, though. He's got my unit number if he wants to make something of it. But fuck him if he can't take a joke." She stepped between their two rigs to brush accumulated snow off her trailer's tail lights. "That won't last long," she called back at Rob as she walked toward her cab. "Enjoy them while you can see them."

141

The rest of the trip to Sault Ste. Marie was an adventure in slow — and snow. At times, Rob could barely see the lights on the back of Lady Bison's trailer, and the back doors of the unit were completely coated with a thick layer of the white stuff — perfect camouflage in the prevailing blizzard conditions. Whenever the road ran right beside the lake, the visibility was so bad that they were doing less than thirty kilometres per hour.

The snow finally eased off as they entered the north end of the Soo. It was still snowing, but more like a Christmas card scene than a winter disaster movie. The Bison rig pulled off at the Petro-Can truck stop on Great Northern Road and Rob gave her a touch of air horn as he passed. Fourteen minutes later he pulled in under the big Canadian flag at the Husky on Trunk Road at the other end of the city. He picked his way past the big-rig fuel pumps behind the restaurant and parked between a couple of west-facing transports that appeared to be shut down for the night — probably waiting for the highway to open again.

"Great job, Flyboy. How are you feeling?" Webb asked as the diesel went silent.

"Huh … almost four hours to do a two-and-a-half-hour drive. I love driving, Rick, but I don't know how truckers can do a thirteen-hour day in conditions like that. I sure hope those OSL guys are ready to take over."

"Well, the sergeant called when we were around Havilland Bay and said they were hanging on to us pretty tight most of the way, after the Silverado pulled the Ford out of the snowbank. Let's go grab a coffee and something to eat. Maybe that will help facilitate their acquisition."

"Be right with you, Rick. Need to update my log. Have to keep up appearances, right?"

Chapter 25

1435 – Husky truck stop, Sault Ste. Marie, Ontario

Jason Mead had followed the transport's tracks as much as the truck itself. He didn't want to lose sight of it, but if he'd kept close behind the trailer, he would have been travelling in a continuous swirl of blinding snow. That would have been impossible — even with the tail lights for reference it was distracting. He drove much of the way white-knuckled and was relieved to finally arrive in the city.

Zak was asleep in the back seat and Willie was just starting to wake up in the front passenger seat when Jason turned into the Husky. He parked at the convenience store end of the building, out of sight of the restaurant at the other end and the transport parking at the back. He stepped out of the pickup and pulled on his parka, stretched and yawned as he grabbed his and Willie's overnight bags from the back seat.

Raymond was parking nearby when Willie, Zak and Jason started to walk toward the transport parking area. Raymond and Kyle Roach caught up with them before they got to the first rows of parked rigs.

"Grab a wet squeegee at the fuel pumps when we go by, Zak," Willie said, and traded with Jason, a pair of magnetic door signs for his bag, as they walked.

"Okay guys," Raymond said. "This is likely their last stop

before North Bay. We gotta take it back now or we're screwed for sure. If one of them's stayed with the rig, Jason, you go back and get your pickup. And when we take the guy down, we'll stuff him in the back seat and you and Zak get him out of here. The rest of us will rename the rig and start down the road.

Willie gave the front licence plate to Raymond. A small cordless screwdriver appeared from Kyle's pocket. There, between the third and fifth rows of parked transports sat their Kenworth. The group paused a second until a man disappeared around the corner at the other end of the row. He appeared to be heading toward the restaurant.

Did that mean one of the wardens was still holed up in the cab? Raymond and Willie sneaked closer. Raymond pulled a big pistol from his pocket and motioned to Willie to unlock the passenger side door. When he opened it, the interior light came on and Raymond hoisted himself up in one fluid move, ready for action.

"All clear. They're both gone. Let's do it."

With no further hesitation, the team moved in on the company's rig as if they owned it.

Willie climbed in and adjusted the driver's seat forward. The game warden who'd been driving had much longer legs than his. He started the diesel and made the necessary entries in his log. By the time he'd checked the instruments for fuel and DEF, air and oil pressure, Zak had squeegeed the dirt off the OSL logos on both doors. Jason slapped on the magnetic signs displaying a different company logo, and Raymond and Kyle replaced the front licence plate. The rear tractor and trailer plates could wait. They were covered in salt and snow. Highways department enforcement officers never expected to be able to read those during a snowstorm anyhow. Three minutes after the OSL men arrived at the truck, Willie and Kyle rolled out in the rig now identified as Riesling Transport, Kitchener, Ontario.

Riesling was a small outfit that OSL had bought from the widow of the original owner several years earlier. After they'd parked the Kenworth that came with the business — nearly identical but needing major work — Derek Cheney had kept its registration up to date. It gave him two convenient identities for his one operational truck for occasions such as this. Not one bit legal, but easy enough for officials to overlook unless an officer took the time to verify vehicle identification numbers during an inspection — a step frequently ignored at busy weigh scales.

Raymond and Jason took off ahead of the newly named rig in the black Silverado. Raymond was not taking any chances this time. He had decided to run interference ahead of the transport all the way to BC, somewhat reminiscent of the 1970s movie, *Smokey and the Bandit*, but without the high-speed antics. He didn't want the guys to get snagged in any more roadblock situations.

Willie headed the rig east. With the highway closed between Sault Ste. Marie and Wawa, they'd have to take the long way around. But with three drivers, including whoever happened to be the passenger in the Silverado, aside from food and fuel stops they'd be able to drive non-stop all the way to the coast without any of them logging over their legal duty hours.

Zak was headed back home to Scarborough — it was his job to return the rented F-150 to Avis as soon as he switched back to the original Tennessee licence plates. Timely return of the rental would suggest that the three men out on bail had complied with the requirement to return home until they were called back for court.

—

145

In the Husky restaurant

Webb and McNabb came out of the men's washroom and were about to pick a table when Webb's phone sounded. It was a summons to get out to the parking lot. The bad guys were on the move.

"Aw, shit," McNabb sighed. "Four hours on the road and not even a break for coffee."

Webb led the way out of the restaurant. In the parking lot, they approached Detective Ian Selkirk and a woman they'd not seen before.

"Guys, this is my boss, Detective Sergeant Sally Aldridge. Sal, meet Rick and Rob." The sergeant was a mid-sized woman in her mid-forties, chestnut hair, greying and cut short. Despite being a woman in a traditionally male-dominated organization, every officer she supervised, male or female, all swore allegiance to the woman. She was one of those inspiring leaders everyone hopes to be able to work with at some point during their career.

"Sorry about the short notice boys. Rob, you're coming with me. I followed the procession down from Wawa … had the least stressful driving conditions, so you get the first few hours to sleep. Since Rick's been on vacation since leaving Regina, he can drive the first shift with Ian.

"We've got fresh rides and a supply of food and coffee in each vehicle." She saw McNabb's face light up with that news. "The OSL truck is now travelling as Riesling Transport. The transmitter Ian tagged it with can send as far as ten kilometres, but we'll try to keep one vehicle within a kilometre at all times."

"Excuse me, Sergeant," Rob interrupted. "But being in uniform isn't going to be very helpful if we end up at the same refuelling stop as the OSL crew. We're not exactly in plain clothes mode."

"We've got that covered, Rob … and it's just Sally, or Sal. Your head office folks gave us your uniform sizes, and the Soo team that picked up our replacement vehicles and groceries, also hit Value Village for a couple of changes of clothes appropriate to the role of weary long-distance travellers … meaning, practical, but nothing fancy. So, unless there's anything else…."

Webb asked, "We'll report the truck stolen? So they don't twig to the idea we just gave it to them?"

"The base team here will call it in," Selkirk said. "And truckers, being the brotherhood that they are, will get the word out even faster than the mainstream media. You can be assured that it will be treated like the real thing … although a lot of them might get a chuckle that it was snatched from law enforcement."

Sally pressed on a key fob to unlock the doors of a white Jeep Compass parked right there. Ian led Rick to a dark green Subaru Forester parked across the lot. Two minutes later, both cars were heading east to catch up with their prey.

Rob chose to sit in the reclining back seat so he could change clothes and then stretch out and get some shuteye. But first he went to work on a three-piece chicken dinner and a couple of sugary apple fritters. While he ate, Sally told him she worked out of the provincial headquarters and had been a detective for twelve of her twenty years in policing. She had been with the Major Case Section for the last three years, dividing her time between training new detectives and taking part in actual field operations.

She and Selkirk had flown up to the Soo last evening, right after the cash had been discovered in the tires. They'd grabbed four hours of sleep in a local hotel before driving north to wait for the truck to go by in White River.

"Then you've got to be running on empty by now, too," Rob said. "I can grab a quick nap to recharge and take over in

147

an hour or so if you can keep going that long."

"Don't worry, Rob. Us old folks don't need as much sleep as you young pups," she directed a smile at the rear-view mirror. "When you've been in the business as long as I have, you learn to pace yourself ... and drink lots of coffee."

"Uh, that can have its drawbacks too, Sal."

"Yeah, it can at that. By the way, one of the first detectives I trained, transferred up your way ... and then jumped ship. I hear she's a CO now."

"My partner, Lizzie Cheechoo ... you trained her?"

"Yeah. A real sharp cookie."

"She sure is. She was seconded to us when my first partner was murdered during a poaching investigation that went all to hell." He paused when the memory of it brought a lump to his throat. "Anyhow, she literally saved my ass that time."

"I hear you were one of the heroes that day too."

"So was my wife. The accolades were split three ways."

"She's the redheaded, fireball bush pilot?"

"Yeah, that's Sam alright. That's what the TV news anchors called her. Me, I wouldn't dare."

As they chatted, he changed into a red flannel plaid shirt and a pair of faded blue jeans he fished out of the Value Village bag. There was an acceptable winter coat too. It was a size larger than he would have needed as a civilian, but it would nicely camouflage the extra bulk of his Kevlar vest and the 9 mm Glock 17 pistol in his shoulder holster.

"Oh, I should mention, Sal, the OSL guys will probably want to stop for fuel before heading north again. We had more than enough to get to North Bay, but I'm guessing they'll refuel sooner than that ... whichever route they decide to take."

Before they had started out, he'd adjusted the front seat forward for maximum leg room in the back. Now he reclined the back seat and stretched out, wondering if he'd be able to sleep — and was gone within minutes.

—

Webb was at the wheel of the Forester, steering single-handed while eating a ham and cheese sandwich with his free hand. Constable Selkirk was filling him in on his family history with exaggerated gusto in a strong, put-on Scottish accent.

"Aye lad, me family be descended from the famous black sheep, Alexander Selkirk of Markinch, in the Kingdom of Fife, do ye ken? Me auld great, great, great, great granddad Alex is reputed to be the tearaway who ran off to sea after fighting wi' his brother on the Sabbath … a dreadful sin in the eyes of the elders of the auld kirk. Aye and when he returned tae the auld country years later, it is said that the author Daniel Defoe based his story, Robinson Crusoe, on the exploits of yon Alex.

"And that's all the Scottish accent I can manage without permanently straining my tongue and my larynx. Nor have I set foot in the land of my wild ancestors. Yet."

Webb had already learned that the detective was in his mid-thirties, divorced after a horrendous ten-day marriage, and now married only to his career. "Lots of girlfriends, though. All the fun with none of the commitments."

Chapter 26

1610 – Blind River, Ontario

Willie Eardley parked the transport between the A&W and the Esso gas bar at the east end of town. It wasn't a refuelling stop for the rig — they planned to refuel and change drivers farther along, but Willie desperately needed to make a pit stop and he was beyond being hungry. Famished was more like it. They hadn't eaten since grabbing breakfast before six that morning in White River. Raymond stopped at the Esso to refuel his pickup. Jason got out of the Silverado and walked back to join the others as they ordered their meals.

The revised driving team was much more professional now with Zak gone. Kyle Roach was a seasoned truck driver with well over a million kilometres behind him. Swapping out the excitable Zak for Roach was something Raymond had planned from the outset regardless of the idiot kid's relationship to the boss.

Even though the late afternoon temperature hovered around -10°C, they ate their takeout burgers outside, pacing up and down the parking lot at the same time. The non-stop drive to the west coast would take four tiring days. Exercise during food and fuel stops would be essential to keep them going.

"So, do you want to head north on Highway 144 at

Sudbury, Kyle?" Raymond asked as he rejoined the group. He accepted the combo dinner that Jason handed him.

"Nope. Even though it's a couple hundred klicks shorter, there's no point travelling on secondary highways with few services when the major truck route's available. So, unless weather or road wrecks change the situation, we'll take 11 all the way around to Nipigon.

"Besides, driving the rig through North Bay where the game wardens were taking it anyway, is sort of like poetic justice." They all chuckled at the thought. "And they're not likely to be looking for us heading towards their own destination." They'd already heard the reports of the stolen OSL truck. The truckers' grapevine had been busy ever since the word came out when they passed through Bruce Mines. But word of the stolen OSL rig had nothing to do with the guys driving a Riesling Transport. Of course, like everyone else, they'd keep an eye out for it. That was all part of being in the brotherhood.

"By the way, I figured out why the office lost track of these guys, Ray," Kyle continued. "The game wardens popped the GPS fuse. Guess they didn't want us looking over their shoulders. But she's working now."

Raymond thought about it for a moment. "Nope." He took another bite out of his Papa Burger and chewed thoughtfully, then without swallowing, spoke with his mouthful. "Pull the fuse again, soon as you get back in." He swallowed, then continued. "I don't know if the wardens can get hold of the code to log into the unit or not. Maybe from the manufacturer … maybe not. But let's not take any chances. Be best to stay under the radar for this run. If we need GPS coverage when we get out to the coast, we can use our smartphones."

"I'll pull it now." Kyle set his burger in its cardboard tray on the running board and climbed into the cab. He was back to eating in less than thirty seconds, by which time Conn had his phone to his ear. He was still pissed off at Derek Cheney, but knew that the guy should be kept in the loop.

"Yeah, Kyle was just telling me that it was the game wardens shut down the location feed. Pulled the fuse on the GPS."

"Shit. They must know you were watching them. You be careful. Keep your eye out for the bastards. They're probably watching you now."

"Wouldn't make sense then, for them to shut off the feed. They've probably got some computer geeks or the cops who could pick up our signal, Derek."

"Just keep your fuckin' eyes peeled anyhow."

"Will do, boss. Will do."

—

Across the road at the Blind River Tourist Information Centre

McNabb and Detective Sergeant Aldridge made a pit stop of their own. The sergeant did a few stretches before adjusting the front passenger seat so she could get in. Rob got behind the wheel, refreshed and ready to go. He'd slept solidly for most of the hour and three quarters since they'd left the Soo.

They watched the OSL outlaws come out of the A&W. Rob was ready to start the Jeep but sat back and waited when it became obvious that they were "dining out" and not leaving just yet.

Webb and Selkirk in the Subaru were twenty kilometres ahead of them by now. Sally called Ian on her cell. "You guys should find a snowbank to write your initials in. It might be a long time before your next pee break. Subjects have stopped for a bite and are pacing the lot while they eat. They are still keeping company with the black Silverado. No sign of the Ford, though."

"We'll wait for them in Spragge, Sal. There's a carpool parking lot across from the weigh scale. Those boys will more likely have their eyes glued on the government facility than on us when they go by ... we'll be as good as invisible."

"Okay, we'll pull out just ahead of them when they get ready to leave here, and you can drop in behind after they go by." Tailing someone from ahead is a technique often used by surveillance teams, although there are usually more than two cars in a tailing team. The lead vehicle can even start down alternate routes on speculation, returning quickly enough to drop in behind the parade if the subject vehicle doesn't go that way.

"Roger ten-four, boss."

While they sat watching, Rob made a quick phone call to Sam and found her back home in Moosonee. Moose surveys were out of the question due to cloud cover across the northeastern corner of Ontario, and with conditions predicted to remain the same for the next forty-eight hours, it was pointless to wait in Hearst.

As a result, she got home in time to hear little Lottie's first word, "Da." Sam's disappointment at not being the first one named soon dissolved when the toddler began pointing and calling everyone in the room "Da," including the cat. Katie Burke suggested it might be the toddler's attempt at asking, "what's that?" which led everyone to take turns naming each person or item that Lottie pointed to.

Chapter 27

Detective Sergeant Sally Aldridge woke up as McNabb took the left turn from Highway 17 onto 11 and headed up the big hill.

"Gonna need to stop at the top for gas," Rob told her. Both police rentals were following behind the transport now — Webb and Selkirk were just ahead of the Jeep. They had refuelled the Subaru recently and were good to keep going.

When he got to the top of the hill, Rob pulled in at the first gas station — just in time to see all the lights go out. But it wasn't closing time — it was supposed to be a twenty-four-hour operation. However, when they looked around, the lights were out on every building they could see. Streetlights too. The power had obviously failed, but over how wide an area? It could prove to be a problem for them.

"Got enough to get to Temagami, Rob?"

"Nope. It says we've only got sixty-four kilometres left. The computers aren't necessarily accurate, but I sure wouldn't risk trying for a hundred."

"Okay, go back toward town. I'll let Ian and Rick know."

McNabb pulled out onto the highway and started back down the hill. In front of him, the whole city of North Bay lay cloaked in darkness. But there was a faint glimmer of light back to the west.

"Looks as if Nipissing First Nation still has the lights on, Sal. We'll try there." He had to backtrack nine kilometres to the Eagles Nest Gas Bar. Extra care was needed at each of the four major intersections, which by now were snarled with bewildered motorists, helpless without the guidance of the traffic lights. But somehow, he got through without incident. The power was still on at the Eagles Nest and the gas bar was open.

Twenty-five minutes after their first run up the hill, they were northbound again. The sergeant was behind the wheel once more. "Amazing, I got two hours of undisturbed sleep while you were driving," she said. "There aren't many drivers I trust enough that I can sleep while they drive. You're a smooth wheelman, McNabb."

"I think it was more likely just a case of sleep depravation on your part, combined with my boring company. And, no offense, but at the hundred and thirty klicks you are doing now, this is a bit too exciting for me to try for my next round of shuteye. You *do* know that there are some seventy-kilometre curves on this stretch of highway, right?"

"No sweat, Rob. This car's got four-wheel drive."

"Yeah, I know. I also know that if you go off-roading in the deep snow with a two-wheel drive vehicle, you'll only need a tow truck to pull you out. But if it happens with a four-by-four, you'll need a bulldozer or a log skidder or a crane. And it's not the snowy bushes that worry me so much as the rock cuts."

At just that moment, the little Jeep drifted into the oncoming lane on a curve to the right that would have been challenging at one hundred km/h. The amber caution sign, two hundred metres back, had suggested seventy, just as McNabb had forewarned. Fortunately, there were no oncoming vehicles.

A few long seconds after she brought the vehicle back under control, Sally said, "I don't find your company one bit

155

boring, Rob. But maybe we'll try one-twenty for a while." She continued pushing northward and blew through the fifty-kilometre speed zone in Temagami without noticeably slowing down.

—

In the Silverado approaching Latchford, Ontario

Raymond Conn's phone warbled. It was Willie calling from the Kenworth.

"Yeah?"

"Hey Ray, Kyle says he has the feeling we are being followed. They're keeping a long way back, but they always seem to be the same distance behind. Been there since North Bay."

"Okay, we'll check it out," he said and pulled into the gas station just north of the bridge. A minute later, the Kenworth rolled by and less than another minute passed before a green Subaru wagon went by. The driver must have had some ice built up on his windshield wiper blade because he was running the washers and had his arm out the window, grabbing at the blade each time it swept close to the outer edge of the windshield. There was nothing to suggest the occupants were cops.

—

"Smooth move, Rick," Selkirk grinned at his driver's quick reaction.

"Hey, I saw the black pickup as soon as the gas station came into view. Could have been anyone. But as we got closer, the guy standing beside it was looking at us … not gassing up. The place is closed. Instead of staring at you trying to read his plate I thought maybe I could catch his attention by pretending to clear an iced-up wiper blade … something probably everyone has to do once in a while, driving in the winter."

"I only got part of his plate number, but it matches," Ian said, just as the Silverado ripped past them on the way to catch up with the company transport. "Okay, he just gave me the rest of the number. It is Mr. Conn's truck. I doubt he would have ripped past us like that if he thought we were cops. So, we're in the clear for now, Rick."

—

2230 – New Liskeard, Ontario

Halfway down the long hill on the final approach to town, Sally caught up with Rick and Ian in the green Subaru. She stepped down on the brake pedal, slowing the Jeep to match their speed.

"Let them know it's us, Rob."

McNabb speed dialled Rick's number and put his phone on speaker. Ian answered. Rick was still driving.

"We've just touched down behind you guys."

"She give you a good flight?"

"Did you say 'fright'? … The seatbelt sign stayed lit the whole time and there was some major turbulence just after North Bay, but she put it into an awesome sideslip manoeuvre to save the day and my heart rate is almost back to normal, so yeah, I think we survived."

"Hey, that's why you drew the short straw and I'm in this car. You should ride with her sometime when she's in a hurry. The guys at HQ call her Mustang Sally … probably something to do with her personal choice of wheels, too."

"Enough of that, Constable Selkirk," Sally cut in, grinning. "Show some respect for your superior officer."

"Sure, boss. I'll try to remember that. Anyhow, the OSL boys have been keeping a steady pace. The guys in the Silverado dropped back in Latchford to check us out, but quickly lost interest. There's been no excitement other than that. Whoever took over the wheel of that rig in Nairn Centre is a flawless driver.

"Speaking of which, Rick has been at it since we left the Soo, so we're going to switch here in New Liskeard. Are you two okay giving us a time out? We both need to make a pit stop."

"We'll be fine Ian, as long as your boss knows how to poke along at a hundred and four klicks."

"Just make sure she doesn't dose off. High speed is like caffeine to her. And by the way, in case you haven't heard, the forecast says we'll be running into some snow between here and Cochrane. Same weather system we came through earlier, south of Wawa. But they say it won't get as bad as what we got back there."

"No, it shouldn't, and I'm not driving this leg. Not yet anyhow. Do you have any valium with you?"

"For you or for Sal?"

"I haven't decided yet. Anyhow, we'll talk later." Rob disconnected the call.

He and the detective watched the OSL truck turn right into the Husky truck stop, and Webb and Selkirk went left into the restaurant across the road. Sally continued three and a half kilometres up the highway and pulled in at the government weigh scale there. It was closed, and she parked the Jeep out of sight behind the office to wait for their quarry to continue north.

It was only four minutes before the white Kenworth rolled by, right behind the black Silverado. The OSL team had simply switched drivers. Bathroom breaks were unnecessary for guys who peed into empty windshield washer fluid containers while they drove.

Sally let them get out of sight before taking up the chase.

Chapter 28

Webb and Selkirk entered the restaurant to pick up a takeout coffee and to use the washroom but there was a lineup for that. A long one. Bunch of guys dancing around with their legs crossed because it was a one-hole bathroom and someone in there was taking their time.

"I'm going to use their snowbank out back," Webb said and turned to leave.

"Go ahead, but I need more than a snowbank."

Selkirk returned to the car twenty minutes later and climbed into the driver's seat. "They *really* need more than one crapper in there. Been another minute longer and I'd have needed a change of underwear. Guts are still rumbling, but we've got to push on."

He put the car in drive and headed back out onto the highway. The snow had started to fall and was beginning to accumulate on the pavement, but with its winter tires, the four-wheel drive Subaru stuck to the road as advertised. He picked up the pace to a hundred and fifteen, knowing that it would take a while to catch up with the other chase car and their quarry.

Webb was tired and hungry after his long stretch at the wheel. He wolfed down a couple of egg salad sandwiches followed by a lukewarm coffee chaser, then reclined his seat and soon drifted off to sleep. He slept soundly for almost an hour and a half, but on a long straight stretch of highway just past

Ramore, he was awakened by Ian's sudden exclamation.

"Shit, shit, shit ... this is going to hurt!" An oncoming pickup truck — going way too fast — had lost traction on the snow-covered road surface and was coming toward them, spinning into their lane completely out of control. Ian kept his foot pushed down on the brake pedal and the antilock braking system was chattering hard, doing its job. But the approaching truck kept on coming — still out of control. He was forced to choose the only escape route available to avoid a head-on crash. He aimed for the snowbank on his own side of the road. The Subaru hit the snowplowed ridge at almost forty kilometres per hour and was temporarily lost in an explosive cloud of the newly fallen white stuff thrown up by the impact.

When the air cleared, the green wagon was completely covered by a layer of snow. And inside, except for the pale glow of the instrument cluster, the world had gone dark.

Webb was the first to move. He tried opening his door, but it was wedged hard against the frozen snowbank. "Can you open your door, partner?"

Selkirk still had his foot pressed hard on the brake pedal, but the engine had quit, and the car was stopped. "Oh ... the door ... yeah ... good idea." He shook his head to clear it.

The detective hooked his fingers on the latch handle but had to put his shoulder to the door to get it to budge. A shower of snow fell from the roof, down the back of his neck as he forced the door open wider. "Shit, that's cold."

After a couple more shoves he managed to open his door enough to climb out. He looked around. There was no sign of the pickup he had dodged. No sign of it having left the road either. Just some dramatic skid marks in the snow where it had passed. "Assholes just buggered off," he swore under his breath. "Probably drinking, or uninsured or suspended ... or all three."

He stepped down onto the travelled portion of the highway and surveyed the scene. The car was sitting high on the snowbank and leaning over somewhat toward the passenger side. There was no traffic in sight — no one to offer assistance. The tail lights showed as a faint glow through the snow that covered the back of the wagon, so he climbed the snowbank and gave the back end a quick brush off with his bare hands to clear the lights.

"Hit the four-way flashers on your way out, Rick, and bring my phone. We're going to need a ride. This buggy isn't going anywhere without a winch."

Webb crawled over the console and exited the car through the driver's door, dragging his parka forward from the back seat as he did. He handed Selkirk his phone and then got to work forcing the back door open on the driver's side. One of the coolers had upset and fallen open during the sudden stop. Ian's parka was buried under an avalanche of sandwiches, snacks and water bottles.

"Hey, Sally … we ran into a bit of a problem here," he gave her a quick summary of the incident. "We were probably only about ten minutes behind you when it happened. I've been pushing to catch up."

"Don't sweat it, Ian. Murphy's Law guarantees shit like that happening. We'll come back and pick you up. Have all your worldly possessions out on the roadside ready for a quick transfer. We'll be there in ten minutes."

"And the car?"

"Don't lock it. Leave the keys in the console. We'll call to get it towed. Don't worry, those OSL guys aren't going anywhere fast. We'll be on their asses again before we hit Cochrane and we'll pick up a couple of fresh rides there as we'd originally planned."

"Thanks boss."

—

2355 – Hwy 11 just south of Matheson, Ontario

McNabb grabbed onto the passenger assist handle above his door as Detective Sergeant Aldridge did a sliding U-turn and headed back to rescue the others. She set new land speed records for a Jeep Compass over snow-covered roads. At least the highway there was relatively free of curves, and even the few they came to were well engineered gentle bends. But Ian had been mistaken in his calculations. It took fifteen minutes, not ten, to get back to pick up the marooned officers. And in those few extra minutes, the snow began to fall much harder.

Two minutes was all it took to load the snowbound stragglers, and they were northbound again. The Compass wasn't as responsive now with four hundred additional pounds of law enforcement bodies and baggage on board, so it took her an extra ten seconds or more to return to white knuckle speed. And at that speed, even Mustang Sally began to find road conditions a little hairy, so she dropped back to one hundred and twenty km/h. And then she slowed even further to one-ten. At that speed, McNabb almost felt safe, but as the snowfall got heavier, he wasn't so sure. Before long, conscious of deteriorating road conditions, Sally dropped back to just under eighty km/h.

Backtracking to pick up Selkirk and Webb had put them more than half an hour behind the OSL truck. But with the long distances yet to be covered to the west coast, it shouldn't be an insurmountable setback. However, even a minor problem now had the potential for putting the tailing officers farther behind than ever. And of course, the tracking device on the transport was now hopelessly out of range.

Chapter 29

Jason Mead was pushing the pedals in the Kenworth. Kyle Roach was riding shotgun beside him. Raymond and Willie were about a kilometre ahead of them in the Silverado and had just passed the first of two exits leading to the former pulp and paper mill town. Out of the snowy gloom ahead, flashing red, blue and white emergency vehicle lights came into view.

Raymond phoned the guys in the Kenworth as he pulled to a stop at the scene.

"Take a right onto Highway 67, Jay. It's the south entrance into town. There's a tank-truck on its side, right across the road up here."

Kyle Roach took the call. *"Got it boss. Just in time too … we're right there."*

"When you get into town, go left on Victoria and left again on Anson. My GPS shows it coming back out to the highway past the wreckage. We'll backtrack and catch up."

Because of the short notice, Jason took the corner fast and wide, forcing a pickup to take to the snowbank just as it was entering the intersection. The driver leaned on his horn and gave Jason an emphatic, one fingered salute as the Kenworth rushed by him with only inches to spare.

"There's one pissed off citizen," he said.

Kyle just shrugged his shoulders. "Shit happens. But don't dawdle through town. If there are any spare cops around … we don't need that." After a few minutes, he pointed ahead. "There's Victoria Street now."

Mead took the left and accelerated to the fifty km/h speed limit. He didn't see the series of severe potholes in the road ahead because they were covered by the fresh snowfall. The Kenworth hit them hard.

"Going to need new fillings in my teeth after that, Jay."

"They need a bump sign there."

Beneath the tractor and the trailer, massive cakes of accumulated frozen slush and snow jarred loose and fell to the road. Imbedded in one departing sixty-pound ice cake was the magnetic tracking beacon that Detective Selkirk had slapped on in Wawa.

—

0030 — Hwy 11 just north of Matheson, Ontario

The Jeep Compass and its four officers arrived at the junction with Highway 101 only to discover that Highway 11 to the north, was barricaded. A police constable emerged from his cruiser and waved them down with his flashlight as he sauntered toward the approaching Jeep. Aldridge had her window down even before she got the car stopped. She was digging in her purse for her badge — McNabb whipped his out of a shirt pocket and passed it to her.

"Police. We need to get through. We're following a transport that's the subject of a major drug investigation."

"I'm sorry ma'am … uh, conservation officer …?"

"His badge," she pointed at McNabb, seated beside her.

"I'm DS Aldridge, Major Case Section out of GHQ. We need to get going ... *right now!*"

"I'm sorry Sergeant, the road is not just closed, it's impassible. There's been a major wreck at Iroquois Falls and the plows have been taken off the road till morning because of the heavy snowfall. But 655 is still open, north from Timmins, if that's any help."

"Shit," she gave a frustrated sigh. Digging through her purse once again, she came up with a business card which she handed to the constable. "Okay, thanks. Not your fault. Would you please pass the word on up the road that we need any reported sightings of a white tractor-trailer combo, last identified as Riesling Transport, Kitchener, Ontario. Don't approach, interfere or follow. We just need to keep track of it until we're back on their tail."

"Sure, Sergeant. Right away," he said and strode back to his cruiser with more purpose than he'd left it a minute earlier.

Sally ran her window back up and hit the gas. The Compass spun its tires as it turned left onto Highway 101, headed westbound for Timmins. Normally it would be a forty-five-minute drive, but if road conditions remained the same as this all the way, they would be over an hour getting there.

"Ian, get on the phone and arrange for new rides in Timmins ... if they can do it before we get there. If not, we'll need them in Kapuskasing."

—

0110 – Cochrane, Ontario

It was snowing hard when the Kenworth rolled into Cochrane. Despite the terrible driving conditions, a faithful Ministry of

Transportation inspector was on duty at the weigh scale. And the amber lights were flashing: "All Commercial Vehicles Report for Inspection."

"Oh, shit," Jason groaned. "Tonight? … in this?" But he pulled off the highway and eased the rig onto the scales. Instead of getting the green light to leave, the red light came on. "Oh, fuck."

The inspector zipped up his parka as he exited the scale house and headed for the cab. Jason ran down the window and pulled his driver's licence from his wallet then reached for the phoney truck documents from above the sun visor.

"Good evening driver, where are you headed?"

"West coast."

"Your logbook up to date?" the man asked as he reached up and took a quick look at the offered documents.

"Yes, sir." Jason reached for the book and started to pass it out the open window.

"Naw, keep it in there. It'll just get snowed on and soggy out here." He gave the offered documents another quick scan, then handed them back up to Mead. "Okay, you are good to go. But take care, now. Highway's not in very good shape tonight." And he walked back toward his office.

"Thank fucking god."

"You did good, boy," Kyle told him as he watched a cop, sitting, parked in his cruiser near the highway entrance. Jason replaced the documents and noted the stop in his logbook before moving off the scale.

Chapter 30

Sally Aldridge wheeled into the Independent Grocery Store at the junction of Highways 101 and 655. Selkirk leaned forward in the back seat and pointed to a quiet corner of the parking lot. "They're over there but let me off by the main entrance. Gotta make another pit stop."

Aldridge dropped him at the door then headed over and parked between their two replacement vehicles. One was a brand new, dark blue Ram pickup and the other, a silver Nissan Pathfinder. Both were four-wheel-drive vehicles. Both, common makes and colours. As with their earlier rides, they were generic vehicles — the sort driven by anyone in the region — intended to not draw attention.

Vehicle keys were exchanged, and road conditions updated. One of the delivery drivers provided a fresh supply of coffee for each vehicle. Five minutes later, they were on the road again, northbound up 655, hoping to somehow find and reconnect with the OSL truck when they got back to Highway 11.

McNabb and Aldridge took the Ram — Rob's choice — and he was behind the wheel again. Rick Webb took the wheel of the SUV while Ian Selkirk reclined in the passenger seat beside him. Said he was feeling a bit "off." Grabbing cat naps was his preferred way to stay fresh on stakeouts and long tailing jobs, so he figured some shuteye was all he needed.

Twenty minutes after pulling out of Timmins, Webb was searching for an FM radio station as he drove. The road was straight and level. Kilometre after boring kilometre. The tail lights of the Ram were like a fixed beacon about two hundred metres ahead of him. The effect was almost hypnotic. Any radio station would do. Even country music.

"Stop the car! *Stop the fucking car!*" Selkirk shouted as he sat up and grabbed for the door handle even though they were still moving at a good clip. Webb got the Pathfinder pulled to the side of the road and stopped just as his passenger bailed out and lost his supper on the snowbank. The detective stayed there, retching for several minutes before he could speak.

Up ahead, the Ram's tail lights initially drew away, but didn't completely disappear. McNabb had seen the Nissan fall behind and figured that waiting would cost less time than having to backtrack if the guys had had a breakdown.

"Aw, shit, Rick, don't eat the tuna sandwiches. My guts feel like shit. Gotta be fuckin' food poisoning." He stayed hunched over, his face pale and sweaty. He waited to see if his stomach had settled or would erupt again.

While his disabled partner paused a moment longer, Webb phoned Sally. Explained the situation. "I think I should run him back to the hospital in Timmins." They were stopped about halfway between Timmins and Highway 11.

Detective Aldridge offered an alternative. *"There's also a hospital in Smooth Rock Falls, Rick, if Ian is willing to wait a little longer. It's a smaller facility, but I hear they've got a good ER there."*

"Stand by, I'll ask him." Webb looked at the detective who was a picture of abject agony. "Sally's suggesting the option of Smooth Rock Falls, Ian, but it's almost twice as far. I'll take you back to Timmins if you'd prefer."

His patient eased himself back into the passenger seat, groaned and uttered a couple more expletives before answering. "Let's keep going, Rick. It's going to be tough enough for you guys to keep a tail on that rig without losing another hour or more by the time you drive me back and try to catch up again … just hurry."

"We're continuing north, Sal. But let's see if we can cut down on travel time. He's in agony here."

"*Step on it, Rob,*" Webb heard over the phone. "*Don't spare the horses until we get to the Smooth Rock hospital.*" And out ahead, the Ram became lost in a vortex of swirling snow. Webb stomped down on the gas to catch up.

—

0210 – In the blue Ram

"Well, shit," Aldridge said after disconnecting from the second call in as many minutes. If it's not one thing, it's two others." She took in a deep breath, held it a few seconds, then blew it out. That call had come from the police communications centre. "The officer in charge says that the transport went through Cochrane at ten past one and was seen again in Smooth Rock Falls fifteen minutes ago. That was the good news … or at least it's better than no news." But the tailing team was still about sixty kilometres from Smooth Rock Falls and the rig would be as much as another twenty to twenty-five kilometres west of there by now.

"And then the dispatch sergeant had the nerve to give me the bad news. Instead of the heavy snow we've been fighting, a band of freezing rain swept through to the west of Smooth

Rock. Highway 11 is closed for the night from Smooth Rock Falls to Kapuskasing. But the transport went by five minutes before they closed the road.

"He said they'll let us through, but if we go off the road, we'll be on our own. They aren't allowing any service trucks out until the highway contractors have sanded, salted and scraped the road bare again. Said it's already looking like an auto graveyard out there.

"And now, with Ian down, I've got to see if we can pick up another driver along the way. There's no way we can safely continue a two-car tail, with just three drivers … not for more than a few hours, anyhow. But I'm not dropping down to one chase car unless there's no other option. That would just double the risk of losing the truck for longer periods, if not completely. Guaranteed we'll tangle with Murphy's Law sometime before we're done."

"I think he's already onto us," Rob pointed out. "Had a few dealings with old Murphy myself. Busy guy during the winter here in the north."

—

0225 – Moonbeam, Ontario, 41 kilometres west of Smooth Rock Falls

Jason Mead was still driving the Kenworth. The road had been snow-covered most of the way from New Liskeard to Smooth Rock Falls, but between Strickland and Fauquier it had transitioned to glare ice in a matter of two or three kilometres. As long as he made no sudden manoeuvres, the weight of the rig provided reasonable traction. And luckily, there were no hills and few curves on this part of the highway. Still, forty kilometres per hour was as fast as he felt comfortable driving. It was obvious from the number of vehicles parked in the ditches that other drivers hadn't thought of slowing down. They saw two of them resting on their roofs.

His biggest struggle at the moment was trying to keep the Kenworth's windshield clear of ice. The freezing rain had almost stopped, but there was still a fine drizzle, and on the glazed road surface there was enough moisture that the front tires threw up even more spray. With the temperature already well below freezing, it all froze instantly on contact with the glass.

Frequent applications of windshield washer antifreeze helped a little, and Kyle Roach had turned the cabin heat up to the maximum setting in defrost mode. They were holding their own, but only just barely, and they were now peering through small semicircular clear patches of windshield just above the defrost vents. As they entered the reduced speed zone in the town of Moonbeam, the windshield washer fluid ran dry.

"*Shit!* Out of juice. We've gotta stop. Call Raymond, Ky," Jason said as he pulled over in front of a darkened furniture store. "Ask him if he's got any spare washer fluid."

When Kyle got off the phone, he climbed down and helped Jason force the bent moose bars forward. They had the tractor's hood open by the time Raymond and Willie returned in the Silverado.

"I've got half a jug here guys. We're only about twenty minutes from Kapuskasing … well, it would only be twenty minutes if the road was bare. We'll buy enough there to finish the trip."

While Jason poured the windshield washer fluid into the reservoir, Kyle mentioned something that had been bugging him since they had left Smooth Rock Falls. "Ray, there was a cop watching us as we pulled out of the weigh scale in Cochrane. I wouldn't have thought any more about it, but there was another one who did sort of a double take when we came through Smooth Rock. D'you think we've been made?"

"Hmm … shouldn't have been. Other than the fact they'll all be watchin' for a white Kenny, we haven't given them any reason to suspect us with our new logo. The Riesling sign's still on your door?" Kyle nodded and Raymond thought about it for a minute, frowning. "Maybe let's change our identity while we're here anyhow." He returned to his pickup and pulled an envelope and another pair of magnetic signs from the back seat.

"Just got one more name change left after this. If we need to change again, we'll be all out of aces.

"Here Willie, make yourself useful … switch these out. Jason, here's your new CVOR package." He waited while Mead capped the fluid reservoir and dropped the empty plastic jug on the road. Then he handed him a manila envelope containing a new set of falsified commercial vehicle operator documents. Raymond was a whiz at photo-shopping realistic false documents on his office computer.

"Now you're driving for St. Lawrence Express out of Cornwall. The truck is leased from a numbered company … I forget the exact number … ah …something Ontario Limited in Kingston. Got no new plates for you, so if you are asked about it, you can tell them that the leasing company just bought the truck a couple days ago, and the new registration is caught somewhere in the COVID web. There's a copy of the fake bill of sale and an authentic looking insurance slip in there to match.

"You guys are keeping your logbooks up to date, right?" The drivers all nodded. While Raymond talked, Kyle climbed up on the driver's side front tire and scraped off a large patch of ice. With the truck idling and the heat still full on, it came off in big sheets. It wouldn't stay that way for long, but it would be good for a few kilometres.

"Okay," Raymond was saying, "so it'll be a pain in the ass, but you'll each need to start a new log now, under St. Lawrence Express. Start your entries from North Bay ... same time entries as your Riesling log. Whoever's got his done first, can switch off with Jason when we stop in Kap." They always carried spare logbooks with them. This wasn't the first time they'd switched identities on the run.

"We can't afford any more fuckups, guys. We'll be out of rope for sure if they stop us for anything at all." He looked at each of his drivers. They looked good to go. "Okay, we're done here. Let's roll. Coffee, fuel and washer fluid in Kap. Drive careful."

Chapter 31

Considering the poor road conditions, Rob McNabb had made good time coming up the northern half of Highway 655. The road was familiar to him, and the truck was a newer version of his own personal vehicle. And it was running on winter tires. Rick Webb had struggled to keep up in the SUV. It was equipped with all-season tires which weren't nearly as effective in true winter conditions. But he arrived white-knuckled at the junction, just a couple of minutes after the Ram.

Highway 11 had been plowed, and both vehicles cruised easily on the packed snow surface. The continuing sounds of agony coming from Detective Selkirk inspired Webb to pull out and pass the Ram when he caught up with it. He put his foot down and found that the Pathfinder had no problem cruising at one-twenty-five on the hard-packed snow.

Other than two sweeping curves, the highway was straight and level the rest of the way. It took him only thirteen minutes to get from the junction to the hospital in Smooth Rock Falls where he parked in front of the emergency department entrance and grabbed a wheelchair from inside. He was pushing Selkirk in through the door when McNabb and Aldridge pulled up in the Ram.

"You guys go on," he said when Sally came barging in.

"You'll never catch up to them if you stick around waiting for him to be seen." And to a nurse who had just come to the desk: "He's a provincial police detective. Likely got food poisoning. Been bothering him a bit all evening. Got a lot worse when he lost his supper about forty minutes ago."

"Thanks Rick, but he's my detective," Sally said, then held out her hand. "Give me your keys and climb in with Rob. See if you can make up for some lost time … but keep it between the snowbanks. I'll wait here until they wheel him into an exam room, then I'll do my best to catch up. Flash your badges and use my name when you come to the roadblock. They'll let you through."

"Get well soon, buddy," Webb gave Selkirk a reassuring pat on the shoulder, then turned and left the building. Selkirk paid no attention, making a dash for an open waste basket he saw across the room.

———

"Just when you think things are running smoothly, think again," Webb repeated Rob's first rule of trucking as he climbed into the passenger seat in the Ram. "Sally says 'Go.' And she's the boss. Or did you want me to drive for a bit?"

"No, I'm good to go. Only been driving since Timmins."

"Just as well. If we go off the road, it's you who'll get to fill out the 'rainbow form,'" he ribbed his junior partner. The ministry had been using a multi-coloured, self-carboned accident report form ever since the beginning of time and the document had kept the nickname through the generations. Press Hard – You Are Making Five Copies was printed in bold across the top.

As soon as they pulled onto the highway, they could see

the flashing lights of a lone police cruiser parked on the near side of the bridge. Rob ran down his window as they approached.

"Road's closed fellas."

"We know," Rob said as he flashed his badge. "Detective Sergeant Aldridge is our official secret password. She'll be along after she gets one of our team members settled at the hospital."

"Accident?"

"Medical emergency."

"Sorry to hear it. Okay, the road's covered with snow hardpack from here to Strickland, but after that, you'll be running on glare ice until you get past Kap. Watch for pedestrians wandering around out there too. There's a whole bunch of vehicles parked in the ditches, and some of those folks are bound to be looking for a pull back onto the road. Just ignore them. Maybe one day they'll learn to slow down on glare ice."

"Gotcha, thanks."

McNabb's window went up, and after he manoeuvred around the barricade, he said to Rick, "We can go like stink for the first few kilometres. I just hope the OSL guys drove across the ice as slowly as we'll have to, or we may not catch them again until Longlac. We must be at least a good hour behind them by now."

"And our rig could be one of the ice victims too."

"Huh, that would be a real pain in the ass for both the good guys and the bad."

"Yeah, it would that. I'll keep an eye open for them as we go."

Over the first eighteen kilometres Rob was comfortable doing a hundred and ten km/h, still running on smooth-packed snow. But after rolling through Strickland, the road became every bit as treacherous as they'd been warned. Fortunately, someone ahead of them had been equipped with tire chains. The early twentieth century invention had chewed up the icy surface just enough to improve traction for the Ram pickup. It wasn't great, but Rob crept his speed back up to fifty km/h before deciding that any faster would be pushing his luck.

Twenty-five minutes later, Rick's phone rang. "Hello."

"We're on our way, guys. What's the road like?"

"Icy with a capital I," Rick said. "But right now, we're following someone who chewed up the glaze with tire chains. If you stay in their tracks, you should be able to make half-decent time. How's Ian?"

"Surviving and feeling half-alive, he says. They got him in quick. The ER Doc agreed with his diagnosis. But the beds are all full of COVID clients tonight, so they gave him a shot of something to settle the nausea and gave him back to me. He's going to have to sleep it off though. Won't be legal to drive until it wears off later this morning."

"Good to know we didn't lose him."

"How are you guys holding up?"

"Well, Rob's got his second wind and if I can get my head down for an hour or two, I can switch with either one of you. Between the three of us, we should be okay as far as Thunder Bay, but another coffee stop around Hearst would be helpful."

"Okay, Rick. You get some shuteye while you can. You may end up having to drive for both of us in a few hours. Talk to you later … I've just come to the ice." She disconnected before he could reply.

———

0305 – Kapuskasing, Ontario

The OSL gang *had* been an hour ahead of the pursuit team when they brought the St. Lawrence Express into the Flying J Truck stop, but the situation changed soon after they finished topping

177

up the fuel and washer fluid. Willie Eardley got behind the wheel to take his shift. Kyle Roach was at the back of the trailer checking tires and cleaning snow off the tail lights while Willie started the diesel and began an entry in his log. The senior driver walked forward to the cab and reached up to open the driver's door.

"How's your air pressure, Willie?"

Willie paused his entry, looked at the dash and shook his head. "Only seventy PSI. It's taking forever to come up, Ky. Nowhere near the green yet."

"We've got a bad line at the back. Probably damaged when a chunk of frozen slush broke free. Park it over there, away from the pumps and I'll see if the guys in here can drum up a mobile mechanic."

"Yeah right. Fat chance at this time of night."

Roach headed for the convenience store to speak to the gas bar cashier. He paused at the Silverado to let Raymond know about the problem. Willie set the diesel on high idle and watched the air pressure begin to creep toward eighty pounds per square inch — the minimum needed to operate the airbrakes.

Inside at the counter, the cashier was talking to a local insomniac who visited every night for a coffee or two — or three — during the wee hours. Roach's request to find a mechanic was nothing unusual to the men on either side of the counter. Big rigs seemed more prone to breakdowns in the dark than during daylight hours. Especially in the winter.

"Ah oui, my friend Cloutier, 'e is garagiste. I will call 'im now. 'E is not busy this winter ... most the log trucks, they har parked ... the Coveed, you know? 'E will be glad for getting some work."

"Thanks. It's the white Kenworth parked over by the billboard."

Chapter 32

As Rob drove through town, Rick kept a lookout for the OSL truck — sporting a Riesling Transport logo. The tracking receiver was turned on — had been plugged into each of the vehicles they'd used ever since leaving Wawa. But Ian's tracking bug was not in this town, and the only white Kenworth they saw was a St. Lawrence Express unit parked at the Flying J truck stop. A mobile mechanic's utility truck was pulling away from the trailer as they went by.

"Want to pull in for a coffee, Rob?"

"Naw … I'd just have to take another bladder break in half an hour. How about you?"

"No, I'm good. I can wait until Timmy's in Hearst."

The highway conditions in town were an improvement over what they'd experienced since Strickland. Municipal crews had made fast work of the section of the highway through town, and when they got to the western outskirts, they followed a sander for a couple of blocks. But it wasn't doing any sanding or salting. The icy surface was already decaying, the result of a heavy dose of road salt laid down earlier. Rob pulled out and passed the saltshaker and was soon rolling along at a comfortable ninety km/h.

—

Fifteen minutes after McNabb and Webb passed the Flying J truck stop, Willie Eardley drove the OSL rig back onto the highway to follow Raymond's Chevy pickup west once more. The mobile mechanic had wasted no time fixing their problem and a company card had paid the bill.

They'd heard of the highway closure behind them, but they had paid no attention to the westbound Nissan Pathfinder that went by just before they pulled away from the truck stop. It was just local traffic.

—

In the Ram pickup approaching Mattice, Ontario

By the time McNabb drove through Opasatika, the outside temperature had fallen toward -20°C. After that, the road was bare and dry. There had been neither snow nor freezing rain through the area. He'd set the pickup's cruise control at a hundred and ten.

While the others had gone into the hospital in Smooth Rock Falls, he had synchronized his phone with the Ram's Bluetooth system. DS Aldridge's next call came at 0455.

"*Rick?*"

"He's sleeping right now, Sal … I'm hands free with the volume down. What's up?"

"*Where are you?*"

"Coming to Mattice in a couple."

"*I'm almost caught up then. But no one has seen our rig go by since the last sighting in Smooth Rock.*"

"Crap. Passing through several of these small towns I've

seen black and whites lying in wait, so it's not for lack of observers. I wonder if our bad guys have changed their identity again?"

"That's entirely possible. But we can't have uniforms stop all the white transports on the road. Whatever clever solution we come up with, we can't let those clowns know we are following them. All we can do for now is keep pushing on. It may be easier to spot them in the daylight later this morning. You said the front bumper is a little crooked?"

"Yeah, but hard to see if they go rolling by at a hundred klicks. Not a reliable identifier. Almost impossible at night. I do have a better idea, though. Can you get us an aircraft?"

"I already asked … got zip. What did you have in mind?"

"Damn. Sam marked the trailer roof with blaze orange paint when we were in Terrace Bay. And in the morning, she said it was easy to spot from two thousand feet overhead."

Webb was awake now, and sat up, joining the conversation as he raised his seatback.

"Rick, here, Sally. Let me call our folks downtown. They promised to help with logistics if we needed a hand. Judging from what I've just heard, this would qualify."

"Go for it. Call me back with the results."

Webb hit the speed dial to call the secret squirrels' office on his own phone as Aldridge disconnected from Rob. A one-minute conversation with the night shift ended with: *"We'll get right back to you."*

—

0515 – Hearst, Ontario

Fifteen long minutes passed before the return call came from head office. McNabb had just parked in front of the Tim

181

Horton's in Hearst when Webb's phone rang. It was Nora Johnson calling from the Major Case Unit. She was the staff superintendent in charge of the secret squirrels.

Before the conversation even got started, Sally Aldridge pulled the SUV in next to the Ram, and at Webb's beckoning, she hopped into the back seat of the pickup.

"Go ahead, Nora. We've got DS Aldridge here with us. She's our boss for the moment."

"Okay Rick. I had to shake a few grumpy folks out of bed, and I think I may have promised my first born to one of them, but things are coming together better than I thought they would. We've got a Turbo Beaver lined up to meet you in Thunder Bay when you arrive there this morning.

"Going by your location when you called, I'm estimating you should arrive there between ten and ten-thirty this morning … does that sound reasonable?"

"Barring the unforeseen, I'd say that's about right. Where are they coming from?"

"Moosonee. It was the only bird available on short notice. We are arranging to get her refuelled the moment she lands, and once she's topped up, she is at your disposal for as long as you need her."

"That's great Nora. Sure do appreciate it, thanks."

"You need anything else, just call," she said and disconnected.

"Poor Sam," Rob said to the others, shaking his head. "She hates to be wakened in the middle of the night."

"Is that going to be a problem, Rob?" Aldridge asked.

"Oh, no. It's just the early wakeups that piss her off. No, once she gets airborne, she'll want to escort us for the entire length of the Trans-Canada to B.C."

"Well let's go grab a quick coffee," Sally said. "We've got a plane to meet."

They each ordered bagels and large coffees and took turns in the one available washroom. The women's room had a plugged toilet. Ian Selkirk woke up and came in long enough to use the washroom but had absolutely no interest in food.

They returned to their vehicles fifteen minutes after they had arrived. Rick drove for Sally — Rob was alone in the Ram, still enjoying his second wind and loving the new truck. They headed west once again.

If they had left two minutes later, they would have seen a black Chevy Silverado leading the St. Lawrence Express past the restaurant.

Chapter 33

It was still dark. Sunrise was more than an hour away. McNabb was in the lead, listening to tunes from his MP3 player routed through the pickup's multi-speaker sound system. Sugarloaf was singing *Green Eyed Lady,* a favourite of his. It conjured up warm thoughts of Sam.

He was floating along the highway at one hundred and fifteen km/h when he was caught by surprise. In the middle of the dark road sat a dark car blocking his lane. It was slightly askew and showing no lights. He braked hard — both feet on the pedal, or at least that was his instinctive reaction. Coming to a stop right behind the vehicle, he put on his four-way flashers. The disabled car was a compact SUV.

"Someone's having an off night." But it was worse than an off night. Something bad had happened here, and as soon as he got out of the truck, the situation became clear. Using the flashlight app on his cell phone, he saw that a cow moose lay dead, sprawled across the hood and windshield of the vehicle.

The accident must have happened in the last few minutes. Steam was rising from under the hood and a growing puddle of engine coolant and moose blood was spreading across the pavement under the front of the vehicle. He could hear the ticking and pinging of hot engine parts cooling down. There was no sign of the occupants outside of the crippled car.

Webb and Aldridge came to a stop behind the Ram and joined him as he tried to force open the driver's side door. It was jammed of course.

"Hello," Aldridge called through the narrow opening that used to be the driver's side window. "Can you hear me?" There was no response. "This doesn't look good, guys."

Reaching in through the gap, the sergeant folded back a loose flap of the now deflated side curtain airbag. She directed her cellphone flashlight inside to reveal a shoulder and the back of a head. Judging from length of hair and the victim's choice of clothing, it was probably a woman. She snaked her hand in to feel the victim's neck.

"Got a pulse, here," she said as she checked her cell phone. But there was no signal.

"Rob, there's no cell service here. Have you got….?"

"Yeah, it's in my bag. I'll call it in." McNabb returned to the truck for his government satellite phone, dug it out of his overnight bag and was pulling on his parka just as Webb managed to force the lift gate open at the back of the wrecked vehicle. He climbed in and was wriggling forward over the back seats when Rob connected with a 911 operator.

Sally Aldridge hurried back to the Nissan to retrieve her regular flashlight and parka, and she pulled a reflective, roadside emergency vest from her bag. She looked inside to ask Ian Selkirk if he could lend a hand, but he wasn't in the SUV. He was still under the weather — busy heaving his empty stomach over by the snowbank.

As she hurried back toward the wreck, Aldridge saw a vehicle approaching from the west. She flagged it down and spoke to the driver, who pulled over into their lane and parked behind the Ram and the Pathfinder.

Harry Headliss was a trapper from Longlac. He was on his way out to spend the day checking his trapline. The inside of his truck cab was an untidy jumble of gear. The pickup's bed was covered by an old beat-up camper shell and was just as untidy as inside the cab.

When Aldridge asked about some tools and equipment, he said, "Sure do, Ma'am." He had a collection of most of the things one needs to forge a living in the bush. The old fellow, short, lean, and sporting a long, unkempt beard, looked as tough as an outlaw biker. He stepped out of his pickup and followed Sally to the victim's car.

Webb managed to wedge his head through the gap between the two front seats and found himself face to face with a young woman. Her mouth was moving, but at first, no words came out. Then after a moment, she gasped, and straining from the effort to catch her breath, she managed to croak, "Help … please help me. I can't move. What happened?"

"You've hit a moose." He couldn't see any way of freeing the woman. The roof was crushed down almost to her head, and she was squeezed between her seat and the steering wheel. The dashboard was pressed down against her thighs and knees. In her present situation there was no way to reach her to assess for injuries or perform first aid, and at that moment she was still disoriented.

"I'm Rick Webb. I'm a conservation officer. What's your name?"

"Mel … Melanie Ramsay … I'm a nurse in Cochrane." She began to breath more freely.

"Are you travelling alone, Melanie?" he asked.

"Just me and my baby," she answered, beginning to sound tearful.

Chapter 34

A baby! Alarmed by that, Rick Webb pulled himself out of the narrow space to look around the back seat and into the infant carrier he had just squeezed past moments earlier. It was empty.

"*Oh God, no!*" said to himself. A dark shadow from his past crowded into Webb's mind. This can't be, he thought. His Melanie, in that car crash, the day she learned she was pregnant. He was at work — hadn't been with her when she died. Despite the passage of time, it was still a raw memory. Now it was as if a scab had been ripped off. Sickened by the thought, he determined that he would stay by this young woman's side until help came. He would not leave her to face this ordeal on her own. But he dreaded having to ask his next question.

"Is the baby in the front seat with you?"

"I'm still pregnant with her. I'm going back home to Thunder Bay to be induced tomorrow."

The sense of relief that her answer brought was tempered by his concern for possible injuries — hers and the unborn baby's — injuries that couldn't be assessed with her pinned in the way she was.

"Are you in any pain? If so, where does it hurt?" He knew it was a pretty lame attempt at a first aid assessment, but there was little else he could do. While she answered, he reached forward and took her wrist to check her pulse. Sally hadn't elaborated other than indicating that there was life there. Heart rate was rapid, but strong. That was reassuring.

"I'm badly squeezed in here. There's lots of pressure, but no, there's no pain."

Rob finished his report to the 911 folks and cut in on their conversation, talking through the broken side windows. "Help is on the way, but it has been a busy night. The paramedics will be a while getting here." He didn't tell them that the "while" would be well over an hour.

"Move aside there, sonny," a gruff voice interrupted McNabb. Old Harry Headliss took one look at the situation and sized up the job in just seconds before returning to his truck. Less than a minute later he called to the others. "Well, give a hand here. Can't do this all m'self."

Sally went back and picked up a large plastic tarp he'd dropped on the pavement and Rob was handed half a dozen eight-foot, two-by-fours as well as a pail containing a hammer and nails. The old man followed them back to the wreck with a camp stove and a twenty-pound propane cylinder.

"Don't smell no gasoline, so we'll tent the tarp over the car and run the stove to help keep the girl from freezin'. This ain't no time to be sittin' in a car with the windas all out." The temperature was hovering around -25°C.

"Grab the jackall out o' the back of my truck, young fella," he ordered Rob. "Oh, and there's a coil of heavy rope on the floor in the back seat. You'll need that too. Then move your truck around front and get that carcass dragged off. Block the wheels, first."

Before McNabb got back to the wrecked car with the things he'd been sent for, the trapper had nailed together a crude tripod over the driver's side of the car. He and Sergeant Aldridge draped the tarp over the frame and across the rest of the car while Rob tied the rope to the moose and repositioned the Ram pickup. The camp stove was burning full bore in the tented area near the driver's door by the time Rob returned from the trapper's truck with a couple blocks of firewood to jam under the damaged vehicle's front wheels. It wouldn't do to have the wreck rolling forward when he tried to pull the moose clear. Less than ten minutes had passed since he and his companions first arrived on the scene.

The trapper had just begun the slow process of cutting the forward window post with a hacksaw when more help showed up. A building contractor and his helper, on their way from Geraldton to Hearst, sized up the situation and went into immediate action.

"Jesse, get the Sawzall and a new hacksaw blade." And when Jesse returned with a cordless version of the popular handyman's tool, the contractor said to the trapper, "Good idea, but this'll work a lot faster." And to Jesse again, "Bring our jackall for the other side." In little more than a couple of minutes he had the first "A" pillar cut through and was moving around to the passenger side.

Meanwhile, between moments of the noise of tortured steel caused by the reciprocating saw, Webb questioned Melanie, trying to assess her injuries. She had collected herself by now and gave him a quick summary of her condition.

"Other than some minor cuts and scratches, I don't think I'm injured … not seriously, anyhow. I've got feeling in my feet and can wiggle my toes. I'm just squeezed in so I can't move."

Dreading having to open the subject, Webb asked if there was any activity from her unborn child.

"She's started squirming. She does that all the time at night. I'm pretty sure she's okay, too." She paused to take in a new phase of the rescue activity.

The trapper set his jack in the driver's side window

opening just inches from the back of her head. He rested the base on the edge of the opening and snugged the lifting head up against the collapsed roof. "Close your eyes, miss, in case the plastic trim pieces shatter."

In a moment, the contractor set his jack in the corresponding position on the passenger door. They began to apply cautious strokes with the handles of their jacks. The door panels began to buckle, but the roof remained rigid.

McNabb asked, "Would it be any help to run the saw across the roof where you want it to hinge? Or just cut it right off."

"Yeah, let's try that … take it right off," the contractor agreed. "Be a few more minutes of racket, miss. Sorry."

A highway maintenance crew arrived and began to direct traffic. Despite the early hour, there were now more than a dozen vehicles on either side of the wreckage waiting to use the one open lane, or at least, half of the available lane and the road shoulder. Part of that lane was taken up by the work of the rescue volunteers.

—

At just that moment, Conn's black Silverado and the OSL crew in the St. Lawrence Express pulled to a stop behind the growing line of traffic held up at the scene. A car, two pickups and five transports were stopped between them and the crash scene.

"Shit, if it's not one thing, it's another," Willie Eardley grumbled. "How long do we gotta sit here I wonder Ky? We'll be a week late getting to the coast at this rate."

"Cheney can't bitch about this holdup, Willie."

"Betcha he will. We wouldn't be here if we … and I mean Zak … hadn't fucked up in Saskatchewan in the first place."

"Guess you're right about that."

A flagman from the highway maintenance crew cleared the eastbound traffic, then waved the westbound lineup to come through.

"There you go, Willie. We're moving again."

—

With little to contribute to the rescue efforts, and on the off chance that they'd gotten ahead of the OSL truck, Sergeant Aldridge took advantage of the lull and ducked out of the shelter to observe the westbound transport trucks idling past the wreck site. She missed seeing the black Silverado ease past less than a minute earlier. More than a third of the commercial rigs going past were all white.

She paid most of her attention to door mounted logos. But if the bad guys had changed their identity again, a new company name would be meaningless. She also watched for bent front bumpers. But like the colour white, a surprising number of the transports that passed, sported bumpers with at least some version of a crooked smile. Winter driving in Canada, she suspected. When the St. Lawrence Express lumbered by, it just blended in with the rest, and the glare of headlights from the following traffic gave her no chance to look for faces in the cab.

"Rob," she called out when she saw the CO also temporarily unoccupied. "There's lots of help here now. You take the truck and go meet the plane. We'll catch up when we can."

"On it, Sarge." McNabb untied the rope from the moose and the pickup and was about to climb in and drive away when the sound of screeching tires and the sickening thump of automotive metal against metal drew everyone's attention.

It was immediately followed by a second impact and a screaming engine, revving out of control just before it died. He climbed into the Ram and drove forward fifty metres to the scene of the action.

A two-ton utility truck had slammed into the back of a pickup, driving it and the car ahead of it into the back end of a dump truck. The pickup and the car, unable to move the gravel hauler, squirted out to the left, completely blocking the westbound lane. The road was effectively closed.

"Aw, shit." McNabb got out to assess the situation. There was nothing he could do that other people hadn't already begun. Unimpressed by their changing fortunes, he got back in his truck and backed up to the moose collision to report to Aldridge — who was equally unimpressed.

"Road's blocked both ways. There's two people injured but half a dozen Samaritans claiming first aid training are hovering over them, so I didn't stick around to add to the confusion. Two of the drivers are engaged in a heated argument about each others' family ancestry. But since we're undercover, I left them to discuss their genealogical research on their own."

Meanwhile, the highway maintenance crew got word that the ambulance was going to be further delayed by at least another hour. But Melanie insisted that she didn't need an ambulance ride back to Hearst — just regular transportation — a ride forward to Thunder Bay.

"Honest, I'm not significantly injured. I'm just pinned in here," she repeated as she watched the roof being lifted from above her head.

"Can you reach the seat adjustment control?" Webb asked.

"Yes, but it's a power seat and nothing is happening. I

already tried."

Another new bystander announced himself as an apprentice mechanic. "Power seats are always live. They work without the key being on. If it isn't working, you just have to jump power to it from another source.

"If you're sure about that, boy, then make it happen," Harry Headliss ordered. "If we can move the seat back enough, then maybe we won't have to take the whole damned car apart to get her out."

The hood was jammed shut, so the building contractor cut a hole where the budding mechanic indicated — right above the battery. The kid discovered that one of the battery cables had come disconnected during the crash. Should be a simple fix. Pushing hard, he held the connector against the battery post. "Try it now."

Melanie squeezed her hand between the seat and the jammed door and pushed the buttons to lower the seat and run it back. "It's working … I think maybe I can get out now."

Webb crawled back out of the car and climbed under the tarp onto the remaining section of the roof. Someone handed him a blanket to drape over the jagged steel edge left by the Sawzall. "Okay, gently now, and at your own pace, Melanie. I'll provide some lift, but I don't want you to hurt yourself."

Melanie wiggled, Rick lifted and Harry, as gentle as a father with a newborn, reached in and helped her get clear of the wreckage.

"Thank you … Rick and Harry … all of you."

"Oh, it was nothin' Miss," Harry said. "It's just what we do for each other, here in the north country." He turned away for a moment, embarrassed by a tear running down his cheek before he continued. "But when you're tellin' the story to your girl one day, you can tell her she was pulled from a wreck by the

Headliss trapper from Longlac." Melanie smiled and gave the old trapper a one-armed hug as she climbed up to join Rick Webb, sitting on top of the disabled car.

A police cruiser arrived as they talked, its emergency lights blazing. It pulled in close to the wreck, in the space left by the Ram.

—

DS Aldridge flashed her badge and spoke to the police constable as he stepped out of the black and white pickup. She handed him her business card and said, "I don't like to pull rank, constable, but my team and I need to be on the road, westbound, half an hour ago. We've got this wreck resolved … all but the paperwork and the cleanup.

"Mr. Headliss over there is going to claim the moose. The victim, here, is uninjured other than some minor cuts and abrasions, and is coming with us. I can write it up as we travel and email you her document copies.

"And unfortunately, while all this was going on, a subsequent multi-vehicle rear-ender over there has the road blocked both ways. Several injuries involved and a heated debate over blame."

"Understood Sergeant. To start with, let's take a look and see if we can set up a slalom course for you to get through the mess."

Chapter 35

The dump truck that had been rear-ended was still mobile, so they hooked a chain from it to the utility truck that had caused the crash and dragged it ahead far enough to create a gap in the wreckage. The Ram and the Pathfinder snaked between the damaged vehicles and onto the open road.

Rob McNabb was back up to speed, rolling along with the cruise control set at one-twenty km/h trying to make up for lost time. Because of the risk of meeting but not seeing a moose until it was too late, he kept his foot hovering above, but not touching the brake pedal. It wasn't a comfortable pose to hold for prolonged periods, but he knew he could shave valuable fractions of a second from his reaction time that way.

Rick Webb and Melanie Ramsay, the moose crash victim, were in the Ram pickup with him, both quiet, but awake. Detectives Sally Aldridge and Ian Selkirk were right behind in the Pathfinder — the sergeant driving and the constable sleeping again. Longlac was still almost an hour away.

McNabb called home on the satellite phone and talked to Sam while she finished breakfast. Business first — the day ahead — preliminary plans for the air search. The next topic left him feeling uncomfortable — as it had during previous family discussions.

"Mae Ling still insists on changing her name. But Katie finally got her to open up about it. Turns out that a couple of the 'cool' girls at school have been posting racial comments about her online."

"Nasty little witches. Attitudes picked up from their parents, maybe? Or just a lack of parental supervision. Or peer pressure." Rob paused, thinking, and when Sam remained quiet, he carried on. "But changing her name because of that ... gee, I don't know, Sam. It still doesn't sit right with me. Obviously, the decision is hers in the end, but she has such a pretty name. She shouldn't have to hide her heritage because of race baiting by a pair of snooty, trouble-making teens. She'd just be running away from the problem ... but never *getting* away from it."

While he and Sam felt the same way, they were concerned that trying to dissuade Mae Ling could result in her digging in her heels. Teenagers tended to be like that. They had been teens themselves, only a decade earlier. They could relate.

"I mean it's not as if she can't make friends. Madeline and Geneviève are as close to her as they could be without being sisters. And they're not changing their names to hide their French background."

"That's not the same, Rob."

"Yeah, well ... maybe you're right. But it's still not fair."

"Anyhow, I've asked the principal to see if she can discuss the inappropriate posts with the girls and their parents. And Katie keeps encouraging her to phone her friends instead of using Instagram." Rob could hear dishes being stacked in the dishwasher as Sam brought the topic to a close.

"I should get ready to go. I've got the plane to prep. I was going to leave earlier, but I'll have a fifteen-knot tailwind all the way."

"Okay, sweetie, see you in Thunder Bay. Give my love to the girls. And by the way, the weather here is light overcast with a high ceiling ... I can see a faint outline of the moon. It's minus twenty-eight and dead calm right now.

"Don't worry about checking the highway when you are inbound unless it's close to your route. We'll work out how far the truck could have gone if they haven't made any stops. Then if Sally agrees, we'll get you to start the search past their greatest possible distance and work back from there. And while you are doing your air search, we'll be on the road, going on the assumption that they are still somewhere ahead of us."

"Thanks, Robbie. See you later."

—

0910 – At the OSL office in Scarborough, Ontario

Zak Graham walked into Derek Cheney's office and without so much as a "Hi, how are you doing," he plopped himself in the chair across from his uncle. "I need someone to pick me up at the car rental drop-off."

"You're late. Gimme the keys. We'll take care of it." Cheney took an envelope from under his desk blotter and tossed it to his nephew.

"What's this?"

"Your final pay. You're done here."

The young punk opened the envelope and stared at the cheque. "Pay looks kinda short, and where's my bonus?"

"After all the shit you've caused me this month, you expect a *bonus*?"

"Yeah, my trip bonus."

"Trip bonus is for successfully completed runs, not for stupid fucking stunts that get you thrown in jail and my rig fucking seized by the law, you shit for brains idiot! And I'm sure not paying for your time in jail. That comes under 'leave without pay.' No wonder your old man disowned you and threw you out. And your Uncle Jim warned me not to take you on. But no, I had to take the high road. I thought I could make an honest man out of you. But he was right and I was *really* wrong. Fuck. You are nothing but trouble, Zak. Expensive fucking trouble.

"Now, get out of my sight before I throw you through the fucking front door and then open it to see if I need to do it again."

Zak Graham stomped through the office, slammed the counter gate closed and slammed the front door even harder. "Fuckin' asshole. I'll get even with the cocksucker. He'll be real sorry he ever did that to *me*." He marched down the street to wait for a city bus.

—

1027 – Dorion, Ontario

The OSL crew was making good progress. They were on a two-lane stretch of the Trans-Canada Highway — a choke point — where all road traffic from east to west depends on a single highway to keep the nation's goods moving when they arrived at the site of a transport rollover. The police had the traffic stopped in both directions.

The black Silverado and the white Kenworth came to a stop in a line of traffic that stretched seven or eight hundred metres back from the action. Looking down the long straight stretch, Willie and Jason could see a mobile crane and a heavy haul tow truck manoeuvring into position. This was going to take a while.

Willie left the diesel idling but got out and pulled on his parka to stretch and walk around for a bit. Jason got out too. He walked ahead to the Silverado to chew the fat with Raymond and Kyle who were listening to the chatter on the CB radio.

Word amongst truckers close to the action was that they would be stopped for at least an hour. But just when everyone had left their vehicles to stretch or relieve themselves, the crane moved aside, and the traffic began to move, one lane at a time. Eastbound came through toward them first, but soon they were rolling again.

—

1050 – The good guys at the Dorion rollover site

The drive to Thunder Bay was going smoothly. Or at least, had been, until they arrived at the scene of a tractor trailer rollover on the two-lane stretch of Highway 17. Two police vehicles, a heavy lift tow truck and a mobile crane were already there, and the road was completely blocked. The team was stopped behind a line of traffic four hundred metres back from the action.

Ian Selkirk was feeling well enough to walk the distance up to the wreckage. He spoke to a sergeant in charge of the scene. No, there was no way they could let anyone through until the crane had the transport tipped back onto its wheels. It was a tricky operation that couldn't be rushed but he would send a cruiser to escort the team's unmarked vehicles to the front of the line. Best he could do. Ian stuck around long enough to get a look at the wreckage. It wasn't the OSL unit. This one was a white cab, but it was pulling a multi-coloured trailer. One of the big grocery chains.

The crane hoist went better than expected and the team got escorted past the wreckage forty minutes after they had stopped. Better than they had feared, but they were likely still far behind the OSL gang — and would be over an hour late for their rendezvous with Sam.

Chapter 36

The team parked their vehicles in the short-term lot. When they entered the terminal building, Webb and Aldridge branched off with Melanie Ramsay in search of a car rental agency. McNabb and Selkirk found Sam on the airport service apron checking over the Turbo Beaver. Rob and Sam hugged as if they'd been apart for weeks.

It was always the same with them. And in his current state of exhaustion, he would have loved to just hang on and go to sleep standing there with Sam holding him up. But she let go first and introduced herself to Detective Selkirk. Ian was feeling a whole lot better now.

"So, where do you think your missing bad guys have gotten to, Robbie?" Sam was in a hurry to get going. "How far could they go since they were last seen?"

"We did the math while we were held up back at the truck rollover," he yawned. "And based on how far they could have gone since the last sighting in Smooth Rock Falls ... barring any delays, they've got to be closing in on Upsala."

"That'd be half an hour from here in the yellow bird," Sam replied without having to refer to a map.

"Okay, and the half hour it takes you to fly from here to Upsala would put them halfway to Ignace."

"And in the half hour that *I'll* need to get from Upsala to Ignace, they should be arriving there at about the same time as I do." Sam completed the calculation.

"That was what we figured. Of course, that's if they barreled straight through without a single delay. I'm guessing they won't be nearly that far along yet."

"So, you want me to start a few more klicks past Ignace and work backward?"

"That's the plan."

"Okay, Flyboy, I'm on my way."

Sam hugged her man again, then swung up into the pilot's seat and went through her pre-start check list. She was on the radio to Thunder Bay tower by the time the turbine came up to speed. She got clearance to take off as soon as a regional passenger flight from Winnipeg landed.

McNabb and Selkirk re-entered the terminal building and caught up with the others at the car rental counter. Melanie's husband was a heavy equipment operator at an iron mine on Baffin Island. He was arriving on the Winnipeg flight for three weeks of home time and she was arranging replacement transportation.

"So, to get down to business," Sergeant Aldridge said. "What's happening, Rob?"

"Sam will be airborne in just minutes. She's heading west to cut the guys off at the pass. Or at least, see if she can find them. So, I'd suggest that we grab something to eat and then hit the road."

"Sound thinking. Let's do it."

Chapter 37

Detective Sergeant Aldridge was in the lead, driving the Pathfinder with Conservation Officer Webb sound asleep, stretched out in the passenger seat. Detective Constable Selkirk was sticking right behind, driving the Ram pickup, and once they were out of town and back on the open road, he had no problem matching Sally's hundred and thirty km/h average speed.

McNabb was not sound asleep, although he sure could have used the shuteye. The highway, for the first thirty-five kilometres past Kakabeka Falls, was a hilly stretch, with a few curves that were not designed to be taken at such speeds. McNabb had visions of a repeat of Aldridge's fancy sideslip action north of North Bay. This stretch of the Trans-Canada didn't become straight and boring until just past Raith.

"Ian, you're driving like the damned sergeant."

"She's the one who taught me to drive, Rob. My old man was a klutz with a wheelbarrow and mom could barely manoeuvre a bundle buggy. Didn't Sal tell you? ... she's my aunt."

"Must have slipped her mind."

"Admittedly, we don't bring that up at work too often, so I guess you're forgiven for not knowing."

"No, no, it's entirely my fault. I should have recognized

the family resemblance from your wheelsmanship."

Selkirk chuckled. "Taken as a compliment. So, after Sal turned me loose, I refined my skills doing five years on traffic enforcement, running down hopped-up Hondas, Beemers and other Hot Wheels idiots on the freeways around Toronto. Now I just wish Mustang Sally would speed up so we can get eyes on our missing truck again."

McNabb decided with a driving resumé like Selkirk's, it would be reasonably safe to catch a few winks on a quiet stretch of the Trans-Canada in northern Ontario — even travelling at close to Mach 1. He drifted off within the next couple of kilometres.

—

1145 – near Raith, Ontario

It seemed to McNabb that he had just fallen asleep when Sam phoned, but forty minutes had already passed. It was just over an hour since the Turbo Beaver had taken off from Thunder Bay. Selkirk answered the call. Rob was awake but remained reclined in the passenger seat.

"I flew as far as the Atikokan turnoff guys, and I've started back your way. Saw nothing the couple of times I crossed the highway on my way west. I'll let you know as soon as I spot them."

The road to Atikokan left the Trans-Canada Highway fifteen kilometers past Ignace.

"Thanks, Sam," Rob answered from his resting pose, then asked, "Where are we now, Ian?"

"We're between Raith and Upsala," he said, answering McNabb's question for them both. "Thanks for the update, Sam. Happy hunting." He disconnected the call and Rob returned to sleep soon after.

The next time McNabb woke up, only fifteen minutes had passed. Sam was on the phone again.

"*Hey, I found them. They're about halfway between Upsala and Ignace. I'll go high and dawdle along behind them until you guys catch up.*"

"Good job, Sam. Stay on them," McNabb said, then disconnected the call.

Ian flashed his headlights to catch the sergeant's attention, and at the same time flicked on the turn signal to pull into a snowplow turnaround they were approaching.

Both vehicles wheeled into the spot and parked side by side, window to window.

"Found them, did she?" Sally asked.

Selkirk said, "They're about a hundred klicks ahead of us."

"Good show, but we need to know how long she can stay on them. With our luck, God knows what other delays we might run into."

McNabb played his fingers across the Ram's touch-screen display. "Call Sam," he told the digital lady inside the dashboard. While the truck and his phone worked together to connect the call, Rick and Sally left the Nissan and stood by the driver's side window.

"*Hey, Robbie, what's up?*"

"It's Sally Aldridge, here with the others, Sam. How are you for fuel? … What I mean is, how long can you escort the transport?"

"*Got lots yet. I'm good for the rest of the way to the Manitoba border easily if I can refuel in Kenora afterward, but poking along at their pace, I'm going to have to alternate circling clockwise with counter clockwise soon. I'm starting to get dizzy up here. Where are you now?*"

"We've pulled off for a quick conflab at the beginning of

205

the central time zone … less than twenty minutes from Upsala. We'll get back on the road in a minute and we'll keep you posted on our progress so we can set up to take the hand-off."

"Roger that. Talk to you later."

—

1110 Central time

The Ram and the Pathfinder pulled back onto the highway with Mustang Sally still in the lead. She put the pedal down hard and Detective Selkirk had to scramble to keep up. Then he called the police communications centre to let them know there was an unmarked high-speed convoy headed west on 17. They didn't want any delays from being pulled over by an eager constable in a black and white. Now that McNabb was used to the high-speed ride, he dropped off to sleep once more.

In the Pathfinder, Rick Webb did some quick calculations based on Aldridge's 130 km/h cruise speed and the OSL transport's maximum speed. "We're looking at arriving in Dryden about half an hour behind them, Sal. But … just a sec … gotta make sure I've done this right. Yeah, we should be almost caught up when they hit the Manitoba line."

—

1245 – over Dryden, Ontario

Sam Williams circled the Turbo Beaver three thousand feet above the town and watched the bright orange dot on top of the OSL transport pull into a truck stop. A look through her binoculars verified the corporate identity of the facility before she phoned the guys in the Ram.

"Hey Robbie, they've arrived in Dryden. You may have caught a break. The rig just pulled into the Petro Pass Truck Stop and there's a bit of a lineup at the pumps."

"That's great, Sam. We're about half an hour out ... still following Sally at warp speed. We're going to need gas there too, but that shouldn't take us as long as it does for them."

—

1314 — Over Dryden

Sam reported that the OSL gang had refuelled and parked away from the pumps. She had tried to watch the black pickup as it left the truck stop. Lost it briefly, but she was pretty sure she saw it pulling into the McDonald's south of the highway.

The high-speed tailing convoy rolled into town. Aldridge managed to get her speed down to the legal fifty km/h limit as she coasted past the Walmart. Selkirk, at the wheel of the Ram, flexed his shoulders to ease the tense muscles that three hours of tailing his high-speed boss had caused. Both chase vehicles headed to separate gas stations near the west end of town. The Pathfinder — running on fumes — pulled in at the first one and the Ram with a quarter tank left, took the next. They filled their tanks and drained their bladders and an unmarked police cruiser delivered coffee while they waited for the OSL rig to move again. Sam kept it in view as she continued to circle high above town.

—

DAVID G. FERGUSON

1130 Pacific standard time (1330 central) — The Strait of Juan de Fuca

The Canada-United States border between Vancouver Island and the state of Washington runs down the centre of the Strait of Juan de Fuca. Internationally agreed upon shipping lanes dictate that inbound ships use the American side and outbound ships keep to the Canadian side.

Because of the questionable nature of so much of his cargo, Captain Chang kept *Ocean Princess* to the Canadian side of the border by almost a mile, inbound though she was. This was not a problem for the marine traffic control folks when shipping traffic was light, as it was right then. In fact, for Chang, keeping to Canadian waters was a prudent choice. He knew that the U.S. Coast Guard regularly patrolled the American side of the strait. In U.S. waters, vessels as distinctive as *Ocean Princess* were automatically targeted for detailed inspections.

The United States Coast Guard was an agency tasked not only with search and rescue duties, but it was also a law enforcement agency, well known for boarding ships and seizing illicit cargoes. The Canadian Coast Guard, on the other hand, was primarily a search and rescue agency, tasked also with emergency pollution abatement duties.

U.S. Coast Guard vessels were well armed and capable of enforcing compliance. Some Canadian Coast Guard vessels did carry members of the Royal Canadian Mounted Police, but any fire power was limited to police small arms.

At that moment, *Ocean Princess* was making barely four knots while the chief engineer fretted over a hot propeller shaft bearing. Jordan River, on Vancouver Island, lay six miles away on her port side. The chief told the captain that they could probably make it to Vancouver without stopping if they continued to creep along at that speed. Captain Chang was accustomed to such requests, given the vessel's general condition, and had no option but to comply. As a result, he began to edge the old ship even farther into Canadian waters. He needed to build an extra margin of safety in case the mechanical problem worsened. He was determined to stay clear of U.S. waters.

Fortunately, arrival on schedule was not a pressing concern for the captain. The questionable cargo would be offloaded and available for pickup whenever he arrived. The customer for one of his two most lucrative containers — the drugs and ivory — was also running behind schedule but had assured Chang, during a brief satellite phone call, that the transaction would proceed despite the delay.

After offloading the contraband and collecting his fees, he would relocate to a government approved docking facility in the heart of the city to unload the remainder and load the cargo for his return trip. That cargo, too, would be late arriving in Vancouver. A full load of containers carrying luxury autos and SUVs from eastern Canada, was held up behind a train derailment somewhere in northern Ontario. Unlike so many of his cargos, this vehicle shipment was completely legal. He didn't plan to leave without it.

Chapter 38

After gassing up the Pathfinder, Rick Webb parked it with a view of the highway and waited for the OSL truck to pass by. "Get ready for it," he told McNabb over the phone. He sat in the driver's seat with his binoculars ready to train on the passing traffic. "Sam says the black pickup and the Kenworth are right behind a red and white Manitoulin Transport. They are the only two westbound rigs in this part of town right now."

The two transports went by less than thirty metres from where the Pathfinder was parked. A Manitoulin truck, a dirty black Silverado and a dirty white Kenworth pulling a dirty white trailer.

Webb got a good look at the new name on the Kenworth's door. The new sign wasn't as dirty as the rest of the cab. Hadn't been exposed to the road salt for nearly as long.

Aldridge had her phone connected to the MNR pilot in the Turbo Beaver. "Thanks for everything, Sam. We're on it."

Webb said to the officers in the Ram, "We're on the tail of the St. Lawrence Express now guys." Then he chuckled. "Rob, you should have taken me up on the offer to stop for coffee in Kapuskasing."

"*Why's that?*"

"We drove right by those guys last night. That was the rig

parked at the Flying J truck stop."

"*Well, shit.*"

Webb pulled out and followed half a dozen car lengths behind the OSL rig and allowed himself to get separated when a traffic light turned red. The delay gave them a more comfortable gap — they wouldn't be right on the truck's tail. When several other vehicles pulled in front of him, it was better still. McNabb, who was driving the Ram once again, followed one red light cycle later.

—

1740 – Approaching the Ontario-Manitoba border

Ian Selkirk was asking McNabb about his big polar bear poaching bust as they rode along. They were about half a kilometre behind the Pathfinder. "So where were you when the guy started shooting at …." He was interrupted by a call from Sally.

"*Keep an eye open for a silver Chevy Impala. Them're the good guys. That will be our RCMP tail. They said they'd be joining us near the Falcon Lake Campground as we go through Whiteshell Provincial Park.*"

"Thanks for the word, Mustang Sergeant, ma'am," Selkirk answered. At the same instant, his own phone chimed to announce a weather alert. "Oh … *this* could be fun, guys." He read the automated text while Aldridge was still on the line.

"An Alberta Clipper is advancing across southeastern Saskatchewan and will be moving into southern Manitoba during the evening, bringing high winds and heavy blowing snow to affected areas. Road closures are possible."

"*Just when you think things are running smoothly, think again,*" came over the phone from Webb in the Pathfinder.

"Rick's been listening to too many old truckers' tales," Rob explained.

—

1905 – Hwy 1 approaching the last exit before Winnipeg

Kyle Roach was driving the Kenworth. Jason Mead rode with him. All they had seen of the black Silverado since sunset had been the distant glow of its tail lights ahead. But now its brake lights came on as it appeared to merge with a lot of other brake lights.

"Hmm. Traffic's backed up under the overpass," Kyle commented. To the high mileage trucker, it was nothing exciting — nothing unusual. For anyone who spent as much time on the road as he did, traffic holdups were not uncommon. "No flashing red and blue lights anyhow."

Whatever was holding up the traffic didn't appear to extend beyond the other side of the bridge. When he caught up, he eased the rig forward to stay behind Raymond's pickup. Traffic was stop and go — sometimes more stop than go.

As they got closer to the overpass, they could see someone in a reflective emergency vest directing some of the traffic toward the exit ramp. Kyle and Jason watched as the redirected vehicles crossed the bridge and re-entered the highway eastbound, heading back the way they'd come.

"Strange. Some being sent back … others continuing on."

"What're they doing?" Jason asked.

"Don't know. We'll find out when we get there." And he eased the transport one more car length ahead.

It soon became obvious that the passing lane was fully

blocked off. A concrete barrier had been placed across the outer lane and the boom truck that had delivered it was parked just beyond. All traffic was forced into one lane and being stopped by a group with flashlights and more emergency vests.

"Damn Indian roadblock again," Jason speculated. But before Kyle had a chance to offer an opinion, a commotion broke out at the barricade. People emerged from vehicles ahead of them and drifted toward the action.

"Sit tight, Jason. It looks like a clusterfuck, but it's none of our business unless they make it so."

The traffic sat, blocked. Nothing moved. Ray and Willie climbed out of the Silverado and walked back to the Kenworth. Kyle ran his window down and shut down the diesel so he could hear what Ray was saying.

"Just heard it on the radio. Bunch of citizens pissed off that COVID infested folks are comin' in from Ontario. They're turnin' back anyone who's been there or got Ontario plates. The cops are aware of it, but they're already tied up dealing with a major demonstration gone wrong, downtown. So, I've got an idea. Jason, smear the plates on my Chevy while Willie and I go and deal with this. Then pick us up when the traffic starts to move."

Mead reached under the sleeper bunk and pulled out a small tub of drywall joint compound. Like false licence plates and multiple logos, it was another tool of their trade. He opened the container after he stepped down from the truck. Using a plastic spatula that lay on top of the compound, he smeared enough of the product onto the back plate of the Silverado to obscure the letters and numbers. He repeated the process on the front plate, closed the container and climbed into the driver's seat of the pickup to wait. The stuff would freeze or dry and fall off soon enough, or they would knock it off at their next gas stop. But for now, the Silverado was travelling incognito.

Raymond and Willie began to walk toward the blockade. Raymond had the sawed-off shotgun in his parka pocket and Willie tucked one of the AR-15 rifles they bought in Regina inside his long coat. Kyle stayed in the Kenworth.

—

It didn't take Sergeant Aldridge long to see the potential for a dangerous development. She got on the phone to the folks in the Ram, and spoke to Webb, sitting beside her, as she instructed them.

"Webb and Selkirk, follow the two OSL guys who are walking toward the barricade. They are trying to hide it, but they appear to be armed. Follow them but blend in with the crowd. We don't want to show ourselves for who we are unless you are absolutely certain that lives are in danger. McNabb, the Mounties are stopped two cars behind you. Go get them and relay my message."

Ian Selkirk caught up with Rick Webb as he strolled toward the action amidst the other looky-loos. Selkirk had his pistol in his coat pocket. Webb left his in his shoulder holster. The outer layer of fabric of the coat they'd bought him was thin, and anyone looking would clearly see the outline of the pistol if he pocketed it. Besides, his winter firearms qualification required drawing from inside a closed parka. Webb was good at it, and he was already at step two — his coat was unzipped to his waist.

Selkirk sized up the situation as they walked. "The way they are trying to conceal them, it looks like a long gun on the right and a handgun in the other guy's pocket. Which do you want to cover?"

"From the body language, handgun looks like the guy in

charge. I'll cover him. It's the underlings who are usually the loose cannons. You're the copper … I'll let you have him."

—

By the time Conn and Eardley walked the ten car lengths to the blockade, all eyes were on the commotion. There was a whole bunch of yelling and shoving going on and a flurry of flying fists in the middle of it all, so no one — except the law — noticed Raymond Conn climb up onto the concrete barrier. He nodded to Willie who let out a sharp, almost ear-splitting whistle that did absolutely nothing to quell the uprising. The roar of a shotgun blast, however, resulted in quieting most of the mob, but the two men in the centre of the cluster were still engaged in a heated argument. It took another shot fired in the air to bring total silence.

—

McNabb led the Mounties forward as fast as they dared without looking too obvious. After he pointed out Webb and Selkirk to them, Corporal Sneed sidled up to Detective Selkirk who had a good line on Willie Eardley from the other side of the road.

Looking like two strangers passing judgment on the action in front of them, Sneed walked away, taking up another vantage point. Constable Dunphy similarly made contact with Webb, who deferred to the constable's jurisdiction and full police powers. "Glad you could make it. You've got the authority, but I'll have your back."

Rob McNabb chose to lean against the front fender of an unoccupied pickup at the front of the line. It was the driver of that vehicle who had started the commotion. There was no one else in the cab. From this position, Rob had a clear sightline to Conn and Eardley. The five lawmen in plain clothes, with pistols still concealed, watched the two outlaws, their guns revealed, confront an angry crowd with two different agendas. The lawmen hoped that the gunmen would show restraint.

McNabb took out his phone and activated the camera in video mode. He pressed the record button and slipped the phone into the outer breast pocket of his coat. The camera lens peaked over the edge of the pocket, picking up a grainy video due to the low light, but a decent quality soundtrack.

—

"Excuse me, folks," Raymond Conn called from up on the concrete barrier. He spoke loud enough to be heard by all, but not in a threatening manner. He didn't need to sound aggressive. He held the shotgun in full view of everyone in the crowd. And standing beneath him, in front of the barrier, was the solid hulk of Willie Eardley with the AR-15 rifle at the ready.

"My buddies and me, we've got a job to get to out in Alberta, see. But you guys in the fancy vests are holding up the traffic. So, as of now, this roadblock is over." He popped open the action on the old shotgun. The two empty shotshells fell to the road and he slipped in two live rounds to replace them. He closed the gun's action with a flick of his wrist. "Can I trust we'll have your full cooperation?"

There was some grumbling heard from several of the emergency vests, and at least one "fuck you." Audible gasps came from some of the delayed travellers and when McNabb saw Eardley begin to swing the rifle muzzle toward the crowd, he reached inside his coat and slid his pistol halfway out of its holster. Step two and a half of three. In his peripheral view, he caught Selkirk changing his stance as well. He noticed someone in the crowd watching him, so he started wiggling his hand as if he was scratching an itch. The person's gaze went back to the man on the barricade.

Then one of the emergency vests spoke for the rest. "Let's get them through, folks. We don't want anyone getting hurt. That's not why we came out here."

"Thank you, sir," Conn gave the spokesman a casual salute. "Everyone get back in your vehicles. The yellow jackets here will stand aside and let everyone through." Moments later, the nearest vehicles began to creep forward.

—

Webb returned to the Pathfinder as Sally unlocked the doors and got in the driver's seat. She had just completed a different mission.

"Success," she said. "I got the tracker attached to the rig when the guy in the cube van behind the transport, got out to join the rest of the crowd. You guys did well."

"We didn't have to shoot anyone."

"Exactly."

As soon as she started the engine, Webb phoned McNabb and Selkirk who were back in the Ram, half a dozen cars behind them. "It must be nice to work for an organization unencumbered by policies on the discharge of firearms. A couple of well-timed warning shots sure can get folks' attention … certainly had the right affect on that mob."

Selkirk came back with: "*Yeah. Sawed-off shotgun. Add another to their growing list of offenses.*"

"*Got it all on video, too,*" McNabb added.

"And we've got them on a leash again, folks," Sally added.

"The tracking device is deployed and we're receiving a clean signal, so we'll be able to spread out a little. We don't want our cover to get burned crossing the prairies."

Aldridge phoned the Mounties in the Impala to thank them for their presence. Traffic rolled slowly toward the blockade.

"Not at all, Sergeant. Your Ontario guys had it well covered. We've got openings for them all out here any time they're looking for a change."

"You'll never get them, Corporal. The detective constable is beholden to me for life, and I keep trying to entice the MNR guys to join my shop, but they won't budge, not even for the thirty-thousand increase in pay. Go figure."

"Gotta be kidding. Truly devoted to their calling, I guess."

—

Jason Mead stopped the Silverado at the barricade just long enough for Conn and Eardley to get in. The Emergency vests stood by, helpless, as more than twenty vehicles slipped through their grasp. They would have to wait for a break in the traffic before they could re-establish control.

—

Once everyone was on the Perimeter Highway, Sally positioned the tails where she wanted them, sending the Mounties to run ahead of the OSL vehicles with instructions to top up their gas at the first available pumps. She would rotate each of the units out for refuelling before they got any distance away from the city. With a snowstorm coming, it wouldn't do for them to run short of gas out in the middle of the prairies.

Chapter 39

The U.S. Coast Guard cutter *George H.W. Bush* circled slowly in United States waters, waiting for the *Ocean Princess* to drift across the border.

The beat-up old freighter was stopped dead in the water. During the last four hours, she had slowly drifted closer to the international boundary. That the ship found itself there was entirely the fault of the catastrophic failure of the overheated propeller shaft bearing. The bearing *and* the outgoing tide.

In the engine room, the chief engineer had removed the bearing and was driving wedges under a wooden trestle he'd constructed to provide temporary support for the shaft. One of the stokers was slathering grease between the shaft and the wooden structure. If all went well and they used only enough power to move the ship along, the repair would easily get them into port. When he was satisfied with the work, the chief phoned up to the bridge and informed Captain Chang that they were ready to proceed.

On the coast guard cutter's bridge, the VHF radio squawked. "*Coast Guard Cutter George Bush, this is Ocean Princess. Thank you for standing by. We do not require assistance. Minor mechanical problem is repaired. We will be underway momentarily.*"

James Sherman Taylor III, the skipper of *George H.W. Bush*, picked up the microphone and replied, "Ocean Princess, you have mistaken my intentions. This is neither a courtesy call, nor an offer of assistance. Unless you regain power shortly, you will be in United States waters. Please prepare to be boarded for inspection upon arrival. Over."

"Coast Guard Cutter Bush, we will not be staying in United States, captain. We are returning to Canadian side of channel. There is no obligation for inspection. We are not disembarking any cargo or persons in your country."

"Regardless of your intentions, sir, once we confirm that you are entirely in United States waters, we do have the authority to board and inspect your vessel, and we fully intend to do so."

Captain Taylor was a patient man. He would make no move on the disabled ship until he could sail his patrol vessel between it and the international border with room to spare. And even then, he would circle the Chinese vessel several times before acting. It was the best way to avoid an international diplomatic incident — and all the attendant administrative grief he would no doubt face when politics came into play.

Ocean Princess continued to drift inexorably toward the invisible boundary line at barely more than half a knot — the speed of the outgoing tide. She finally arrived at the invisible line and began to float across, into the cutter's jurisdiction. The cox'n on the cutter's bridge watched the ancient ship's progress on a video monitor. Its image was transmitted from a camera mounted on a drone hovering directly over the ship, and the cutter's GPS receiver provided a superimposed image representing the international boundary.

When three quarters of the *Ocean Princess* was on the United States side of the line, the officers on the cutter's bridge watched a plume of black diesel exhaust belch from the Chinese vessel's funnel, but she continued her slow drift across the line. When the overhang of the bow was the last portion of the ship that could claim to be in Canadian waters, a languid disturbance rippled the water behind the slowly turning propeller and signalled that the old freighter had restored power, or at least enough power to stage a slow return to Canadian waters.

Just as the ship began to move forward, its exhaust discharge turned even darker. The engineer had applied a touch more power. His decision had immediate dire consequences.

Sound travels through the water with surprising clarity, and everyone aboard the coast guard vessel could hear transmitted through their own steel hull, the tortured machinery in the old freighter as it came to a screeching stop. The ship coasted halfway back into Canadian waters before losing momentum. Ten minutes later she was fully in U.S. waters. Dead in the water. The propeller shaft had snapped, overstressed by the heat of the failed bearing. In his hurry to make his temporary repair, the chief had failed to notice the hairline crack. No jury-rigging would fix it now. It was a job for a shipyard — or a trip to the breakers.

Chapter 40

The snow had started to fall before the OSL gang and their law enforcement shadows passed Portage la Prairie. But it wasn't bad for the first twenty minutes. Then the wind picked up, and the snow began falling horizontally. And it got heavy.

McNabb found it easier to drive with the fog lights turned on and the headlights off. The veil of snow reflected less glare from the lights set low in the front bumper.

Other than a few drivers who must have thought themselves immortal, most of the traffic rolled along between fifty and sixty km/h. But there was a generous sample of those who didn't think mortality rules applied to them. Most of those could be found jammed into the snowbanks on either side of the two westbound lanes.

Ian Selkirk checked the tracking device monitor. It showed the transport to be a little over half a kilometre ahead. They weren't gaining and they weren't falling behind. They were keeping pace in their assigned position.

McNabb's phone rang. The Ram's touchscreen display showed Katie Burke calling, the friend who was taking care of his daughters. His heart skipped several beats. Katie wasn't normally the sort to call him at work, so there had to be something wrong at home.

He touched the connect button on the steering wheel. "Hi Katie. What's up?"

"Dad, Mom isn't answering her phone." It was Mae Ling. She sounded breathless. Rob's heart skipped several more beats. What had happened at home?

"She's probably taking a long bath in her hotel room, Mae Ling. What's happened?" Rob held his breath until she spoke again.

"Tiffany and Meaghan came over tonight to apologize. They said they didn't think about their posts hurting my feelings. And they want to do chats with me and Maddie and Vivi online. They said they don't want me to change my name, either."

He exhaled, relieved. It was her excitement, not an emergency, that had her wound up. She said she was using Katie's phone because hers was taking forever to do a system update.

His heart melted each time she called him Dad. With Sam and him being only twice her age when she joined the family, they had suggested she could use their given names, and at first, she did. But when they constantly referred to themselves as Mom and Dad with the baby, Mae Ling soon began to honour them with the same titles.

Rob had to swerve to avoid a fishtailing SUV and took a moment to reply as he watched it clip the front fender of the pickup it had just cut off ahead of them. The offending SUV spun into the snowbank just as Mae Ling spoke again.

"Are you okay, Dad?"

"Yeah … I'm fine sweetheart. I'm driving through a bad snowstorm right now and some of the other people aren't very good at winter driving.

"So, you are okay with that … with Tiffany and Meaghan's apology? … Oops, that one's in the ditch too." The clipped pickup was off the road now, on the other side and facing the wrong way. Driver must've overcorrected.

"Hi, Mae Ling, it's Ian Selkirk here with your dad. Things just got a little crazy on the highway, but I can see from the smile on his face that he is really happy for you."

"*Hi Ian. Where are you now?*"

"Good question. The last sign that I could read said we are almost at Brandon, Manitoba."

After a brief pause: "*Oh, I can see that on Google Earth. The next place you will pass after Brandon is Kemnay. But it is very small, so you might not be able to see it in the storm.*"

"Right now, sweetheart," Rob managed during a lull in the excitement, "about all I can see are the tail lights of the car right in front of me. But thanks, it's good to know what's ahead."

"*You sound busy Dad. I will let you go. Be safe. And yes, I will keep my name now.*"

"Mae Ling … my Beautiful Bell. I'm really glad to hear that. It's a good decision. I love you and thanks for calling. Give Mom another fifteen minutes then try calling her again. I know she will be pleased to hear your news too."

"*Love you too, Dad. Bye Ian.*" She ended the call. Despite the stressful road conditions, Rob felt a load lifted from his shoulders.

"She's growing up, Ian, and she has come a long way with her English. When we rescued her a year and a half ago, all she had was broken, pidgin English … she was polite, but her vocabulary was most definitely learned on the streets. She caught a real break with the foster parents who took her in during the four months before she adopted us. They were retired English teachers and they gave her a great start. She's a smart and sweet kid … uh, young woman."

McNabb was halfway through another relieved sigh when the car ahead came to a sudden stop. The pickup ahead of the car was stopped too, with its four-way flashers going, and Rob thought he could see even more lights flashing beyond that. He got the Ram stopped without hitting the car ahead, or getting rear-ended by the pickup behind, but judging by the sound of the thump that followed, that guy wasn't so lucky.

"The bad guys are stopped too, Rob," Selkirk said, looking at the tracking monitor. "It'll either be a pileup or a road closure."

"They'd close the highway and just leave us out here in this?"

"It's happened before."

McNabb's phone rang again. It was Aldridge this time, and Selkirk answered. "We're here, boss."

"*The highway's closed for the night, guys. Our two Mounties are at the head of the line, and they say everything's being directed off at the second exit into Brandon. The big truck stop is already full, so we are all going to be parked at the Walmart until further notice.*"

"The Mounties are ahead of the OSL gang, then?"

"*Yup. The horsemen said they'll manoeuvre for a spot with a direct line of sight as the rig pulls in. We'll have to do the best we can without drawing attention to ourselves.*"

"Ten-four, Sarge. We'll see you in there."

Chapter 41

The half of the Walmart lot farthest from the store was mostly filled with stranded motorists while the inner half, now almost deserted, had been kept open for local customers and store employees. The local police had coordinated with store management and the parking operation had gone off without a hitch.

Now, nothing moved. Snow was still ripping horizontally across the lot and the storm wasn't supposed to subside for a few hours more. And that's when the temperature was supposed to drop to the mid-minus thirties.

McNabb and Selkirk wrapped themselves in the cheap sleeping bags that Aldridge had bought earlier and were reclined in their seats in the cab of the Ram pickup. Neither of them cared to risk sleeping in the vehicle with the engine idling during a snowstorm. There was always the risk of carbon monoxide poisoning. They had just settled in following the midnight to 0300 shift watching over the OSL trucks and crew. The RCMP officers had drawn the 0300 to 0600 shift.

Rob was already sound asleep, and Ian was just drifting off when someone knocked on the driver's side window. McNabb was startled out of his sleep and not really pleased about the interruption.

"Crap." He opened his eyes to see Aldridge outside, brushing the snow from his side window. One push of the Ram's start button activated the accessory mode, and he rolled the window down a few inches, just enough for Sally to speak through. Still, a flurry of snow blew past her and landed on him.

"Sorry to wake you guys, but I'm doing a bed check." She chuckled. Rob and Ian didn't. "Actually, I'm here with news of another twist in the bad guys' plot."

"Oh?" from Rob.

"What's up?" from Ian.

"The inspector just called. OSL's ship has arrived in the general vicinity of its expected destination, but it has sort of ... been lost to us."

"It sank ... or sunk?" from Rob.

"It lost power in the Strait of Juan de Fuca and drifted across the border ... into the arms of the U.S. Coast Guard ... the one agency no one thought to notify to leave it alone ... not that it would have mattered in those circumstances. They've boarded and inspected it, found a variety of infractions and contraband and have seized it. They are towing it into an American port as we speak."

Selkirk sat up and said, "So, whatever OSL was going to buy from them...."

"Is no longer on the market."

"Shit," McNabb said. "After everything we've gone through to get this far."

Rob and Ian raised their seatbacks. The junior detective suggested a group meeting as McNabb started the engine to get some heat back in the cab. "Seeing as how we're wide awake now."

Sally walked back to the Pathfinder to fetch Rick Webb and Ian called the Mounties in the Impala. The Mounties said they'd keep it as an audio meeting. COVID distancing would be impossible for six bodies in a pickup cab, and the corporal suggested that the four Ontario officers couldn't be trusted to be disease free. Funny guy.

"So, what do we do now?" Rob asked when the meeting opened. As the junior member of the Natural Resources contingent, he assumed that it was all over except for repossessing the transport load of fur. But he also knew that the police would be reluctant to blow a lengthy investigation just because a drug deal fell through for the bad guys. They would probably want to wait for another opportunity.

Sally Aldridge was the senior officer on the road trip, but her inspector would have the final say on any decisions they made.

"We've got two options at this point. On one hand we could march over there right now and take them down for a whole slew of crimes. They've stolen a transport loaded with wildlife evidence — evidence tampering. The possession of the sawed-off shotgun and the assault rifle brings firearms offences into play as well as discharge of the shotgun in a crowd. They're in possession of almost a million U.S. dollars in cash ... no doubt laundered. They've stolen a snowplow and a log truck ... destroying the latter, blocked the Trans-Canada Highway ... am I missing anything? Oh yeah, two of them have violated the conditions of their bail and they've got a raft of charges against them for their original stunt in Saskatchewan and I'm sure if I was properly awake, I could come up with lots more.

"Or, on the other hand, we can see what their next move is. I'm sure they'll get new marching orders sometime between now and the morning if they haven't already. I know what *needs* to be done, but I'm open to suggestions. What do you guys think?"

"Count me and Rob out of the decision-making process," Webb said. "It's largely a police matter. We're just in it for the warm fuzzy stuff."

"Corporal Sneed, I realize you guys were dropped into this at the last moment … Any comments?"

"Well, Sergeant, in theory, I'm supposed to leave any decision making up to my detachment commander, but he hates being wakened up at oh-dark-thirty on cold winter mornings, so I'll go out on a limb and suggest letting your bad guys make the next move.

"If we take them down here, you've lost any chance of getting them on a drug buy in the foreseeable future. Furthermore, in a parking lot full of non-combatants, we could end up with collateral damage. I'll vote for leaving them alone and seeing what happens. Constable Dunphy, with me here, doesn't have a say in this. He's still a rookie … but he says that's his vote anyhow."

"I, too, would suggest letting them make the next move," Selkirk agreed.

"And that," Aldridge concluded, "was my inclination too. Are you okay with that, Rick … Rob?"

McNabb spoke first. "I'm guessing the alternative for us two would be to get out now and walk home, would it?" he asked, tongue-in-cheek. "But I didn't bring my snowshoes." The cops all laughed, but he went on. "So, don't you dare … *any* of you, under *any* circumstances … do *not* tell Sam that I'm about to break our Post Apocalyptic Vow … again."

"What's that, Officer McNabb?"

"Well, Constable Dunphy, both my good woman and I have already been through several life-threatening situations in the line of duty. And we've each been saved by the other's brave actions several times now. But since the arrival of our two daughters, we took a vow to never willingly get ourselves into situations that could result in a … well … another life-threatening situation. In other words, as Sam would so eloquently put it, no more hero shit. Unfortunately, those events sometimes do come with the job."

"*Oh.*"

"And Rick?" Aldridge asked.

"Never took any oaths with the missus, and if she hears about this, she won't be too pleased either, but like we said just a couple of days ago … somewhere around Terrace Bay I think … we signed up for the original delivery, so I guess we'll see it through … at least until the next hiccup."

—

At the same time – fifty metres away

Raymond and Kyle were reclined, asleep in the Silverado when Derek Cheney phoned. An unforeseen turn of events had left the boss furious. And, of course, he said it was all Raymond's fault — even though Conn had no influence over the United States Coast Guard, or the mechanical fitness of a Chinese ship several thousand kilometres away. When he disconnected the call, Raymond was seething. He phoned Willie and Jason in the Kenworth, and they trudged through the snow to gather in the pickup.

"Shit, Ray, I finally just got to sleep. Those fuckers stole the mattress from the sleeper, and that bunk is real hard. And Willie snores … real loud."

"Stop your bitchin' Jay. We just got recalled. Fuckin' Chinaman got his ship seized by the U.S. Coast Guard. So now there's nothin' to pick up out there. We'll pull out and head for home as soon as the highway is open again. But from the look of it, that ain't goin' to be for a few hours yet.

"And Cheney says when we get back to Ontario, leave the rig in the same place we took it from in the Soo. Says it'll make the game wardens look foolish, and he figures the lawyer'll be more likely to get it back for us if it simply gets found. If we run it all the way home, we'd have to give it a whole new permanent identity or we'd never get to use it again.

"Now you can go back over there and get some sleep."

"Yeah, right. No snorin' this time, Willie. 'Least not until I'm asleep." The two of them bent into the wind and stumbled back to the rig.

As soon as they left, Raymond told Kyle that he'd had it with Cheney. "The guy shits on me every time someone else screws up, but he never gives a word of thanks to any of us when we come up winners." He looked at the wheelman for a moment before he continued. "You know, I've got a cousin in Minnesota who keeps in touch. He's looking to put together a team. You interested?"

"Yeah, Ray, I'm in. Derek's goin' off the rails more'n more lately. Don't like that. Not one bit. Yeah, I've had enough for sure. If you pull out, I'll come with you. I'm not one for working up a plan like you can ... I just like the drivin'. But the way that A-hole is goin', *we're* likely to get jammed up with the cops because he was havin' a tantrum instead of fixin' a problem along the way.

"Even with all the shady shit I done over the years, I ain't never been caught. I sure don't want that to change now."

"Okay. I've got an idea I want to think through for the return run. But in the meantime, don't say anything to the boys. You okay with that? They've got no passports anyhow. And they sure won't qualify for one after their Saskatchewan screw-up goes through court."

"No problem, Ray. Be like old times ... you and me

together." Kyle grunted as he shifted to recline his seat again. He was asleep in less than a minute. He was a doer, not a planner. Sleep came easily to a guy with an uncluttered mind.

Raymond reclined his seat too. He could hear a nearby front-end loader shuttling back and forth, getting an early start at snow clearing. He lay there, expanding on the idea of jumping ship. Yeah, Cheney could go fuck himself. And unlike his young drivers, Conn knew where there was enough cash to start fresh in a new location. The B team was never told about the money in the tires. Someone else had always handled the cash transactions when they arrived in Vancouver.

Chapter 42

The snow had stopped falling and the wind was calm. The temperature was -36°C. The local radio station's weatherman went on about a polar vortex that was causing the bitter cold all across the prairies and northwestern Ontario.

To everyone else in Manitoba it was just another February morning. Several minutes later, the morning DJ announced that the highway would be open again by eight o'clock.

Rob McNabb and Ian Selkirk walked back to the Ram, each with a takeout breakfast they'd picked up at the McDonald's outlet in Walmart. The clouds formed by their condensed breath followed them across the lot, and Rob's fingers, still damp from washing up inside, wanted to freeze to the door handle on the truck.

They watched the OSL crew sweeping snow off the Silverado and the Kenworth. The Kenworth's diesel was running again. Along with other big rigs in the parking lot, it had been run intermittently all through the night. Without a place to plug in their block heaters, it could have been a challenge to start some of them from stone cold if they hadn't taken that precaution.

Rick and Sally left the Pathfinder to pick up breakfast as

soon as Rob and Ian returned to their ride. The two Mounties had been ready to go since 0700.

At 0810, the OSL team pulled out of the parking lot. The tailing vehicles mingled with the rest of the departing crowd. They spaced themselves randomly in the traffic flow as everyone headed back out to the highway. It was no surprise to the law enforcement team that the Kenworth took the ramp to the eastbound Trans-Canada. Most likely heading back to the stable.

—

0910 – OSL office in Scarborough, Ontario

Sylvia was handling the early dispatch calls as she did every morning. Bea didn't start work until ten. After arranging for a transport to pick up a load of plumbing supplies in Mississauga, she used a quiet moment to send a brief text.

Derek Cheney stepped out of his office just as Sylvia tucked her cell phone back into her purse. And in that instant, something that had been lurking in the back of his mind — the seeds of a thought he hadn't been able to put his finger on before now — came together with total clarity. He took no time to plan his approach but acted instantly.

"Give me your phone."

"What for?"

"Who were you texting?"

"My brother."

"Bullshit. Show me your phone." He grabbed her purse, dumped everything out on her desk and took the phone. "You've been passing information to someone, haven't you?"

It had to be that. He knew it now. Why else would the U.S. Coast Guard just magically choose to show up and stop the ship that had his cargo aboard? And if the information had gone that far, then the local police must already be in the loop and prepared to move in on him at any moment. He'd had the nagging feeling for days that he was being watched, but he had never found any evidence of it until now.

Sylvia sat, aghast. She pleaded with him that she was just telling her brother what was going on at work. She wasn't snitching to anyone.

"What's your brother's name?"

"Andrew."

"Why is this text you just sent, going to a phone number and not to him as a named contact?" He was looking at the message history screen.

"He just got a new phone and new number. I haven't had a chance to create a contact for him yet."

Cheney looked at the last text message. It had been sent less than a minute ago. Despite all the texting abbreviations she had used, he deciphered a list of much of what had transpired with the delivery crew yesterday afternoon — locations and times: Winnipeg roadblock, winter storm, Brandon layover....

"Shit! Come with me!" Again, he didn't wait for her to act, but clamped an iron hard hand on her upper arm and hustled her out of the office. Across the yard there was an old warehouse. The interior was divided into three concrete bays, each bay just large enough to accommodate a forty-foot transport trailer. Obsolete now, it had provided secure storage for bonded loads in a bygone era. Each bay was closed off from the main space by a heavy steel door in addition to the exterior overhead garage doors that opened on the parking lot. The building was long out of use except for some personal storage, including his 1971 Chevy Camaro — a restoration project he'd never gotten around to. Other than that, the place was empty.

Cheney escorted the terrified secretary to the bay farthest from the street and shoved her inside. The steel door closed with frightening finality. Sylvia's heart almost stopped when she heard a heavy padlock snap shut. There was an overhead light but no windows and nothing at all she could use to escape or draw attention to herself. It was cold in there, too. Just below freezing. Too cold for the light sweater she was wearing in the office.

Five minutes later, Cheney opened the door long enough to throw her purse and her winter coat in on the floor. How considerate of him. Of course, it wasn't out of consideration. He needed all evidence of her presence gone from the office when Bea arrived for work. It was no surprise to Sylvia that her phone wasn't in the purse.

Cheney had taken the phone out to the parking lot and ground the life out of it with the heel of his boot and then thrown the remains into a dumpster before stomping back into the office. He had some serious plans to make. Right away.

Getting out of the country was his first priority. He'd get his brother-in-law to fly him to a private airstrip they sometimes used just across Lake Ontario in upstate New York. From there, he would make his way to South America where an old German friend of his father's had once told him he could live in luxury while hiding in plain view. The old guy was still alive, and Cheney slid Otto's contact information from under the desk blotter and stuck it in his wallet.

He pulled out all the cash from the wall safe behind his desk. He had fifty thousand Canadian dollars and just over half a million in U.S. funds but was annoyed that the other nine hundred thousand was hiding in the Kenworth's tires. He would have to make nice to Raymond and get him to rendezvous with the cash somewhere in the States. He realized that he'd ridden him pretty hard lately. But he'd have to give it a shot. Maybe offer him a hundred grand to bring the money-bearing tires across the border. Yeah, leave the money in the tires to get it across the border ... tell customs he was just delivering replacement tires for a company truck parked with a couple of blowouts. That would work. Sure hoped it would.

—

0955

Derek Cheney had just finished talking to his brother-in-law on the phone when Bea arrived for work.

"Good morning, boss." She looked in his office door as she hung up her coat. He looked edgy, she thought. But then again, she'd known him to have wild mood swings on any given day. And edgy seemed to be the pattern most days now.

"Hey, Bea." He tried to appear occupied as he normally would be when she arrived for work.

"Where's Sylvia?"

"Called in sick."

"Poor girl. Probably her brother again. Andrew's a real worry for her." She sat on Sylvia's desk chair to pull off her winter boots as she continued talking. "Got Down's syndrome and he needs constant attention. I think he's got some other health issues too. And after her mother passed, she didn't have the heart to put him in an institution, so he's been living with her. She has to keep calling him and sending texts to keep him occupied. It's gotta be tough on her," she said as she went to her desk. Without skipping a beat, she put on her headset and took her first call. "Overnight Shipping. How can I help you?"

Cheney sat at his desk, stunned by the realization of what

he'd just done, accusing the wrong person — if there was even a right person to accuse. Maybe there wasn't a snitch after all. Certainly not Sylvia. Maybe he was just being paranoid. "Fuck. How do you dig yourself out of this hole?" he asked himself. "Sylvia, Sylvia, Sylvia, what the fuck do I do now? Shit!"

It was not like he could just turn her loose and say he was sorry. She would hardly return to her desk and greet Bea as if nothing had happened. When a former driver had made sexually suggestive comments to her last year, she'd torn a strip off the guy and demanded that Derek get rid of him. The guy had been a problem anyhow, so he did. But he knew she'd go to the police for sure the moment she got out of there. And while he'd had Raymond and the guys make an occasional "problem" disappear over the years, he wasn't about to do that to the girl.

Well, she had her coat, so she wouldn't freeze out there. Someone would find her soon enough. Meanwhile, his flight to the other side of the lake was set up for mid-afternoon. His brother-in-law had commitments he couldn't put off, so he'd agreed to meet him at Buttonville airport at three thirty. Until then, he had to make himself scarce. He stuffed the cash into the attaché case he kept under his desk, and then put on his coat and headed for the door.

"I'll be out for the rest of the day Bea. Hold the fort, will ya?" he said as he went through the front office on the way out to his Audi. Just as if it was any other day on the job.

Bea acknowledged with a wave and a nod while talking with a client, and at that moment — the very instant the front door closed — something at the foot of the coat rack caught her eye. Sylvia's boots! She had been showing off her new boots yesterday afternoon while she was getting ready to go home. So, why were they here now if she wasn't?

Bea got up and walked into Derek's office while still

talking to the client. Her wireless headset worked from anywhere in the building. The wall safe behind his desk was left ajar. She used a pencil to swing it fully open and looked inside. Other than a couple of documents, it was empty. She had no idea how much money he kept in it, but according to Raymond, there was always a sizable cash "float" stored there. Even as she finished with the client on the phone, she had her own cell phone out and whizzed through her contact list. She selected Sylvia's number and pushed the call button.

After the seventh ring tone, the system told her that the party she was calling wasn't available or was out of the service area. "Please leave a message after the tone." Bea knew that Sylvia never shut off her phone and never went anywhere that there was no service. Caring for Andrew kept her tied down and in cell range full time.

Chapter 43

At that instant, Bea shed her matronly dispatcher persona. The seasoned police detective that she really was, went into action. She punched a number into her phone; her call was answered on the first ring.

"There's trouble in the camp. The rabbit is on the run and his wall safe has been emptied. He left in the Audi five minutes ago and there's a fresh tracker in his briefcase … I replaced that on Tuesday."

"Okay, Bea. We've got his signal … going north on Warden Avenue right now. I'll tell his tailing squad and notify Sally in the travelling road show out west. They've left Brandon, heading back east. I see in the log that you've been made aware that the west coast rendezvous is off."

"Roger that, boss. Before you go, there's been one other troubling development here. His personal secretary is missing. She wasn't here when I arrived. Sick day, he said, but it doesn't check out. I'll investigate while I've got the place to myself.

"Okay, stay on site and we'll send the backup team over to help. They should be there in a couple of minutes." Ever since the undercover operation had begun to look shaky, backup officers had been providing surveillance while fronting as a failing carpet cleaning business. They were located in a similar rundown building

located diagonally across the street.

Bea started going through the drawers in Cheney's desk. She was looking for keys for the old warehouse. Unlike many businesses, there was no key rack in the OSL office. Any time people needed a key, they went to Derek for it. Whether he kept the few keys that were needed in his pockets or in the desk, Bea had never been able to determine. She'd been given a key for the front door when she started working there because she was frequently the last person to leave, so she had never had the opportunity to ask for one. There were spare keys for the office door but none for the warehouse. She threw on her coat and met the backup team as they pulled up in their carpet cleaner's van.

"Get the big key. We need to get into that building." She pointed and walked ahead. Tried the door. Locked, as she expected.

"Got a warrant?" one of the backup officers asked as he heaved a battering ram out of the back of the van.

"Don't need one. Exigent circumstances. Besides, I'm an employee here, and the boss just left me in charge for the day. This is a consent search." She would have grinned if the circumstances were different. The two brawny male cops swung the ram at the door. It took three mighty whacks — the steel door was tough. The door and the lock had been purchased with a tough neighbourhood in mind. When the door sprung open, the ram clattered to the pavement and the three officers rushed into the warehouse with their guns drawn. Just in case.

"Sylvia," Bea called out as they moved across the floor.

"Help. Bea, I'm in here," came from the far end of the building. Bea and the backup team rushed to the farthest steel door.

"Hang in there Syl, we'll have you out in a flash."

"Honkin' big mother of a lock on that, Bea," one of the detectives said. "I'll be right back." Their carpet cleaning van was well stocked with equipment for dealing with such circumstances and he returned in less than a minute with a high-speed cutting tool. The lock fell open in little more time than it had taken to fetch the machine. A bolt cutter would have just gotten a sore jaw trying to chew through the heavy lock.

—

1040 – Trans-Canada Highway near St. Anne, Manitoba

Raymond's pickup was just a black dot on the horizon, two kilometres ahead of the Kenworth on the straight, totally mind-numbing section of highway. The snow had been cleared off the travelled surface, but plows were still working on winging back the high drifts and snowbanks built up on the shoulders. Every couple of kilometres there were stranded vehicles half-buried on either side of the road.

Willie Eardley was driving the rig. He and Jason Mead were both grumbling about doubling back east again and being on the road for so long without any chance now of completing the run to Vancouver. No chance either of getting the trip bonus that Derek always paid following a successful run. They'd just get their regular basic pay for days worked — and none for their time locked up in Regina. Jason had a car payment due, and Willie's woman was on his case about wanting to move to a slightly less crappy apartment that they could ill afford, even if he had received the bonus.

"How many days ago were we last here, going in this direction, Jason?" Willie asked, hoping to lighten up the mood a little.

"It was just yester ... oh, eastbound ... fuck, I don't remember, and right now, I really couldn't give a shit. The days all seem to run together."

Willie didn't have the energy to try again, so they both lapsed into a long silence.

Chapter 44

Rick Webb was driving the Nissan Pathfinder several kilometres behind McNabb and Selkirk in the Ram. The Mounties in the Impala had been withdrawn from the tail when the parade re-entered Ontario. The corporal and his rookie constable had been willing to carry on but were disappointed that their staff sergeant's recall trumped their enthusiasm.

Detective Sergeant Aldridge was on the phone to her team in Toronto. It was the umpteenth call she'd been on since pulling out of Brandon. Everyone, from Bea the undercover operative, to the provincial police commissioner had become involved. Since the drug and ivory transaction was off the table and Derek Cheney was on the run, everyone agreed that the entire OSL crew should be arrested and taken out of play simultaneously.

While the big prize of a drug bust was now out of reach, the team did have lots of evidence on them for their other multiple breaches of the law. There was enough to put each one away for at least a few years. The takedown teams had eyes on everyone, and it would be best to grab them all before someone found a crack to crawl into.

Now it was just a matter of waiting for the prickliest target, the team with the transport truck — and the guns — to arrive at the takedown site. The police had held off until Raymond Conn escorted the rig back into Ontario. That placed everyone in the same provincial jurisdiction, simplifying one of many legal hurdles they had yet to get over.

A location between Vermillion Bay and Dryden had been chosen for the takedown. The highway was straight as a ruler but ran over a steady succession of rolling hills in an area of open farmland. The roadblock was set up at the bottom of one of the hills where it wouldn't be seen until it was too late for the OSL transport to turn around.

A cell phone signal blocking device was ready to be activated so that Conn in his pickup, who would be the first to come over the hill, wouldn't be able to call back to the transport.

Because of the blockade-running history of the guys in the Kenworth, some heavy-duty hardware had been positioned at the takedown site. Four dump trucks were waiting to physically close the road at the chosen spot. Two in front and two more to box them in from behind. Extra police bodies came in from Kenora, Fort Frances and Atikokan to bolster the takedown team. It looked as though everyone would be in position before the arrival of the OSL gang.

—

1238 – Approaching the Trans-Canada Highway junction with Hwy 71.

Raymond Conn phoned the guys in the Kenworth.

"*Yeah?*" Jason Mead picked up the call.

"We're taking a right, onto Highway 71, Jay. Cheney's run into another problem, so we've changed the plan a little."

"*Sure, Ray. Whatever you want. We're just following the leader.*"

Conn disconnected the call without elaborating. Kyle

245

Roach had been driving the Silverado all morning while Raymond took several urgent calls from Cheney and placed several of his own to his cousin in Minnesota. Plans were coming together nicely with the cousin. Yes, he could use a couple of experienced hands in his organization. And in response to the calls from Scarborough, Raymond had led Cheney to believe that he would meet him down in Columbus, Ohio in several days to hand over the tires. Big bonus in it, Cheney had promised. It was a promise Conn had no intention of keeping. His mind was set on a much bigger bonus.

—

1239 – In the Ram

Rob McNabb was behind the wheel and following half a kilometre behind the OSL rig. There were three civilian vehicles between them — two pickups and a subcompact car. Because of the hilly terrain the transport wasn't always in view, but anytime he had a clear line of sight, it was there. Selkirk was snoozing with his seat reclined, and Rob was listening to his tunes, the volume turned low. The Manhattans were halfway through singing *Kiss and Say Goodbye* when he crested the hill overlooking the Highway 71 junction. At that instant he saw the transport signal a right turn.

"Oh boy!" he sighed. This wasn't good. He punched the Bluetooth call button without hesitating. "Call Sally Aldridge," he instructed. The call connected.

"*What's up, Rob?*"

"Bad news, Sal. The boys turned south on 71. We're well behind them. I don't think our cover has been burned, but they are obviously going to miss out on your big reception."

246

"*Crap!*" There was long pause. "*I've no idea why they would take the long way around, but that's immaterial now. I'll have to see what we can set up down 71, or on Highway 11 when they get there.*"

Selkirk sat up and joined in when he heard what was going on. "I'm wondering, Sally, seeing as how their boss appears to be set to run off, maybe Mr. Conn has decided to withdraw his pension from the tire fund and skedaddle across the border."

"*Good thinking Ian, but Rick is reminding me that they won't be able to go over the border with a load of undocumented fur. Even if they've fudged a good set of papers for the rig, they never had anything to cover the load of fur.*"

"They don't need the trailer," McNabb said. "The fur would just be a nuisance to try to sell in a regulated market like the States. Almost impossible. And they don't need the tractor. If he's retiring, all he'll be interested in will be what's in those tires. If they don't have the tools to do it themselves, they can just find a tire shop. With all the pulpwood trucks around Emo and Fort Frances, there've got to be a few of those in the area."

While they talked, McNabb pulled off to the side of the exit ramp and stopped for a moment. He made sure that the OSL truck was well out of sight before he completed the turn onto Highway 71. "Brief change of topic, Sal. Maybe you guys should follow them for a while. If they are paying any attention at all, they might think it too much of a coincidence to have a blue pickup trailing behind them when one followed them for almost a hundred klicks out of Manitoba … even if it is a common colour."

"*Yeah, our rides are probably reaching their best before dates soon. We'll take the handoff. Good call, Rob. Be with you in a few minutes. In the meantime, I've got to make some calls … change some plans.*"

1242 – In the MNR Turbo Beaver C-FOEY over Lake of the Woods

When she had landed at Dryden the day before, the local air service manager called Samantha Williams into his office and reassigned her to a local job for a couple of days. The pilot who was supposed to have taken the flights had called in sick.

Today she was flying Conservation Officer Rylie Birks and provincial police Constable Ricky Ho around the big lake. They were checking ice fishing parties. There had been complaints that some of them had snowmobiled across the closed international border from Minnesota. Constable Ho was along primarily to enforce public health COVID quarantine orders.

"Come in low over that island Sam," Birks said, pointing to one of the many islands dotting the large lake. It was a long narrow island, oriented east to west and located in the southwestern part of the lake about three kilometres from the U.S. border.

"There's almost always a group there that crosses from Minnesota to fish the south side, right close to the island. If they are there, land as close to them as you can … as fast as you can. They don't like me much and are likely to run. I've caught them with over-limits before."

As she put the Beaver into a descending glide over the island, Birks picked a group up with his binoculars and confirmed it was them. They were off to the left, no more than a quarter mile away.

At the same instant, two snow machines blazed past the group, barely a hundred metres offshore. The noise from their high-performance machines would easily drown out the sound of the Beaver's idling turbine, leaving Sam's plane in stealth mode for a few critical seconds longer.

She banked the plane hard left, fully extended the flaps and set it down no more than two hundred metres from the fishermen. Slush was not a problem. Three other landings they had already made on the lake were all on solid ice, covered by flat crusted snow. There was an inch of fresh powder on top.

Applying full reverse thrust, she not only managed to stop the plane right beside the group, but also created a minor blizzard of loose snow that threw them into temporary disarray. Might have upset them a little, too, but hey, they were breaking the law. Her enforcement team was out the plane and onto the group in an instant.

Sam was about to shut down the turbine when one of the men — he appeared to be not much older than a teenager — looked as if he was planning to run. She kept the turbine running at idle speed. While the two lawmen were talking to the other three men in the group, the young fellow mounted his snowmobile, turned the key, and sped off.

—

Same time – In the Pathfinder

Webb told Aldridge, "From what I recall, this road is a steady succession of curves and hills for three quarters of the way to Highway 11. It might seem a bit weird if we keep showing up in their rear-view mirrors intermittently, but not gaining on them. Everyone out here drives faster than that.

"It might be a good time to see if we can get some aerial observation going again. That way we can keep out of sight at least as far as Nestor Falls. There's nowhere they can go other than on down the road, but if they pull off for a pee break, we might unknowingly cruise on past them … again."

"You want to call your people while I piss off mine? Your connections seem to be better at coming up with air support." she said, her phone poised, ready to dial.

While Aldridge was upsetting a staff sergeant in Dryden, Rick was on his phone to Jacqui in the office of the secret squirrels. "I'm calling in for another favour. Nora assured us that you guys were at our beck and call."

"*That's what we're here for, Rick. Let's have it.*"

"Can you provide us with a couple more hours of air support? We could use the help right about now. Be closest if it comes out of Dryden."

"*What's your 10-20?*"

"We've just started south from the Trans-Canada on Highway 71. The subject took an unexpected turn. It's a difficult stretch of road to keep a uniform distance behind the subjects without tipping them off to a tail."

"*You're going to love this, Rick. Sam Williams got held over there to do a couple days of patrols on Lake of the Woods. Right now, she's got a CO and a police constable on board checking anglers. She can't be too far away from you guys.*"

"She's going to get tired of us cutting in on her other assignments."

"*I understand that she considers any job in her Beaver to be a slice of heaven, and if it has any connection with McNabb, she's on cloud nine. I'll call the air service and get her over there A.S.A.P.*"

"Thanks Jacqui." They disconnected the call just before Sally Aldridge finished the call she was on.

"Air support coming up shortly."

"That's the good news, then. Mine is not so. The cavalry is all lined up behind us now, getting farther behind by the minute. Manpower and equipment are going to be limited when we get down to Highway 11. They'll scramble a couple of high-speed units, but timing might be tight. We'll have to improvise somehow."

"We could always take a page out of their book," Rick looked at Sally, smiling. When she returned with a questioning look, he said, "Tip a load of logs onto the road in front of them."

"Last resort, Webb. Only as an absolute last resort." She chuckled. "It would be ironic, though, after they tried to do it to you guys."

"Well, fret not. Sam is bringing another CO and a constable with her, so we'll have a little more strength than the bad guys."

Chapter 45

When Sam Williams had stopped the Turbo Beaver beside the group of fishermen, the plane was already pointing east, and she had kept the turbine running. As soon as the young man started his snowmobile and bolted, Sam boosted the Beaver to full power and was airborne in an instant.

She kept her skis a few feet above the snow and pulled back on the power as she flew up beside the fleeing snowmobile, forcing him to continue parallel to the island — eastbound, not south toward Minnesota.

Meanwhile, Conservation Officer Birks commandeered one of the other snowmobiles from the group. He chose the fastest sled, and soon caught up with the fleeing machine, edging toward it from the opposite side.

Wide-eyed, the runner watched Sam's Beaver flying along beside him. He was mesmerized by the sight of it. The wheeled skis of the aircraft were right there, at shoulder height, less than ten feet away from him.

If he'd kept his wits about him, he could have easily outmanoeuvred the aircraft by applying his brakes and turning behind it, heading south, toward home. But instead, he kept going at full throttle in a futile effort to outrun the Beaver. He kept watching the plane and steering straight ahead. In doing so, he failed to notice Birks move in close on his other side to grab the emergency shutoff tether cord and give it a jerk. The engine quit and the machine coasted to a stop; the driver helpless to do anything about it. Birks had the tether in his mitt.

Sam climbed the Beaver away from the spot and circled once, then landed, pulling up and shutting down beside them. The runner was now handcuffed, and Birks had just read him the official police caution — the one that American folks call their Miranda rights.

Sam got down from the cockpit and opened the back door. She helped Birks guide his restrained prisoner up the ladder and into a back seat in the aircraft. "In you get and watch your step. Those ladder rungs can be slippery in snowy conditions," she said, then turned to Birks. "Here, Rylie, stick a mask on him and make sure he's properly belted in."

"What about my sled?" the guy asked.

"You should have thought about that before running," said Birks. "The other guys in your group can figure out how to get it back home. Bad enough that you're being charged for obstructing a peace officer and unlawfully crossing the border *and* fishing without a licence *and* not wearing a helmet. But as my little gift to you, I'm not seizing your machine today."

Instead of lifting off, Sam taxied the Beaver the three miles across the smooth ice surface, just below air speed. Coasting to a stop near the main group, she saw Constable Ho handing someone a ticket and one of the other men standing, hands on his hips, glaring at the aircraft. Someone's upset, Sam thought. This could get ugly.

When Birks got down from the plane, the man looked past him at the restrained passenger and started, "That's the *last* fuckin' time you come fishin' with us boy. After pullin' a stupid hairbrained stunt like that, I'm ashamed to admit that you're my son. Do you have *any* idea how much more trouble we are in because of your stupidity? If these officers were going to cut us any slack at all today, that went out the window when you ran."

"You takin' him in, warden?" the father asked Birks. "I'd almost consider it a favour."

Birks gave him a slow smile. "Somehow, I think a father-to-son chat might be just as effective at this point. That and Constable Ho's COVID quarantine ticket and a couple more I've got to write him at the same time."

"Well, the boy works for me, officer, and it'll be comin' outa his pay, that's for damn sure. And you can be sure, it will get paid. If it didn't, we wouldn't be allowed back, and I surely do love your country. I should make him walk back for them sleds, but since you are kickin' us out today, I guess we'll double up and fetch 'em back on our way out."

As Birks unlocked the young man's cuffs and returned the snowmobile keys to the father, Sam overheard an incoming VHF radio call.

"*Oscar Echo Yankee, it's Dryden calling, over.*"

"Dryden, OEY," she replied.

"*Roger OEY, your assistance is once again required following the high priority orange dot, whatever that means. Are you in a position to respond?*"

"That's affirmative, Dryden … at least, if it's back in this part of the province we can. We're just finishing up with a contact group here on the ice. We'll be airborne in a few minutes after the lawmen make some more money for the Crown. What's the location of the rabbit? Or have they lost it again?"

"*No, it's still within reach, but the hounds say they might spook it if they follow too close going through the briar patch. Do those game wardens always speak in code?*"

"It's a job requirement," she smiled as she replied.

"So, when you're done there, head east to the first blacktop. They are somewhere near the north end of Highway 71, driving south, over."

"Roger that. Let them know we're coming, and we'll give them a call when we pick up the scent. OEY, out."

"Dryden clear."

—

1310 – In the air over Hwy 71 north of Sioux Narrows, Ontario

"There they are Sam." Birks pointed ahead toward the highway on his side of the Beaver.

"Yeah, I got 'em, thanks. Now we climb to two thousand feet and follow. This is the boring part, guys," she said as she put the Beaver into a wide climbing turn, keeping it above and behind the OSL transport. "I followed them like this for over two hours when they were westbound yesterday. Wish they'd make up their minds."

After they'd finished with the fishermen on Lake of the Woods, Sam had explained to Birks and Ho the situation with the OSL gang. Phone conversations with Detective Sergeant Aldridge kept them appraised of the situation on the ground.

The four officers on the road had discussed and agreed with Selkirk's prediction that Raymond Conn and at least one other member of the group probably planned to retire from the business and cross into Minnesota.

Now it was just a question of which crossing they would choose — turn left and cross the river at Fort Frances or go right and cross at Rainy River.

So, despite the officers aboard the Beaver facing an hour and a half of slow circling over their prey, there was the growing likelihood of some action before the afternoon was out.

—

1340 – Scarborough, Ontario

The carpet cleaners delved into a detailed search of the OSL office and warehouse. Bea sat working at the dispatcher's desk but had routed all incoming calls for OSL to the automated answering system — not that the company would be arranging any more shipments.

Instead of returning to the task force headquarters in downtown Toronto, she was now searching for any meaningful information stored on a laptop they found at the back of Cheney's bottom desk drawer. The machine was old and slow, but it coughed up a list of business contacts as well as a family contact that might have something to do with his planned departure. She got on the phone to her office.

"Inspector."

"*Yeah Bea?*"

"What's Cheney up to?"

"*He drove home after he left the shop. Came out ten minutes later with a suitcase, and now he's driving random loops around the city with occasional stops at coffee shops. His tail team aren't sure if he's just killing time or trying to figure out if he's being followed. But they don't think it's the latter.*

"*How are you guys making out, Bea?*"

"From what we've found, it looks like Cheney's brother-in-law, a James Wright, has a plane out at Buttonville. It's a Cessna 185, registration CF-WTF. They appear to have made occasional clandestine trips across the lake in the last couple of years. And he keeps a car in a shed at a small private airstrip near Barker, New York.

"Can you send someone to sit on the in-law's plane? If

Sally can't snag the transport before Cheney boards that plane, we're going to have to move on him, regardless … or go through a whole lot of extradition bullshit when the Americans grab him."

"We're on it, Bea. Good find."

Chapter 46

"They've turned right, Sergeant," Sam told Aldridge over the phone. "The highway between here and Rainy River is mostly flat and straight as a ruler. I can land the airborne division on the blacktop just about anywhere you need them. Constable Ho says he won't even write me up for the violation."

"Okay, Sam. They're committed to crossing the border now for sure. There's no other reason to go toward Rainy. Just stay high and inconspicuous for the time being. They're going to have to stop somewhere between here and the bridge whether they plan to open up those tires to get at the money or just take the tires with them. It would be a lot easier to pass themselves off as essential workers at the border with a couple of heavy truck tires in the back of the pickup."

"Sergeant Aldridge, it's Constable Ho here with Sam. I know the guys at the U.S. Customs and Immigration checkpoint on the Minnesota side. Do you want me to call them with a heads-up? Just in case?"

"Good idea, Constable. Yes, go for it, please. Meanwhile, since you guys still have eyes on them, we're going to hang back two or three kilometres. There's no point in us ratcheting up the tension any sooner than necessary."

—

Same time – In Raymond Conn's pickup.

Conn was on the phone to Willie and Jason in the Kenworth. "So, after we get the tires off, you guys spin the nuts back onto the remaining two wheels and head back east to drop the truck in the Soo. We'll run these tires across the border and meet up with Derek." He had told them about the money stashed in the tires and improvised a story about a drug buy that Derek was going to make in Detroit.

Willie had already guessed about the money in the tires. It was one of those open secrets at the shop, but no one said anything. And it had been pretty obvious on his one successful trip west.

The Vancouver dockworkers had taken the truck inside their warehouse, but they had kept the OSL drivers out using bodyguards even bigger and meaner than the OSL guys. But anybody who's been around big rigs knows the universal sounds of a tire shop. And that's what they could hear inside the dock terminal.

Changing the subject, Eardley asked, *"Will we be okay running single wheels on a dually axle?"*

"You've got a small load on. Won't hurt a thing." He really didn't give a damn, but Willie didn't need to know that.

"How do we get home from the Soo?"

"Rent a car. Jason's still got the company card, right?" He disconnected the call and didn't mention that there might not be a job, or even a company to return to when they did get home.

"Gotta keep staff morale up, Ky. What else could I say?"

Roach just grinned and reset the cruise control for a slow run through a lengthy sixty km/h speed zone across a First Nation territory. The sign had a long Indigenous name, and he only got to read the first three syllables before he was past it.

259

1520 – In Conn's pickup

Hwy 11 through Rainy River cuts a straight line across the town from east to west. Railroad tracks, less than seventy yards to the north, run parallel to the highway for the whole distance. The railroad station museum and a vehicle repair garage are the last two buildings in town and lie between the highway and the tracks. The bridge to Baudette, Minnesota is one kilometre to the west of the repair shop.

"There, Ky. Pull in on the far side of that garage. It's got a big parking area plowed out." Raymond got on the phone to Willie. "Follow us in here Willie, and park beside us." Although the snow had been removed from the large parking lot, he didn't realize that much of the cleared area was glare ice. It was the result of a warm spell and a day of rain which froze solid when the temperature dropped.

Conn parked there anyhow, in the northwest corner of the lot, next to the snowbank that paralleled the railroad tracks. Even as the Kenworth idled up alongside the Silverado, Raymond was shuffling toward the back of his truck on the icy surface. He almost went down but steadied himself and raised the pickup's rigid tonneau cover to reveal a collection of tools, ropes, chains and scrap ends of some wooden planks. They were leftovers from a deck building project for a friend.

Conn grabbed a couple of short two-by-ten boards and told Roach to do the same. He shuffled around to the driver's side of the Kenworth, and Kyle stayed on the passenger side. Willie eased the rig forward and stopped when Conn signaled. Conn and Roach each stacked their boards, one on top of the other, and laid them in front of the inside tires on the tractor's rear axle.

Conn stood up and signalled Willie to go forward again.

The two inner rear tires began to climb onto the boards but spit them out like tiddlywinks on the icy surface. Roach grabbed a nearly empty bag of sidewalk salt that Conn used at home and poured a handful on the ice before laying the boards down on top. He slid the bag under the Kenworth to Raymond, who repeated the process on his side.

On his next try, Willie got the wheels up on the boards, but proceeded to roll off the other end before getting stopped. Roach shook his head and opened the passenger side door. "We'll be here all day if you keep this up. Let me up there." He worked his way around the front of the Kenworth and climbed in as soon as Willie was clear. With one gentle shunt in reverse, the inside rear tires climbed and stayed perched on the boards. The manoeuvre raised the outer tires on that axle about three inches off the ground. Now there was no need to lift the axle with jacks to remove the outer wheels.

Even as Roach engaged the parking brakes, Willie already had a heavy-duty socket wrench fitted onto the first lug nut on the driver's side. It took a few bounces with his weight on the wrench handle to begin to loosen each nut, and there were twelve nuts to loosen and remove on each side of the truck.

—

1525 – In the Pathfinder, entering Rainy River.

Sergeant Aldridge called her headquarters to tell them they would be ready to move on the OSL road show in about ten minutes. As soon as she disconnected, she took a call from Constable Ho who was on Sam's phone again. She motioned Webb to contact McNabb and Selkirk on his.

"*Okay Sergeant, both vehicles have just pulled off in a parking area west of the train station. It's on the right side of the road at the western edge of town. Everything there is as flat as the prairies … not much cover anywhere. There's the station, then a truck repair garage and your bad guys are parked on the far side of the garage. Everything to the north and west is wide open. Sam says she can land between the highway and the tracks. It's open and reasonably level all the way west to the river."*

"Okay, give Sam back her phone, and tell her to stay airborne for the moment," she switched phones. "Ian, are you on the line?"

"Ten-four Sal, what do you need?"

"You and McNabb go west, past the rig. Doesn't sound like there's any cover there, so pull off the road and make like tourists doing a driver change or trying to find your passports or something to kill time. You'll be in full view of the subject group. Webb and I need to evacuate the business next door to the takedown site without making it look like that's what we're doing.

"Then when Rick and I are ready to move, we'll get you guys to make a U-turn and roll into the parking lot to bracket them."

"Ten-four. We're coming into town just behind the cube van that's on your tail."

Sally switched phones again. "Sam, when we are ready down here, we'll get you to land the airborne troops, but don't park within gunshot range of the bad guys. Remember your Post Apocalyptic Vow. Your man was adamant about that during one of our recent meetings."

"Roger that, Sally. Looks like a stiff west wind down there, so I can make an easy short-field landing and put the guys close to the action. Then I'll taxi a few hundred metres more to the west."

"Thanks Sam … and everyone else, remember, this is a high-risk takedown. In fact, extra high risk without a proper recon and briefing. Remember your training, keep your partner in view and keep this call connected for now since we don't have enough compatible comm sets to go between us."

She reached for her seatbelt release as Webb wheeled into the railroad museum parking lot and pulled close to the east wall of the repair garage, out of sight of the OSL crew. The two of them entered the shop through a door marked "Employees Only" and found themselves in the parts department. Aldridge flashed her badge at the first two people they encountered: a middle-aged man in clean blue coveralls and a young woman dressed in casual office attire. The woman was busy searching an online auto parts catalogue. The man was unpacking a case of oil filters.

"Good afternoon, folks, I'm Detective Aldridge, this is Conservation Officer Webb. We need you to evacuate the premises right away so that we can apprehend an armed group that has gathered around an eighteen-wheeler in your far parking lot. Is one of you the owner or manager?" she asked.

"Yes, I'm the owner, ma'am," came from the man.

"How many people are in the building right now?"

As Webb headed into the repair bays, the man answered, "Five of us and two customers."

"Okay, we need everyone to leave quietly, without making it look like a mass exodus. The last thing we want is for the fellows out there to get excited. Can you get all your people together and maybe walk them over to the museum?"

"It's closed at this time of year, Detective."

Rick Webb gathered the three mechanics in the service bays and two customers from the waiting area at the parts counter in time to hear the last bit.

"Is that school bus running?" Webb asked, looking over his shoulder at a modern twenty-passenger unit with tinted windows.

"I just brought it in to do a six-month brake inspection," said one mechanic.

"Is it roadworthy?"

"Runs great. It just needs recertification, is all."

"Okay. Everyone on the bus," he told the group. "Go for a long coffee break somewhere downtown."

"You heard the officer," said the owner. "Let's go."

"Good call, Rick," Aldridge said as the school bus backed out of the bay and the owner ran down the overhead door. "Now, I'll call in the airborne troops and you get Rob and Ian moving."

As soon as Webb gave the go-ahead over the phone, McNabb did a snappy bootleg turn and headed for the parking lot. He hesitated just short of the entrance and waited until the Turbo Beaver passed low overtop of the Kenworth before he drove into the parking lot. He stopped the Ram thirty metres from the rig. The pickup was angled forty-five degrees from the front of the road tractor with a clear view of the driver's side and the front of the rig. The OSL people were still looking up at the low flying bush plane. None appeared to connect the aircraft's appearance with impending trouble.

Not until Selkirk shouted, "Police … Freeze!" did any of the bad guys react to the situation. Their attention left the Beaver and snapped toward him.

"And that goes *double* for us," Sergeant Aldridge barked from the back of the OSL trailer where she and Webb stood for cover. McNabb and Selkirk stood behind the open doors of the pickup. All four officers had their guns drawn. They knew these characters were armed. How heavily armed, they had yet to discover.

Chapter 47

"Hands on top of your head," Aldridge ordered.

McNabb didn't wait for them to comply. He left the cover of the Ram to get eyes on the far side of the transport. He could see a pair of legs moving between the trailer and the Silverado. He should have kept his full attention on that pair of legs, but he was also watching the Beaver, praying that Sam would taxi out of gunshot range.

Unfortunately, his divided attention cost him. As he advanced, he slipped on a sloped patch of ice that he should have noticed and he went down hard. He cursed his hard-soled work boots as he fell. Hard rubber on ice — poor traction.

He landed on his back and lost his grip on his pistol. It skittered several metres away from him toward the front of the Kenworth. He was still more than twenty metres from the rig and never got to see who was on the other side.

Nobody moved. Not for a moment. Not until Kyle Roach released the parking brakes and dropped the Kenworth's transmission into drive. Just running at an idle, the big truck began to roll slowly toward the fallen officer. At the same instant, Jason Mead, who was on the far side of the rig, opened a storage bin beneath the sleeper cab and pulled out one of the AR-15 rifles they'd bought in Regina. He slid it under the tractor on the ice to where Willie Eardley was still crouched — still loosening lug nuts and not yet halfway done the first wheel.

As Willie snatched up the rifle, he swung it toward Selkirk, who saw it coming. Before Willie got his finger inside the trigger guard, the detective commanded him to drop the gun. The swing continued and the finger moved to the trigger. Selkirk saw it, fired three rounds at him. Willie went down — dead.

At the same time, Raymond Conn pulled a Colt .45 semi-automatic pistol from his belt and dived under the trailer, snapping off two rounds toward the back, in the direction of Webb and Aldridge. The two officers had already taken cover behind the back wheels, crawling forward to keep pace with the rolling rig. The heavy mudflaps took the hits and did some serious dancing, but neither officer was hit.

Having broken the OSL gang out of their momentary trance, Roach stopped the transport again and grabbed the sawed-off shotgun from between the front seats. But he stayed inside. He preferred the high vantage point from the cab.

Mead pulled the second rifle out of the bin and jumped up into the bed of the Silverado for better cover. He fired a few quick rounds under the transport, toward where he assumed Selkirk and McNabb were standing. Like McNabb, he had seen legs over there. But Selkirk had already rushed to take cover behind the Ram when he saw the driver's side window on the Kenworth opening and the double barrels of the 12-gauge shotgun point in his direction. It went off just as he ducked low behind the tailgate of the pickup.

When Zack had sawn the barrels short, he'd intended to use it at very close range — mano a mano. But it was way too short for the shot Roach had taken. As a result, the heavy buckshot pellets in the cartridge spread in a wide pattern across the parking lot. Two hit the Ram, causing minor body damage. Dimples only. None hit Selkirk. The second blast followed in less than a heartbeat but had no more effect than the first shot, other than chipping the pickup's windshield in one corner.

Selkirk popped up from behind the tailgate and began firing 9 mm rounds at the Kenworth while Roach stopped to reload the shotgun. He had only two rounds for each reload. The detective had seventeen. But Roach had lowered the air-ride seat and ducked down out of sight, and Selkirk's rounds did not penetrate the tractor's door. Raymond had modified the cab several years earlier with steel plates inside each door. It was by no means an armoured truck — it was simply intended to stop small calibre rounds. It was doing exactly that.

Less than two hundred metres west, Sam brought the Turbo Beaver to a hurried stop. The reverse thrust of the propeller threw up a blizzard of soft snow. CO Birks and Constable Ho simultaneously leapt out on opposite sides of the plane and ran, half-crouched, toward the action. The wind-blown cloud of snow stirred up by the Beaver followed them and provided some cover as they hurried toward the protection of the snowbank at the near edge of the parking lot.

As soon as Sam heard the shooting, she abandoned the idea of moving the plane farther away. Instead, she shut off the fuel and master power switch to kill the engine and dived over the seats to get to the rifle case while the turbine was still winding down. She didn't know what to expect, but she and McNabb had experienced enough life-threatening challenges together that she wanted to be prepared for anything.

With the 30-06 semi-automatic hunting rifle in hand, she climbed down from the aircraft and moved back to the tail. She leaned forward and rested her elbows on the tailplane. Even without looking through the rifle scope, she could see that the situation in the parking lot was in turmoil, but there were no immediate safe targets available. She snapped the first of her two loaded magazines into the rifle. Five rounds in each mag. She dumped the remaining ten rounds from a box of shells into her parka pocket while she waited. Shooting at people wasn't her intent. It wasn't in her DNA — not even shooting at dangerous criminals. But she was a deadly accurate shot, and given the chance, could cause enough distraction to keep at least one of the bad guys pinned down.

Birks and Ho took cover behind the frozen snowbank at the near end of the parking lot. They were crouched between Sam and the gap between the Silverado and the Kenworth. The two officers appeared to be urging McNabb to join them.

Rob would have loved to be able to do that, but by lying on his side where he'd retrieved his pistol, the big rig kept him out of Jason Mead's line of fire and the front wheel provided partial cover from Raymond Conn. If he moved to join Birks and Ho, his route to the snowbank would be fully exposed to the AR-15 and possibly to Conn's pistol as well.

Instead, while he lay there, he finally saw an opportunity to contribute something to the fight. Mead poked his head above the bed of the pickup several times and turned his attention to fire at Webb who was crouched behind the rear tires of the transport trailer. McNabb got to his knees, then stood, crouched, and raised his pistol to shoot.

Conn was lying under the trailer between the Kenworth's back wheels and was trying to get a clear shot at Sergeant Aldridge. As he loaded a fresh magazine into his pistol, he glanced behind him, toward the front. He was just in time to see McNabb crawl forward and get to his feet, about to take a shot at Mead. Conn fired a quick single round at the game warden before turning his attention back to Aldridge.

"Robbie!" Sam saw McNabb slammed backward by the shot and go down.

Chapter 48

The pilot nearly dropped the rifle to run to her man. Nearly, but not quite. Instead, with a lump in her throat and tears in her eyes, she raised the rifle, determined to make someone pay. If she knew who had fired the shot that hit him, she might have made an exception to her rule about not shooting even a bad guy. But she didn't know, so that wasn't going to happen.

She ran a gloved hand across her face to wipe her eyes dry, then peered through the rifle scope. Her first round went through the windshield of the Silverado. Whoever had been shooting from there needed to be subdued. She placed the bullet through the windshield at the exact point of the rear-view mirror mount.

The bullet hit the windshield and drove the wrecked mirror through the back window. A hailstorm of broken glass and hardware raked the raised fibreglass tonneau cover that Jason Mead was sheltering behind and under. It made a tremendous racket. Hitting the cover at such a shallow angle, it didn't penetrate, but Mead dropped to his knees then lay on the bed of tools and scrap lumber, not knowing if the next round might pierce the tonneau and hit him.

At the same time, Kyle Roach peeked through the Kenworth's windshield and saw the downed game warden, still in front of the truck. The guy still appeared to be moving, so he dropped the transmission in drive once again, and while keeping his head below the windows, he began to roll the truck toward the prone body of McNabb.

With the snowbank obstructing her view, Sam couldn't see Rob; had no idea how badly injured he was, or if he was even still alive. But when the truck started to roll forward, she knew she had to stop it. What she *didn't* know was, where the most vulnerable parts were positioned under the hood of a highway tractor, so she fired a barrage across the front of the grill. Each round was spaced a uniform distance apart.

The radiator, air conditioning condenser and transmission cooling coils were punctured with the first three rounds, but those wouldn't disable the rig right away. She had one round remaining in the first magazine. She adjusted her aim a few inches to the right and fired again then switched mags.

Rickie Ho realized what Sam was trying to do and tapped Birks on the shoulder. "Pour covering fire into the pickup." As soon as Birks opened up on the Silverado's grill and windshield, Ho scrambled over the snowbank. He stayed low and scrambled to where McNabb lay gasping. Sam's last rounds were whizzing just yards away, above and to his right, but looking at the pattern she was making, he was confident that he would not be hit.

Sam fired again, and when her next round hit the Kenworth, the diesel died instantly. She had hit the fuel injection pump. But the transport continued to coast forward, still at a crawl — now silently — ever closer to Rob McNabb. When Ho reached him, McNabb couldn't talk, but pointed to his chest, and then at the snowbank. There was no blood. Under his civilian clothes, he wore his body armour. But the shot had left him badly winded, disabled by the hit. He'd been hit right over his solar plexus, a crucial nerve centre in the body.

The constable grabbed Rob's parka by the hood and dragged him back toward the snowbank, meanwhile, adding his own 9 mm barrage to the engine compartment and cab of the Kenworth. With all the shooting, it sounded like a war zone. Raymond Conn got a snapshot off at Constable Ho. His arm was hit by Conn's rushed shot, and it took him a few seconds to realize his coat was in worse shape than he was. The bullet just grazed his upper arm. With no further thought to his own pain, he grabbed McNabb's hood again and pulled him several more feet before losing traction and falling on the ice himself.

Ian Selkirk took advantage of Sam's barrage to edge out from behind the Ram and begin pouring his next seventeen-round magazine into the Kenworth's rear tires near where Raymond Conn was sheltering. And he had his second spare mag clenched between his teeth ready for a seamless reload.

Webb ducked out from his place behind the OSL trailer and began to pour rounds into the back of the Silverado. He knew that one of the bad guys was hiding there, so he put his first shot through the far side of the tailgate and placed each subsequent round three inches to the left of the last one.

Jason Mead saw the progression of new holes in the sheet metal creeping ever closer to him as the 9 mm bullets broke through. His magazine was empty, and he'd left his other spares in the Kenworth, so he couldn't return fire. He was done, so he threw the AR-15 over the side of the pickup bed and raised both hands over the side. Webb held his fire but remained ready to shoot again if the guy in the pickup changed his mind.

The transport was still rolling ahead. Raymond Conn was about to try another shot at Constable Ho but found himself suddenly exposed. His cover between the back wheels of the tractor had moved on. Sgt. Aldridge saw him looking at her and she aimed straight for his eyes. "Drop it!" she yelled.

Whether or not he heard, over the melee, she couldn't tell, but it was obvious that he knew he'd never get to shift his aim back to her again before she shot. He dropped the Colt on the ice. And knowing that she wouldn't be satisfied with it lying just six inches from his hand, he used his other hand to slide the gun toward her, then raised his hands.

The Kenworth kept rolling. One front wheel was about to roll over McNabb's right knee when the truck suddenly stopped. The front tires of the trailer had come up against the boards that Conn and Roach had laid down to raise the tractor's rear tires. The boards almost dislodged, but the rig rocked backward, and they held in place. The truck rocked eerily back and forth several more times but remained stopped. And the shooting stopped too. Almost all of it at the same time. The silence was deafening.

Selkirk advanced on the cab and ordered Kyle Roach out. The driver dropped the empty shotgun out the open window and climbed down from the cab to surrender. The detective got him handcuffed as Aldridge ordered Conn out from under the trailer and placed him under arrest as well. A moment later, Webb led Jason Mead around the back of the trailer to join the other perps.

With the shooting suddenly over, Sam, in tears, laid the rifle on the Beaver's tailplane and ran the two hundred metres through knee deep snow toward where Rob lay. As she got closer, she realized that Birks and Ho were bent over working on him. He must be alive, but she was still terrified, not knowing how badly injured he might be. When she got close and scrambled over the snowbank, she didn't see any blood on his clothes or on the ground. Thank God for that.

Even wearing his Kevlar vest, the hit to his solar plexus had totally immobilized him, but by the time she knelt beside him, he was beginning to take shallow breaths.

"Now I have an idea how you felt that time, Sam," he

managed to gasp.

"Robbie McNabb, what about our vows?"

"What, you want to get married again?" He began to chuckle but held his hand to his chest and winced as he struggled to regain control of his breathing. "After all I put you through? Here, help me up."

"Screw that, Flyboy! You lie there until the paramedics arrive." As angry as she sounded, she knelt beside him on the ice and hugged him and shed tears of relief.

Ricky Ho and Riley Birks left them and shuffled across the ice to join the others. Birks went looking for a first aid kit. Ricky Ho's arm was leaking red stuff. His coat sleeve was wet with his own blood. And since Selkirk, Webb and Aldridge all had live prisoners to guard, Ho went to verify that Willie Eardley was truly deceased. He took the opportunity to put cuffs on him too. Standard operating procedure since the Waco, Texas massacre, where bad guys, thought to be dead, still came up shooting.

Two of the police cruisers that had been up at the original takedown site near Dryden finally caught up with them and rolled up in time to take charge of the scene. After the shootout, and with one man dead and two of the good guys injured, the original takedown team had to step aside for others to investigate. The staff sergeant was shaking his head as he got out of the first cruiser.

"Holy *shit*," he said as he walked around the bullet-riddled trucks. "Looks like we just missed seeing Riggs and Murtaugh filming a Lethal Weapon sequel."

Chapter 49

The constable assigned to watch Cheney's brother-in-law's Cessna 185 did a commendable job of watching the wrong aircraft. A simple miscommunication had him watching over a bird the same colour, with almost the same registration — but the letters were inverted. No one showed up at the aircraft registered as CF-FTW. So, when Derek Cheney and Jim Wright arrived, they loaded Cheney's luggage into CF-WTF and prepared to leave. Wright's plane happened to be parked on the opposite side of the busy airfield.

The four unmarked police vehicles that had been tailing Cheney had been delayed by a car wreck that blocked their exit from Highway 404 and they'd had to continue to the next exit north before doubling back. They converged on the airport just as the Cessna was taxiing toward the southeast end of the main runway.

When they discovered the registration SNAFU, Bea, who was riding with two plain clothes constables, on a jump seat in the back of the carpet cleaning van, phoned the boss to ask him to contact the airport and shut down the runways. The boss got back to her immediately and said his call had been put on hold. "You are on your own. Get the son-of-a-bitch, but don't cause any collateral damage. There's a lot of expensive equipment parked there."

"Light up your bubble, boys," Bea told her team, "and get us across to that plane before it takes off." The constable on the passenger side pulled a mini-light bar from under his seat. He turned it on as he leaned out the window and stuck it on the roof. The other three cars followed suit and Bea told the passenger to radio the other units. "We'll run down the taxiway behind him. Get the other cars to parallel us, three abreast down the runway ... and go like bats from hell."

The Cessna arrived at the end of the taxiway and rounded the corner, ready to pull out onto the runway once the pilot, looking to his left, checked for incoming aircraft. The tower hadn't yet given him the go-ahead. But at that moment, Derek Cheney was looking the other way. He was alarmed to see three cars showing emergency lights, racing toward them down the runway.

"Shit Jim, get her airborne *right now*!

Jim took one look. "Ah, *fuck*. It's too late Derek! We'll meet them before we reach airspeed."

Less than twenty seconds later, the four vehicles converged on the Cessna. Bea's carpet cleaning van pulled up right behind it and the other three, still inline abreast, blocked the runway. Bea and the passenger ran from the van, pistols and badges on full display as they rushed to either side of the Cessna.

While the runway itself was blocked, the ground to the far side of the runway was wide open. Beyond that lay a long level stretch of dried grass ... the snow had all melted the previous week. Wright opened the throttle.

"Hang on Derek, I'll take off on the grass, but it might be a bit rough." But even before he let off the brakes to begin the takeoff roll, he felt the plane settle on his left side. He looked out the window to see a stocky, middle-aged woman hanging on to the outer end of the port wing strut. She had one arm hooked over the strut and her free hand was pointing a Glock 17 pistol directly at him.

Even if she hadn't had the pistol, he wouldn't be able to take off. With such an imbalanced load, the wing on the unweighted side of the plane would reach airspeed much sooner than the side with the woman hanging on to it, and the wingtip on the side with the extra weight would drop to the ground. Not only hard on the woman, but a guaranteed wreck too.

"Sorry Derek. No can do." James Wright pulled the throttle back to an idle and killed the engine.

"Shit," Cheney cursed. "I never would have suspected that woman." Which was exactly why she had been chosen as the plant inside his organization.

"Out you get, fellas," Bea commanded. "Derek Cheney, you are under arrest for assault and forcible confinement for starters. But don't worry, the list is much longer than that.

"James Wright, you too, are under arrest for the same charge as an accessory after the fact." She read them both the police caution, then to the carpet cleaning crew, "Take them away, boys."

The men were handcuffed, searched, and taken into custody. The uniformed officer who had been watching the wrong plane showed up in a city cruiser with a cage. Cheney and his brother-in-law were put inside and taken downtown to be processed.

One of the tailing team drivers was a pilot. He fired up the engine and taxied the Cessna to a secure government parking apron where it was searched for evidence. The briefcase full of money was the most interesting find. But there was also an aircraft maintenance log that showed the plane was almost a year overdue for renewal of its Certificate of Airworthiness. Nothing to do with Derek Cheney's activities, but possible leverage for the purpose of loosening Mr. Wright's tongue when questioned about his brother-in-law's unlawful business practices.

Chapter 50

1610 – Rainy River

The takedown site was marked off with crime scene tape, and two constables were parked in front to secure the area while they waited for a crime scene unit to arrive.

McNabb had been checked over by paramedics, and although he'd sustained an ugly bruise that was tender beyond belief, he was declared to be of sound body. In fact, he insisted on it. He was feeling a little left out, in that he was the only one of the good guys who didn't fire a single shot. He felt that maybe he'd let the team down.

Constable Ho had his wound dressed and patched up. He hadn't lost much blood. It just looked bad the way the material in his parka acted as a wick, spreading the blood stain in dramatic fashion. Just a scratch, he claimed.

Raymond Conn, Kyle Roach and Jason Mead were locked in the cells at the back of the local police detachment and the good guys were sitting around the squad room, taking their turns giving their statements to the officers who had arrived right after the shooting had stopped.

The local staff sergeant was grilling Samantha Williams in his office. He was old school. One of the dwindling number of members of the old boys' club — from an era when cops were men and women belonged at home raising children. He wasn't conducting an interview to take a statement. The man was upset that a civilian — a woman at that, untrained in police tactics — had the temerity to fire multiple high-powered rifle rounds in his community during a police takedown. Fair enough that he should be concerned about public safety, but he was entirely unprofessional in his approach. Most of all, his nose was out of joint because his small detachment wasn't invited to the fight. But it was the Natural Resources pilot who was taking the heat.

Sam felt like a child being subjected to an angry school principal's scorn. She'd been there as a kid. The staff sergeant was a big man. Tall and stocky, he stood and looked down at Sam who was sitting in a straight-backed chair. He was truly intimidating. All he lacked was the principal's leather strap.

McNabb could hear it all going on through the closed door. He was getting angrier by the minute. Sam shouldn't be getting chewed out for trying to save his life. He was at the point of boiling over and was about to get up and head to Sam's defence, but Sally Aldridge put a restraining hand on him. She could hear Sam giving back as good as she got.

"I'll get this, in a minute, Rob. I think Sam has got his measure now. Listen."

—

"Well, you weren't there, *Staff* Sergeant." Sam spit out his rank with particular venom. She was livid. "*If* you had been there, you would have seen an officer go down in front of a fifty-thousand-pound transport truck whose driver was obviously intending to run over him. Would you have stood there with your hands in your pockets? Even as old as you appear, I think even you would have taken action too.

"If I had wanted to shoot the driver, I would have hit him

279

with my first shot! What I aimed to do, was kill the engine. Which I did. But I've never seen under the hood of a Kenworth before, so it took me five rounds to hit something vital. Yes, I kept count. And when the diesel quit, *I ceased firing.*"

"Yes, but you've already admitted that the man down was your husband. At that point you were angry, acting out of revenge, not for the good of anyone's health."

"*Damned right I was pissed off....*"

"And *furthermore*, you saw another officer go over the snowbank to help. You could have stopped firing then. You put him in danger of getting hit by friendly fire."

"On the contrary. Constable Ho called for covering fire from CO Birks. He moved out *between* Birks's fire and mine. But I saw Ho take a round from the guy under the transport and go down. So that meant there were two officers in danger of being run over by the rig. It didn't matter who it was. I *might* have even acted to save your life if it had been you who'd gone down, *Sir.*" Without waiting either for his reply or his permission, she stood up and walked out of his office — fuming. Totally in character with the flaming red hair.

The staff sergeant was standing there with his mouth open when Sally Aldridge entered, closed the door and quietly stood in front of his desk.

"Something you should know, Sir: Several years ago, Samantha Williams received a provincial commendation for saving a group of school children by taking that very same action against a speeding pickup truck." She laid a fresh printout of the commendation on the man's desk and left as quietly as she had entered. Nothing more was said.

—

1715 — Rainy River takedown location

It was getting dark by the time the group left the police detachment. They were under orders to overnight in Fort Frances so they could be interviewed by the Provincial Special Investigations Unit in the morning. Everyone got a lift back to the takedown site where a CSI team had just finished setting up.

With floodlights covering every angle, it did look like a movie set. The Ram, a minor victim of gunfire, had to stay, but McNabb and Selkirk were permitted to take their personal gear with them. The Turbo Beaver and the Pathfinder were cleared to leave. Rob went with Sam and the others piled into the SUV.

Sam used the Beaver's landing lights to augment the fading daylight as she got the aircraft airborne. When unmarked vent pipes from an unmarked natural gas pipeline poked through the snow in the Beaver's path, she had to haul back on the control column to force an early takeoff just seconds before the aircraft would have lifted off on its own.

"*That* could have hurt," she gasped. "Haven't seen a single pipeline sign to warn us, either." She flew the remaining half kilometre to the river and found one lonely warning sign — facing the Minnesota side. "Lot of help that one is," she shook her head, then turned east.

Twenty minutes later they touched down at the Fort Frances airport. A taxi carried them to the Super 8 in town where accommodations had been arranged for everyone.

"Ah, finally. Just the two of us. A night together in a hotel, Sam. Just like being in Niagara Falls. You did say you wanted to renew our vows."

"Not right now, McNabb." She gave his bruised chest a poke that made him gasp. "I'm still pissed off at the way that guy chewed me out."

281

"Sally and I thought you did a great job backing him down, sweetie. His door isn't soundproof."

"Yeah, well I'm still pissed. What have you got in that bag to drink?"

"Not a drop. But Boston Pizza is right next door. After I soak my tortured body in a hot bath for half an hour, let's walk over and get a table for the gang and order pizza and a beer … or two. Government's buying." She climbed into the tub with him, and they stayed there until the water began to cool.

—

At Boston Pizza, dinner with the rest of the team was a somewhat subdued celebration. They had brought down the OSL team, both here in northwestern Ontario and in Toronto, but they had fallen far short of the intended goal. There'd be no drugs or ivory to show for their lengthy and expensive investigation.

Tomorrow they'd all be grilled by the provincial Special Investigations Unit, called in whenever someone died or was injured during an interaction with police. Aldridge would probably be hauled up on the carpet for her hasty takedown and would take a licking for involving four Natural Resources employees in the shootout.

Next week, the load of fur would be shipped to North Bay and Webb would go there to put together that case while the police returned to Toronto to lick their wounds and lay what charges they could against OSL and its employees. Williams and McNabb would return north and resume their regular duties.

Part 2

Chapter 51

Saturday, February 8, 0730 – Moosonee

Rob McNabb woke to his phone vibrating on the bedside table. He had remembered to turn off the ringer for once. Following ten days of non-stop action away from home, this was going to be a sleep-in morning.

Except, that plan was about to crash. He fumbled with the phone. Couldn't find the connect button for a moment, with his eyelids still glued shut.

"Yeah?" he managed, only half-awake. Sam stirred beside him

"Good morning, Rob," Detective Sergeant Sally Aldridge's cheerful voice brought him up to the next stage of wakefulness. "Got a job to go on if you are interested."

"Jeez Sal, we just got back from Fort Frances last night. I thought this was going to be a long weekend. Isn't it Family Day or something like that?"

"That's two weeks from now, buddy. Yesterday, while we were waiting to give our statements, you told me that you find conducting interviews to be more difficult than collecting physical evidence … which I hear you excel at. So, I'm offering you a training experience you won't want to turn down."

Sam was awake now. McNabb put his phone on speaker. "Okay, what's the catch? Can't I just conduct my interviews like the Rainy River staff sergeant?" Sam gave him a poke, shaking her head at the memory. She left him momentarily speechless — she'd poked his solar plexus again.

"Yeah right," Aldridge continued, laughing at the memory. "How to win friends and influence people. No, there's no catch, Rob. Our entire takedown team at the Toronto end got exposed to COVID. They're all at home isolating and frantically shoving test swabs up their noses. But Mr. Cheney is in jail and the guy needs to be interviewed. He's impatient to make bail. And there's a bunch of physical evidence to go through too, and Ian and I are on our own. You are welcome to join us, and maybe hone your skills. I'm a pretty good teacher. And honestly, we're in desperate need of help digesting the evidence."

He looked over at Sam who was lying on her side looking at him. "Go for it, Robbie. She's right. You've always said you don't feel totally confident interviewing bad guys. Well, those guys are among the worst."

"When do you want me?" He had his mind set on Monday.

"The air service is sending the Beechcraft King Air up to get you. Be at the airport at ten o'clock."

"Oh, crap. No rest for the…." He failed to come up with a substitute word as he rolled out of bed.

—

1015 – Moosonee airport

When McNabb made his way up the airstair into the government's executive aircraft, the first person he saw after being greeted by the pilot was Detective Sergeant Sally Aldridge.

She could read the surprise on his face.

"Rob, we're running on a tight timeline … cranky defence lawyer issues. So I thought I'd brief you on the fly, so to speak. We really need to hit the ground running."

"Could you skip the part about hitting the ground? I'm not entirely comfortable with the image, seeing as how you are going to give me this briefing at thirty thousand feet."

"Point taken, Flyboy," Aldridge paused and chuckled. "I also invited Rick Webb to join us … we do make a good team … but he tells me he just got word of a transfer and a promotion. He and his wife are going to be looking at housing for a few days in Sault Ste. Marie before heading to North Bay to deal with the seized furs."

"The Soo job. I didn't even know he'd bid on that one."

"Never mentioned it to me either in all the hours we spent on the road together. So, back to business. Your transport truckload of furs is on its way to North Bay in the care of a commercial carrier. The money-bearing truck tires were flown down with us in the police Twin Otter yesterday.

"Mr. Conn and his surviving road warriors are being detained in Fort Frances, since that's where they held their last stand. There's more than enough to hold them in custody on just the shootout alone. Detectives out there have been fully briefed on events leading up to their arrest and they will coordinate with us after completing the interviews up there.

"The bullet-riddled transport and Conn's pickup are being retained as evidence there as well and will be laid to rest or sold for parts after we close the case. I'm told both vehicles are write offs."

"Hey, don't blame me. I didn't put a scratch on them."

"Still feeling left out, eh? By the way, did you bring any civilian clothes? One of the defence lawyers cries 'intimidation' any time one of his clients is interviewed by a uniformed officer … especially one wearing a pistol."

"Yes, jacket and tie … decent casual. My staff sergeant already warned me. But I wanted to look professional in uniform when I entered your headquarters."

"It's Saturday, Rob, and we are set up at an offsite facility. No doubt the cleaners will be impressed."

Chapter 52

The Beechcraft executive plane's cabin was impressive, done up in the manner of an office, but not fancy like a rich guy's toy. There was a separate cabin at the back. A small office, or a sleeping compartment for overworked cabinet ministers maybe. McNabb didn't know what it was, and there was no time to explore — the twin turbines stayed running during the brief stop to pick him up and Aldridge was already fastening her seatbelt.

"Okay," she began as the aircraft taxied toward the runway. "So, you already know a lot of what the OSL gang was trying to accomplish before their ship failed to come in." She handed him a three-page case summary. "The owner and boss of the company is Derek Cheney. He's built much like Raymond Conn, only a couple sizes larger. Lots of tattoos and an arrogant attitude ... at least with the police personnel he's dealt with so far. But Bea, our undercover operative, said that other than some unpredictable mood swings, he was an acceptable boss. Most of the time.

"The legitimate side of the business is ... or was ... brokering and dispatching freight, mostly for independent truck owner/operators. But he played his cards close to his chest when it came to the drugs and more recently, the ivory side of his enterprise.

"We were originally alerted to his west coast drug purchases by a disgruntled employee a little over two years ago.

The guy was an ex-con who was enjoying his freedom so much that he didn't want to do time again. We offered him immunity in exchange for his cooperation. Unfortunately, we mismanaged the situation and he disappeared just as we were getting the ball rolling on our investigation."

"Mismanaged?" McNabb asked.

"We fucked up, would be the more correct terminology. We let the guy get killed. Some of us still have carpet burns resulting from visits to the commissioner's office.

"That aside, at around the same time, Cheney advertised for a dispatcher to handle the freight brokering side of the business. Enter Bea. She's a senior detective from Thunder Bay closing in on retirement. She had done some undercover work years ago. And in civilian life before going into policing, had done exactly that same job, dispatching for a trucking company. Who would suspect a matronly woman of being an undercover agent?"

"So, she's the one who was feeding us information while we were on the road?" McNabb asked.

"Yes, but by then, she wasn't sure if her cover would hold. Cheney was getting cranky about even the smallest problems, and he was smarting after his showpiece wife left him for her lover last Thanksgiving.

"For the last couple of weeks, he had become short-fused and paranoid. Then, to make things worse, the blockade running stunt pulled by his road crew in Saskatchewan left him thoroughly pissed off. Bea figured that any hint of outside interference could blow her cover. And the disappearance of the original informant was still fresh in our minds. That's one of the reasons we were making life so difficult for you guys those first three days on the road."

"Is he running a drug trafficking network, then?"

"That's where we've struck out so far. He didn't appear to have anything to do with the drugs after the truck returned to Ontario. Might have just been a mule, but we're pretty sure that's not the case. Bea picked up a lot of useful intel during her undercover time, and she learned that a few previous loads also included a quantity of ivory with the drugs.

We believe the load picked up by the U.S. Coasties was the second half of his December order. But we don't know that ivory was on the menu on every west coast trip. Cheney was totally lips sealed when it came to that side of the business. After a run to the coast, the truck would show up in the yard, all washed and waxed … and empty. Left him looking squeaky clean. On the surface.

"So, the next stage of our plan kind of evolved while you and Rick were with us on the road following his people back west. By allowing them to take back the rig, we had already set them up to make the buy on the coast. That was where we originally planned to take the guys down. But that changed when our commissioner and the RCMP liaison superintendent, plus several chiefs of police in southern Ontario wanted to take the risk that we could stamp out the marketing end here while we had the fish on the line.

"I know … we led you guys to believe that the takedown was going to be in Vancouver, and you'd get to seize the truck there and bring it back. That *was* the plan for a couple of days, but under the revised plan, you guys were going to get to seize the Chinese ship with *its* new cargo of illegally exported furs and we would tail the truck back to Ontario, once more. We did have the approval of your chief to carry on, as long as you and Webb were willing. Of course, that plan got pooched when the ship drifted into U.S. waters."

"Hmm. You were willing to keep us in the dark? While

working a joint task force project as important as this? That really stinks! Especially when our chief told us that the police were taking us on as equal partners ... 'not as excess baggage' she told us." He paused, thinking quickly through his options before he spoke again.

"Take me back to Moosonee now, please." He was really steamed that he and Webb hadn't been told the whole story while they helped tail the OSL rig back out of Ontario toward the west coast.

"Honest, Rob, that pissed us off too. We all felt you guys should have been given the full picture, but it came from someone way above us. And no, not someone in your organization, or mine either. Some bean-counter deputy minister in a non-enforcement federal agency didn't think much of COs. He probably has a record in your system.

"He told our commissioner that he felt, and I quote, 'game wardens are just a bunch of glorified dog catchers,' and he ordered him to keep you two out of the loop, or he'd withhold the funding for this project. But I assure you, everyone on our team appreciated having you two guys work with us, and we were all pleased that you pitched in as if you'd been with us all along.

"And saving the best for last; when we were flying home yesterday, our superintendent told us the guy is no longer with that ministry.

"Now, I *can* take you back if that's what you want. You sure didn't deserve to be treated like that. But I'll tell you Rob, Ian and I really do need your help. Remember what I said to the RCMP corporal when he was trying to recruit you two. I would take you onto our team in a heartbeat. And that's the truth."

McNabb knew that screwed-up directives were often sent down from high levels in government, and if the directive hadn't come from either the provincial police or his own ministry, then he couldn't hold it against Aldridge and her people. "Okay, Sergeant, I'll take you at your word. Let's keep going. We've got work to do."

"Thanks Rob." Crisis averted. Aldridge was relieved. "Now, with the illegal fur export file still being open, you may want to probe Mr. Cheney for some answers. That might be a good subject to broach during our getting acquainted session with him.

"And for the main event, as short-handed as we may be, our mission is to determine the intended destination of the drugs … and the ivory … and pull on each of his loose threads to see what unravels. Even without whatever he was expecting to get off that freighter, there's got to be evidence of some kind, leading us to what he did with his previous shipments.

"For now, we've charged and cautioned him only for the assault and abduction of his secretary, so we will *not* discuss, or ask him any questions related to those charges. We need him to feel that things aren't as bad as they might seem … without actually telling him that."

Rob turned over his copy of the handout she'd given him and was drawing the beginnings of a link chart. Inside a circle he drew on the left-hand side of the page, he wrote "*Ocean Princess.*" He drew another circle to the right of it and named it "Cheney" and drew a line connecting the two. He drew lines to two more circles to the right of "Cheney." One above the other, they were labelled "drugs" and "ivory" respectively. The sergeant watched, saying nothing.

"Sorry, I know this is basic detective 101 stuff for you, but I like to visualize. I'm a hands-on guy. The link chart helps."

"We've got a great big whiteboard in our conference room, Rob. I'm hoping you'll get to draw a whole lot more circles on it before we're done."

"Okay, before we interview the guy, is there any chance I could look at his office? It's the visualization thing again."

"Before we do any interviews, the three of us have got a whole pile of evidence to go through. We'll probably all have blurred vision by the end of the day. His entire office is packed in boxes, now in our possession. Bea's team gathered it all at the task force HQ on the day of the takedown, and that was when they learned that there had been a probable COVID contact.

"Six sick dicks make for a big hole in our task force. The husband of one of the clerks developed symptoms that day, and of course he would have been contagious for several days before that. He's in an ICU right now and she has tested positive. So, the team is self-isolating and getting tested every couple of days."

"Why didn't the team leave the office set up the way they found it?"

"We're too short of bodies to secure the location, Rob. As messy as this makes it, the decision was made to secure everything in our own workspace."

The King Air landed at Toronto Island Airport an hour and forty-five minutes after leaving Moosonee. The two officers took the island ferry across the harbour to the Bathurst Street terminal and were driven to the task force headquarters in a waiting police shuttle.

Chapter 53

Detective Sergeant Aldridge punched a code into a keypad and they entered a conference room that had been rented in a downtown hotel. It had been purpose-built as a venue for events requiring extra-secure facilities. It fit the bill for a task force headquarters. Detective Constable Selkirk caught up with them just as they went through the door.

The room was large enough to hold a dinner event for almost fifty people. There were six round tables that would each seat eight bodies. They were arranged in two rows of three. Two long rectangular serving tables were placed against one wall. Three computers were set up on each of the serving tables with a landline telephone beside each desktop. The straight-backed dining chairs were stacked in one corner but there were half a dozen comfortable rolling office chairs scattered around the room.

"Sorry, Rob, it's baptism by fire," Sally told him. "Lunch is being delivered. We'll eat on the fly. Just don't spill anything on the evidence. When we pack it in for the day, we've got rooms here in the hotel. Each time we enter or leave this room, we sign the log."

Rob looked around — impressed, but also a little bewildered. "Where do we start, boss?"

Sally got them to give her a hand arranging five of the round tables in a circle around the sixth. She pointed at a stack of sealed cardboard boxes sitting inside the door. "Each box represents a different part of Cheney's office. Three for his desk, one for the walls and bookshelves and the wall safe. And one with all the contents of Raymond Conn's desk. The secretary's desk is boxed up too, but for now, after a cursory inspection, we don't expect to find anything she hasn't already told our people.

"Sort the items from each box on its respective table. Anything that looks even remotely like it could be evidence gets placed on the centre table. I'll mark it off into sections with masking tape.

"Rob, can you start with what was on top of his desk? Ian can start on the centre and right-hand drawers, and I'll take the left. The boxes are labelled. And when you come to the card that says, 'laptop computer,' Ian, Bea took that home with her. She is cataloguing everything that is on it, there. She'll email us the file when she's done. We also downloaded its hard drive onto a portable drive which you can access on any of the computers in here, but his files are a disorganized jumble. Better to wait for Bea's sorted version."

McNabb found the box containing everything that was taken from the top of Cheney's desk. After setting it on one of the round tables at the back of the room, he appropriated a coasting chair and a yellow pad of lined paper as well as a couple of pads of small pink sticky notes. Before returning to his worktable, he booted up the nearest PC for later use.

Everything from the box, he arranged on the table as if it were a desk. He stood for a moment and stared at the result. "Sally, were there pictures taken of the office before this stuff was touched?"

"Yeah. In ... just a sec ... ah ... this folder, Rob."

He leafed through a stack of several dozen glossy prints. Found three that included the desk and returned the others to the folder. Laying the prints out beside his simulated desktop, he reorganized several items. Most commonly or recently used items would probably be closest to Cheney. He ignored those to start with in favour of eliminating some of the least likely items first, beginning with a soup can filled with pencils and pens. He dumped the contents out on the table and found nothing of interest in or under the can. A coffee mug still had a quarter cup of cold sludge in it, and he held it high enough to see that there was nothing on the bottom.

There was a double tiered, In & Out tray. Several invoices to clients waited in the In tray and a stack of them, already signed by Cheney, sat in the Out tray. All the invoices appeared to relate to the legitimate side of the business, but he scrawled a question mark on a sticky note, slapped it on the top invoice and put them all on the evidence table. Just in case. A battle-worn stapler had no apparent evidentiary value. It had little value of any sort since McNabb couldn't get it to work.

An old-fashioned Rolodex caught his eye. That, some loose pencils and pens and the desktop blotter were the only items remaining. The blotter was covered in doodles and random numbers and dates. If any of it had any meaning for Cheney, it was Greek to McNabb. Another sticky note with a question mark — another item for the central table.

The Rolodex looked as if it had come from the 1950s or '60s. The tabs on many of the buff-coloured index cards were dog-eared and worn, and the once white contact cards had yellowed with age. McNabb raised his coaster chair all the way up and rolled it close to the table to examine the old-fashioned rotary contact list. He started with the first card he saw. It was probably the last address card that had been looked at.

Windham. An 800 number. Maybe reservations for the hotel chain. Cheney had possibly been planning his getaway. Rob confirmed that's what the number was with a quick phone call. He put a sticky note on that card.

He moved on and began to check each card that contained entries. Wing's, a Chinese restaurant. Then came the XYZ index card. Not one entry there. Not many names begin with the letter X. Even though there are names starting with Y and Z, apparently none of Cheney's contacts did.

Acme Tire Store came under A. So did Aunt Jane. A phone call there proved to be a restaurant — not a family member. The B section was empty. Conn, Raymond was the only card under C. There was no card for Captain Chang. That was disappointing.

He worked his way around the Rolodex wheel, finding business names and company employees. Several Asian names showed up — Dr. Hung, Dr. Soo, Nguyen, a grocer, and Lee, Jimmy. But the last name could just as easily not be.

When he got to O, there was a card with a phone number — an international number for somewhere — but no name. He scooted his chair over to the PC and pulled up a reverse phone directory that covered international numbers. It wasn't as simple as looking up a domestic number, but when he found a site, he entered the number. The area code was for Indonesia. It came back with a message "unidentified mobile." He looked across the room and waited a few seconds until Sally appeared to pause what she was doing.

"Alright if I call an unidentified international number, Sally? It's Indonesian."

"Sure, Rob. Don't identify yourself unnecessarily. Just be prepared to listen for a greeting, then hang up. But if it is appropriate, introduce yourself and add 'Detective' to your title.

Someone in that part of the world might not know what a conservation officer is. But everyone knows detectives."

He punched in the number. The phone rang six times with no pickup. Oops, middle of the night on that side of the world. Someone's going to be pissed. McNabb hoped it would go to voice mail — that could at least give him a name — but halfway through the seventh ring, someone picked up.

"*Hello?*" a male voice answered. North American English. Didn't sound half-asleep — or upset — just cautious.

"Hello," McNabb replied. This could go nowhere fast, he thought. Neither of us wants to ask who nor give anything away. But he took a stab at it. It *was* his call, after all. International number — maybe the ship's captain? "Yes, I'm trying to reach Captain Chang," who, Rob knew, was in custody. In North America.

"*And who, may I ask, is inquiring?*"

"This is Detective Conservation Officer Robert McNabb calling from Toronto. And to whom am I speaking?"

"*Special Agent John Mitchell in Seattle. I'm with the U.S. Fish and Wildlife Service.*"

Thank goodness, he'd found a fellow game warden. "I take it, Agent Mitchell, that you folks have a Captain Chang and some of his worldly possessions in your care?"

"*Yes, Officer McNabb. Between me and the Coast Guard we have the man himself and a whole shipload of goodies ... and a rusty sieve named Ocean Princess, which is long overdue for the scrapyard.*

"*I'm glad you called. We have been trying to determine who, in Canada, to send a copy of the inventory of his cargo. The two numbers we have for you folks keep going to voice mail.*"

"Probably the desks of the group that got sent home for a stretch of COVID isolation. I can give you an email address right now and you can use this phone number to contact us."

He gave Mitchell his own government email address and presumed the agent had caller ID on the captain's phone for the phone number.

"*Okay, McNabb. I'll send it immediately and give you a more secure number to call if you've got any questions after you've absorbed the list. We've got a lot of things to sort out between us. The captain isn't cooperating. Documentation is non-existent for some of the containers, and he won't tell us who those cans are destined for. Says it's none of his business … he just drops them on the dock when the receiving party comes up with the appropriate payment. You might have some answers at your end.*"

"We're looking for drugs and ivory, but goodness knows what else our bad boys might be into. We're literally just getting started here."

"*Okay, the document is on its way.*"

"Thanks Agent Mitchell, and you can call me Rob."

"*Ten-four, and I'm John.*"

"Later, John."

They disconnected and Rob opened his email account to wait for the incoming message. In the meantime, he coasted his chair back to the table he'd been working at and moved the Rolodex to the centre table, he pencilled "*Ocean Princess*" on a pink sticky note and attached it to the nameless card under the letter O.

Chapter 54

Ian Selkirk struck out with the contents of the centre and right-hand desk drawers. Aside from the card labelled "laptop computer," there was a pair of badly worn golf shoes, a quarter bottle of Canadian Club whiskey and a bottle of antacid — empty but for the last swallow — in the bottom drawer.

The top drawer contained a stack of old *Road and Track* magazines piled on top of as many issues of *Hustler*.

The centre drawer was a nest for pens, pencils, paper clips, a ruler and several sizes of sticky notes. There was also a framed 8X10 family picture, turned face down. It was a wedding picture of Cheney and his trophy ex-wife. And there was nothing between the layers inside the frame. One never knew what might be stashed between a picture and the carboard backing.

He moved on to sort through the box of things taken down from the office walls and was presently removing those pictures from their frames.

Aldridge had saddled herself with the left-hand drawer. There was just one drawer on that side, a drawer the height of a file cabinet drawer. It had contained file folders full of timesheets for all the OSL employees. She was sorting through the time sheets, looking for names of workers they hadn't yet encountered. Found several and added them to her section of the centre table. And the whole stack could end up being useful for verifying alibis — who was working on any given date.

Fortunately, they were filed in chronological order.

As soon as the email arrived from Seattle, McNabb sent the attachment to the printer. He made three copies, dropped them onto the centre table and picked up a burger, which was getting cold. He ate it without bothering to reheat it in the microwave.

"The ship's inventory is in, folks."

"Familiarize yourself with it first, Rob," Sally said, looking up from the timesheets for last May. "That way we don't all have to repeat the same learning curve. You can brief us on the highlights when you are done."

"Ten-four, boss," he said, and he began to read through the five-page printout. The *Ocean Princess* had been carrying sixteen containers, all twenty feet long or smaller, plus a number of crates and boxes stacked in the centre hold. She was built before containers became the common mode of moving goods, and forty-foot sea cans just didn't fit on her decks. On arrival at the Coast Guard facility, each container had been removed from the vessel and opened for inspection. The most shocking was listed first.

"Holy shit," Rob said, more to himself than to the others, but Ian heard him and noticed a pale, sick expression on his face. The container had housed twenty-four Asian girls and young women. They'd probably been told they were bound for a new life in America. In reality, some criminal organization in Canada was going to be missing its latest shipment of sex slaves.

The Coast Guard inspectors couldn't find any documentation aboard naming the receiving party. Surprisingly, the girls had all survived the trip, but some of them were in terrible health. Because *Ocean Princess* was days behind schedule, they had run out of their meagre food and water supplies long before being rescued.

Selkirk set down a landscape print he was dismantling and came over to look at what McNabb was reading. Rob shook his head and looked up at the detective. "That's how they brought Mae Ling into the country, Ian."

"I kind of gathered that, Rob. But she's safe with you and Sam now, and those girls will be taken care of too." He'd already picked up on McNabb's sensitivity about human trafficking any time he talked about his adopted daughter, Mae Ling.

"Yeah, but it shouldn't be happening at all. There should be an international crackdown on sex trafficking. Not just empty promises the politicians keep making."

"Limited resources Rob … just like us. Pretty cruddy excuse though, isn't it?" He patted McNabb's shoulder and paused beside him until Rob took a deep breath and nodded his thanks. Then he went back to what he called his art project, removing a poor-quality Lauren Harris print from its frame.

McNabb paused for a minute more before he resumed his perusal of the list of cargo from the *Ocean Princess*. The next four containers documented were loaded with cheap kitchen utensils bound for a nationwide discount store chain. Three more units were listed as containing suspected counterfeit designer handbags and shoes.

The next item on the cargo list caught McNabb's eye the moment he read the heading. It was another twenty-foot unit. Contents listed as 1127 kilograms of ivory. The coast guard folks had counted and weighed 146 elephant tusks. McNabb paused a moment, shaking his head as he contemplated the horrible deaths of seventy-three elephants. Murdered just to satisfy some perverted sense of human need.

When he returned to the cargo list, he saw that hidden under the tusks at the front of the container, they had found a package containing ten kilograms of heroin.

"Yeah, this is what we wanted to see, guys," Rob said as he scribbled some numbers in the margin of his copy of the list. Then he used the calculator on his phone to make a couple of quick calculations.

"Based on the latest black-market prices, it looks like about a million U.S. dollars split roughly 50/50 between heroin and ivory. I'm guessing the load of fur was to top up the nine hundred thousand hidden in the tires." Sally wandered over and looked at his work.

"Now you've done the easy part, Rob. That's a great first step. But we really need to tie it to our bad boys. I doubt there will be a label stuck on the container door saying, 'Please deliver this to Derek Cheney.' But somewhere there has to be something tying it to the man."

Ian came back over to look and asked, "Were there any notations other than names and addresses on the Rolodex cards, Rob?"

"Nope. Nothing that looked like any kind of a code, either."

"What else was on his desk?" Sally asked.

"Pencil holder, blotter, coffee mug, In and Out baskets, Speedy Auto Glass scratch pad, a bent stapler...."

Ian and Sally were already going over the desktop items as he spoke. Nothing immediately stood out for them until something caught Selkirk's eye. He gave McNabb a friendly swat across the head with a rolled-up copy of the cargo list.

"Robbie McNabb, you need a seeing eye dog, or reading glasses at the very least." He unrolled the printout, laid it down on the blotter and circled an alphanumerical string of four letters followed by six numbers. TCLU 296315. On a corner of the blotter, amidst a variety of doodling, he pointed to a like string of letters and numbers — the exact same letters and numbers and a date and question mark, "Feb 1?" circled beside it.

"Shipping container identification, Rob. It's a unique identifier. The only container in the world with that ID. And isn't February first about when the OSL team would have originally arrived out there … if they hadn't gotten jammed up in Regina?"

Sally looked relieved. Now they could tie the container of heroin and ivory from *Ocean Princess* to Cheney's operation. "You each get a gold star. Rob can polish his after he cleans his new glasses.

"In the meantime, call your contact at the U.S. Fish and Wildlife Service and see if he can send us a picture of the container, clearly showing the ID. Ian, you grab a couple shots of the blotter. One wide angle and one zoomed in on the ID string.

"Once we print all those off, I think we should go and introduce ourselves to Mr. Cheney."

"Is that a good idea, Sally?" Rob asked. "Before we're finished here? We still have no idea where he is delivering his treasures."

"Making that connection without help might be a long shot. Let's see how he responds to an introductory interview, Rob. He may well clam up, but on the other hand, being locked up all by himself in a cell for two days, he might be glad of the company. He might let something slip that gives it to us on a platter.

"But first, let's check in at reception and get settled in our rooms. I could use a shower and you need to change into civvies. We'll meet back in the lobby in half an hour."

Chapter 55

Ian Selkirk drove the three of them from the hotel to the holding facility in a rented minivan. While he drove, Aldridge gave McNabb a brief rundown on how they would conduct their first interview with Derek Cheney.

The man was waiting in a drab interview room when they walked in. He was handcuffed and wearing institutional orange coveralls, but he'd rolled up the sleeves to his biceps, making sure that his tough guy tattoos were on full display. At Aldridge's request, he had not been chained to the table. But there was a mean looking jailhouse constable standing outside the door.

Aldridge spoke first, hoping to set a conciliatory tone. "Sorry to keep you waiting, Mr. Cheney. I'm Detective Sergeant Sally Aldridge, this is Detective Constable Ian Selkirk … and that fellow is Detective Conservation Officer Rob McNabb." Rob was pleased that she had beefed up his title again. Like she had said earlier, everyone knows what a detective is.

Cheney just grunted in reply.

"We will be recording the interview so that no one can later claim that either party misunderstood the other. Do you understand?"

"Yeah," he growled.

"Before we get started, can we get you something to drink

… coffee, tea or a soft drink or water?" Sally asked.

"Nope. Let's get on with this fuckin' sideshow. I need to get out of here. Got stuff to do."

"Okay, these two have a few questions to ask about your westbound cargo. I'll be back shortly," she said. Three officials facing an unaccompanied defendant would be construed by a cranky defence lawyer as intimidation. They didn't need that. Instead, she let herself out of the room and joined the audio-video tech in the next room to watch the proceedings on a monitor. There was no one-way glass in the interview room.

"Derek … may we call you by your first name?" McNabb took the first turn.

"Whatever."

"So, I'm sure you are aware that we played tag with your transport load of furs for almost a week. West to east … then west again and back east once more." McNabb watched as Cheney came close to a smile and appeared to loosen up just a little. "Can I ask you about the source of all that warm fuzzy stuff your guys were hauling?"

"Came with the contents of a business I bought out."

"You bought the business and bought their inventory?"

"No, just bought the business … a mom-and-pop trucking company. After the old guy died, his widow put it up for sale. I bought it for the business name and for a Kenworth tractor that was an exact match for mine. When we went out to pick up the Kenny, the woman said I could take whatever was in their barn. She wanted the building emptied so she could sell the place.

"We went in to load a complete set of new tires for the rig that I'd seen there when we were still negotiating, and there was this big walk-in cooler, still running. Looked inside and there's this mountain of fur. I asked, and she said I could have it … said the fur was all bought legally … from legal trappers. Said the market was poor but she didn't have time to hang on to it until prices went up.

"There was way too much for my pickup, so we came back the next day with our rig and loaded the tires and the fur and some truck parts we found. We took a couple of pickup loads of junk to the dump for her too, and that was it. I had a buyer for the fur lined up in China, but you guys fucked that up for me."

"Derek, there were no export permits in the truck with the fur. Your drivers wouldn't tell the officers anything about the source of the load. And the name and address they gave for the purchaser, don't exist. Raw furs can't travel out of province, let alone to another country, without export permits."

"Huh!" Cheney flared up. "You have any idea how hard it is to get any kind of government permit during this fuckin' plague? My rig is still two months overdue for its licence renewal with the transportation ministry. They just said keep drivin' … It'll be along soon. Fuckin' pandemic shutdowns. Lazy fuckin' government employees is more like it. Pain in the fuckin' ass."

"That I can understand. My own pickup is waiting for its renewal too, but the export permits come from a different agency … one that's still open for business."

Selkirk took his turn. "Do you have a fur dealer's licence, Derek?"

"I'm not a fur dealer."

"You just said you were going to sell them to someone in China. That would constitute dealing in furs … and would therefore require a dealer's licence. Who did you buy the furs from?"

"I already told you. I didn't buy them. She gave them to me."

"So, can you tell us her name?"

"Sure. Hilda Riesling. She's out between Kitchener and Cambridge. They ran Riesling Transport."

"Okay. Did she give you any paperwork with the furs?"

"Yeah, like I said, the furs were all bought legal, from real trappers … with licenses. Stuff's all in an envelope on my dining room table." He stopped and looked as if he'd said more than he had intended, then he added, "You can't go in there without a search warrant."

McNabb took another turn. "We know that Derek." He looked at Selkirk, who nodded his agreement to the next question he knew was coming.

"Do you have a cleaning lady, or a neighbour you trust to go into your place?"

"Yeah, why?"

"If you would consent to that person accompanying us into your house, directly to your dining room table to pick up that envelope, it would sure help us square this situation away."

"No fuckin' way. No sir. I want to talk to my lawyer."

"Okay, no problem. Someone will be in to see you to your cell." As McNabb and Selkirk stood to leave, Detective Sergeant Aldridge entered the room and declared the interview suspended. The big jailhouse constable followed her in to take Cheney back to his cell. The video technician stopped recording.

—

It was the easiest search warrant application McNabb had ever filled out. One item to search for in one location revealed voluntarily by the subject of the warrant. An on-call Justice of the Peace issued the warrant without any hesitation and another constable drove McNabb and Selkirk to Cheney's Scarborough home. Twenty minutes from door to door.

Using a house key McNabb obtained from Cheney's possessions taken at the time of his arrest, they entered the house, took the shortest apparent route to the dining room and within seconds, found a big manilla envelope with "Riesling papers" written across the front. The only other items on the table, besides dirty breakfast dishes, were a grocery list and a message to a Mrs. McCabe, saying that he would be away for a while, and could she keep an eye on the place.

Back outside, while McNabb locked the front door, Selkirk spoke to an elderly lady who had confronted their constable as he waited outside for the others to return.

"Rob, this is Mrs. McCabe. I was just asking her if Mr. Cheney ever received deliveries that came in large trucks."

"No," the woman chimed in. "Like I told him, nothing bigger than the courier vans that drop off Amazon boxes. I put those inside for him as soon as the vans leave. I often wish I had shares in the carboard box companies, though. Some big boxes arrive but don't seem to have any more than one or two items rolling around in the bottom. I get packages like that too. It's such a waste."

"No deliveries arrive late at night?"

"No, I'm kind of a night owl. I've never seen anything arrive during the wee hours, other than Derek and his fancy car."

"Does he get a lot of visitors?"

"No, none at all since his wife left him. Imagine that, leaving her hard-working husband and running off with a weightlifter. She should be ashamed."

"Thank you for your cooperation, Mrs. McCabe."

"Is he in a lot of trouble?"

"We are still investigating, so it wouldn't be appropriate to say at this point," Selkirk told her.

Chapter 56

Rob McNabb sat, yawning. He was leafing through the stack of pictures of Cheney's office one more time, hoping to see something — anything that might give them a clue as to the final destination of Cheney's load of ivory and the drug shipment. Every time he thought about the seventy-three elephants murdered for the tusks in that one small shipment, he became even angrier. And, of course, there were thousands more of the majestic creatures being slaughtered every year.

During supper — an actual restaurant meal for a change — he, Ian and Sally had agreed that they wouldn't get any more out of Cheney about the furs. Didn't need to now. They had enough to lay charges for export without permits and selling, or attempting to sell, without a dealer's licence. The furs were being inventoried and graded by the folks at the auction house in North Bay and the final tally would be in their hands in a couple of days. Webb would process those charges when he got to North Bay. Wildlife enforcement was in the MNR's jurisdiction — not a police matter.

The three of them had gone back to the conference room after the meal and pored over the big file emailed to them by Bea. But while the contents of the old laptop from Cheney's desk drawer covered a lot of shady dealings, there was nothing they could see that helped follow the heroin or the ivory. Almost all the activity on the laptop had occurred two years ago and earlier. They had already decided that he probably wasn't using the device anymore. Bea had noted that in her covering email, too.

Aldridge said she would turn the device over to a forensic auditor to examine. There were bound to be other offenses waiting to be uncovered there. Revenue Canada would probably be interested in some of his business dealings. Strange thing was, they hadn't found a newer laptop in their search of his office or his car. Another warrant to search the house would have to wait for some compelling evidence, or an admission of its existence in the next interview.

Aldridge and Selkirk had returned to their rooms at around ten o'clock. McNabb was sitting alone, first googling some of the names in Cheney's Rolodex, and then back with the office photos. He had them spread out over three tables. But after an hour and a half, he decided he wasn't getting anywhere; too tired. He was in the process of signing out, ready to lock up and go to his room. He started turning out the lights, his fingers running across a row of four standard light switches. From the farthest to the nearest. As he snapped the last toggle down and the room went dark, a light came on in his head.

"Well shit." He quickly switched the room lights back on again. He rushed back to the table with the pictures. A quick look at one of the photos confirmed his lightbulb moment, and with picture in hand, he went to the table where Selkirk had been sorting articles removed from the walls in Cheney's office. What he wanted wasn't there, not that he expected it would be. If it was here, Ian surely would have put it on the centre table.

He rebooted the computer he had been using earlier, and at the same time used the hotel house phone to call Selkirk's room. The detective answered with a yawn.

"Sorry, Ian, did I wake you?"

"Turned out the light just seconds ago. What's up?"

"I found something peculiar. In the pictures. Do you mind coming back down?"

"Two shakes of a ram's tail."

On the computer, McNabb opened the digital images of Cheney's office while he waited for Selkirk. He found the image he wanted and enlarged it to show the item in detail, then started an entry in the conference room log so the detective had only to initial it when he came through the door. Which he did almost before Rob finished writing.

"Initial your sign-in, then take a look at this." He showed him one of the pictures. He had already circled the item with a Sharpie. Didn't think Selkirk would want to be playing twenty questions so late at night.

"Light switch cover. Decorative. What of it, Rob?"

"How many switches?"

"Just … the one. Hmm … it is rather large for a single switch, isn't it? Okay, you've got my attention." Instead of a standard metal or plastic switch cover, the light switch at the entrance to Cheney's office had a large decorative cover. It appeared to be an image of the Toronto skyline in relief.

"There's more to it than that, Ian, but easier to see on the big screen." He turned to the image on the computer. "Look at this. The slot for the light switch flange looks irregular, like a rough do-it-yourself job; not machined or molded in a factory. And it is cut right through the CN tower."

"Yeah, I see what you mean. Who would make a decorative image of the Toronto skyline, and then cut a slot out of the city's centrepiece landmark?"

"And look at the colour, Ian, sort of like ivory … maybe

a little yellowed. Age, dirt … cigarette smoke maybe? Finally, there are no screw holes. How did they attach it to the switch?"

"Good question."

"I looked for it among the things you sorted through that were hanging on the walls. They never thought to bring it with the other seized items."

"Well, they took the ceiling fixture apart," Ian countered, "because sometimes you can stuff things like drugs or money up there, but there's no room inside a single light switch box." He stood, thinking for a moment. "So, how does this solve the case, Rob?"

"Doesn't … yet. But it is a curiosity that could be hiding something. Evidence of something. And, if it *is* ivory, then it means we might have picked up the trail. So, first thing in the morning…."

"Why not now, Rob? Other than the door locks and police tape, the place is unsecured. Leave it too long and either someone from his team, or vandals could get in and take it or wreck it."

"Okay, what about keys?"

"The team left us an entrance key." He walked to the table with the check-in log and pocketed the key. After they'd signed out and locked the door, Selkirk threw the van key to McNabb. "I'll text Sally while you drive. Should let her know we are going CSI-ing."

—

Twenty-seven minutes later, they were standing in the OSL office, staring at the light switch cover. It was an artist's concept of the Toronto skyline, as viewed from out on the islands. It measured six inches high by eight inches wide — far larger than a commercial decorative cover for a single light switch.

The structures sculpted in relief stood out from the background by more than an eighth of an inch, making the overall thickness over three eighths of an inch in places. Tool marks on the piece, though tiny and refined, were visible.

"This didn't come off of a factory mold, Ian."

"It's definitely not plastic," Selkirk agreed.

"My grandmother has some antique ivory carvings," McNabb said. "She used to let me play with a couple of them when I was a kid. This sure has the look and the feel of ivory. I wonder what she'd say now if I suggested she had contributed to the murder of elephants? And to think, our grandparents question the values of our generation."

It was readily obvious that there were no screws holding the cover in place, but they could see a slim gap, maybe a thirty-second of an inch, between the cover and the wall.

Selkirk gently pried at it with his fingernails and the space widened slightly but returned to its original width as soon as he let go. "Must be glued on. Maybe we just cut out the drywall to get behind it."

"Here," McNabb said. He pulled out his pocketknife. "Let me try some gentle persuasion first." He slid the blade into the gap at one end, being careful not to apply too much pressure. He could detect a little give, a touch less resistance, and as he eased the blade farther in, could hear the adhesive backing coming unstuck. He moved the knife farther along and repeated the process.

Selkirk put his head close to the wall and looked in the side that was coming away. "Looks like strips of double-sided tape, Rob."

McNabb continued to work with the knife, and the space between the cover and the wall widened with each repositioning of the blade. A minute later, Selkirk pulled it free from the last section of tape. But they found nothing in there. Just bare wall and the exposed light switch box. No space to hide anything. Nothing bigger than a flash drive, anyhow. But there was nothing. Not even a flash drive.

"Poop."

"Rob. Look at this." His partner turned over the cover so McNabb could see the back side.

Hand Crafted at Jimmy Lee Specialty Arts – 44°38.9'N 78°40.3'W was etched into the smooth surface, along with a few words written with a felt pen: *Thanks Derek. Great material. Keep it coming.*

"Now we're getting somewhere, Ian. Jimmy Lee is in the Rolodex. And those coordinates are somewhere down around this part of the province."

Selkirk pulled an evidence bag from his pocket and dropped the cover inside. "I've got a friend at the crime lab who owes me a favour. She's working nights this week, so we'll swing by there on the way back. I'll get her to put a rush on it."

Chapter 57

Despite their late-night evidence gathering excursion, Selkirk and McNabb met Aldridge in the task force room right after breakfast. The detective sergeant was already there when they signed in. She was standing, looking at a link chart that had appeared on the whiteboard overnight. She detected McNabb's touch.

"Don't you ever sleep, Rob?"

"Oh … that? I just did a quick and dirty version after we got back from our little tour of Cheney's office." It was a remake of what he had drawn on paper during their flight down, yesterday. But now, as well as employee names added in circles of their own on the chart, he had added a circle for Jimmy Lee, connected directly to the ivory circle.

Aldridge got the coffee maker started while Rob and Ian briefed her on their discovery in Cheney's office.

"Good work, you two. You still sure you don't want to join my team full time, Rob?" She got a head shake for an answer before she continued. "Too bad. I won't give up asking, you know.

"In the meantime, assignments: Rob, locate the Jimmy Lee operation, wherever it is, and then determine the best way to get there."

"Ian, I need you to see what you can put together on Jimmy Lee himself. So far, all we have is the Rolodex entry and the note on the switch cover," Aldridge said. "Meanwhile, I've been summoned to go and brief the superintendent before he goes to church this morning. And as soon as I get back, we'll prepare for our second interview with Cheney. His lawyer has agreed to a meeting after lunch." She handed them each a mug of coffee, then signed out and left.

McNabb already had a leg up on his assignment because he'd checked out the coordinates on Google Earth just before he finally got to bed. Now he needed to make some calls.

Selkirk had an inkling he had seen something that might lead to Lee in the briefing notes left by the team that was out on COVID leave, but it didn't come to him immediately. However, when he got to the last page, there it was. James Leeson Wright. Derek Cheney's pilot and brother-in-law. His sister's husband.

He picked up a bright pink marker, pulled off the cap and highlighted "James" and the "Lee" part of Leeson. Then he dug through the file and found the man's arrest record. Two phone numbers were listed there. He retrieved the Rolodex from the centre table and rotated the knob until the card for Jimmy Lee came up. The second number listed on the arrest record — James Leeson Wright's mobile phone matched Jimmy Lee on the Rolodex. "Bingo, Rob. It's the brother-in-law."

McNabb was on the phone to someone and raised a hand to acknowledge Selkirk's statement. A moment later, he hung up and rolled his chair toward the detective. "Found the place … working on logistics. You were saying?"

"It's Cheney's pilot brother-in-law. If we are going to search his art facility, we also need to hit his residence in Pickering. But we don't have enough in the way of grounds to obtain a warrant for the house. Nothing at all, really.

"So I'm thinking, after the Cheney interview, I'll spend the rest of day out there nosing around. I can scope out the property … ask folks about his comings and goings. There's gotta be at least one disgruntled neighbour willing to stir up some shit. There always is. Has his Cessna been searched, yet?"

"I don't know, Ian. When she was briefing me on the way down yesterday, Sally said it was grounded for lack of a valid Certificate of Airworthiness when they arrested him. Should still be at Buttonville. But I assume that either the Mounties or Transport Canada would maintain custody of it until he complies. And wouldn't it be seized as evidence in Cheney's attempted run?"

"Should have been. I'll check on my way east."

Chapter 58

When Detectives Aldridge and Selkirk entered the room, Derek Cheney and his lawyer, William Spender, were already seated. Aldridge made the introductions and Spender half rose to introduce himself and gave them each a soft, wussy handshake.

"Thanks for making time to meet with us on a Sunday," Aldridge said.

"I'll do whatever it takes to get my client cleared and released on bail. You people have violated his rights, keeping him here this long. The delay will not look good in bail court tomorrow morning."

Aldridge didn't rise to the bait but turned her attention to Cheney. "Last night, Derek, my team came up with some interesting evidence. Tell me, who does the heroin and the ivory go to when you get it back to Ontario? Do they go to the same place?"

"I don't know nothin' about no drugs or ivory. I just handle freight for other people. I don't know what's in their loads."

Rather than wasting time listening to more denials from the man, Selkirk began to lay out the evidence. He placed copies of 8x10 photos on the table and turned them toward Cheney. They were pictures of the container with one door open to show the elephant tusks inside the unit and the other door closed to show the shipping container identification number, plus closeups of the ivory and the package of drugs inside the container.

"Your ivory and your drugs," said Aldridge.

"Not mine."

Next, just like dealing playing cards, Selkirk laid down the pictures of the desk blotter. One was the image of the entire blotter, and the second, a closeup of the blotter showing the container number and the circled date.

"Your blotter … your container number … your ivory and drugs," said Selkirk. A run of three.

"Just doodles. Don't prove nothin'."

The deal went to Aldridge, who laid out photos of the money inside the tires. "Nine hundred thousand in U.S. funds, Derek. Do you always carry that much cash in your truck tires?"

"Not my money."

"Well, no … not any more it isn't. Not unless you can prove legitimate ownership. Reverse onus applies here. The person in possession must prove lawful ownership of large sums of cash discovered during an investigation. Otherwise, it is forfeited to the Crown. So now it belongs to our poor starving federal government." She could see the sudden alarm in Cheney's eyes. But he said nothing.

"So … all that money … what, Captain Chang doesn't accept certified cheques or bank drafts or wire transfers? Or is this just a safe place to keep your petty cash?"

"I don't know any Captain Chang or *Ocean Princess*. My guys were just delivering a load of fur to the coast to be shipped to China." He'd slipped up and didn't catch his mistake. Gave her too much information; Aldridge hadn't mentioned the name of the ship yet.

"And the cash?"

"Like I said, it's not mine."

"Who is Jimmy Lee?" Selkirk took over again, placing his elbows on the table as he leaned forward.

"Don't know no Jimmy Lee or Captain Chang or any other damn Chinese."

And that was McNabb's cue to enter the room. He was carrying the Rolodex in a small carboard box. And in a file folder, he had the light switch cover plate. The crime lab had referred them to an expert, and just before lunch, a curator at the Royal Ontario Museum had met with them and positively identified the material as ivory — African or Asian would require further testing, but definitely ivory. Also in the folder, were several documents and a Google Earth printout showing the location indicated by the coordinates of Jimmy Lee Specialty Arts.

"Good afternoon, Derek." He looked at the lawyer, Spender, and introduced himself, then took a seat between Aldridge and Selkirk. That put him directly across from Cheney. With his lawyer present, the defence could no longer claim three-on-one intimidation.

"Just who *is* Jimmy Lee, Derek?"

"Like I told these detectives, I don't know any Jimmy Lee. You guys keep asking me about all these Chinamen I never heard of."

"Do you recognize this?" McNabb pulled the Rolodex from the box and set it on the table between them.

"Hey, you can't have that. It's mine," Cheney complained.

His lawyer touched his arm to get his attention. "I'm afraid they can." He explained the search warrant and subpoena issued on his office contents.

"Who is Dr. Hung?" McNabb asked.

"My dentist."

"And Dr. Soo?"

"Family doctor."

"Nguyen?"

"Corner market. Vietnamese, not Chinese."

"Fēicháng hǎo," McNabb said. Very good, in Chinese. Cheney opened his mouth to respond but caught himself. Not quickly enough to go unnoticed though. McNabb's best buddy in high school had immigrated from Hong Kong and McNabb had picked up some basic phrases. More from Mae Ling, too.

"So, you *do* know some folks of Chinese origin and you know the difference between Asian nationalities. Okay then … let's go back to Captain Chang," he paused. "Still doesn't ring a bell?"

"Fuck you. Already told you no."

McNabb spun the Rolodex to the letter O. He turned it so that Cheney and Spender could see the phone number with no associated name. He took out his own phone and brought up the number from the recent call history. He showed the number entered on the display to the lawyer. "Same number?" Spender nodded, acknowledging that it was.

McNabb pushed the call button and put the phone on speaker then laid it on the table between them.

"*Hello.*" The call was answered immediately, on the first ring. McNabb had arranged the call before going to lunch.

"Yes, it's Detective Conservation Officer Robert McNabb from Toronto. To whom am I speaking please?"

"*This is James Sherman Taylor of the United States Coast Guard. I'm the captain of the Coast Guard cutter George H.W. Bush.*"

"Captain Taylor, on whose phone did you receive this call?"

323

"This is the phone we confiscated from a Captain Chang at the time we took his vessel, Ocean Princess, *into our custody."*

"And did Captain Chang indicate ownership of the phone you seized from him?"

"Yes, he raised a royal stink about needing his phone to notify his business contacts."

"Captain, do any recent calls to area codes 416 or 905 show up in the call history?"

"As a matter of fact, yes." Captain Taylor listed three outgoing calls to two different numbers — two to Cheney's office phone and one to his mobile. *"In addition, there are four incoming calls from the second number I gave you."* Cheney's cell phone.

"Thank you, Captain Taylor. You've been most helpful." McNabb ended the call and looked at Cheney. "It would appear that you have at least a passing acquaintance with the good captain, eh?" And to emphasize the point, he laid down a photo received from the coast guard captain, showing the call history screen on Captain Chang's phone.

The three investigators watched the belligerent expression disappear from Cheney's face. His angry flushed skin tone faded to grey.

McNabb slid the Rolodex to Selkirk. It was his turn. McNabb's phone chose that moment to vibrate, indicating an incoming email, but he ignored it and put it back in his pocket. Didn't want to interrupt the energy flow at the table. Cheney could fold at any moment and Ian had the goods to make it happen, right there in the folder.

"Okay, lets go back to Jimmy Lee. Any hints, Derek?"

He looked at Cheney, and when he made no reply, he said, "Alright, we'll do it the hard way again." He turned the Rolodex cards until they stopped at Jimmy Lee and turned it to show Cheney and the lawyer. "You know this fellow?"

Cheney shrugged his shoulders, then said, "You're the detectives. You fuckin' figure it out."

Spender tapped Cheney on the arm and whispered something in his ear. But Cheney shook his head and said, "I've had enough of this shit. They can go fuck themselves."

"I guess that's what we'll have to do, then ... the detective part, anyhow." Selkirk smiled and looked at Aldridge, who took over.

"He's right, Derek. I'm sorry you didn't want to bring things to a conclusion here. It could have helped you in your upcoming court proceedings if you had cooperated with our enquiries. But as you said, we're the detectives. It may take us a little longer, but you may rest assured that we can do this without you. This interview is concluded." The three detectives rose as one and walked out of the room.

McNabb felt a little uncertain as they left. After they were out of earshot of Cheney and his lawyer, he asked the others why they had ended it without putting more pressure on Cheney. They still had the light switch cover and the documentary links to Jimmy Lee.

"We would have introduced those things if he had willingly given us the ivory shipments and the drugs, Rob. That would have helped close the case. And for him, at that point, there would be no going back. But as it stands now, if we give them everything we know, either he or his lawyer could get word to the brother-in-law, and the whole operation might evaporate before we move in on them," Selkirk explained.

"Oookay ... I see what you mean. I guess in the excitement over finding the location last night, I could have given the show away. Sorry 'bout that."

"No, you did your part well, Rob," Aldridge said. "You sure caught his attention when you spoke to him in Chinese.

Caught me off guard too," she smiled. Looked impressed. "And you struck a raw nerve when the coast guard skipper spoke to you on Chang's phone. But Cheney has his heals dug in too deep to back down now. Some people cave in when you catch them out like that, but others fight you to the bitter end. I'm guessing that Mr. Cheney falls into the latter category. So, now we have to get up to that Jimmy Lee location before they get the word that the heat is being turned up."

"Alright," McNabb said. "This morning I called one of the COs in Minden to find out about access to the place. I talked to Joel Hershey — we went to college together — and I asked him what he knew about the place. He says it is the site of a former commune of ill repute, near Burnt River, north of Lindsay. Got bunkhouses, a cookery, a generator shed and some other outbuildings, but the one time he saw it, he says it was all in pretty rough shape.

"I asked him about access, and he said last time he went past on the county road, the access road into it was snowed in. But he said he'd check it out this morning and get back to me. That might have been the email that buzzed while we were in there." He pulled out his phone and called up the message.

"Hmm, he says the road in still isn't plowed, but he flew his drone over the place and says to check out the video," which McNabb clicked on. What they saw was impressive. "We should view this on a bigger screen."

"Let's go back to our shop," Aldridge suggested. "We need to draft a really good application for a search warrant and call up some additional resources for this."

"Are the Feds going to join us for the ivory takedown?" McNabb asked. "I don't think that I have any authority to handle CITES cases." Enforcement of the Convention on the International Trade of Endangered Species was normally handled by the Wildlife Enforcement Directorate, a branch of Environment Canada.

"Like everyone else these days, Rob, most of the federal wildlife officers are tied up helping other agencies with COVID issues. Last I heard, they'd almost all been seconded to help several provinces with contact tracing for their public health agencies. But this morning your chief got the environment minister to appoint you as an officer in the interim."

Chapter 59

1450 – Task force conference room

Aldridge, Selkirk and McNabb sat in front of a large screen monitor and watched the drone footage that Rob's friend, Hershey, had taken that morning. Once the camera was turned on and tested, the drone rose quickly, focusing on the officer. According to an altitude readout in a corner of the screen, the unmanned flying machine climbed to four hundred feet before it transitioned into level flight. After circling Hershey's location once, it began to follow a snow-covered bush road that snaked through the trees.

Ten minutes later, a large clearing came into view, and the drone camera revealed three long buildings sitting side by side near the north edge of the clearing. They looked like elongated residential bungalows with small windows, spaced the way they would be in a bunkhouse. Six smaller outbuildings were scattered in random fashion nearby. There was smoke coming from the chimneys of two of the larger buildings.

But what caught everyone's attention was the aircraft parked near the most westerly of the bunkhouse buildings. "Looks like a Cessna 185," McNabb suggested.

He paused the video and enlarged the image of the aircraft. The registration letters on top of the wing showed up in big print on the screen: "CF-WTF."

Aldridge flicked through the other team's briefing notes. "That's Wright's plane."

McNabb looked puzzled. "As the expression goes, WTF! I thought it was impounded for lack of a valid Certificate of Airworthiness."

"That's all they were holding it for. But if he has an aircraft mechanic friend and there was nothing that needed upgrading, Rob, he could have had that done in a matter of hours. Even from the comfort of his jail cell. His one call to his lawyer could have included that little detail. He could still face a fine for late renewal, but with the COVID backlog, they might not bother."

"Hmm. Well anyhow … as far as getting in there," Rob said, returning to the logistics of approaching the art compound, "I was originally thinking in terms of snowmobiles. It's only about four kilometres from the maintained county road. And Joel said he could provide rides for at least eight raiders including himself. But now that we know there is a plowed or packed airstrip, there is also the option of flying in. Or are you going to tell us that you still can't get any aircraft, Sally?"

"Flying in would be good. But I'm told that the provincial choppers are both tied up and the force has no large, fixed wing birds. However, I will do what I can. And before I forget, I need to touch base with the Crown attorney. We have to keep Cheney locked up until we can search the brother-in-law's house and art colony. No bail for at least another couple of days.

"Spender will probably go ballistic, but if you can't piss off an occasional defence lawyer, this job wouldn't be nearly as much fun as it is. In the meantime, Rob, you start to draft our search warrant applications. One for each location. Leave the residence one open until Ian does his neighbourhood canvass. Ian, you better get going."

329

1830 – In the hotel restaurant

Detective Ian Selkirk arrived back at the hotel in time to catch supper with the others. He was grinning as he entered the dining room to join the group. They had a corner table, far enough from the few other guests that they could talk without being easily overheard. Aldridge and McNabb had already ordered their meals, but the server came back and took his request, bringing him a beer to start with.

"So, our Mr. Wright lives in the wrong neighbourhood … at least, wrong for his own good. I took the carpet cleaners' van around and tried to drum up some business. Nothing doing. Most folks have either gone back to hardwood or forward to laminate flooring. But if you don't push the hard sell, you'd be surprised by the unrelated topics folks are willing to discuss with a chatty tradesman. The short version: he lives there with his wife. Kids are all grown and living away. No large vicious dogs, but one small harmless yappy one, I'm told.

"Details worthy of note: A retired couple across the street have seen late-night deliveries made by the OSL transport … about once every five or six weeks. They never saw what was arriving, but whatever it was, it was arriving, not leaving.

"The guy next door caught his own Labrador retriever dragging a small elephant tusk from Wright's garage one day. The dog must have pushed the man-door open to get at it. Tricky latch that doesn't always catch, he said. When he carried the dog's trophy back into the garage, he said there were dozens of them in there. Some, bigger than he thought they grew. He didn't know they were illegal to possess, so he didn't report it to anyone. But, considering the globally declining elephant populations, he wasn't very happy that Wright had them in the first place. They're not really on speaking terms with our Jimmy.

"The thing that has most of the neighbours bummed out though, is the steady succession of vehicles coming and going from the place most evenings. Seedy characters driving cars that are way above their class, knocking at the front door, entering, then leaving minutes later. Always in the evenings, except Sunday and Monday when he's away. And evenings because Wright leaves most mornings and doesn't return until suppertime. No one has any idea what he does for a living, either.

One neighbour is a retired transit cop. He has been recording licence plates, and since he was going to be my last stop, I told him who I really was, and swore him to secrecy. In exchange, he let me copy his list. Three of the first four names I checked are convicted street dealers. Haven't got to the others yet, but Wright gets my vote for Drug Distributor of the Year."

"Good work Ian," Aldridge said. "Our road trip to the near west spruced up your game."

"Nothing like endless hours cruising Canadian highways in the dead of winter to refocus your mind, boss."

"That should give us what we need to search the house, and garage." Aldridge smiled, relieved by the bounty of knowledge scored by Selkirk's afternoon in the field. "The information was looking impossibly thin until now. But there's no way a warrant application can get turned down with info like that."

McNabb's phone chose that moment to warble. He excused himself from the table and answered it in the lobby. When he returned five minutes later, he was shaking his head, but at the same time, he looked amused.

"Man, we can send humans into space and back successfully. We can even do complex communications like Zoom meetings and not screw them up too badly, but some pipeline company executives are demanding a personal meeting on Tuesday with the director of the air service to explain why Sam landed a government aircraft on their pipeline right-of-way in Rainy River. The director has asked Sam to come to Toronto and attend the meeting with him.

"First, she gets chewed out by a grumpy old staff sergeant for trying to save my life. Then it turns out that the staff sergeant has a next-door neighbour who is a supervisor for the pipeline. The word worked its way up the corporate pipeline, and now some cranky executive desk jockeys want a piece of her hide for risking damage to their underground infrastructure. Thing is, she says there's no pipeline shown on either the aeronautical charts or the aircraft GPS. How was she to know? The only evidence we saw was the unmarked vent pipes sticking up through the snow when we were taking off.

"The inquisition is scheduled for eleven that morning, and she says the director, who's really pissed off at the pipeline folks, won't allow the meeting to go on until noon. He says he and Sam will walk out if they try to drag it out any longer than half an hour. So, I think I can find us a Tuesday afternoon flight into the Jimmy Lee compound … if you agree with that method of ingress, Sal."

"Sounds good, Rob. I'll call the air service director after we've eaten and invite myself to the inquisition. After all, I'm the one who told her to land there. And I didn't see any signs saying, 'No Bush Plane Landings Allowed.' Rob, can you officially requisition the flight for us?"

"Can do."

Chapter 60

Detective Constable Ian Selkirk and a team of ten uniformed police personnel, plus a drug detecting dog and her handler, arrived without fanfare. They travelled in regular marked police vehicles — no lights or sirens. Two members of Environment Canada's Wildlife Enforcement Directorate arrived with them driving a rented cube van.

A UPS courier driver was walking down the driveway with a package he had just picked up at the house. Selkirk produced his badge and detained the man on the spot. After showing the driver a copy of the search warrant, he beckoned to a constable and one of the wildlife officers to come and check out the parcel.

Selkirk moved on to the house and knocked on the door. No battering rams were used. None were needed. Mrs. Wright — Derek Cheney's sister — answered the door. Jim Wright was not at home, she told them. He spent every Sunday, Monday and Tuesday "up north." Wasn't due back until later.

"Mrs. Wright, I'm Detective Constable Ian Selkirk. We have a warrant to search the residence, garage and any outbuildings located at this address." He handed her a copy of the document. "You are not under arrest, but Constable Wiebe, here, has been assigned to stay with you for the duration of the search. Any interference with the search team will result in your arrest. Do you understand?"

"C'mon in. That's Jim's business. Not mine. I wondered how long it would take someone to get curious. Can I offer the constable a drink?"

"Coffee please, if you have it, Ma'am."

The search team split up. The second federal wildlife officer led two constables to the garage. The defective latch on the side door allowed them easy access and they were simultaneously elated and disappointed by what they found in the back of the garage. Six large elephant tusks were leaning up against the back wall. Another ten smaller ones were lying in a pile in front of them. That was all there were. But it was a good start.

The tusks were numbered, marked with indelible marker, and dated. Even though a gap in security had allowed the theft of a major shipment of raw ivory, the Chinese government officials had been meticulous in their record keeping. Their country was one of the strictest nations when it came to clamping down on the international ivory trade.

The markings indicated that the tusks were part of a shipment that had been on the way to being burned — the internationally agreed upon plan for stamping out the illegal trade. But even the best security can be breached by smart, bold criminals, and these tusks had somehow avoided the bonfire.

The dates marked on the tusks were important. While many countries outlawed the sale of ivory outright, Canada was one of those nations slow to adapt, and still allowed possession and sale of ivory taken before 1990. Each of the tusks in Wright's garage was dated 2013 or later, several of them only two or three years back.

The first federal wildlife officer, trailed by the unhappy UPS driver, brought the reopened package into the garage to show his partner. Everyone there paused to admire the replica of Mount Rushmore, masterfully reproduced in ivory. It was addressed to a retired U.S. senator in Texas.

"I'm sorry driver. We'll give you a receipt for the seizure, but this is one item you won't be delivering. And no, it's not your fault. Here's my card. Have your supervisor contact me with any questions."

"But it was in my care. The minute I signed for that package I became responsible for it."

"Well, our respective lawyers can argue over this sir, but it was still on the property covered by the warrant when we apprehended it. And now, with my signature on this receipt, the responsibility passes to me. You are off the hook."

When the driver left, talking urgently into his phone, the two police constables assisted the wildlife officers in cataloging the find before they loaded everything into the cube van. The garden shed and a portable garage in the back yard contained nothing of interest to the law.

Meanwhile, inside the house, the search for drugs was progressing well. James Wright did little to hide his stash. Heavy duty residential entrance doors and an elaborate alarm system protected the house. That false sense of security had allowed him to become too casual for his own good.

The house was a brick-sided split level, built in the early 1960s. Under the living room was a four-foot-high crawlspace. In the adjacent recreation room, a bookshelf on rollers was all that concealed the entrance to the area. The drug sniffing dog led the team right to it. Inside the crawlspace, a variety of illicit recreational drug products was kept in a set of old kitchen cupboards from another era. The cupboards were not locked.

Other members of the search team entered Wright's office and came up with paper and electronic documentation of his illegal enterprises. An Excel spreadsheet contained a list of ninety-three orders for ivory carvings. The list included names and addresses of the clients and thumbnail pictures of those items which had already been shipped.

The biggest challenge was gaining access to a safe imbedded in the concrete basement floor in the office. But two of the officers who'd been sidelined by the COVID contact five days earlier, had tested negative twice and were back on the job. They arrived with the carpet cleaners' van around four-thirty and went to work on the safe. With appropriate tools and a strong dose of enthusiasm, it took just over an hour to open the strongbox. Unlike Wright's orderly record keeping, the safe was literally stuffed with cash. Rolls of money were jammed in there.

It took the search team until nine o'clock that night to sort the money and perform a hand count. Even after being manually straightened and pressed flat, much of the money was too creased, wrinkled and folded to run through a mechanical counter. When they were done, they tallied $359,875 in a mixture of Canadian and U.S funds, in denominations from fives and tens up to one-hundred-dollar bills.

Chapter 61

Samantha Williams flew the Turbo Beaver in a wide circuit, well away from the Jimmy Lee Art Colony before lining up on final approach to the snow-packed runway used by James Wright. His Cessna 185 was parked next to the most westerly building in the compound, just as it had been in the video taken on Sunday morning.

On board the Beaver were Aldridge, McNabb and four provincial police constables. Their landing was timed to coincide with the arrival of three snowmobiles over the snowbound access road. The snow riders included three more conservation officers and three police constables, riding two-up. Their timing was impeccable.

Sam coasted the Beaver to a stop in front of the Cessna, effectively blocking it from making a getaway. At the same time, the snowmobiles dropped a constable at the back door of each bunkhouse building before circling around to stop at the front.

Aldridge, McNabb and his friend Hershey each led a small team of officers through the front door of the three bunkhouses. The entries were simultaneous. There was no polite door knocking, but none of the doors was locked. Less than thirty seconds after arriving in the yard, they all entered their respective targets with copies of the search warrant in hand.

They were ready to counter any resistance and to redeploy the forces as needed. It was assumed that Wright would be in the building closest to the parked Cessna, so Aldridge assigned an extra constable to her team.

On entering the most westerly building, the first thing the officers noticed was a trestle table just inside the front door. There, in plain view, lay half a dozen small and medium-sized elephant tusks.

Detective Sergeant Aldridge soon picked out the man she presumed to be Mr. Wright. He was sitting at a desk on a slightly raised platform in the corner on the left side of the large room. He sat with his back to the door and had his cell phone pressed against his right ear and a finger stuck in his left. He hadn't yet noticed his visitors — hadn't heard the arrival of three snowmobiles or the approach of the Beaver's idling gas turbine over the noise inside the building.

An old-fashioned cast-iron wood stove, its side plates heated to a dull red, stood between Wright's desk and the door. A large floor fan, running at full power behind the stove, rattled, hummed, and clanged continuously from the effort of pushing warm air to the far corners of the room.

Sitting at two long worktables were fifteen Asian men and women, every one of them appeared to be of advanced age, and every one of them was intent on carving and shaping intricate designs into pieces of ivory on the tables in front of them.

In the back corner, farthest from Wright's desk, two much younger, tough-looking Caucasian men were using an electric band saw to render a pile of smaller elephant tusks into pieces suitable for whatever projects the ancients were working on. The noise caused by the saw's overheating blade kept Wright's attention fully on his phone call. And the pungent odour raised by the cutting operation, caught in the throats of the officers the instant they entered.

In the middle bunkhouse, Hershey and his small team found an old man and an old woman, both Asian, chopping up vegetables and some unidentified small mammal carcasses. It was obviously the cookery and dining hall, but the place was way too warm for the safe handling of meat and not clean by anyone's standards. The smell was nauseating.

Hershey spoke into his headset mic and Aldridge told him to join her and leave a constable to watch over the old couple. After securing all the sharp knives they could see, Hershey and the other CO went back outside. They called out to the back door constable to join them.

McNabb's team discovered that the third building was a filthy bunkhouse. A large woodstove sat in the middle of a central common room, but the fire was out. The stove was stone cold — as was the building. It was obvious that the place was in use, but no one was there. He too, reported to Aldridge and got orders to bring his team to the first building.

The passage of eight more bodies through the front door did get Wright's attention. Couldn't help but do so with the burst of cold air that temporarily displaced the heat from the stove.

Aldridge waved the search warrant at him, and McNabb turned off the noisy fan so the sergeant could be heard. "Police, Conservation Officers and Federal Wildlife Agents, Mr. Wright. We are here to search the premises."

"You've got no right. This is a private art colony and a shelter for aged immigrants." He stood up and came around his desk toward the crowd of uniforms.

"This warrant gives us the authority, sir," Aldridge said.

McNabb had seen the tusks on the table by the door when he entered. He followed the sergeant's lead and exercised his newly appointed authority as a federal wildlife agent. "James

Leeson Wright, you are under arrest for engaging in the importation and trade of an endangered species. And looking around this place, I'm guessing there may be a few more charges to add before we are done." Wright towered over McNabb's six feet by another seven inches, but the CO wasn't in the least bit intimidated. He stepped behind the man, and before Wright could react, he had him in handcuffs.

McNabb was just beginning to give him the official police caution when the two men working the saw in the far corner bolted out the back door. He continued reciting the caution without pause as the constable waiting outside the back door managed to grab one. But the other man took off through the knee-deep snow, wearing only running shoes and indoor clothing. One of the other constables crossed the room and hurried outside to take up the chase.

The ancients, who had been working quietly until then, suddenly all began jabbering in what Aldridge could only presume was a Chinese dialect. Several appeared pleased to see the arrival of all the uniforms, but most of them cowered, terrified by the arrival of the authorities.

Rob McNabb searched his memory for a few appropriate Chinese phrases. He called out in what he hoped would be passable Mandarin and told them to put down their work and stay calm — that it was Jimmy Lee they had come to see. He knew his instructions would sound broken and somewhat uncertain, but the pandemonium faded to a murmur. Hoping for a break, he switched to English.

"I am Conservation Officer Robert McNabb. Do any of you speak English?" No one spoke, but seeing that Rob had calmed down the workers, Aldridge and Hershey grabbed Wright, with the help of one of the larger constables, and hurried him from the building.

Chapter 62

The moment Wright was out the door, one wizened old man raised his hand. "I am Martin Yee. I speak English. I and three others here are Canadian. But the rest were brought into the country illegally. That is why they are afraid." The man could have been in his seventies or his nineties, McNabb couldn't even begin to guess. He asked Mr. Yee why they were all working there under such poor conditions.

"The apartment that we four Canadians were living in was sold and was being demolished. We have since come to the conclusion that it was Mr. Wright who arranged that … in order to take control of our lives. Rent elsewhere in the city was far beyond our means. You see, I am the only one with a work pension. He promised us a safe home for our retirement, up north. We were assured that we would be able to live out our days in comfort, doing things we enjoyed, to fill our idle hours." He paused and gestured at the room. "This sweatshop is the recreation hall and craft room. We have been enslaved here since a year ago December."

"Wait," McNabb interrupted, "why didn't someone just walk out and get help?"

"Mr. Wright … 'Jimmy Lee' he likes to be called … flew us here, two at a time, all the way into the wilderness in the back of his airplane with the windows blacked out and supplies piled to the roof behind the front seats. The flight took over three hours after we left Toronto. From my knowledge of Ontario, after flying one hundred and fifty miles an hour for that much time, we are a long way up north. He warned us that we are many miles from the nearest highway, and when we got here, he took our winter jackets away and said he was getting them cleaned. But they were never returned." The old man was wearing summer clothes, sandals and no socks. "In the summer, he assured us that if we tried to escape, the mosquitoes would drive us mad, long before we reached civilization.

"And then his guards," he nodded in the direction of the two who had fled. "They never let us out of their sight. They even follow us to the outhouse. In short, there was never an opportunity to escape."

McNabb was sickened by the horrific conditions these people were being forced to live and work in. Sickened too by the lies Wright had told them to get them here and keep them once they had arrived. Flying them in endless wide circles for three hours with the windows blacked out would certainly give them the impression that they had come a long way.

"Martin, after the lies he told you about your accommodations here, I feel badly telling you that the township road is only four kilometres west of here. And Toronto is no more than an hour and a half away by road. This place is just north of Lindsay." McNabb stopped while the old man translated for the others.

While he waited, he picked up several of the nearest ivory carvings. They were not yet complete, but the detail was exceptional. One piece, a traditional oriental dragon, was created in the mind of the woman who was carving it. The other, if McNabb's memory served him, was a representation of the Seattle skyline. For that, the artist referred to printouts of three pictures laid out on the work bench in front on him. They were taken from different angles, allowing the artist to create the 3-D carving.

Martin Yee saw McNabb admiring the pieces. "All of our work is commissioned by Mr. Wright's clients. For the landscapes, he brings us pictures to work from, either provided by the client, or from his own research."

"Does Mr. Wright pay you for this work? His clients must pay him a fortune for these beautiful pieces."

"We create these works to pay for our room and board, such as it is. Each of us worked with ivory before it became illegal to sell. For me and my wife and our two friends, it was a hobby, but the rest of them are the true artisans. It is their trade. That's why he smuggled them into the country."

"Well, we've got some serious business to conduct with 'Jimmy Lee' this afternoon, and then we'll see what we can do about getting you folks back to civilization." McNabb felt bewildered by the magnitude of the injustice these people had suffered.

"Thank you, Officer McNabb. Where did you learn to speak Mandarin? I am afraid your pronunciation needs improvement," he smiled, "but we were able to understand what you were saying."

McNabb smiled back. "It's a struggle, but I picked up some from a high school friend who came from Hong Kong. And our adopted daughter is trying to help me improve on it. Your English, on the other hand, it's far ahead of my Mandarin … Am it correct to assume you were born here?"

"My grandfather helped to build the Canadian Pacific Railroad. He stayed afterward. I am the third generation here. I was a librarian before I retired."

Chapter 63

While McNabb was with the Chinese elders in the rec hall, Aldridge led James Wright toward the cookery. She paused outside to instruct Hershey and the other two conservation officers to begin their search of the outbuildings. Badly maintained like the main buildings, they were strewn in a haphazard line opposite them. If this were a pioneer settlement, the area between the main buildings and the outbuildings would be a primitive main street. Not narrow, but not wide, either.

Hershey divided the team and headed to opposite ends of the row with a plan to work toward meeting in the middle. At the near end, closest to the rec hall, was a workshop, well stocked with all the tools needed to maintain such a facility. But it was unlikely that any tool had felt a human touch in a number of years. Next to it was a four-seat outdoor toilet that was in regular use but also sorely lacking in maintenance and was close to overflowing.

At the far end of Main Street sat the generator shed. It housed an antique diesel dynamo that was, with a steady rattling growl, contributing more energy to the establishment than the inhabitants contributed to its well-being. The continuous sound of the generator was probably why the inmates had never heard traffic passing on the nearby county road. Wright must have kept it running full-time with that purpose in mind.

A small, ancient bulldozer sat next to the generator shed. It was nominally covered by a ratty tarp, and the block heater was plugged in, ready to start up and tow its heavy roller up and down the runway after the next snowfall.

Several other shabby sheds contained a mixture of unused garden tools and a derelict riding mower, but other than the crime of gross neglect, no further evidence of unlawful activity was discovered until the two teams met at the entrance to the final building.

Directly across from the dining hall stood a frame building the size of a single car garage. It leaned close to ten degrees to the east. A heavily trampled path across Main Street led directly from the parked Cessna to the building. When Hershey and a stocky constable tried to tackle the pair of outward swinging doors, the one on the right was frozen to the ground. When they dragged the left-hand door open, they hit pay dirt. Leaning up against the back and side interior walls of the building were several dozen large elephant tusks. Half of them were longer than Hershey was tall. The three COs and two constables who were assisting, stood in awe of the largest tusks.

"Imagine the massive animals needed to carry those suckers around and make it look easy," one of the police constables said, shaking his head.

"Think of the thousands slaughtered by poachers just to provide us arrogant humans with carved figurines and nick-nacks," Hershey added. "It sickens me to think about it." It was said with a catch in his normally strong voice. He took a moment to compose himself, then got into delegation mode.

"Okay guys, judging from all the foot traffic, at least some of these came from the Cessna since it last arrived. Let's go and give his plane the full CSI treatment. There's dried blood on the base of some of these tusks, so we might find some traces flaked off in the plane. I sure do love it when we get to seize an airplane."

Sam Williams, idle until now, hauled a big evidence collection kit from the back of the Beaver and carried it to Hershey as he approached the Cessna. He and the other two COs climbed into disposable coveralls and snapped on latex gloves before opening the doors on Wright's aircraft.

—

As the search of the Cessna began outside, Aldridge paused her interview of James Wright in the dining hall to take an incoming call from Ian Selkirk. She had switched her phone to speaker mode even before Selkirk announced his good news. The instant he began to speak, she could tell by the confident tone of his voice that Wright was in big trouble. And because he had clammed up as soon as he was arrested, letting him hear the conversation was intended to wear him down.

"Hey, boss, don't know what you are finding up there, but even if you strike out, we've got your Jimmy Lee fellow dead to rights on drugs and elephants. Lots of stuff here and his wife openly admitted that it was entirely Mr. Wright's business. Says she has nothing to do with it. Too busy knitting stuff for refugees and grandkids."

"Good work, Ian. No drugs turning up here yet, but the game wardens hit the big time in the ivory trade right from the start. They are working over his Cessna as we speak and knowing how those guys are at gathering evidence, I'm guessing the government is going to come into possession of one more bush plane before suppertime.

"Also, when you are done there, can you arrange for accommodations for seventeen seniors? These are victims, not perpetrators. Four are Canadian. The remainder are Chinese national artisans smuggled into the country by Mr. Wright. Put them up in our hotel if you can and lay on appropriate security. We'll need to interview them all. And when you've done that, notify the Canadian Border Services folks that we've got some business for them too."

"*Need me to arrange for translators?*"

"No, Rob McNabb has got it covered. Two of the Canadian victims are willing to provide that service for us."

James Wright sat on the sidelines, temporarily ignored by the police officers as they listened in on the conversation.

At just that moment, the Chinese cook and her husband became agitated — in a mixture of English and their own language. The woman had come up with a wicked looking carving knife that was missed in the initial search. Now she was waving it and threatening the uniforms in broken English. She had everyone's attention.

Sitting there, basically unattended, Wright noticed that one of the women must have dropped a hairpin on the chair next to the one he was sitting in. He had watched an online video once, of a man using a straightened hairpin to free himself from handcuffs. Wright hadn't been consciously preparing for such an eventuality; it was just something he'd come on while surfing the net. And neither McNabb, nor the constable who had taken charge of Wright, had taken the time to engage the locking pins on his cuffs. They had been in a hurry to get him out of the sweatshop when McNabb appeared to have brought the workers under control.

While Aldridge and two police constables manoeuvred to deal with the knife-wielding cook, Wright tried his luck with the little flattened piece of metal. Three times he managed to start the tiny blade into the slot, but without success. The fourth time, the end he was using got jammed and was bent out of shape.

That end was useless for any further attempts. Switching ends behind his back was tricky enough on its own and he began to think he didn't have what it took to perform a Houdini escape. But when he pushed the fresh end in this time, he could feel it slip between the ratchet teeth and the little spring-loaded pawl that held the arm closed. Just like that, one wrist was suddenly free. He was free. The other one didn't matter for now. He pulled his jacket sleeve down over the remaining cuff, slipped the loose cuff up the sleeve and waited for an opening.

The commotion with the female cook ramped up to a new high as she backed farther toward the other end of the room and grabbed a hot, cast-iron frying pan from the stove. It had nothing in it, but it could deliver a lot of pain just as it was. Now the husband got involved. He saw the officers edging closer to his woman, two with pistols drawn and one with his taser out. He yelled excitedly at his wife to stand down and pleaded with the police, in broken English, not to shoot.

When the distraction was at its peak, James Wright slipped out the front door unnoticed, and headed for one of the Natural Resources snowmobiles. His Cessna, blocked in by the Beaver and crawling with game wardens, was obviously off limits.

But the key had been removed from the first snowmobile. The other two machines were parked too close to the Cessna to risk trying.

Chapter 64

Samantha Williams had nothing to do during the arrests, or the searches, or the interviews, so she gravitated toward those who appeared to have the most interesting assignments. She had lingered over the collection of tusks in the garage for a few minutes, but then the COs who were searching Wright's Cessna asked her advice on the best non-destructive methods of removing the seats and interior panels in the passenger/cargo area.

When they discovered they needed a different type of screwdriver, Sam walked over to the workshop to get one. In the meantime, the searchers concentrated on removing what they could.

For such a rundown facility, she was amazed by the great selection of quality tools she found in the professional grade tool chest. Everything was dusty, but other than that, very much like new. She had just opened the tray containing the screwdrivers when James Wright grabbed her from behind, put a hand over her mouth, and held a very sharp wood chisel to her throat.

"Looks like the Cessna's not available right now, missy. So you are going to fly me out of here in your Beaver. And if you don't feel like cooperating, I'll fly it myself. Got it?" He could have done it himself if he had known the start-up procedure for a gas turbine engine, but his flight training and experience was limited to piston engine aircraft. And he would have needed a hostage anyhow, to keep the others at bay.

"Mhhmf," was all she could say with his hand clamped firmly over her mouth. But right then, her mind was racing to come up with something she could do to stop him, or at least draw attention to herself once he led her from the shop.

When he pushed her through the door and out into the yard, she could hear the continued commotion inside the kitchen over the rumble of the diesel generator. All eyes in that building were turned inward. The group searching the Cessna was blocked from view by the Turbo Beaver. She could see no sign of activity through the small front window of the rec hall.

"Just walk quickly to the Beaver. You won't get hurt if you don't draw any attention to yourself." He held her far enough away from his body that she couldn't grab or kick him with any force, and he was more than a foot taller than she was, so a head butt was out of the question.

In the meantime, McNabb had solicited the help of Martin Yee and his wife to write down the names of the enslaved artisans. Progress was slow. Not all the people came from the same region of China. Several spoke a dialect that even Yee had a difficult time with, but when he brought McNabb the list, he stopped and pointed out the window. "Look, look!"

Rob turned in time to see Wright pushing Sam in the rear passenger door of the Beaver on the side facing away from the Cessna.

"Shit, where are all the other cops?" he asked, but he didn't wait for an answer. Instead of a head-on approach, he ran out the back door, hoping to make it around the building and come up from behind the Beaver.

The constables who had stayed with him and the ancients, scrambled out the front door and they could see Sam being pushed into the pilot's seat. It appeared that Wright was settling into the seat immediately behind hers, but even from thirty feet away, they could see him holding something shiny to her throat.

One of the officers keyed his headset mic as he watched. "Hostage taking in the yellow bird. Happening right now. Wright has our pilot."

Inside the kitchen, the officer with the taser heard the transmission. It was time to end the stalemate with the angry cook. It was difficult enough handling one crisis at a time. More than one and the situation could turn to shit in a hurry.

"Taser, taser, taser," he shouted. The others backed clear, and the woman went down. One zap was all that was needed. Aldridge grabbed the big knife from where it fell to the floor and warned the husband to stay clear. The third officer cuffed the old lady while the taser operator stood by, ready to reapply if needed. It wasn't needed and the husband complied.

"You two stay with them," Aldridge ordered as she rushed to the front door. The group who had been searching the Cessna now surrounded the Beaver with their guns drawn. McNabb was the last to arrive and stood, ready to open the back door on the pilot's side of the plane.

Belted into the seat behind Sam, James Wright told her to start the turbine and tell the people to back off. The first pair of seats behind the pilot and co-pilot did not have a side window. He felt less exposed there.

In her side mirror, Sam could see McNabb standing by the back door. She began the start-up sequence, and as soon as the turbine fired, she pushed open her door. She waved her arm and shouted out over the increasing noise of the turbine and the spinning propeller to those standing on her side of the plane. "Back off," she yelled, but with her hand, she pointed at the back door. She hoped McNabb would take the hint.

With the noise and the pungent stink of turbine exhaust rolling in the open door, Wright didn't notice the back doors on both sides opening. He didn't notice until it was almost too late. But his peripheral vision caught movement behind him and he turned in time to see a cop and a game warden already halfway inside. He yelled at them and gestured with the chisel he was holding at Sam's throat.

The two men retreated and closed the back doors as they left. Wright shook his head. "The nerve of those assholes," he said to himself. And to Sam: "Get this fucking thing in the air."

Sam's heart sank. The guys should have stayed on board. Even with the chisel held to her throat, Wright would have been in a no-win situation. With a cop and a CO both pointing their guns at him, he would have had to back down eventually, or die — and he didn't seem the suicidal type. Reluctantly, she increased the power and applied the right wheel brake. The Beaver pivoted around to line up with the snow-packed runway. The law enforcement personnel stood clear, and she started her takeoff run.

Chapter 65

Wright leaned forward into the cockpit and switched off the VHF radio. "You won't be touching that unless I need you to. Head south," he ordered. His next stop — Sam's last — was Barker, New York. The car that he and Derek co-owned was waiting in the hangar they rented at the private airstrip there.

Sam banked the plane into a gentle left turn. Wright relaxed a little and sat back in his seat as the Beaver climbed away from the compound. The hand holding the chisel rested on his knee, nowhere near Sam's neck. So his heart almost stopped when he heard the voice behind him.

"*Freeze, or you die*, asshole." Rob McNabb pressed the cold muzzle of his 9mm service pistol into the side of Wright's neck. Proper police procedure and etiquette fell momentarily to the wayside. McNabb was there to save the woman he loved.

"Drop the chisel *now!*" After a brief pause, the tool hit the cabin floor. "Put your hands behind your back, one at a time. If I detect *any* muscle movement other than a slow, deliberate compliance, you will die *right* here … *right* now. I'll even volunteer to clean up the mess.

"Just so you know, that's my wife you have taken hostage. *Nobody* does that to Sam Williams and gets away with it." The first wrist, when it came around the seatback was already cuffed. Oh yeah, my own cuffs, he remembered. Attaching the second one was a two-handed job and required him to tuck the gun under one butt cheek until Wright was secured. But the man took him at his word. Never made a wrong move. McNabb pulled his cuff key out of his pocket and pushed home the locking pins. No Houdini hairpin tricks would set him free this time.

Holding his gun to Wright's neck once more, McNabb reached above his seat with his free hand and grabbed an intercom headset. He fitted it over his head and keyed the mic. "Sam, you've got the plane. I've got Wright. Let's go back to the compound."

"How did you do that Robbie?" She didn't sound as surprised as he thought she might. Just relieved.

"We knew he'd order everyone off when we came through the back door, so after the other two guys rushed in, I crawled in under Hershey and stayed put while he was backing out. Wright couldn't see me through the seat behind his."

"I wondered what you were doing when you weren't standing there with the others watching me leave. You saved my life again, Flyboy. Thanks."

"No problem, sweetie. Danger is no stranger to a ranger, ma'am."

"Yeah, but we came awfully close to breaking our Post Apocalyptic Vows … again."

"We've pretty much trashed them this past week, haven't we? Maybe it's time we turned in our guns and badges and Beaver keys and got full-time desk jobs, Sam. Wha'd'ya think?"

"What, and get crushed under a falling filing cabinet? Screw that, McNabb. Now, do up your seat belt. We're almost back."

While Sam began a circuit to line up with Lee's airstrip, Rob began to recite the police caution. "James Leeson Wright, you are under arrest … once again … for escape lawful arrest, assault, forcible confinement and hijack of an aircraft…."

"You can't arrest me for that. You're not even a cop."

"Jimmy Lee my man, if that's a problem for you, let's just call this a citizen's arrest. Furthermore, as a lawfully appointed and highly trained peace officer, my employer has seen fit to arm me with this deadly pistol. From this point on, if you endanger the lives of either me or our pilot, I can legally take appropriate lethal defensive action. Now, let me finish giving you the caution, before I forget where I was."

The Beaver kissed the snow strip just minutes later, and Sam coasted the plane to exactly where she had parked it before. Through her open side window, she flashed a thumbs up to the waiting police and COs. Then she feathered the propeller and shut down the turbine.

At the same time, Wright's second guard, the one who had run out the back door of the rec hall and taken off through the snow, was escorted back into the compound. He'd given up after the constable who followed him had walked him into the ground two kilometres away. Rather than trying to chase the man down immediately, the constable followed at a comfortable pace — comfortable for her, anyhow. Keeping in great shape with her daily ten-kilometre runs meant there was no contest. After fifteen minutes of breaking trail through knee-deep snow, the guard, normally a tough, mean, short-tempered fellow, hadn't the energy to resist. On being returned to the compound, he was handcuffed to the cold iron stove in the cold sleeping quarters along with his partner.

As the situation wound down, the police and the COs began sorting out how to move Wright and his two henchmen with sufficient police escorts, plus the cooks and fifteen artisans back to civilization. Sam's Beaver could only take seven passengers at a time. Even if she just flew them the short hop out to Lindsay, she'd still be shuttling people until after dark. And the Cessna couldn't be used even if they had a second pilot. It was seized as evidence — lots of ivory traces and fragments had been picked up in the search. It would be taken over by the federal wildlife officers when they turned up. The provincial police had no transportation available other than a Cessna traffic aircraft — two, maybe three passengers at a time.

One of the constables spoke up, offering a suggestion. "A De Havilland Buffalo would work great." When everyone turned and looked at him, he elaborated. "I'm in the RCAF Reserves. We fly those out of Trenton on search and rescue missions. I'm a loadmaster. I might be able to talk our major into sending one up for us if they aren't already tied up on a job. It's a big bird and will take everyone here in one load plus have plenty of room for all your seizures. Even then it will still be running light."

"What about this short runway?" Aldridge asked him.

"With what we need to move, it'll have about the same flight capabilities as this guy's Cessna," the constable said.

Samantha added: "If the constable has any trouble convincing them to spring one loose for a couple of hours, I'm on good terms with the major in charge of the Rescue Coordination Centre too. We did them a favour a while back."

—

It was twilight when the military Buffalo dropped onto the runway. Reverse thrust on the big twin turboprops brought the search and rescue plane to a stop well short of the Cessna and Sam's Beaver. The pilot pivoted the aircraft to face back down the runway, and the air force reserve constable guided the pilot as she backed it up to the chosen loading zone.

While two constables finished stringing yellow crime scene tape around the facility, the conservation officers and four of the military air crew loaded all the raw ivory, the finished works, and other seizures aboard the Buffalo. Just behind the seized goods, the three prisoners plus the two cooks, restrained for the moment, were guarded by the four police constables who had flown in with Aldridge and company. The fifteen artisans followed, all relieved to be leaving what had been for them, a primitive labour camp for over a year.

Epilogue

It took two weeks for the police task force to build back up to its full complement. But eventually, everyone returned with negative COVID tests. During that time, McNabb had stayed on to help Aldridge, Selkirk and their slowly rebuilding team put the case together. Neither Wright nor Cheney would make any statements. The physical and documentary evidence the team gathered, plus statements willingly offered by Conn and his road crew would form the backbone of the prosecution's case.

Raymond Conn, Kyle Roach and Jason Mead faced multiple charges of attempted murder and related firearms offenses over the gunfight in Rainy River, but in a move to save his own skin, Conn fingered Derek Cheney as the person who gave the orders to "disappear" the ex-con driver who was going to go undercover for the police. Roach and Mead provided corroborating statements.

The whole surviving road crew, including Zak Graham, faced additional charges for possession of prohibited weapons as well as their abortive roadblock attempts. And Graham and Mead still had unfinished court business in Saskatchewan.

Derek Cheney was charged with first degree murder for ordering the death of the undercover driver. And as the man who had led the OSL crew to commit all the crimes they were charged with, Cheney faced the same charges as an accessory, both before and after the fact. And of course, he faced still more charges for the assault and forced confinement of his secretary.

As for the transport load of fur that had brought the conservation officers into the mix at the beginning, Cheney was charged with exporting raw furs without permits and attempted sale of furs without a fur dealer's licence. The last that Rob McNabb heard, federal wildlife officers were still working up charges for Cheney's CITES offenses involving both the ivory and the wild fur.

James Leeson Wright faced a whole docket of charges too. In addition to his major federal wildlife charges for his involvement in the ivory trade, his unlawful confinement of the artisans as well as the human smuggling he would be tied up in court for ages. He also faced a whole other set of charges relating to importing and trafficking illegal drugs.

Half of the smuggled Chinese workers accepted their deportation orders and willingly returned home. The rest asked for asylum and were taken in by the Greater Toronto Area Chinese community who provided them with the legal representation required handle their claims. While they waited for those to be processed, their sponsors set them up in the comfortable and dignified retirement accommodations that they deserved.

About the Author

David Ferguson's career as a conservation officer (CO) with the Ontario Ministry of Natural Resources (MNR) spans almost thirty years and began in eastern Ontario as a deputy CO when he hired on as a fish hatchery technician in 1970. He became a full-fledged CO in the MNR's former Moosonee District in 1975.

He served in that capacity, making his way south, first to Elliot Lake and then Minden, from where he retired in 1999. During his career, he came into contact with thousands of people. By far, the greatest number were law abiding folks. Of those he encountered breaking the law, many would politely accept their fate, causing no problems for the officer. But there were also some of the kinds of people you didn't turn your back on — men of the sort, frequently known to the police.

David retired with his mental warehouse full of memories that could be fictitiously woven into the fabric of his stories. His believable characters are composites of the many people he has met over a lifetime. The places he has lived, worked and travelled, provide the realistic settings for his fictional stories. This is his fourth such book.

He lives with his wife Pat in northern Ontario.

www.ingramcontent.com/pod-product-compliance
Lightning Source LLC
Chambersburg PA
CBHW061308170626
46817CB00001B/108